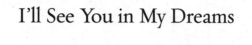

I'll See You in My Dreams

I'll See You in My Dreams

William Deverell

McClelland & Stewart

LIBRARY AND ARCHIVES CANADA CATALOGUING IN PUBLICATION

Deverell, William, 1937-
    I'll see you in my dreams / William Deverell.

"An Arthur Beauchamp novel."
ISBN 978-0-7710-2716-1

    I. Title.

PS8557.E8775I44 2011   C813'.54   C2011-902103-X

We acknowledge the financial support of the Government of Canada through the Book Publishing Industry Development Program and that of the Government of Ontario through the Ontario Media Development Corporation's Ontario Book Initiative. We further acknowledge the support of the Canada Council for the Arts and the Ontario Arts Council for our publishing program.

Published simultaneously in the United States of America by McClelland & Stewart Ltd., P.O. Box 1030, Plattsburgh, New York 12901

Library of Congress Control Number: 2011925619

Cover art: Alfred Gescheidt/Getty Images
Typeset in Minion by M&S, Toronto
Printed and bound in Canada

ANCIENT FOREST
FRIENDLY
This book was produced using ancient-forest friendly papers.

McClelland & Stewart Ltd.
75 Sherbourne Street
Toronto, Ontario
M5A 2P9
www.mcclelland.com

1   2   3   4   5   15   14   13   12   11

Dedicated to the First Nations people who survived, defied,
and exposed the Native residential school system.

A THIRST FOR JUSTICE:

The Trials of Arthur Beauchamp

A BIOGRAPHY

BY WENTWORTH CHANCE

FOREWORD

AT TIMES THERE SEEMED MORE LABOUR than love in this labour of love, yet I can now sit back with weary satisfaction at having realized a long-held dream: capturing the tumultuous journey of Arthur Ramsgate Beauchamp from awkward familial beginnings to early triumphs and losses, and, despite years of alcoholic despair and cuckoldom, finally securing a reputation as one of the leading trial lawyers of the past hundred years – sharing the throne, in my respectful opinion, with Clarence Darrow. (A.R.B. will forgive me for giving the edge to Darrow, with his more strenuous commitment to social justice.)

Before you proceed on, dear reader, please practise with me this aid to pronunciation. It's *Beechem,* not *Beau-chom,* and certainly not *Beau-champ.* The name came to England with the Normans, but the conquerors were stubbornly met by the Anglo-Saxons' insistence on hard syllables.

I am indebted to many, first among them Margaret Blake, Member of Parliament for Cowichan and the Islands, Green Party leader, and, of course, Beauchamp's life partner, the liberal yin to his conservative yang. Thank you, Ms. Blake, for filling in so many of the gaps that your overly cautious partner shied away from.

Many from Beauchamp's firm, Tragger, Inglis, Bullingham, had anecdotes to tell, particularly retired partner Hubbell Meyerson, who offered several humorous tales, and Gertrude Isbister, Beauchamp's long-time secretary. Without the aid of Beauchamp's daughter, Deborah, I might never have been able to bring alive his self-destructive decades with her mother, Annabelle, who, though she otherwise cooperated with this enterprise, recalled only happy memories, insisting that the rest was "history, best forgotten." Legal beagles Augustina Sage, John Brovak, and Maximilian Macarthur III offered lively anecdotes. April Wu should not go unmentioned, nor should Ira Lavitch, Nick "the Owl" Faloon, or Tony "the Angle" d'Anglio.

A collective thank-you to the good folks of Garibaldi Island, where Beauchamp has entered into a relaxed, bucolic retirement. Reverend Al Noggins, our hero's ally and spiritual adviser, shared confidences if not confessions. The island postmaster, Abraham Makepeace, and the editor of the *Island Bleat,* Nelson Forbish, were unsparing of their time.

It would be inappropriate not to extend my sincerest gratitude to the subject of this biography, and I do so unequivocally, despite an unaccountable chilling of friendship that followed his reading of the final draft. And finally, I acknowledge the unrelenting support of my publisher and its editors, publicity staff, and lawyers.

My onions are shiny, my peaches plump, my bean pods crisp and fresh. All the entries are cuddled in foam in the back of my beloved 1969 Fargo, ready for the drive to the community hall tomorrow and the judging at the 2011 Garibaldi Island Fall Fair.

Pacing on the veranda, I try to pump myself up: this year the Mabel Orfmeister Trophy for Most Points in Fruits and Vegetables must be brought home to Blunder Bay, where it belongs. Doc Dooley has ruled too long; he must be overthrown.

I will wait half an hour before heading out. I don't want to get there too early. I don't want to appear anxious. I often felt this kind of tension as a lawyer, at the outset of a trial. I hope my beets and cukes will speak with the eloquence I displayed in court.

I go inside and flop into my club chair, reach for the poems of Catullus, recite aloud a favourite line: "No fickle lusts, no rooting between other sheets – your husband will lie only in the valley of *your* breasts." Emphasis added, as if for Margaret's ears. Has anyone else been lying there, in that valley? I have been playing with that worry lately. A stupid concern, obviously false, unworthy of me.

Now my hand reaches out to *A Thirst for Justice: The Trials of Arthur Beauchamp.* This opus has been sitting beside the chair since its pre-summer release – presumably it was considered to offer light reading for the beach or cottage.

I have tossed away the book's cover jacket with its repellent illustration, my beaklike nose in profile, a frightening sight for those of tender years. I have marked up pages, written marginal notes of the kind that crazies scribble in library books. So many flagrancies, so many wounds exposed, so much grist for the Garibaldi gossip mill. Locals who snaffled early copies are having trouble making eye contact with the impotent cuckold.

From time to time I suffer a masochistic urge to tell the whole story, shout it to the world, bold and uncensored. But I have contented myself with vocalizing to my club chair, or to the goats, the sheep, and Bess, the milk cow. I can't find the courage to do anything but ruminate (as Bess does her cud, chewing again what has already been chewed and swallowed).

Astonishingly, the biography has won plaudits for Wentworth Chance, my self-proclaimed official biographer and (I'd thought) champion. It was seen as "candid" and "brave." The *Toronto Star* considered it "a remarkable story of self-redemption." Who knew that shy Wentworth could speak so loudly on paper? Who could have guessed that A.R. Beauchamp, Q.C., so wise, so wary, would have posed so nakedly for those interminable taping sessions?

I leaf through it again, seeking to recognize myself, wondering who this fellow could be – so accomplished in the courthouse, so mired in insecurity outside its walls. My years as a tormented, self-doubting alcoholic. "The Wet Years" is my least favourite section, but one I've reread often, mainly because I have a mental blank about the drunken episodes that Wentworth makes seem almost heroic – hurling insults at a judge at a Law Society dinner, dousing a prosecutor with my gin-spiked water jug, my raucous barstool recitations from the Song of Solomon or the *Rubáiyát. A flask of wine! A book of verse!*

"Where the Squamish River Flows" is the poetic title of one of the early sections, complete with black-and-white photos of the cast: young Beauchamp himself, in the apparent guise of Ichabod Crane, Gabriel Swift, Professor Dermot Mulligan, Ophelia Moore. To kill time I return to it, though I've read it until its print smudged, looking for shadowy clues to what truly happened on the shores of that misty river on the Easter weekend of 1962. *Evil, unforgivable evil . . .*

PART ONE

———

THE CRIME

From "Where the Squamish River Flows," *A Thirst for Justice,* © W. Chance

IT WAS JUST AFTER THE 1962 EASTER WEEKEND when Beauchamp's first murder file landed on his desk. Only twenty-five, he was in his fourth year of practice and still regretting his choice of criminal law over pursuit of a doctorate in classical studies. So it was a matter of extreme irony that the case that finally tilted him toward the law involved the death of his respected – nay, idolized – tutor in the Greek and Roman classics, Dermot Mulligan, D.Th., Ph.D.

Let us put this life-shaping event in context. His firm, Tragger, Inglis, Bullingham, was perhaps the most conservative, the most staid of Vancouver's major law offices, and it regarded its small criminal division almost with embarrassment, its staff as untouchables. This is where Beauchamp toiled, in a windowless office on the fourteenth floor of a West Hastings bank building.

By the spring of that year he had built a creditable record of victories, but only one of note: a dangerous driving charge against the Highways minister, Phil Gaglardi. Many had been cases from the Legal Aid Society, earning a paltry thirty-five-dollar per diem. Occasionally, to the disapproval of his seniors, he would even act pro bono – a beggar, a vagrant, a street drunk. He was a pushover for the sad stories of the oppressed.

Earlier that year he'd finally escaped from the stifling oppression of his parental home on University Hill, to a West End bachelor flat. One might often see him having a fifty-cent breakfast in one of the busy diners on Denman Street, or on lonely walks by English Bay: gangly at six foot three (friends called him Stretch), hair clipped short, sombre of expression, his lugubrious eyes and heroic nose combining to give an impression of craggy world-weariness.

Picture him on a chill and misty April morning in Tragger, Inglis's requisite uniform – overcoat, hat, dark suit, black shoes – striding beneath the pink-blossoming trees of the West End toward the crypt, as he called his windowless office, to prepare the cross-examination of a young woman whose front teeth had been knocked out by a detested client . . .

A h, yes, Schlott – Hugo Schlott – that was his name. A beefy, red-faced, post-pubescent progeny of a doting, disbelieving mother who was paying my fee. The chief of the criminal section and my immediate superior, Alex Pappas, had handed it off to me with a smirking "Do your best, pal."

Truly the Schlott case represented the low point of twenty-five years of a life poorly lived, spent in random wandering without clear direction. It offered stark proof I had taken an ill-conceived detour from the path of enlightenment to the path of shame. The doors of academia had been opened wide, bounteous scholarships offered. Instead I was bound upon my barrister's oath to defend an odious bully.

I had no stomach for the trial, and I fully intended not to punch in that day. Instead I would march into the den of the managing partner, Roy Bullingham, and announce I would be applying to Cambridge to complete my thesis on *The Aeneid*. I owed that to Dermot Mulligan, for he had opened those academic doors and I had failed him. Dr. Mulligan – author, classicist, philosopher, mentor throughout my master's program at UBC – had disappeared on Easter weekend, only a few days before, from his retreat by the Squamish River, and it was feared the river had taken him to his death.

That it was a pleasant spring morning seemed only to add to my malaise. That I entered my building amid a hurrying group of pretty secretaries only made me feel more lonely. Members of the intimidating other sex tended to spurn this socially dysfunctional sad sack; I'd never known the touch of Venus, that which they call love.

For no accountable reason, those few moments in the rattling elevator stick in my mind (though withheld from my prying biographer as too delicate for his omnivorous ears). I'd plastered myself to the back wall of the crowded cage behind the comely Gertrude Isbister: nineteen, newly hired, among the loveliest of the flowers that adorned our secretarial pool. As the lift lurched in ascent, she made a misstep while adjusting her skirt. Without thought I reached out to steady her, my hand resting for an electric second on the fluffy fabric of her tight angora sweater.

I said, "I truly beg pardon. Excuse me" – something like that, my face aflame. Whether out of shyness or reproach, she did not respond, though she didn't move away and continued tugging at her skirt. We were let out on the fourteenth floor (in reality the thirteenth, which, according to local legend, was the haunt of ghosts wailing from the air conditioners). As Gertrude preceded me, I saw that her right stocking was poorly aligned, puckered at the knee. Staring rapturously at that juncture of skirt and knee, I barely missed colliding with Geoffrey Tragger as he exited his office.

"Steady there, son," he said, adjusting his glasses. "Beauchamp, isn't it?"

"Yes, sir. Arthur Beauchamp." I was surprised. This absent-minded senior partner, a corporate tax specialist, rarely recognized, let alone spoke to the forty-odd inferiors in practice there.

"You're on the criminal end, are you not?" (These and following conversations are reconstructed as best I can remember; do not call it creative non-fiction – I seek to offer a fair rendering, without gloss.) "Your name was mentioned this morning . . . Yes, Mr. Bullingham wants a tête-à-tête. Something that's been in the news . . . Well, never mind. He's waiting for you."

Bully's secretary showed me straight in. He was seated behind his massive oaken desk, a gaunt man of middle years, a skin-deep sheen of affability disguising the Scrooge within. Lolling in an easy chair across from him was Alex Pappas, wearing a rumpled suit and a vanity hairpiece, fleshy wattles quivering below a stubbly chin.

"We got something for you, kid," he said.

"Alex believes you're up for this," said Bully. "Your first murder."

I had rehearsed an exit line from Pliny: *Multi famam, conscientiam pauci verentur.* Many fear their reputation, few their conscience. My conscience (I might have added) will not let me defend a violent misogynist, sir. Fie, I say, to reputation. But my tongue was tied. A murder? Something that had been in the news? I trolled through the possibilities: the gangland turf war then adorning the front pages, or maybe that psychotic who'd mistaken his mailman for the Antichrist.

Bully was sifting through the papers in a thin folder. "You really think he has it in him?"

"He's streaky," Pappas said. "Won five straight, dropped the next two. Then four wins – charity cases."

"Yes, I've heard of his penchant for defending life's losers. Noble intentions, I'm sure, but we can't have too much of that. What about Crawford?"

Pappas lit a cigarette. "Too lazy. Arthur is the best of a poor lot. Not much jury experience, a couple of cases. He's not afraid of work. Seems to have some innate tools. Almost unconsciously eloquent at times."

I might not have been there. I retain an image of myself shifting from foot to foot, hands hanging loosely, staring at a framed photograph of a younger Bully greeting my hero, John George Diefenbaker, the famed orator, criminal lawyer, and then prime minister. A similar photo, Bully clasping the hand of Louis St. Laurent, had disappeared after the Tories submerged the Liberals four years earlier. Another campaign was underway that year, Dief fighting to hang on to his job. (By the mid-sixties Lester Pearson had replaced him on Bully's wall.)

"Am I to be allowed in on the secret?" I asked boldly. "Which murder case is this?"

Pappas blew a stream of smoke. "Dermot Mulligan."

My mouth fell open. "Dermot Mulligan? *Murdered?*"

"Read the papers much, kid? Some loudmouth Indian got charged yesterday. Maybe you should tell him to shut his yap before he talks his way to the gallows."

13

I stammered, "I . . . I can't take it on. Professor Mulligan was . . . I knew him. I took courses from him. A hugely respected scholar. I'd be fouling his memory."

I was met with incredulous stares.

On the Saturday of Easter weekend, Mulligan had disappeared from his hobby farm – ten acres along the Squamish River, across from the snow-capped peaks of the Tantalus Mountains. In late March he'd begun a sabbatical there to write his memoirs; he was later joined by his wife, Irene. They were both about fifty, and childless. But I'd heard speculation from mutual friends that Gabriel Swift, a young aboriginal, had taken on a filial role, and that the Mulligans had begun to dote on him.

I was aware from news accounts that Swift was twenty-one and had worked a few years as their caretaker, looking after their A-frame cottage when they were at their Vancouver home. For the term of Mulligan's sabbatical, Swift had moved back to the Cheakamus Reserve, though he returned daily for chores: splitting wood, operating a small tractor, tending a pair of riding horses. Shortly after Mulligan's disappearance he'd been arrested, questioned, and released. But apparently on Easter Monday – just yesterday – he had been detained again, and this time charged with Mulligan's murder.

A theologian and philosopher, Dr. Mulligan was also famed as a translator and expositor of classic literature, which he had taught me to love. A rebel within his once-revered Roman Catholic Church, he was a bit of an oddity, awkward and jumpy, slightly fey. His lectures were often brilliant, yet peppered with anecdotes that rarely seemed on point. A powerful scholar, he'd published nine books on philosophy, religion, and morality, the best of them meditations on the ancient gods and the poets who'd praised them.

Thin, balding, given to wearing heavy horn-rims, he was a man reclusive in habits, rarely appearing outside home, hobby farm, and lecture hall. But I'd shared a glass of Madeira with him, had been among the privileged few to be invited into his book-lined den. Had I been his favourite? I wanted to believe so.

"I revered him . . . It's hard to explain."

"Well, as long as he wasn't going up your ass, I don't see a problem." That salacious innuendo from Pappas I recall distinctly – I was contemplating ripping the toupée from his head.

"All the better that you hold a reverence for the deceased," said Bully. "The jury will be the more impressed that you would defend his killer."

This eye-popping presumption of guilt was, I think now, Bully's effort to shock me, to force me into waving the flag for presumption of innocence. In putting my sense of justice to the test he thought to bend me, break my will.

"One must occasionally do the charitable thing," Bully continued. "The image of the grasping lawyer is all too prevalent. So when the Legal Aid Society calls upon us to show our good heart, we do not demur, particularly for a high-profile case. And there are rewards beyond printer's ink. They have offered an unusually generous hundred dollars per diem, plus a smaller amount for your junior counsel."

"Out of curiosity, whom do you have in mind?" I asked.

"Ophelia Moore," Pappas said. "Spin this baby out and we may even turn a profit. And maybe you'll get laid in the bargain."

The female staff called Pappas "Mister Hands" behind his back. It was all around the office that when he squeezed Mrs. Moore's rear, she'd grabbed his testicles so hard he yelped.

Bully scowled at Pappas. "We don't suggest you'll win, young man. The odds are stacked against you. Eminent scholar slain by a hot-tempered Native with, doubtless, your typical drinking problem. But justice must seem to be done, and you, young Arthur, are the one who must seem to do it."

There was more along this line. It was the ethical duty of counsel not to turn away the impoverished supplicant. This would be my chance, even in defeat, to embellish a growing reputation. A career-maker. Winnable cases would follow. Tragger, Inglis had its eye on me.

Despite my reservations, I felt challenged – I'd been worked over well. And I was intrigued; I had dreamed of putting what skills I had to the supreme test. A murder, a hanging offence! Maybe I owed Dr. Mulligan this – after all, he'd been not only an opponent of capital punishment but a vigorous supporter of Native rights. In his early years he'd been the principal of one of the Native residential schools that he later spoke of so scathingly. I suspected Swift had been his project of redemption.

Pappas stubbed out his smoke. "He's waiting to meet you at Oakie." Oakalla, in Burnaby, the regional prison.

"I have a trial. Hugo Schlott."

"That bum? You'll have to find some way to put it over, pal."

"It's set peremptorily. I've adjourned it seven times."

"Mr. Pappas will be pleased to do it in your stead." Bully's expression warned that he would not hear debate. Pappas looked as if he'd taken a boot in the groin.

~~~

Before heading off to Oakalla Prison, I squirreled myself away in the Crypt with the file and several back issues of the *Sun* and the *Province*. The file was skimpy indeed: a legal aid form and a sheet of paper with some phone numbers – no details, no police report.

The news stories (still extant, crisp, yellowed, and well-fondled by Wentworth Chance) revealed little. After Dr. Mulligan's disappearance, some clothing, presumably his, was found by the riverbank half a mile from his cottage. They were being examined for bloodstains. Irene Mulligan was speechless with grief, secluding herself and refusing to be interviewed by the press.

A person of interest had been questioned, held, and released, but Swift's name wasn't mentioned until his re-arrest. In his remarks to the press, Staff Sergeant Roscoe Knepp of the Squamish RCMP had used the typically prolix phraseology of his trade: "I can only affirm at this point in time that the arrested individual had been in the employ of Dr. Mulligan for approximately two years and five months. A formal charge of murder in the first degree has been preferred against the aforesaid individual. We are pursuing further investigative leads."

Press photos showed Swift being bundled into a cruiser: a young, slender, bronze-skinned lad in rough clothes, a pair of braids, sparking black eyes. He'd called out to reporters that he was being "framed by a fascist f—ing cabal of racist brownshirts." That gave me a jolt. Such bluntness would gain him little sympathy in a white man's court. What in God's name had I gotten myself into?

Swift was obviously a much-politicized young upstart. He was a farmhand, a labourer, a son of the Cheakamus tribe, born on its reserve, educated in a church-run school. No interviews with his friends or family decorated those pages, though encomiums for Dr. Mulligan filled columns.

The few neighbours who would speak of Swift – all white and working-class – claimed to know little of him. Thelma McLean, who lived across the road with her tree-faller husband, had often seen him "lazing about on their porch with a book," a curious observation, implying an association between reading and laziness. "I can't remember speaking to him, but he seemed troubled, always hiding in a book." Mrs. McLean and other neighbours were attending to Irene Mulligan, shielding her from the media swarm outside her house.

Before slipping the file into my briefcase, I looked through the contacts Pappas had jotted down. Staff Sergeant Knepp's number was there, and that of the court clerk in Squamish. The final name caused me tremors. M. Cyrus Smythe-Baldwin, Q.C., the lion of the criminal courts, had been named special prosecutor.

From "Where the Squamish River Flows," *A Thirst for Justice,* © W. Chance

IN 1962 THE PUNISHMENT FOR CAPITAL MURDER was to be hanged by the neck until dead. This sat heavily on Beauchamp's mind as his Volkswagen Beetle sped him toward the regional jail and a first meeting with Gabriel Swift. Two executions had already been scheduled for that year (both were ultimately carried out, before Christmas), and the nation's mood vigorously favoured retaining the death penalty.

Only three years earlier, a fourteen-year-old boy named Steven Truscott had been sentenced to the gallows for a rape-murder conviction based on circumstantial evidence. (Though his sentence was finally commuted to life, it took fifty years before it was found he'd been innocent all along.) This case was to torment Beauchamp throughout his defence of Gabriel Swift. If a grade seven student with a blameless history could be condemned to hang, what chance had an angry militant Indian who, it was alleged, had cruelly repaid Dr. Mulligan's affection and generosity?

Beauchamp held a cynical view as to why he'd been chosen for this defence. Pappas hadn't wanted to sully his own reputation, nor the reputations of his more favoured underlings, by taking on a loser. He resented the young upstart, resented his greater skill, and Beauchamp was being asked to pay the price of his boss's vanity and jealousy. However well defended, a trial that ended with a sentence of death would be a crushing reverse, one that would forever soil Beauchamp's career.

He was torn in another, deeply personal way about defending the suspected killer of a man who'd been his professor and mentor. He wondered if he'd be able to give it his all, especially since he felt it unlikely that Swift was innocent. In all events, he knew he had to level with this militant aboriginal about his affection for Dr. Mulligan.

Beside him that afternoon in his 1957 Beetle, driving through the sprawl of suburban Burnaby, was the divorcée Ophelia Moore, the sole woman among the forty-three solicitors of Tragger, Inglis. Though almost a decade older than Beauchamp, she'd been called to the bar only six weeks earlier, and since the partners didn't seem to know what else to do with her, she'd been seconded to be his junior counsel. Short, slightly heavy but pleasingly so, rosy dimples, blue eyes, and blond curls – the kind of attractive package that tended to cause Beauchamp distress . . .

A distress I couldn't account for, and have never really understood. It has something to do, I'm sure, with the guilt-ridden yearnings of one persuaded in childhood that sexual desire is dirty, the act unspeakable. Strong inferential evidence suggests that my tutors in that regard stopped sleeping together soon after the supposed miracle of my conception. As if in disgust at what they'd produced, they had quickly retreated to separate bedrooms off the echoing upstairs hallway of their split-level rancher.

Their house was only a stroll from the UBC campus, where Thomas Beauchamp was chief librarian and Mavis Beauchamp taught Latin. As their only child I was not deprived, but I was their compliant prisoner, dependent on their support through eleven years of private schooling and seven of higher learning, with only scholarship money to pay for fripperies like movies, books, and the occasional draft beer. It wasn't until January of that year, after the firm had given me a Christmas bonus, that I could afford my own digs: a West End bachelor flat in a stately old manse converted into suites. It was cramped, with a linoleum-floored kitchenette and an oil stove, a small bedroom and shared bath, but boasted wide windows and views of Stanley Park with its vast acreage of emerald sward, brown sand beaches, and towering conifers. Released from the constant cold appraisals of the *pater* and *mater familias*, I'd thought I might burst forth like a flowering plum tree in April. There would be adventures, maybe romance . . .

Not so. I was a freak of society, an unreformed wonk (even back then students were categorized as wonks, wheels, or jocks), incapable of normal human interaction, confused by the rules of the mating game. And barely able to communicate, by words or gesture, with Mrs. Moore, whom I addressed as such, unable to tongue those four wee syllables *O-phe-li-a*. Fair Ophelia of the plump red lips. She was thirty-four, older than me by nine years, but – help me, Sigmund Freud – I was bewitched by her.

At the first blush of our acquaintance, in the Hotel Georgia's cocktail lounge, an oasis frequented by the firm's bottom-rung lawyers, I had committed a double gaffe. She had been enjoying the attentions of Erlander from Estate Planning, Kruger from Corporate, and Bixbee from Personal Injury while I, the only un-attached male at the table, sat beside her nervously knocking back whisky sodas. Finally, as Bixbee went off to piss and the other fel-lows lost themselves in hockey talk (the Leafs were on a roll with Mahovlich, Keon, and Shack), she turned to me mutely, as if daring me to open my mouth.

I said something like (the words are severely garbled in recall): "It must have taken great courage to enter a male profession. You should be proud of yourself."

She looked at me sadly – writing me off, I assumed – then said, "How come you're the only guy here not trying to get into my pants?"

The crudity both shocked and thrilled me. "I, ah, really don't see you in those terms." That was the second blooper, as well as a lie.

She nodded. "I get the message." I took that as a response to what she supposed was a coded communication, that I was, in the current usage, a homo. She seemed to relax and explained her tres-pass upon the male domain: she'd got "screwed" in divorce court; a law degree would enable her to pursue her well-to-do ex for in-creased support.

Unfortunately, on that day in late April as we motored down Boundary Road, she still seemed to think I was not attracted to women, and that we were therefore freed from the games opposite sexes must play. It was warm in the car, and she'd taken off her suit jacket. A cautious side glance took in the outlines of a bra beneath her gossamer blouse. Sheer nylons beneath a skirt that had ridden above her knees.

"So, Arthur, what do you do for fun," she asked, "when you're not defending the dregs of society?"

"I mostly read books."

"It's about the only lonely pleasure left, isn't it, unless you count self-abuse. Have you read *Tropic of Cancer?*"

A sexually explicit novel banned beyond the borders of France, and particularly in chaste Vancouver, where several months earlier the morality squad had seized copies from a local bookstore. "I can't say I have."

"I'll slip you mine. Please don't use it as a sexual aid – it gets the pages sticky."

I braked hard at a red light that seemed to come out of nowhere. When she raised an arm to brace herself, she exposed a bed of hair in the gully of her armpit, which, *horribile dictu,* caused an arousal reaction, a tugging below. I worried that I was deviant in some way, the armpit outscoring the breast as visual stimulator.

(Pause here. That vaguely fetishistic interlude is something I feel bound to get off my chest. After all, Mr. Wentworth Chance has already stripped off much of my protective cover, so I may as well go naked. But since I intend this account never to see the light of day anyway – so many secrets, so many privileged truths and lies – it doesn't matter. It's merely purgative.)

We were in the Burnaby hinterland by then, and ahead I could see the spirit-deadening ocherous four-tiered architecture of Oakalla Prison, on Deer Lake, whose beach on the opposite shore was a preferred destination for escapees able to swim.

"Do you have – how do I put it? – a special friend, a companion?"

"I hope I don't disappoint you if I confess to being heterosexual, Mrs. Moore."

Her laughter was melodic and seemed to come from deep in her throat. "It disappoints that you call me Mrs. Moore." That prompted another glance to my right, earning a glimpse of nyloned knee as I gripped the shift knob, trying to gear down.

Lady, shall I lie in your lap? whispered a prince bolder than I to his Ophelia.

~~~

"How's the sacroiliac, Jethro?" I asked of the moustachioed old boy in charge of admissions.

"Haven't set down in ten days. This lovely young lady with you?"

"Ophelia Moore has just finished her articles. You may be seeing more of her."

"How much more of her?" An unabashedly lewd grin. She gave him a wink, playing along.

I was an Oakalla regular by then, known to the staff, so the process of signing in was casual. While Jethro made pleasant with Ophelia and tried to see through her see-through blouse, I flipped through the visitors' registry.

Swift had been transferred there yesterday after being re-manded in Squamish police court. He'd had a visitor that even-ing: Jim Brady, a name familiar to me from left-wing labour circles. Brady had come with a lawyer, Harry Rankin, an eloquent socialist, hero to the destitute of Vancouver's rough streets. I as-sumed I had lost Swift as a client, and was surprised at how dis-appointed I felt.

Swift's only other visitor, earlier that day, was Celia Swift – his mother, as I later learned.

Usually in a murder case, lawyer interviews were held in rooms the size of wardrobe closets, but all were in use, so Ophelia and I were led to the gymnasium-like visitors' hall with its long central table, its array of smaller tables and chairs bolted to the floor, most of them occupied by inmates with parents, girlfriends, lawyers, or probation officers.

One of the green-clad convicts called, "Hey, counsellor, you're the slickest," and proudly pointed me out to his mother.

"Got him off a warehouse break-in," I told Ophelia. "That en-couraged him to do it again."

We found a free table near one at which a woman was softly crying, her incarcerated boyfriend showing annoyance that she refused to let him touch her. Among the other lawyers in the hall were Harry Fan, infamous for his baffling, impenetrable sub-missions, and Larry Hill, beloved for his stirring, alcohol-fuelled courtroom orations. He'd just dismissed a client and was awaiting another; while the guards were looking elsewhere, he grinned at me and sneaked a drink from a flask.

Too many of Vancouver's best criminal counsel were problem drinkers in those days – maybe a majority. That made a damning statement about the stresses of this rarefied, ill-regarded area of practice. I had sworn (believe it or not) never to fall victim to the curse of drink, though I tied one on occasionally to signal I was one of the guys.

As Swift shuffled to our table – he was shackled but not cuffed – his dark eyes were firmly, unwaveringly fixed on me. Decorating one of them was a purple bruise, and welts appeared elsewhere on his face and arms, badges likely earned within these brutal walls. He seemed taller than in the news photos I'd seen, and stringier. His hair was in handsome braids that hung well below his shoulders.

He declined my hand as he sat. Affronted, I said, "Do you know who I am?"

"Arthur Beauchamp." Astonishingly, he pronounced my surname correctly. "Why are you here?" he asked.

"Because I was asked by the Legal Aid Society to represent you. This is Ophelia Moore, also from my office. My junior." I felt silly calling her that.

"Hello, Gabriel." Her big, dimpled smile.

He frowned as he studied her, as if taking exception to the brightness of her lipstick, if not her blue eyes and blond tresses. He brushed from his forehead strands of his own jet-black hair, then dismissed her as irrelevant to the discussion. "Why would you want to be my lawyer?"

A good question. Why would I want to represent this impolite young brave with his pointed refusal of a hand extended? This jail alone was full of the poor and the desperate who would weep their thanks for legal aid from the up-and-comer Beauchamp.

"I haven't asked to be your lawyer, Gabriel. But you unquestionably need a lawyer. You are charged with a capital crime."

"I turned down Harry Rankin. Why would I choose you instead?"

I felt like telling him there was no point in holding out for Clarence Darrow, as he was no longer of this earth. "If you propose to defend yourself, Gabriel, you will have a fool for a client. Trite but true."

"I won't be gagged by an attorney. I intend to speak with my own tongue."

I was about to say adieu and rise, but pride held me back. I was not going to walk out like a chump, insulted, defeated. "And what would you talk about with your own tongue?"

"The colonial structures of our supposedly free society, the rampant racism, the victimization of the poor."

Ophelia couldn't hide her astonishment but I was prepared for this. "Then it will be a judge who will gag you, Gabriel. The prosecutor is Cyrus Smythe-Baldwin, the most able counsel of the West Coast bar. You will be meat for his grinder. Your political rhetoric will win you no friends on the jury, which will surely convict. You will then be free to declaim against the ills of our society until you are led to the gallows."

Gabriel smiled slightly at this, maybe cynically, maybe in appreciation of my bluntness. "People around here say you're a straight shooter. But you've never defended a murder."

"No, I haven't."

"How many jury trials have you done?"

"Two."

"Did you win either?"

"The second." I didn't tell him they were two-bit offences: an illegal firearm, drug possession.

The warehouse thief, my fan, was parting ways with his mother. He called out to Gabriel, "You got the best throat on the coast, man, and he don't charge an arm and a leg."

Gabriel studied me again. "You seem to have a high consumer rating in here, Mr. Beauchamp."

"Call me Arthur, as you might an equal, because right now I stand in no other relation to you. I am not your lawyer. You are free to reject my services, and I can give you a substantial reason to do so. Dermot Mulligan was my professor. He instilled in me a love of the Greek playwrights and the Roman poets. He was a great man – a little eccentric, sure, as brilliant people often are – but he was like a god to me."

Gabriel lost his stubborn, sardonic expression, and his lips trembled. I looked away, uncomfortable, and saw the woman who'd been sobbing at the next table slip something under it, a white packet.

Gabriel gingerly touched a bruise. Ophelia spoke softly. "Were you assaulted in here, Gabriel?"

He seemed not to hear that, still absorbed in my curt speech. Then a perplexed look. "Assaulted in here?" He swung an arm about. "Can you see how many brothers are in this joint?"

Most of the inmates there were Native. I had got so used to their disproportionate presence in the criminal system that I'd put on blinders against that uncomfortable reality.

"I'm in debt to Sergeant Knepp for this." Gabriel pointed to his bruised eye. "We have a bad history." He pulled up his shirt: a raised yellow mass on his left side below the ribs. "Constable Jettles felt he had to chime in as an act of solidarity, but he only kicked me once."

"Where did this happen?"

"In the cells. No witnesses." There was a moment in which he was obviously struggling to contain himself, all his face muscles tightening. I sensed he had a short fuse and knew it, knew he had to avoid igniting it. A deep breath. "I got my licks in." He splayed his fingers. His knuckles were bruised and scraped.

He steadied himself, getting a fix on me based on his new information. "Arthur . . . Yeah, it comes back. Dermot mentioned you a few times. He was pissed off at you. You threw your life away by choosing law over literature." A sudden smile, more proof of a mercurial temperament. "Wish you'd gone to Oxford instead, Arthur?"

"Cambridge."

"If Dr. Mulligan was your god, what do you think he was to me?"

"I'd hesitate to say."

He nodded, thoughtful, solemn. "You're wondering if I murdered him." His gesture, an expansive arc with his hand, took in Ophelia as well.

"I'm not ready to ask you that."

"How would you go about defending me?"

"By forbidding you to talk about this case with anyone but Ophelia and me, including Jim Brady and Celia. She is your mother?"

"Yes." He was an only child, he said, rare in an era of large families. Celia was a traditional artist in fabric. His father, Bill, had taken to drink, embittered after losing a leg in a logging accident. Both were victims of what he termed "residential school syndrome," a phrase I'd not heard before.

"Jim Brady . . . he's the union fellow?"

"Organizer with Mine, Mill, Smelter. An activist. A teacher. A man I trust."

"Because he's also Native?"

"Maybe."

"Did you say anything to the police?"

"I told those lying shits to fuck themselves." Another shift, a fierce look, his eyes sparking.

"The next thing I would do is photograph your injuries."

On Pappas's advice I always carried a small flash camera in my briefcase, and I quickly took shots of Gabriel from different angles. He raised his shirt and I clicked at the damage allegedly done by Constable Jettles's boot. The flashes aroused one of the patrolling guards from his reveries, and he descended on us, hot-faced, stammering, demanding that the camera be surrendered to him.

"If you touch this camera," I said, "I will have you charged with obstructing justice."

"Hey, Screwloose," called a grizzled inmate. "You know who you're tangling asses with? That's Arthur Beauchamp, the best young throat in town." A kindly review, given I'd never met him.

The guard stilled his reaching hand. "I'm taking this up with the deputy warden."

"Observe the injuries my client has suffered. If you'd like to be called as a witness, I'll arrange it."

The camera went back into my briefcase. The guard went back to his duties, glaring at the laughing inmates. Gabriel pursed his lips, presumably reflecting on the interaction but saying nothing about my use of the proprietary phrase "my client." Visiting time was ending, the room emptying, prisoners being returned to their cells for the pre-dinner count.

"Today is Wednesday. I'll return on the weekend."

"Can you bring me some reading material?"

"In particular?"

"Woodcock's *Anarchism*. Camus's *Resistance, Rebellion, and Death*. The new collection by I.F. Stone. The latest *Monthly Review*." The last I recognized as a dense Marxist publication. The Mulligans' neighbour, Thelma McLean, had recalled him "lazing about on their porch with a book." *Lazing* seemed hardly appropriate. This was a complex fellow; I could see why Dermot Mulligan was attracted to him.

Somehow, without formal words of agreement, we both understood, Gabriel and I, that I was his lawyer now. At least for the time being.

This time he shook my hand.

From "Where the Squamish River Flows," *A Thirst for Justice,* © W. Chance

THUS THE YOUNG LEGAL EAGLE (a befitting descriptor for the beak-nosed barrister) found himself, at twenty-five, taking on a challenge as formidable as any faced by his heroes – such masters of the craft as Winnipeg's Harry Walsh, Toronto's Joe Sedgwick, Vancouver's Angelo Branca, and, not least among them, the eloquent Cyrus Smythe-Baldwin, who would be playing an unaccustomed role this time, as the attorney general's hired gun.

Beauchamp was apprehensive but thrilled – even a bit full of himself – as on the drive back to Vancouver he drank in the applause from Ophelia Moore over his clever handling of his new client. Having silenced the guard who tried to confiscate his Kodak, Beauchamp had quickly cut through prison red tape: in ten minutes Gabriel Swift was in the infirmary having his injuries looked at by the prison doctor.

Though Beauchamp found Swift's brashness hard to take, he'd been impressed by his intellect, and in the end had few qualms about representing him. He regretted not pursuing Swift's rhetorical question, "If Dr. Mulligan was your god, what do you think he was to me?" *Someone much admired* was the implication, and that comforted Beauchamp and persuaded him Gabriel would be worthy of his best efforts.

He'd been taken aback to learn that Dr. Mulligan had shared confidences about him with Swift, even to the point of declaring he'd "thrown his life away" by choosing law over literature. It was an issue Beauchamp himself had been working through, incessantly. He was only too aware that if he bungled the case it was his client's life that might be thrown away, lost to the hangman. This case was to provide the most challenging moments of his young career, and – though he might not have realized it – would determine whether he'd chosen his lifework well or badly . . . or even disastrously.

It was getting on to rush hour as his vw took them into the turmoil of Kingsway, the neon-lit diagonal scar that runs from the bowels of Burnaby to downtown Vancouver. Notwithstanding the day's lateness, Beauchamp and Moore intended to return to the office and their Dictaphones, to transcribe their notes. But a mischance on Kingsway, on the two-mile motel strip, changed these plans . . .

I had yet to encounter a green light as my Bug toiled up that garish avenue, and the congestion was compounded by an accident ahead, but Chance is not wrong that I was very pleased with myself, savouring Ophelia's compliments – "That guy was right, you are the slickest" – while pretending to shrug them off with modest smiles.

As far as I could tell, the case against Gabriel seemed flimsy: no body, no motive, no indicia to put him at the scene, and nothing to rebut suicide. So weak was the case that I did not discount the prospect of applying for bail, though its granting was almost unheard of in capital cases. No decision would be made until I saw the Crown particulars.

But something was niggling at me, something I'd done or hadn't done, something critical. Maybe Ophelia's exposed knees were distracting me.

"Am I missing something?" she said. "You never asked him if he did it, even though he gave you an opening."

"A counsel ought not to take his client's statement until he has received the Crown's version. If asked too early, it might limit options." Doubtless I didn't use those precise words, but the young Beauchamp did have a tendency to pontificate. I can hear myself – vain, teacherish, telling this newly called counsel how the pros do it.

"Something bothers me." My admirer hesitated, as if finding the matter awkward.

"Please expound, Mrs. Moore." I still couldn't bring myself to call her by her given name.

"You don't think it was odd that he turned down Harry Rankin? For you?"

I felt the air hiss from the ears of my distended head. "What do you read from that?"

"He knows he can't manipulate a top counsel, but maybe he thinks he can get around you."

I braked for yet another red light and looked at her. She seemed to flinch at her own brazenness and, as if in contrition, placed her hand on mine as it clutched the gear knob, and squeezed. Could this be the beginning of something? *Spartacus* was billed at the North Van Drive-in. Did I dare suggest we catch it?

Suddenly the engine coughed and died. I thought at first I'd taken it out of gear but then realized that what I hadn't done (*that* was the worry niggling at me) was stop for gas. Beetles of that vintage had no fuel gauges, only a reserve tank opened by bunting a little lever with one's foot. And I'd forgotten I'd already done that, forgotten I was running on reserve.

So we have a picture of the slick mouthpiece looking about wildly for a gas station as traffic clogs up behind him, finally having to ask Ophelia to take the wheel while he pushed. Mercifully, a pedestrian helped me ease it into the parking lot of the Lotus Land Motor Hotel, which boasted three and a half suspect stars and a beer parlour.

"Fuck it, then," Ophelia said. "Fuck going to the office."

Her casual use of the forbidden word caused me an erotic shiver. This wasn't the way that ladies, in my experience, talked. (Today I would hardly notice.)

"Drink sound good?"

Drink sounded ear-splittingly good. A dense haze of smoke greeted us as we entered by the door marked "Ladies and Escorts" – beer parlours were segregated in those days, not so much to protect the allegedly fragile other sex from freebooting males but to protect the allegedly dominant sex from the wiles of women on the prowl. I remember that the room was horribly decorated with plastic palm trees and paint-peeling depictions of beach scenes.

We found a table away from the din of a speaker. Ophelia flagged down a waiter, and soon four glasses of the *boisson de la maison* – draft beer – were on the table.

During the first hour or so I recall succumbing to Ophelia's questioning about my provenance and, my tongue loosened, telling her of my sequestered childhood, evenings spent in the frigid silence of a loveless home, days in the conservative confines of St. Andrew's Boys' School, skipping grades, graduating at fifteen, lacking friends of a similar age. Mine, I confessed, was a little, closed-in world, without adventure. I suffered from debilitating shyness.

I sensed Ophelia was wondering, though she was too kind to express it, whether this character had ever been laid. Again I caught a tantalizing view of an armpit not shaved – a statement of independence, I assumed, of earthiness.

I carried on at doubtless boring length (because she demanded being briefed on the life thrown away) about my study of the ancient classics, the glories of Greek and Roman culture. At some point, I was reminded later, I began loudly spouting the aphorisms of Publilius Syrus ("We desire nothing so much as what we ought not to have"). And I was getting very loud, talking over Elvis as he begged for the safety of his blue suede shoes. Soon my theatrics were attracting applause from neighbouring tables. It was as if I had shed my carapace and the jovial inner showman had emerged.

I dimly remember people buying us rounds. I remember a pitcher appearing on our beer-slopped terrycloth table cover, but I don't remember it disappearing. Aside from a couple of trips to the men's, the rest is blank, though Ophelia later filled in some gaps – not all – and, more recently, responded to Wentworth Chance's indelicate sleuthing with further details.

WEDNESDAY, APRIL 25, 1962

I was Mars and she Venus, and we were hot and slippery with rut and sweat, nakedly entwined upon the springy heights of Olympus. Hungrily she drew my erect phallus toward her mouth, but I was fearful of entering there; I was unversed at this – it was unnatural, long forbidden by codified law. Then a proxy orifice blossomed open, a thick-tufted nest to hide in . . .

(That I remember that dream speaks not just to its intensity but also to the frequency with which versions of it have repeated over the years, like a bad X-rated film.)

I woke up with not just an erection but a rock-crusher of a hangover, and with no immediate sense of where I was or what day it was, or even the season of the year. An obscene racket from an alarm clock beside my bed announced it was just after eight-thirty, presumably in the morning. I concluded I was in the bedroom of my flat. What wasn't coming back, even fuzzily, was how I'd got there. My single bed was in utter disarray, its sheets on the floor, and I was naked, my boxer shorts hanging, for no apparent reason, on my doorknob.

I pulled them on, staggered out to the shared bathroom for what seemed an interminable pour. My resonating groans of urinary relief must have alerted my hallway neighbour, Ira Lavitch, a beatnik, a coffeehouse impresario. His lazy drawl: "You hanging in there okay, my good man? Hope you didn't use all the hot water." There was a damp bath towel on the rack – one of mine – but I had no memory of using the shower during the night.

On my exit, Ira recoiled from the sight and smell of me. "You must've been really rockin' out last night, Stretch." Late thirties, thick sideburns framing a skinny face with the requisite goatee. Naked, a towel around his middle. "Did I not hear the sweet illegal sound of female laughter?"

I didn't pause to ask what had titillated him through the wall, but I was alert to the alarming possibility that I'd broken the landlord's first commandment: thou shalt not entertain women after eight.

Back in my rooms, when I opened a window to expel the fart-thick air, I saw that my car was parked below. Then I spotted a typed note in my portable Smith-Corona: *I set your alarm. Sweet dreams. O.* Beside it, an ashtray with two lipsticked cork-tipped butts.

I decided that Ophelia had tanked up the Bug and driven me home, for I couldn't imagine I'd been in any shape to do so myself. But then what? In a state barely short of panic, I checked the sheets. No wetness other than from my own sweat, but I did come across a white splotch midway down the mattress sheet. The juices of coitus? Or its disproof, the masturbatory spill of denied desire? (There shall be no censoring of this, the authorized, non-publishable version.)

I fought like a gladiator for memory, but all was a void. I didn't dare return to my erotic dream to seek answers; I'd already sent its images packing, back to the subconscious. I studied the note again, that round, inviting, lusty O. I returned to the washroom for a cold, punishing shower.

Gertrude winced as she watched her shaky boss, eyes as ugly and red as the Canadian Ensign, shuffle into his office. A few minutes later she appeared with a mug of coffee and a packet of breath mints.

"Anything else?" she asked. "Aspirin?"

That she was treating my temporary malady with the casual case of an emergency room nurse confirmed my sense that this sprightly young woman (we called them girls back then, or young ladies, expressions once considered polite) had the stuff of indispensability.

"Mr. Smythe-Baldwin returned your call. MUtual 4-7141. He'll be in his office until ten."

It was nearing that time. I was hardly ready for the great barrister, a crafty veteran with a Hogarthian appetite for the table and an equal lust for a favourable verdict. Smitty, he was called by friends. I had watched him many times take the skin off witnesses and wasn't confident I could salvage my own, even from the other end of a phone line.

I was vulnerable not only because of my weakened state but because I was hugely distracted, my thoughts constantly whipping off to the events of the previous night, to Ophelia, the sheets on the floor, the evidence of seminal discharge. Clearly she had used the shower before leaving. What went on before that? I could barely countenance the awkward but compelling scenario: we had got it on . . . had sexual relations (let's not hide behind euphemism!). My first time – supposedly an event that good men and true never forget – and it was smothered in alcoholic fog.

I had not even the vaguest idea what I might say to Ophelia on our next encounter. It was her land registry day; I wouldn't see her until much later, so there was yet a chance to recover crucial information from my abused brain cells.

My hand hovered above the phone shakily, and I waited until I was able to still it, then dialled. I got Smythe-Baldwin's personal secretary.

"I am returning the call he returned to me."

"And who might you be?" I pictured her as grey-haired, steely-eyed.

"Sorry. Arthur Beauchamp, counsel for Gabriel Swift."

"Please hold."

I did so, for nearly two minutes – a lag lawyers call a power delay. I assumed Smythe-Baldwin was calmly reviewing his file while going through a ritual of unwrapping, clipping, and lighting a five-dollar Cuban cigar, grunting his pleasure at that first tasty puff. Meanwhile, I was wondering if Pappas had wangled me into taking this case because he thought I'd be meat for Smythe-Baldwin's grinder.

When he finally picked up, I introduced myself. He said, "You pronounce your name *bee-chem*, which is not the proper way. *Beech'm* – a single vowel. The English tongue rebels against excessive syllables. Which is why Cholmondeley becomes *chum-lee* – thank God for that – and Magdalen College is *maudlin*." Cambridge's venerable all-male college. I'd won a scholarship there, and I wondered if this was a subtle thrust, he being a British-born Oxfordian. But it appeared he knew little about me.

"So you are the young fellow Pappas warned me about. An aspirant for stardom. I must keep my sword unsheathed and my pencils sharpened." I'm sure he used a more striking metaphorical image. Though his quotes are cobbled from tattered memory, I have tried to capture his lovely fustian articulation. "And how does it feel having been granted the daunting task of representing a defendant whose mouth runneth over rather too illiberally, or so it would seem from the foul imprecations he directed to the arresting constabulary?"

Unlike me, he'd earned the right to be pompous, an attribute the press found endearing. I could offer no comment on those imprecations, I said, not having seen the police report, or any particulars of evidence whatsoever. He promised to send a runner within the hour.

"Rather interesting fact situation. Embittered, short-tempered Native slaps away the spoon that fed him, drowns his benefactor in the Squamish River at flood time, only several miles from where its raging waters empty into the sea. One assumes the sharks stripped poor Mulligan to the bone and left the scraps for the bottom-feeders. Nicely thought out – no mounds of earth, no charred corpse, no bullet holes."

Then an excursus: "I defended a missing-body case myself, Beauchamp, back in – when was it? – forty-nine. Everything else was there: motive, opportunity, blood traces on a chainsaw, a sloppy alibi. Had to settle for manslaughter, but I called it a victory."

If that was a hint of an offer, I wasn't biting. That he even mentioned the option of manslaughter suggested his case was feeble. He hadn't bamboozled me; I was feeling surer of myself. But I couldn't hold back from a little pandering.

"I'd be surprised, Mr. Smythe-Baldwin, if you noticed me watching with awe from the counsel bench during several of your recent successes. It will be an honour to meet you formally next week in the Squamish police court."

"We prefer to call it Magistrate's Court, young man. Else the police will think they run it."

I felt like a chided student. "Sir, your reputation was built as a defender of the innocent, or at least those presumed so. Will you be comfortable prosecuting someone who actually is innocent?" I astounded myself with my effrontery; maybe I was still alcohol-impaired.

"The Attorney General personally urged me to accept his retainer, old chap, having wrongly surmised that the defence would be run by a leading counsel. I'm sure he now regrets being stuck with my atrociously high fees."

I had barely recovered from that slight when his runner showed up at noon with a thick legal-sized envelope.

~~~

A standard RCMP/GRC incident report was the first of a dozen carbon-copied pages I perused over a takeout cheeseburger.

On 21/4/62 at 1925 hrs, undersigned received telephone call from MRS. IRENE MULLIGAN re missing person, her husband DERMOT MULLIGAN, address upper Squamish Valley Road, rural area 10 m. nw of Cheekye. Alleged missing individual went off fishing, exact location unknown, on Squamish River at approx.1400 intending to return for supper and failed to show. Neighbours have been alerted. U/S proceeded to said address at 1945 hrs.
Signed,
Constable Brad Jettles

Jettles hadn't responded to the call with lightning speed. Likely he was the sole officer then available at the small detachment. In 1962 the village of Squamish was a frontier town, and its fallers, riggers, truckers, and sawmill and construction workers tended to be boisterous on holiday weekends.

Jettles's next incident report was longer, hammered out the

following morning, a Sunday, presumably over coffee – there was a brown ring-shaped stain on the reverse side of one of the pages.

On 21/4/62 at 2005 hrs, undersigned arrived at Squamish Valley Road north of Cheakamus Reserve, which is reached by gravel road, area mostly scrub, also some small farms including the above-noted with a hay field, barn, corral, and a few horses and fenced garden plot. Residence is a typical A-frame structure with large addition at the back, on a rise over the Squamish River, which had flooded its banks in places. This is a vacation home which the missing person, a Vancouver doctor, DR. DERMOT MULLIGAN, shares with his wife IRENE when not in Vancouver.

On arrival, U/S met with BUCK AND THELMA MCLEAN, neighbours across from the Mulligans on Squamish Valley Road. They had just finished a search with flashlights along the nearby riverbank where Dr. Mulligan went fishing. Chinook and steelhead were running. They said he went off somewhere in the afternoon on foot with his gear and hip waders.

The McLeans and other civilians hiked up and down beside the river from dusk until it got too dark. They found no sign of Dr. Mulligan. U/S asked if he had a boat, and was informed he has a canoe, which I observed had been pulled from the water and was on high ground. The family vehicle, a 1960 Buick Invicta station wagon, was in the driveway. The only other vehicle present was Buck McLean's new 1962 C120 4x4 International pickup, plus a 1956 Massey Harris 444 Standard near the barn.

Jettles clearly suffered a fetishistic interest in rolling stock. It was a struggle getting through the report, and I didn't know how I would survive until day's end, when I hoped to meet with Ophelia and review – subtly, carefully – the events of the past evening. Gertrude, a mind reader, entered the Crypt with a tall mug of hot coffee, then slipped silently away.

I read on. Mrs. McLean had escorted Jettles into the Mulligan cottage, where a couple of other local women were gathered around Irene Mulligan, comforting her and encouraging her to eat what she could of a re-warmed dinner made for two. The constable, still under the misapprehension that Mulligan was a medical doctor, learned little from her, only that she had warned him not to slip on the mossy rocks and not to be late for supper. She had gone for a half-hour walk that afternoon along Squamish Valley Road, as she often did, then returned home to prepare their meal.

Mulligan was a hardy outdoorsman despite his slight build and donnish way of dressing. This I knew from my own conversations with him, when he'd talked of his love for canoeing, hiking, skiing, and fishing, though he recoiled at the thought of hunting. He'd once confided, somewhat ruefully, that Irene was pretty much a homebody and didn't share those enthusiasms. He said her one passion was duplicate bridge – a hobby not easy to pursue in the wilds of the Squamish Valley. She much preferred to stay in the city.

On further inquiries, U/S learned the Mulligans employ an Indian groundskeeper who also house-sits for them during their absences. Name GABRIEL SWIFT, who is known to the detachment, as is his 1953 Triumph Tiger 650 twin-cylinder motorcycle. When not house-sitting, this individual resides at the Cheakamus Reserve, and according to Mrs. Mulligan wasn't around that day. She insisted he was a "faithful" employee and "entirely honest" and has never been any kind of trouble.

However, in private Mrs. McLean approached U/S to dispute this, and she agreed to attend RCMP Squamish today, 22/4/62, at 0900 to fill out a witness statement form. U/S did not have backup to make inquiries on the reserve at night, and postponed that. Aided by Buck McLean and some other men, we did one more riverbank search to no avail. Dogmaster called in from E Division, with civilian search-and-rescue effort continuing today, Sunday, 22/4/62.
Signed at 1037 hrs,
Cst B. Jettles

Irene Mulligan had been in too distressed a state to be interviewed at length. Obviously I had to talk to her soon, before the prosecution could persuade her to alter her good report card for Swift. She would be a valuable character witness.

Thelma McLean was the neighbour who'd later alerted the press to Gabriel's unsavoury habit of hiding in books, thereby seeming "troubled." In her police statement of Sunday morning, she voiced other grave concerns: Swift had "worked his way into Dr. Mulligan's confidence" and "had the run of the place." He also tended to look at her in a way that unsettled her (she did not describe this look). Swift, she said, had been in the Mulligans' service for thirty months, since they'd bought the riverside farm. "The professor would come most weekends, sometimes longer, two weeks, a month, and Irene, she came less frequent, usually only a weekend or two in summer, but otherwise their caretaker had the place to hisself. Slept in their bed, I believe."

Her statement was made not to Jettles but to Staff Sergeant Roscoe Knepp, whose efforts to draw her out had born dubious fruit. She said the neighbourhood was "a thieves' playground," with "tools and building materials and anything you leave outside your house constantly disappearing, including clothes, even my own underthings and stockings I left on the line overnight."

One would have thought her insinuation that Gabriel stole her underwear would prompt at least a sideways look from Knepp, but instead he prodded her: "Q: Did you observe that he had any sexual problems, or unusual perversions?" Mrs. McLean was likely having difficulty sorting out which of the known perversions were unusual, and could only reply: "I thought he was very spooky."

That seemed so at odds with Irene Mulligan's assessment that I could only conclude that Knepp and his witness were in competition to show who was the more intolerant. Gabriel had told me he and Knepp had "a bad history," which I took to mean the staff sergeant had a grudge against my client. I found a clue to that in Gabriel's blotter, which was stapled to the police reports. In October 1959 he'd been convicted of assaulting a peace officer.

His sheet also showed a juvenile offence for shoplifting (he was fourteen) and two adult convictions under the Fisheries Act. A minor record, paling against those earned by most of the sorry folk I'd defended. The one indictable offence, assault of a peace officer, would provide fodder for my next session with Gabriel. He'd been let off with a six-month suspended sentence. (Some years later the magistrate confided to me over a dram that he had an unsavoury view of Knepp, and had suspended that sentence to stick it to him.)

The mere reading of these reports was wearying. I thought of crawling under my desk for a snooze, but of course that would, by some arcane means, trigger a visit by a senior partner. They liked to poke their heads in to see if the worker bees were putting in their billable hours. I compromised by setting my chair into a semi-reclining position and resting my feet on the desk. I began reading Jettles's next incident report.

He'd shown up at the Mulligans' early on Sunday with two other constables. A score of mountain-hardy men had gathered in the pre-dawn morning – back-country guides, white-water experts – and Jettles had briefed them on their task. Both riverbanks were to be scoured by foot and by boat, five miles each way.

Jettles and his backup team had intended to carry on to the Cheakamus Reserve and seek out Gabriel Swift. But that turned out not to be necessary, for he noticed Gabriel standing among the volunteers, hiking boots on, a rucksack, a rope coiled around his shoulders, a Brooklyn Dodgers cap on his head.

As the search crew began dispersing upriver and downriver, U/S politely asked the subject if we could sit down together. He said he had "no time to sit down" and he "knew where to go." When I ordered him to stay, he used foul language and set off by foot south, downriver, very fast, leaving everyone behind. U/S pursued but lost the suspect and radioed CST. GRUMMOND and CST. BORACHUK to follow Squamish Valley Road south and intercept . . .

~~~

I awoke to Gertrude's nudge and her soft voice. "It's five-thirty, Mr. Beauchamp. I'm going home."

Through sleep-blurred eyes I made out that my feet were still on the desk but shoeless – my black brogues were on the floor beside me. Gertrude was in her coat, maintaining a straight face as she handed me a list of calls she'd intercepted. I managed a hoarse thank-you before she left, and took a few minutes to work the kinks out of my neck.

Among the afternoon callers, my mother, a reminder about Sunday dinner: *Six-thirty, please don't be late.* I recalled that Professor Winkle from the History Department would be there. He'd been a colleague of Dr. Mulligan, so I expected the evening to be even more joyless than usual.

Two calls from a client in constant need of coddling: a Liquor Branch quality controller facing his second impaired driving that year. Jim Brady, the labour activist, Gabriel's friend and political mentor. And finally, Ophelia Moore – but she left no message, no greeting, no offer of sympathy or affection. Gertrude had appended a note: *I told her you were tied up.*

Worried that Ophelia might have assumed I was putting her off, I shod myself, stuffed the Swift file into my briefcase, and hurried down to her floor, the twelfth. I found her office empty. A few overtime toilers were still about, and one called, "Try the Georgia."

My long nap had resurrected me, and I sped on the wings of Mercury to the Georgia Hotel, across from the courthouse. In its street-front bar a dozen young lawyers and articling students were crammed around two joined tables, Ophelia sandwiched between two slavering wolves from Russell, DuMoulin.

She appeared to be enjoying herself with immoderate gaiety. There wasn't room to slide an extra chair in beside her, and anyway I wasn't about to demean myself by joining this sordid competition for her favours. The chief challenger was the dashing Jordan Geraldson, who'd recently won a $150,000 personal injury case, a West Coast record.

I slipped onto a barstool, my back to them, pretending eagerness to chew the fat with Harvey Frinkell, a divorce lawyer. "I heard you sprang O'Houlihan," he said. "Good job." Jimmy "Fingers" O'Houlihan was a slippery gumshoe I'd got acquitted of suborning a witness. Frinkell made wide use of his services against adulterers.

"Hey, I know her," he said, eyes fixed on the mirror behind the bar, watching Ophelia in the reflection. He bent to my ear. "I did her husband's divorce. Pretty good job – she walked out of that courtroom practically naked."

"What were the grounds?"

"O'Houlihan caught her *flagrante delicto* in the back seat of the co-respondent's Studebaker Gran Turismo Hawk. The photos turned out real good. She's a honey trap – she's looking to fuck her way to the top. I heard she slept with at least two of your senior partners just to stay on after articles. Confirm or deny?"

I was too furious to respond. My hands, under the bar, were curled into fists.

"Look at those gazongas."

I did look, and met Ophelia's eyes in the mirror. Her smile faded as she took in Harvey Frinkell leaning to my ear.

I slid off the stool and fled.

From "Where the Squamish River Flows," *A Thirst for Justice*, © W. Chance

HARVEY FRINKELL, THE DIVORCE LAWYER who Ophelia Moore claims "screwed" her in the courtroom, was disbarred in 1974 for sleeping with and bilking a client. In subsequently drinking himself to death he has relieved this author of libel risk, and I can freely say there was ample reason why only six people showed up at his funeral.

Ms. Moore told me she well remembers seeing Beauchamp sitting at the bar, hip to hip with Frinkell, on that late afternoon of April 25, 1962. Her account was forthright: "Of course they were talking about me. Arthur was looking right at me while that noxious worm was practically sticking his tongue in his ear. I have to say I did lose respect for Arthur then – the cowardly way he retreated without trying to set the matter straight."

During my sessions with Beauchamp he balked at repeating his brief conversation with Frinkell. Though he insisted that his reticence about talking about Moore was out of polite discretion, some light is shone on their relationship by a tangle they got into twenty-four years later, when as a high court judge she chastised him for his cross-examination of a sexual assault complainant.

Moore, eighty-three at the time of this writing and eight years retired from the Court of Appeal, still owns one of the tartest tongues in the women's movement she helped pioneer. She vividly recalled her evening with Beauchamp at the Lotus Land's beer parlour ("a hilarious time") and driving him home. But as to whether and in what manner she spent the night, she said dryly, "If Arthur doesn't want to say what went on, I shall not embarrass him."

So we are left to speculate as to whether this, the first of Beauchamp's handful of significant female relationships, played a part in shaping difficulties he later endured with the opposite sex, particularly with his first wife, the effervescent Annabelle Beauchamp . . .

After picking up five days' worth of cups and glasses, balling up the sheets for the laundry, and putting the coffee on the hotplate, I reopened the Swift file and tried to find my place. But my mind fluttered back to the Georgia lounge, that awful moment when Ophelia saw me giving ear to Harvey Frinkell's filthy calumnies.

Early evening was upon the city, the sun dipping behind the blocky apartments of the West End. I had much work to do before my next visit to Gabriel Swift, but I felt stalled, unable to get my brain in gear. I pawed through my LPs, looking for something gentle and melodious – a Mozart quartet, a Beethoven sonata – but all my albums were in disarray, as were my books, my literary journals, my clothes, my unwashed dishes, my entire flat, my life. Anyway, Ira had begun to play his own records on the other side of our thin shared wall. He was into mainstream folksingers, Belafonte, Odetta, but also unfamiliar names he'd hosted in his coffeehouse, names that seemed playful, made up: Ochs, Lightfoot, Hicks, Baez, Buffy.

The hoarse whisky voice of Leadbelly penetrated the wall. "Good night, Irene, I'll see you in my dreams . . ." The plaintive, almost legendary ballad startled me with its ironic relevance: "Sometimes I take a great notion to jump in the river and drown . . ." The Weavers' version, popular in the previous decade, could not have escaped the attention of even a recluse like Dermot Mulligan.

I settled down with my coffee and picked up where I'd left off: Easter Sunday morning. Gabriel Swift has taken off running. Jettles puffs along behind, along with a dozen volunteers, and loses him.

At 0747 hrs the search party led by U/S finally encountered Swift standing by a boulder overlooking the river. He led us down a narrow gap in the rocks overlooked by previous searchers, a steep decline that led to a flat overlook approx. 5 feet above the river. There I observed a number of personal items including jacket, shirt, undershirt, trousers, hiking boots, hip waders, a watch, wallet, ring. There was also an open tackle box and a fishing rod.

This scene of abandoned clothing pointed plainly toward suicide. Jettles was experienced enough not to muck about with evidence, though he did go through pockets. Someone produced a camera and took photos. There seemed a chance of rain, so a canvas tarpaulin was laid over everything to await crime scene personnel.

Jettles seemed not to have had further conversation with Gabriel then, or later, when they got back to the Mulligan farmyard. By that time Constables Grummond and Borachuk had returned from their fruitless search by road, and presently Staff Sergeant Roscoe Knepp and an ID officer showed up.

Gabriel wasn't mentioned for the next few pages of this folio, which mostly comprised interviews with Mulligan's neighbours – only a handful, for there were just five occupied small farms in this chunk of flatland forest north of the Cheakamus Reserve. All responded that they'd noticed nothing remarkable on the previous day. No shouts, no screams, no floating bodies, no strangers, and, said one, "No bands of thieving kids off of the reserve." All knew Gabriel Swift, knew he was the Mulligans' handyman and house-sitter. All knew he travelled about by motorcycle or, because it was frequently in the repair shop, by bicycle or foot. None of the neighbours but the McLeans had more than a nodding acquaintance with Dermot, and they only rarely encountered Irene, usually on her afternoon walks. "She barely acknowledged me," one said. I picked up a slight disdain, a backwoods snobbery toward the hoity-toity hobby farmers.

Irene was subjected to a second interview, in which she remained Gabriel's stout defender, insisting he was "almost like a son to Dermot," had never done anyone harm, never shown signs of violence. That seemed a slight exaggeration, given his assault of an officer and the fact that, as she admitted, she had limited dealings with him.

She wouldn't be much help for a suicide defence. She'd told Borachuk her husband had been deeply involved in "his work" – presumably his memoir – and she discerned no signs of depression. They'd been looking forward to a visit the following week to the newly opened World's Fair in Seattle.

I'd met Irene only twice, on visits as a student to their Vancouver residence. On one occasion, having been invited for a glass of port, I arrived on the wrong day. Dermot was out and she seemed flustered, apologetic, her hair a mess of bobby pins. I saw her staring at me from a window as I left, and felt spooked. In my graduating year I came by to thank Dermot for endorsing me for a Cambridge scholarship. She invited me in, appearing less frazzled, and informed me that Dermot was hard at work in his study but would soon be down. She brought me tea and shyly scurried off, and I waited in their parlour for twenty minutes until my idol appeared, rubbing his eyes, apologizing – he'd obviously been having a nap.

They'd married late, both in their forties. She was now fifty-two, two years older than him, a minor academic from an agricultural college associated with the University of Minnesota. They'd met at a conference there. A laconic woman, rather busty but otherwise shapeless, and somewhat dowdy. I often wondered if he'd married her only to discount rumours that he might not have all his male genes in place, with his high voice and his occasional fluttering manner. But he'd confided to me she was indispensable, a studious editor and researcher who also typed his manuscripts and formal correspondence.

An appended exhibit list offered no clues as to what had happened on that hidden ledge above the river. The only papers found in Mulligan's wool-lined jacket were a six-month-old restaurant receipt and a more recent B.C. Electric bill. Coins, paperclips, and other pocket litter in his pants. The wallet had a driver's licence, membership cards in a few learned societies, an Esso credit card and a Carte Blanche, a pocket calendar, a snapshot of Irene, and three ten-dollar bills and three twos. Curiously missing from Jettles's list of clothing were underpants and socks.

Gabriel was not arrested on Sunday, contrary to media reports, though he was picked up on Squamish Valley Road just after noon, while returning from the riverside search.

On 22/4/62 at 1230 hrs, with Cst. Borachuk driving and undersigned Grummond in the back of a patrol car with Gabriel Swift, the following conversation took place as copied into my notebook shortly after:

Grummond: So what were you up to yesterday, Gabriel?

Swift: I was on our traditional hunting grounds.

G: Bag anything?

S: (shakes head)

G: So you like to do a little shooting, Gabriel?

(no response)

G: Maybe a little fishing too? On the river?

(no response)

G: When did you get back?

S: I was with my girlfriend all afternoon. Anything else?

G: What's her name?

Swift then asked if he was a suspect, and U/S Grummond said we had no reason to suspect him, we just need the whole picture from someone who knew the deceased so we can figure out what happened. I asked him again to state the hours he was with his girlfriend, and he said he had nothing more to say. Subject was released pending further inquiries and told not to stray far.

Below Grummond's signature was a handwritten note: *Later ascertained girlfriend is one Monique Joseph, daughter of Chief Benjamin Joseph, Cheakamus Reserve.*

I was having an increasingly hard time figuring out what the Crown's case was based on. I suspected worse must be coming, but my curiosity was put on hold by a phone call.

"I hope I'm not interrupting anything." She would have said something like that, a typical opener.

"Not at all, Mother." The telephone cord uncoiled as I searched my cabinet for a part-bottle of rye I'd stashed on the top shelf. It was there, but empty.

"Not that there could be anything interesting to do in that hole you call a bachelor suite. What are you listening to?"

"'The Volga Boatmen.' Paul Robeson."

"Such a sad man. Lovely talent, but tainted by his adherence to the great false god. At least he's open about it" – unlike the communist sympathizers who, Mavis Beauchamp maintained, lurked on campus, especially in the arts and science faculty – "I need not remind you of Sunday?"

"Half past six. Professor Winkle is coming."

"I would very much appreciate it if you did not get as potted as when we entertained Dean Prentice. And I don't want you challenging Winkle about his distaste for Lord Macaulay."

"Yes, Mother."

"Another thing – it's in the papers that you're going to represent Dermot Mulligan's killer, so I imagine Winkle will ask about it. They were fairly close, you know, but I beg you not to carry on about it in sordid detail."

"I shall be seen but not much heard."

She finally asked after my welfare and I told her I was eating well – an outright lie. In days gone by I'd always had someone to feed me: the cook came Monday to Friday and on weekends there was takeout or Mother might make something. For that evening's meal I'd planned a tin of sardines with soda crackers, perhaps topped off with a bowl of cornflakes.

I apologized for having to cut the call short. The music from next door had stopped and Ira had come calling.

Ira Lavitch called himself a member of Kerouac's "beaten-down generation" – for short, a beat. He'd fled from Philadelphia a year before, certain that President Kennedy would be calling on him to kill for God and country in Vietnam.

"So who was that lady you snuck in here last night?"

"I must have had the radio on too loud."

A skeptical laugh. "I give food for rides." He pulled on his jacket. "We're serving up some chili at the Beanery." His coffeehouse on Fourth Avenue. "Let's split."

"Split?"

"Be gone, man."

Chili sounded exponentially more appetizing than cornflakes. I wanted a break; my concentration was coming poorly.

As we descended the outer staircase we happened upon Crazy Craznik, as we called him, the bewhiskered landlord, raking trash near the back fence. Ira was sure he'd been a Nazi camp command-ant in the Balkans.

Craznik bent down beside my Volkswagen and rose triumph-antly, thrusting at me a lipsticked cigarette butt. "No ladies! No ladies!"

~~~

We stopped at a gas station before tackling the Burrard Bridge. I hadn't driven the vw since Ophelia brought me home the previous night. Realizing she'd filled the tank, I sheepishly paid thirty cents for a one-gallon top-up.

Ira kept prodding me about the night, the husky laughter, the smutty bumps and grunts. I declined to play along, though I was avid to know if I'd been deflowered.

"Didn't hear the rhythmic beat of the springs . . . Where'd you do it, Stretch, on top of your hotplate?"

Maybe on the floor, where I'd found the sheets. I wished I could tell him it was a night to remember.

"She a pinup? Straight or kinky? You looked so wiped out this morning I got the impression your kama couldn't keep up with her sutra."

My boxer shorts hanging on the doorknob, like a trophy from the hunt. Was that straight or kinky?

"How come I never met her? How did *you* meet her? Not at the Beanery, I hope – only nice girls go there."

Long-haired, long-legged twenty-year-olds, so cool, so mysterious that I hadn't the foggiest notion how to approach them. Different from plump, blunt Ophelia. I vaguely remembered telling her I frequented the Beanery, hoping to impress her with my bohemianness.

We swung off the bridge onto Fourth Avenue – a Kitsilano artery to the UBC campus, low-rent, architecturally bland, but with a few oases affording escape from the confines of academe. Ira often maintained that "a scene is about to happen here, man." The scene was undergoing a slow birth, but there was a bookstore near the Beanery, an art gallery across the street, and nearby, a busker playing a harmonica – curly dark hair, a guitar slung over his shoulder, a glowing cigarette stuck between the frets.

Night had fallen, a half-moon rising. A clutch of people huddled in a darkened doorway sharing a bottle; the Beanery was a no-booze zone, and Ira's window sign made that clear, particularly to the licensing inspectors who often harassed him. Other signs promoted coming attractions: a jazz trio called the Alley Cats, a sitar player from Calcutta, and the Melodians, a smiling, stomping, singing threesome. But those were the class acts, justifying cover charges. Most nights featured raspy, off-key protest singers who played to thin houses and afterwards passed the hat.

Ira wasn't losing his shirt, but he was having trouble keeping it on. Competition was tough in those days, with live acts – Liberace, Tony Bennett, Sophie Tucker – at the Cave and Isy's and the infamous Penthouse, a BYOB club frequented by hookers, gangsters, gamblers, and lawyers.

Ira had scrounged scores of oddball movie and art posters, and they added to the Dada-esque decor of this narrow rectangle of candle-topped tables. Maximum seating was forty-five but only eight were in there, plus Lawonda, an impossibly exotic Ghanaian in charge of coffee, chili, and the till – she was Ira's entire workforce. A chess game was underway at one table, Chinese checkers at another.

Ira jumped on the small stage to do a sound check while I signalled Lawonda to bring me a bowl of the best and a coffee. The busker wandered in, cigarette dangling from his lips. He vaulted onto the stage, knocked the spit from his harmonica, and did some tuning licks on his guitar. A young aspirant marking time before returning to college or his dad's insurance business. Straddling a stool, he began to sing with an unforgiving nasal twang: "Corrina, Corrina."

Lawonda came with a tray and placed before me a bowl of chili that brought impatient groans from my stomach. "I made it special for you, Stretch." She leaned toward my ear. "Ira told me you like it hot."

She was in her thirties, wise, salty, and sexy. Body by Botticelli in charcoal, stunning beyond my dreams, therefore untouchable. She was swathed in a multicoloured wrap, something West African and dramatic. A worldly woman, rumoured to have enjoyed a sinful past, she'd bounced from Accra to the Canaries, then Barcelona and London. Lovers galore, I supposed.

"Who's that kid up there?"

"Dylan – like the poet."

Only nineteen, his first album was out . . . and I can't remember what else she said because I'd been turned to stone, spoon suspended six inches from my mouth as I zoomed in on Ophelia Moore. She had just entered, arm in arm with Jordan Geraldson, the prince of torts.

As he pulled back her chair, she gave him a smooch. I rose unsteadily, my appetite in powerful remission. Lawonda stepped back, startled.

Outside by the curb, I retched, but nothing came out.

~~~

On 23/4/62 at 1120 hours, U/S Cst Jettles attended home of Benjamin Joseph, near Cheekye, Cheakamus Reserve, in company of Cst Borachuk. Benjamin, who everyone on the force calls Ben, is hereditary chief here. Also present was his common-law wife Anna and their youngest daughter, Monique, 16, who is in high school. Ben advised Monique was home all afternoon of Saturday, 21/4/62, and was never in the company of Gabriel Swift on that particular day. Monique also signed a statement to same effect.

This was a photocopied scrap of lined paper titled "unsworn affidavit." One sentence: *I, Monique Joseph, full-time student at Squamish Secondary, state as a fact that on Saturday last I was never in the company of Gabriel Swift, of this reserve.* Dated, signed, and witnessed by its author, Brad Jettles.

Though these words smacked of artificiality – *Saturday last* sounded of cop talk – they came as a blow. So much for the prospect of bail. I blinked away a vision of Gabriel walking morosely to the gallows, betrayed by his lover – for surely she had bent to others' wills. I couldn't see an intelligent man like Gabriel lying to the police, creating an alibi that could be so easily exposed.

This day had already set a record for being the worst of my dismal life. It was near its end, ten-thirty, and I finally managed to eat and keep down my tin of sardines and six saltines, all the while desperately hoping Ophelia hadn't seen me cringing my way out of the Beanery.

There was one last document.

23/4/62, at 1500 hours, transcription of recorded interview with Gabriel Swift, in cells at Squamish Detachment. Present were S/Sgt. Knepp and U/S Cst. Jettles. Suspect not restrained. Suspect looked like he'd been in a brawl, with what we observed as facial bruising.

K: You been cautioned you don't have to say anything. You remember that warning, Gabriel?

S: (nods)

K: You prefer Gabe? I heard on the reserve it's Gabby, which is good, because we'd like to hear you do some talking.

S: This is totally crazy.

K: Okay, we just want to straighten out a few things here, then if everything checks out maybe we can all go home.

S: Home to what? Who's going to pay for garbaging my cabin? I want a list of everything you took. I want it back, every damn book and magazine, my radio and my records.

K: Settle down, son. We just want to ask a few questions about what you were doing Saturday afternoon.

S: I told you. I was with my girl.

K: Uh-huh. Where, exactly?

S: In my cabin.

K: Doing what?

S: I was teaching her chess. We were listening to music.

J: Teaching her chess? That's all you did?

(no response)

J: We just talked to Monique, pal. She never saw you once on Saturday.

K: So it looks like you got some explaining, right, Gabriel?

S: Why am I in this cell, Sergeant? Am I charged with something?

K: Right now, we're just holding you for investigation. You want to rethink what you were doing on Saturday? You were with Professor Mulligan, right? A part of the time anyway.

J: We don't say you did anything, Gabriel, but we heard he invited you to go fishing with him.

S: You heard that from whom?

J: From whom? Whom? Who learned you such refined English, Gabriel? Your fishing buddy, maybe? Professor Mulligan?

S: Fuck off, you fat creep.

K: Whoa, whoa, let's all cool down here, and watch your language. Let's talk about the deceased. What were your relations with him?

(no response)

K: Sounds like you've got something to hide. I'm not saying you and him had a fight; maybe something else was going on between you.

S: Let me ask you a question, Sergeant. Are you making up this case out of pure bullshit because I dropped you for calling me a lippy fucking Indian shit?

At this point interview was concluded, as suspect wasn't willing to cooperate further at this time.

I returned to the prologue of this interview. *Suspect looked like he'd been in a brawl.* Remarkably, during the Q and A session these so-called peace officers hadn't asked how he'd got those bruises.

I was prepared to gamble my soul that Gabriel's version was the gospel truth. Impatient with his attitude, Knepp had delivered a few shots to his head. The sidekick, Jettles, had taken that role literally, aiming a kick below the ribs. Quite a feat, unless Gabriel was down on the floor.

There wasn't much else in the file: a note that the abandoned clothes had gone to Vancouver for analysis, along with various scrapings, tweezered unknowns, and fingerprint lifts.

Framed by a fascist fucking cabal of racist brownshirts, as quoted, more or less, by a *Sun* reporter.

I would head up there on the weekend to undo what damage I could. I would have to skirt around Knepp and his crew and be careful in my approach to Chief Joseph. I would have to reach out to his cowed daughter before her lying words gelled as false memory.

I told myself that Ophelia Moore would only get in the way were she asked to accompany me.

I was committed all day to be legal aid duty counsel at 312 Main Street, which in those days incestuously housed both the police station and the magistrates' courts. Such coziness would be regarded as appalling today, but in the sixties the line between justice and enforcement was fuzzy. The Public Safety Building was (and remains) Vancouver's ugliest structure, an institutional intrusion into skid road, with its strip clubs and beer parlours and general sense of carefree lawlessness.

The fifth-floor cells at 312 were mostly populated by alcoholics and vagrants, who were dealt with in bunches in court – hapless hungover men and women who would troop up to get their week or month or more in custody. It was an offence to be homeless back then (Vagrancy A) or to be in a state of intoxication in a public place (SIPP), and Vag A's and SIPPs comprised the bulk of those who were run through the daily mill in Courtroom Two. The human zoo, we called it.

Occasionally real criminals would be called up, and while their lawyers spoke to bail I'd use the break for whispered conferences with derelicts in the dock. I spent the lunch hour doing quickie interviews in the cells. The work was as exhausting as it was unfulfilling, and Magistrate Scott was grumpy, erupting at poorly prepared counsel.

At day's end I had a couple of drafts next door at the West Coast Central Club, whose "membership only" designation was largely ignored, particularly by the many police who enjoyed off-hours there. Its roof occasionally served as a landing site for escapees roping down from prison windows at night.

When I returned to the Crypt at five-thirty, I was still in a sour mood. Gertrude had kindly waited up for me, but I was peremptory when I asked her to phone Oakalla. "Do it quickly – they go bananas when they don't get notice."

Then I saw, sitting on my desk blotter, copies of Woodcock's *Anarchism,* the Camus, the I.F. Stone, and the *Monthly Review* for April, along with a sales slip. She had hiked down to the People's Co-op Bookstore, a task that I'd promised to do and forgotten, and paid twelve dollars from her own purse.

The top item on my blotter was a note from Ophelia: *This just in.* It was clipped to another RCMP witness report, one long hand-written sentence: *Last Saturday, I would say around 2 o'clock, as I was driving my 1958 Nash Metro hardtop near the Mulligan farm on Squamish Valley Road, I saw an Indian male who I identify as Gabriel Swift, crossing the road with a rifle and going into the bush.* Signed two days ago by Doug Wall, with an address on Squamish Valley Road.

This smacked of devious afterthought by overeager beavers at the Squamish detachment. Some scumbag who owed them a favour. I could see the car buff, the often undersigned Brad Jettles, dictating *1958 Nash Metro hardtop.*

Ophelia whisked into my office. "I guess we have to track down Mr. Doug Wall."

I held my voice steady. "Yes, I was thinking of going up there tomorrow for the weekend. Take my camping gear. Rough it a bit."

"How fun."

"Legal aid – they're pinchy, they won't pay for hotels." Abrupt, decisive, businesslike: "I've arranged to see Gabriel this evening to ask a few questions and keep him informed. I was going to ask if you have some time this weekend to get a more detailed statement from him."

"I can cancel everything but Victor Borge tomorrow night at the Queen E." Letting me know she hadn't left the weekend open for camping trips. She obviously had a date with her new beau. "Do you not want me to go to Oakalla with you tonight?"

"Of course I don't not want you to. I mean, I do, I'd like you to come." The stammering buffoon. "I didn't want to assume you had the time."

"Arthur, is this about what happened the other night?"

"I wasn't being chummy with Harvey Frinkell. He is a revolting skunk."

"Thank you, but I'm talking about the previous night."

A throat-constricting silence. "I'm . . . mixed up about that. Sorry, I'm exhausted. Hard day in court."

"We really should talk. Not now, but after seeing Gabriel. I'll be in my office." She walked off briskly and was soon replaced by Gertrude, holding coat and purse.

"I called Oakalla. They'll expect you at seven. I guess I'm off."

I leaped to my feet. She took a fearful step back before I was upon her, pressing folded bills into her palm, apologizing, currying favour. She'd earned one hundred per cent on the firm's next performance review. National Secretaries Week was coming up – might she be free then for dinner?

She answered with a shy smile. Pretty Gertrude with her crooked stockings. My previous secretary was half as efficient and had the temperament of a mule.

I'd put off too long one more pressing duty: calling Irene Mulligan with words of consolation. I reached her at her Point Grey home, where she was being attended to by a few members of her bridge club. She remembered me as her husband's former student and was pleased I was acting for Gabriel. "He didn't do it," she said in a husky, trembling voice. "I'm just praying Dermot is still alive."

She thanked me for my words of sympathy but wasn't able to continue. The phone was taken by a woman who apologized. "She needs her rest, Mr. Beauchamp. Perhaps in a week or so?"

I'm praying Dermot is still alive. One could hardly blame her for maintaining that hope. The likelier premise of suicide would invite gossip, that he saw it as the only way to escape an empty and unhappy marriage. I settled the phone into its cradle and heard thrumming in my head. *Sometimes I live in the country, sometimes I live in town.* Leadbelly's song had started to haunt me.

~~~

Affecting a desire to catch up with the world, I paid the local news-boy ten cents and a nickel tip for the evening *Sun*, then buried myself in it, silently handing Ophelia the keys to the Bug. This is how I hid my shame at my abysmal handling of our previous chat. Other than to ask if the gas tank was full she didn't try to engage me, but her temper was on display as she directed oaths at rush-hour drivers.

A U.S. nuclear test somewhere over the Pacific. Doctors in Saskatchewan threatening to strike. The federal election campaign in high gear. Howard Hughes still missing.

Running out of news, I toughed my way through the sports ("Koufax Fans 18") and the strips (Pogo, Major Hoople). I tried to keep my eyes off Ophelia, though I could not escape glimpses of hitched-up skirt, bared knees, nyloned legs working the pedals.

We pulled into Oakalla's driveway half an hour later, just as I was reading the want ads ("West Point Grey bungalow, $14,500" – at that rate, could I ever afford my own house?). Walking over to the prison building, I was looking stiffly ahead and almost tripped.

"Careful of the curb," she said, taking my arm.

"Sorry."

She squeezed my hand. I felt much better for that.

In the admissions lobby I immediately sensed tension among the staff. Jethro wanted the deputy warden's say-so before sign-ing us in but wouldn't tell us why. Astonishingly, it was not I but Ophelia who was summoned to the deputy's office. As I twiddled my thumbs I heard a distant, confusing female chorus. "We shall not, we shall not be moved."

I looked through the visitors' book. Gabriel had had another visit yesterday from Jim Brady, the organizer for Mine, Mill. It was a Communist union, and I hoped they weren't trying to use Gabriel for some political end. I had tried to return Brady's call but got no answer.

Ophelia returned, looking purposeful, and took me aside. "There's a sit-in in the women's wing; they're locked arm-in-arm in the mess hall. Something about cockroaches in the soup. The deputy has asked me to mediate. The Sons of Freedom are at the centre of it. Why can't they call themselves the Daughters of Freedom?" She was back to her buoyant self.

"Give it your best." I didn't entertain much hope for her. The Freedomite women were obsessively militant, with arson and public nudity their weapons of choice.

I made my way to a cramped interview room with two chairs and a small table, on which I spread my papers. Gabriel was brought in unrestrained, in his green prison garb. His braids were gone; the prison barber had left just stubble, and quite a few nicks.

"They claimed to be looking for lice," he said. "They were disappointed they couldn't find any. Most guys around here tend to roll with that shit. I can't seem to learn how to do that."

Thus the nicks, I suspected. I tried not to imagine the scene. Again I sensed him working at keeping the lid on. As I went through my briefcase, he studied me with a dark intensity. For what? Weakness? *Maybe he thinks he can get around you.*

"I hope these will satisfy your reading habit for a few days." I handed him the books and periodical. A sudden mood shift, a smile and a thank-you-very-much – I had passed a small test. "Ophelia may not be able to join us. She has been seconded to referee a rebellion in the women's section."

"They've got more balls than some of my brothers on this side. Their pride was beat out of them when they were kids."

"Not you, though, Gabriel."

"I was forged differently."

"How?"

"My dad taught me never to be a good Indian. That's what they want – good Indians. Lobotomized in their religio-fascist schools." He stiffened, then made an effort to relax again; I wondered if he'd had anger therapy. Maybe Mulligan, with his pastoral training, had taught him some tools.

"You used a phrase last time: residential school syndrome. Enlighten me."

"Destruction of pride. That's the concept – break the rebellion before it gets started. Force-feed us religion. Smother our language.

Cultural genocide. God knows how many have died because they couldn't cope, couldn't function."

I supposed he meant suicide. I remember Professor Mulligan railing on about the unholy union of these church-run schools and their government sponsors, supported by a supine press reporting only happy news – like last weekend's Easter edition, with its photo of a cherubic holy man passing out candies to his joyous flock.

Gabriel's discourse about these schools gave rise to a suspicion that he'd chosen me over Harry Rankin not because he thought he could get around me, as Ophelia suggested, but because he needed a convert, someone he could bend to his cause. I would resist with all my heart any effort to make this a political trial, but I felt a need to know him better, to crack the hard shell of his anger in hope of finding a soft yolk. "Tell me about your residential school."

He mused awhile. "St. Paul's. I was seven when they grabbed me – my folks had been hiding me. We were about three hundred kids, and I was number 156. That's what they called me. They could never remember my name." He called out, mimicking: "'One-fifty-six, lead us in the Lord's Prayer.' I survived a lot of shit in there, Arthur, mostly for talking Indian. My anger survived. I don't know if my ability to love survived." As he tried to steady his voice he turned away, toward the barren grey wall. I guess he saw me as a typical uninformed white liberal, and maybe I was.

"My folks suffered worse. They were shanghaied by the priests when they were five and hauled way up north to a school in Alert Bay. Try to imagine: one day you're out picking berries with your mom, the next day the door clangs shut and you're in a prison worse than this, wetting your pants and getting whipped for it. It's an essential part of the white colonizers' plan to destroy Native families. With straps and slaps, hands down your pants. There's no nurturing in a res school, no love. I don't relate to my parents much now, especially my dad. They definitely lost the ability to love."

He disappeared in thought after these final trembling syllables, his eyes wet. I was moved too. My other aboriginal clients had always shied from the subject of their school days, as if ashamed. This was a firm validation of Mulligan's distrust of these institutions.

"Dermot did a stint as principal of a res school on the Prairies. You knew that?"

Gabriel swivelled back to me. "He had writer's block over it – with his memoir." A head shake. "Still in turmoil twenty years later. Something happened there, I think, in Pius Eleven Res School. He left the Church soon after." He added thoughtfully, "When Louis Riel lost faith, he said, 'Rome has fallen.' Dermot used that line a lot, his expression of despair."

I told him of the time Dermot cried out, "Rome has fallen," on running out of his favourite port. He remembered Dermot wailing that phrase in his high, chirping voice on losing a fat trout from his line. It was the first time I'd seen Gabriel give me the benefit of a real smile, lacking in irony. In fact we laughed, then carried on about Dermot and his idiosyncrasies, his quirky, cynical wit, his excited way of talking when he was on a roll. I felt a connection with Gabriel then, keen and deep.

"Let's talk about your relationship with Dermot."

Yet another smile, playful. "Maybe I became the chosen one because he gave up on you, Arthur. After you threw the academic life away, after you chose law instead of Latin."

I found irony in that. Had I not thrown that life away, I would not be trying to save his. "You were lucky – an enviable student ratio, one to one."

Four or five hours a day, he said, for nearly three years, on weekends, holidays, academic breaks. Sometimes a whole day. Before leaving for the city, Mulligan would give him a reading list. He devoured everything, a dictionary at his side, the *Britannica* or an atlas open. I supposed he must have an outstanding IQ. So quick of mind, so hungry to fill it, so coherent in expression.

He explained it was not by happenstance that he'd wound up working for Mulligan. In seeking out an employee, Dermot had burrowed through the records of St. Paul's Residential School – records still extant though the school was closed by then – seeking graduates with superior grades. The brightest and most troublesome was the former Number 156, who was doing probation for assaulting a cop. Mulligan would have admired that rebel spirit. He'd have seen the sharp intelligence in his eyes. Gabriel became his project.

Gabriel saw Irene rarely. "I stayed out of the house the odd time she was there. I was uncomfortable with her, didn't get a sense of welcoming." Mulligan had apologized for her: she was inhibited, wasn't suited to the country, often wasn't well.

I assured him she was on his side and would be a good character witness.

He seemed a little surprised. "Tell her I appreciate that."

Mulligan had arrived for his sabbatical in late March, a month before his death, and Irene joined him a week before Easter. The master and student had spent much time outside, hiking or fishing. "We'd talk and argue . . . I was into Marxist writers, and we fought about that."

I said that Ophelia would be visiting him on the weekend to record a more detailed history, but I needed some data to prepare me for my Squamish trip. I showed him Monique Joseph's statement. *On Saturday last I was never in the company of Gabriel Swift, of this reserve.*

I'd feared he would blow his top, but he just sagged. "Those cop-suckers."

I wasn't sure whom he meant. "You told Knepp and Jettles you were teaching her chess and listening to music all afternoon. I presume you also made love?"

"Well . . . we fooled around. If Monique got pregnant, I was afraid her dad would come after me on a rampage, with a loaded rifle."

The scenario described in Jettles's report hinted at an unsavoury congeniality between the police and Chief Joseph, *who everyone on the force calls Ben.* I needed a credible rationale from Gabriel as to why Monique would lie.

He was still working through the betrayal, frowning, biting his lip. But his voice was steady, his chain of reasoning sound. "Benjamin had ordered her to break off with me. I was too old for her; I was dangerous, political, a troublemaker. Monique would have lied to him when she got home that evening. Afterwards she would have felt compelled to maintain that lie."

I groped for encouraging words. "We'll see how well she holds up on the witness stand. I may try to locate her this weekend."

"Try to get to her away from her dad if you can, Arthur."

As he read Doug Wall's avowal of having seen him near the Mulligan farm that afternoon with a rifle, I could see the fury work through him. This time he couldn't master it. He made two fists, brought them down hard on the table. "Shit! Shit!"

"Easy, Gabriel."

He closed his eyes and sat silently for about fifteen seconds, then slowly returned to me, speaking calmly. "I saw him. I even waved. This was in the morning, miles away, at the south end of the reserve, near where I live. He lives way north of there. I was deer hunting."

"Did you bag one?"

"No."

Too bad; that would have helped. "What do you know about this character?"

"He has half a brain. Some Indian blood, but not enough. Drifts about the valley, does odd jobs when he can. Sells hooch on the rez. Chief Joseph lets him do that because he drops off a courtesy bottle." A shudder, a sigh, and a soft expletive. "I'm going down on this one, aren't I?"

"Not at all, Gabriel. They have a circumstantial case full of holes and fully consistent with suicide. No body, no clear motive, not an inkling of proof you were with Mulligan when he disappeared."

Gabriel shook his head. "Knepp and Jettles have made my hanging their life's cause."

"And that's what I'll strenuously argue to the jury." I dared not tell him Canadian jurors tended to regard members of their fabled force as upright to a man. I asked him about the altercation that brought on his charge of assaulting an officer.

"My dad was off in Squamish, drinking. My mom asked me to

drag him home before he blew his UI cheque. Roscoe Knepp drove up just as I was leading him from the bar, and he started strutting around like a rooster, threatening to throw Dad in the tank. I told him to stuff it. He came on with his lippy-Indian-shit stuff and I put him on his ass with a cut lip."

"You got a break – a suspended sentence."

"Yeah, pissed Knepp right off. But he'll get the last laugh, won't he?" A ghoulish dramatization, yanking up his collar like a tightened noose.

Gabriel had known Thelma and Buck McLean for years; there were no strangers in the sparsely inhabited Upper Squamish. But he was on minimal speaking terms with them. "Thelma is prone to wild accusations, especially about her favourite topic – the thieving Indians that lurk everywhere. There was an issue once over a runaway chicken that she intimated I'd killed and plucked. And something about underwear missing from her line. I'm sorry, I laughed."

A senior corrections officer knocked on the door, opened it. "Ten minutes, Mr. Beauchamp. We need him for the count."

I rose. "What books shall I bring next time?"

"The histories of our nations, our legends."

"I suspect there's not much from a Native point of view. Maybe some oral histories."

"Those they haven't yet obliterated." He stood, speaking intensely. "This is what I want the judge and jury to hear. I want this entire goddamned country to hear it. How we've been neutered as a people, our culture gutted. First came the smallpox holocaust. Then, after stealing our lives, they stole our land. My God, man, your Parliament passed an Indian Act that made it illegal to raise money for land claims, money to hire lawyers." Breathing heavily.

"*My* Parliament? Am I to be assigned the role of collaborator?"

"At least the role of wilfully blind. Like Germans in the 1930s, blind to having imbibed, like mother's milk, the myths of the white master race."

I gave him plaudits for his alliterative eloquence but reminded him that those objectionable laws had long been repealed.

"But we lost a generation to repression because the struggle had to go underground. And after stealing our land, here's the final solution: steal the children, suppress not just their culture but their language. Because with loss of language there is a loss of memory. A people without a history is a people conquered."

"*Intelligenti pauca.*" Few words suffice for he who understands.

"But *do* you understand, Arthur?"

I remember being startled, though I ought to have been aware that Latin had been taught in the Catholic-run schools.

"I mean, God, here's the white man, the colonizer, making damn sure he saves his own precious ancient tongues."

"Am I also to blame for that?"

"Yeah, Arthur, you. *You* plural. Everyone who was raised with a bourgeois class consciousness – and that's practically all of you. I blame you for forcing your history on us. For inheriting what has been taken from us."

However one-sided, this vigorous debate reminded me of some of my tos-and-fros with Professor Mulligan, his many challenges. I had an appetite to continue, to defend poor Arthur Beauchamp with his bourgeois class consciousness, but I was being importuned.

"Gotta cut this short right now, Mr. Beauchamp."

I departed feeling unsatisfied, wounded. I'd been scolded unfairly. I prided myself in being a modern thinker. I had fought against the parental prejudice instilled in me (*their problem is they're all lazy*) and I had conquered it, damn it. Yes, our Native peoples had got a bum deal, but John Diefenbaker would correct all that. (I think I honestly believed that back then, in the days of my naïveté. *Fere libenter homines id quod volunt credunt,* said Caesar. Men readily believe what they want to believe.)

~~~

I drove Ophelia to her home in Burnaby Heights and broke the speed law getting there, hoping to evade her threat, *We really should talk.* She did talk, but not about us. I found it hard to take her ebullience. She was too busy patting her own back to afford me a chance to congratulate her for her coup at the jail.

The women had returned to their cells after Ophelia persuaded Corrections to send health inspectors into the prison kitchen. She'd had no trouble with the Freedomites. They liked her brashness, her confidence. In the parking lot, while I stood by, she'd dallied with reporters, enjoying her triumph.

In turn I offered a spirited replay of my own session. Res school syndrome. The gutting of Native cultures. "He's brilliant, expresses himself vividly. Angry, troubled, wounded. Mind you, he has every right to be in a fury, though I felt he was trying to tutor me. It felt like a political re-education class."

The fact is, he'd challenged me, and I didn't have the answers. I vowed to be better prepared next visit. Though I admired Gabriel, was even a little in awe of him, of his depth of conviction, I was daunted by his intensity, fearful of being used, perturbed by his short fuse.

"Tommy Douglas reigns here." She was referring to the NDP lawn signs in her hilly working-class neighbourhood. I was directed to stop outside a pleasant frame house overlooking the Second Narrows. "I'm in the suite below, so I don't get the view. I'd invite you in but it's late."

"Of course, definitely. Eleven-thirty, must hit the pillows."

She lit a cigarette. I tensed, fearing what was coming.

She turned to face me. "Intercourse did not occur, Arthur. Normal intercourse, anyway. I thought all bachelor suites came equipped with condoms, but apparently not yours." Pausing, looking at me quizzically. "Do you remember anything?"

I swallowed. "Not a great deal, I'm afraid. Nothing, in fact."

"Too bad. The foreplay was awesome. We got tangled in the sheets – it was hilarious. I was going to take you in my mouth but you seemed to prefer my armpit." She blew me a smoky kiss. "*Sayonara.*"

I drove home in a state of unbounded desolation.

T hough mostly quadruple-laned now, the highway to the Squamish Valley was a narrow, twisting affair back then, cut into precipitous cliffs falling away to the surging tides of Howe Sound. A spectacular drive from sleepy Horseshoe Bay past the clanking copper mines of Britannia Beach, past Shannon Falls and Stawamus Mountain, the towering perpendicular cliff-face known to rock-climbers as the Chief. Adding a tingle to the two-hour drive, especially in the rain, was the perpetual threat of running into a rockslide or a logging truck.

Squamish is at the fingertip of a long, crooked fjord at the mouth of the grand meandering river that shares its name, a river that on the day I arrived was at high-water, fed by the melting snows of the Tantalus and Coast ranges, which enfold the rickety town. I did a brief patrol in my Beetle, avoiding the stucco-walled structure that was the RCMP station. I planned to talk to Staff Knepp and his crew only at the end of my stay. Until then they weren't to know I was snooping about.

The black clouds advancing like a fleet of attacking dirigibles informed me I'd forgot to check the forecast. I thought of pulling in to the Kosy Motel but bravely continued a few miles north, to Alice Lake Provincial Park.

My tent up, I repaired to Squamish Valley Road, a gravel stretch that meandered through the Cheakamus Reserve, rimming the wide, rushing river, ultimately to some small holdings north of the reserve. The ancient forest of spruce, hemlock, and cedar had been logged, replaced by big-leaf maple and alder. Nature had lost her battle on the McLeans' one-acre lot, however – it was stripped of all natural cover. Presumably that was Buck in the driveway, about to go off on a job, stacking saws and wedges in his four-by-four International. A growling thick-chested mongrel was chained beside a sturdy log residence. A henhouse, a tool shed.

Across the way, on the river side, was a clear view of the Mulligan house on a rise above the river, an uncouth melding of an older A-frame with a modern picture-windowed afterthought sticking out the back. A Liberal Party election sign was stuck beside the mailbox, near a gated driveway so thick with mud that I dared not attempt it by car. Armed – as a good West Coaster must be – with rain slicker, wellies, and umbrella, I unlatched the gate and slogged past a pasture where two horses grazed near a mini-barn.

Smoke was curling from the chimney, lights were on, muddy boots on the doormat – Irene's relatives, maybe. Dermot had none I knew of, unless there was a distant cousin in his ancestral Ireland.

The door opened to my knock on a burly woman of middle years, a pugnacious set to her round red face. I guessed this was Thelma McLean. Her frown on learning I was Gabriel's counsel deepened into one of confusion when I carried on about how much the Mulligans meant to me. I implied I found my role dis-tasteful but was professionally obliged to take a legal aid case and, regrettably, had to do my best.

"Would you be one of the neighbours? Their good friend Thelma McLean, perhaps?"

Her guard finally lowered, she accepted my hand. "Well, I guess you must've seen me on the TV. They had a crew out here. And both the Vancouver papers and CKNW and the *Squamish Times.*"

"And you came across very well. Do you have a minute?"

"Well, kick off them mud flaps and come in. I have some coffee on."

Most of the living area was devoted to a substantial library on tiers of shelves below the slanting walls. A wide staircase to the book-lined bedroom left little room for furniture – a few arm-chairs, but no sofa where a couple might sit. No television, and the fireplace looked long unused, likely because of the dangers posed by sparks in this book-rich environment.

Thelma attended to coffee in the narrow kitchen and sent me off to the addition, a spacious post-and-beam parlour looking out on misty green mountains. A boxy windowed airtight kept it warm.

A console radio and record player. Dermot had brought a wide collection of LPs and older thirty-fives, including Bach's complete cantatas – music that fuelled his muse, he'd told me, and made him long for God.

I strolled to the far end, with its view of the growling river. This was Mulligan's study – a wide desk and, beside it, shelves of references: biography, history, philosophy, ancient classics. There was a phone on the desk but no typewriter, no other writing tools, no paper, files, or journals; it was polished clean. I sneaked a peek in a drawer. Only some staples, paperclips, and a couple of decks of cards.

As Thelma came in with a tray I closed the drawer with my knee and strolled over to join her, affecting nonchalance. I took my coffee black, found it too hot, told her it hit the spot. I said I'd talked to Irene only the night before. "She's exhausted with grief."

"Poor thing, she never had no close relatives, no kids neither, and her parents are gone, she told me. There's nobody excepting me to help her out. I insisted on looking after the house; it was all I could do. I won't wonder if she sells it. She never felt relaxed here. All them books would drive you crazy."

She added some split alder to the stove. I sat near it, my notebook out.

Mrs. McLean talked easily, clearly relishing her role in this notorious case. "She must've felt like a prisoner whenever she was here. It's not as if the Professor could ever leave his books and take her to town for a meal or bowling or a movie. She didn't have nothing to do except be his secretary and sometimes take a walk in the afternoon, whenever it wasn't pouring. She never answered the door when he was out – can't blame her, with all the thieves around – so you could never go calling. But I'd wander across the road if I saw her and we'd talk about this or that – woman talk, life's burdens. You'd have to say she wasn't real countrified. And she didn't like the horses – they was Dermot's thing. The whole idea was Dermot's thing."

"Irene stands behind this fellow Swift; I guess you know that."

"Well, she just won't believe they made an awful mistake hiring that red Indian. That's what we call him – red Indian – because of his politics. Sergeant Knepp calls him a commie shit-disturber."

That was useful to know, but this was going in the wrong direction. "Okay, we've pretty well covered Irene. What about Dermot? Surely he wasn't always with his books."

"I didn't mean that impression; he just never spent his free time with her. It was always Gabriel. They'd have a heater going in the barn. I don't know what they did in there – maybe just read their books and talk, maybe something else. Or they'd go riding together out onto the reserve, or fishing, whatever. Hiking. They'd take the trail up the Chief. He could've thrown Dermot off that and nobody'd be the wiser."

"Okay, how did you and Buck get along with him?"

"We heard about how he took a swing at Roscoe Knepp and figured him for bad news. We got ourselves a good guard dog just in case, and even then my laundry got swiped right off the line one night, which Gabriel thought was a laughing matter. Mostly we kept out of each other's way."

"I meant Professor Mulligan."

"Oh, him." She fiddled with the poker, added another stick of wood. "I didn't want to say nothing like this to the news people, but between me and you, he was snobby. He had this way of looking at you like you was white trash, like even Indians are better. He's a big intellectual – or was – but he'd talk to us like children, speaking slow, with small words, like we couldn't understand anything over two syllables."

Mulligan *was* rather a snob, with all but his favoured few. A haughty, clipped manner of speaking.

"Some people act distant when they're depressed. Did Dermot seem that way to you?"

"You couldn't tell what he was feeling. He never cracked a smile unless he was around that Indian. Roscoe asked me if they was acting perverted – like homos – and that got me thinking, like, what did they do on their hikes? You'd have to say Dermot was a little funny, if you know what I mean, like, sexually. This is between you and me, okay?"

"I won't repeat it."

Any hope that she wasn't spreading around that despicable theory was quickly dashed. "A lover's quarrel, that's what Doug thinks. Doug Wall – we had a little powwow, Buck and me and Doug. I guess you heard he saw Gabriel sneaking onto that field out there with a rifle. It's all over the valley."

"Do you know if anyone heard any shots?"

"Mrs. Lumley, who's down the road a piece, says she heard a gun fire, but given she's half deaf and they was bucking up timber behind her, I got my doubts. To be fair."

"Yes, we want to be fair." This was a neighbour sent by Satan. She'd been up and down the valley offering salacious opinions and daily updates.

"One theory we're working on, Buck and me, is sexual blackmail. We told Roscoe that maybe Gabriel held that 30-30 on him to get him to pay up. Then he tells Dermot to take off them clothes and swim for it." She points an imaginary rifle. "And then *blam, blam.*"

I wasn't interested in hearing more ludicrous theories. When I showed signs of stirring, she tendered a small redemption, offering to phone Doug Wall. "He's a little distrustful with strangers, but maybe not lawyers, being as he's had a few troubles along the way. Anyway, I'll put in a good word."

I rose. "Thank you for your kind hospitality."

"I just want to see justice done."

~~~

The storm front had arrived in all its petulant splendour; I could barely see through the flapping wipers as I passed through Cheekye, a small cluster of dwellings striving to be a village. A dilapidated lodge on the Cheakamus River looked like paradise compared with what awaited me in a tent. I had to roll down my window to make out the No Vacancy sign.

Farther on, in Brackendale, was the Big Chief Drive-in, a Native-run roadside café and souvenir shop where Doug Wall had agreed to meet me for lunch. I parked behind his fender-crinkled red Nash Metro and made a run for the door. The smells and sizzles in this overheated diner reminded me that I hadn't eaten since the previous night's burger and root beer at an A&W drive-in.

I hung up my coat, which gave off mist in the heat. A jukebox was playing. A couple of families from the Squamish band were sitting by a barrel stove, their lunch done, enjoying refills and bantering, teasing, laughing, the children quietly listening, absorbing.

Among the non-Natives at the tables was a stout, broad-faced fellow, ketchup on his grey whiskers as he attacked a steak. The image was of a bear at a carcass. He nodded at me.

I ordered the buck-and-a-quarter soup and sandwich, then joined Wall, who stared at me awhile, his mouth working until he swallowed, washing everything down with a swig of Orange Crush. "Bo-champ?"

"That's right."

"Thelma told me you're a square dealer. Ain't you awful young to be defending a murderer?"

"I haven't lost one yet."

"You can't be worse than the last attorney I had. Never seen him sober."

"What were you charged with?"

"A fire that someone else started."

I reminded myself to check his record. "Bad luck. How did they set you up?"

He said something with his mouth full, a profanity. Maybe someone had informed on him.

"You know Gabriel Swift fairly well?"

"Yeah, everybody knows everybody around this here valley. He's a agitator, a pain in the ass." He pushed his plate away, swabbed his lips and whiskers with a napkin. "I'm sticking with what I told the bulls. It was in the afternoon I seen him."

He had a liar's stubborn eyes. He'd seen Gabriel deer hunting, that was certain, but surely in the morning. "How do you know it was the afternoon, Doug?"

"I been around long enough to tell morning from afternoon."

"So what time exactly did you see Gabriel?"

"Around two is what I said in my statement."

"Maybe an hour or two earlier or later?"

"Not a chance."

"Were you wearing a watch?" His wrist was bare.

"It got stole."

He glanced accusingly at the Native families – two men, two women, four kids – watching us, speculating. I wondered how the Native community felt about the case. Chief Joseph seemed in the pocket of the RCMP, but surely others had views that sharply differed.

I showed Wall his statement. "Who asked you to write this out?"

"Jettles. Brad Jettles."

"He dictated it and you wrote it down?"

"I said it in my own words, exactly like he asked me to." He thought about that, then added, "Because it's the truth."

"Where were you driving from?"

"I have a cabin up in the back country where I been staying since my old lady kicked me out. I was going down to see some friends."

"Who else did you see while you were on the road?"

"I can't remember. Whoever was there, I guess."

"Mrs. Mulligan? She often takes a walk in the afternoon. Did you see her that day?"

"Maybe . . . I don't know."

There was little point in spending more time with a fellow so determined to be evasive. I would have another go at him at a pre-liminary inquiry, and it would only forewarn him if I asked why he'd waited until Wednesday, four days after Mulligan's disappearance, to come forward. But I fired a final shot. "Everybody knows you bootleg into the reserve. Especially the cops, right? Because they gave you a licence to do it. Roscoe and Brad."

He signalled for his bill. "I got a engagement." As he began to rise, I beckoned to him with a crooked finger as if I had a secret to impart. Curiosity drew him forward.

"My friend, I am going to come after you with all guns firing, and when I prove you're lying – because I've got the goods – the judge will send you up for twenty years on a perjury beef. You've been in the joint, you know what they do to informers in there." It was my hard-boiled voice, but I didn't have to feign anger. In retrospect I'm not sure it was wise to imply I had secret evidence against him, but I wanted to shake him, dissuade him from being so certain on the stand.

Wall's head disappeared into a rain poncho and he went off to pay his bill. "It's on me, Doug," I called. He turned and walked out into the downpour, everyone staring at him.

The young waitress leaned over to me as she served my soup and sandwich. "Good luck, Mr. Bo-champ," she whispered.

"Beech'm," I said.

~~~

I turned north to Cheekye, where Chief Joseph lived, just over the Cheakamus bridge. My little car slithered dangerously near some grazing horses, near a collapsed cedar fence. In this rain-darkened afternoon, lights were on in the reserve's scattered frame dwellings. No one was outside. Everything looked wet and sad.

I had no set plan for the weekend's most delicate task: separating Monique Joseph from her parents, entreating her to tell the truth. She had got Gabriel into a bad pickle by lying to her parents. He could be hanged were she not to recant – that's what she must understand. But she was only sixteen and dependent on her parents, perhaps in fear of them. The cop-suckers, Gabriel had called them.

I was kicking myself for not having invited Ophelia to come when I ought to have insisted. Who better to interview Monique Joseph than the crisis intervener who'd won over the mutinous women of Oakalla?

The cultural centre loomed through the rain, a windowless sawn-lumber longhouse with a few smoke holes in a shake roof. Election signs out front, stuck there proudly – the great white chief, Diefenbaker, had recently granted treaty Indians the right to vote.

Around the corner was a two-storey dwelling, obviously that of Benjamin Joseph. Obviously because an RCMP van was sitting outside it, engine running. I called down curses on my own head for not going there first. They'd wasted no time after Doug Wall alerted them.

I parked nose to nose with the van, whose driver was slouched, wiping a wet nose, pretending to ignore me. Puffy red cheeks and recessed, close-set eyes. Jettles, I guessed.

A girl's rain-blurred face stared from a second-floor window: Monique, confined to her room. The front door opened and Staff Sergeant Roscoe Knepp stepped out, pulling on a rain cape, and came purposefully down the path toward my car. Rugged, handsome, square-chinned – the Sergeant Preston type one saw in the tourist posters. He called, "Step out of the car, sir, with your hands up."

I was astounded at his effrontery. Grabbing my umbrella, I alighted to find him unhooking his handcuffs from his belt.

"I'm afraid we have to impound this vehicle, sir. We don't allow people to drive tin cans on the public roads." A broad grin at my confusion, then a raucous laugh. "Gotcha!" He grabbed my hand. "How're you doing, counsellor? You sure picked some kind of pissy day to come moseying around the valley."

I recovered, attempting a smile. "So what's going on here, Staff?" As if I didn't know.

"Let's talk about it in comfort – we got the heater on. Grab the front seat there, I'll jump in the back." Pushy, but I didn't resist. "Brad Jettles, Arthur Beauchamp." Just a chortle issued from those pudgy lips; he was still enjoying his honcho's little joke.

Knepp leaned toward me from the back. "Last time you were up here, it was over that narcotics roundup, a really big shew – you watch Ed Sullivan? – at one of the camps. I watched some of the trial; you were smooth. I said to myself, here's a fella to watch."

I turned, observed an old yellowed bruise on his cheek. Gabriel had indeed got his licks in, though it would be counter-productive to raise that issue here. "I'm complimented, Staff. I'm here to interview the Joseph family. Individually and in private."

"Look, we want to do what's right," Knepp said. "Normally I'd say no big deal, talk to anyone you want. Doug Wall told us you were here, by the way. I want to be open about that."

"Did he mention I accused him of having a licence to bootleg?"

Knepp shrugged that off, still smiling. "Come on, counsellor, we deal in the real world. If he doesn't sell hooch, some even slimier asshole will. Hey, he came to us with information, what can I say? We want to be straight with you, Mr. Beauchamp . . . That's awful formal – is it Arthur or Artie?" He was battling to save his grin.

"Arthur."

"The situation here . . . Well, Chief Ben and his family, they told me explicitly they don't want to talk to you. These folks don't talk much anyway to whites. Maybe you don't understand their culture – you're dealing with people who are withdrawn. It's in their nature. I'm not saying you'd do anything wrong, Arthur, but some people aren't too quick, if you get my meaning, and their words get twisted. And they're afraid of that, and frankly they told me they won't answer the door to you."

"Cyrus Smythe-Baldwin won't condone this."

"Well, come on down to the station, you can call him on our phone. We got Smitty's private home number, Brad!"

"Have it somewhere. I'll look around." Jettles honked into a Kleenex. "Crap, I hope I'm not coming down with something."

"Follow us in, Arthur. We can talk, show you things. We're playing slow-pitch here, not hardball. We're just country cops looking after folks' safety and trying to be fair."

~~~

The Red Ensign hung limp and dripping in front of the police station. A few officers and clerical staff looked me over as I entered. I tried to avoid Jettles and his worsening cold, but he and Knepp smothered me with affection, helping me off with my rain slicker, hanging my jacket by the radiator, offering coffee. Would I like to try calling Mr. Smythe-Baldwin now? Did I need a visit to the gents' room?

After a piss and prolonged hand-washing, I joined Knepp in the squad room. He had his jacket off but his gloves still on, so I surmised his knuckles had got banged up by contact with Gabriel's face. Jettles was at his desk, as was another constable whom Knepp introduced as Gene Borachuk.

"I won't bother Mr. Smythe-Baldwin now," I said. "Instead I'll take it up with the magistrate." On Tuesday, the remand date.

Knepp looked apologetic. "Walker's off next week. We got a lay magistrate subbing – the local jeweller. A legal argument may be out of his league." To Jettles: "Those serum reports in yet?"

"Lab says it's going to take a couple of days. They want to take a careful look at the pink panties."

Knepp laid a file of photographs before me. "The item here depicted went down to Heather Street on Thursday." RCMP forensics in Vancouver. "Looks like someone tried to toss it in the water and missed."

The first photo showed what looked like a small pink garment caught in the root mass of a windblown tree that had slid down a riverbank. "That's only a few feet below where we found Mulligan's clothes," Knepp said. "Couldn't see it behind the tangle. It was only when the ident guys came back a few days ago, one of them spotted it."

A closer angle showed a pair of panties snagged on a rootlet. Then a close-up of them dangling from tweezers, and finally they were shown spread on a sheet of wrapping paper beside a twelve-inch ruler. Silk-like fabric, flared at the leg openings, which were trimmed with lace and ribbons.

As Jettles and Borachuk got up to hover and watch, Knepp

carried on in his excruciatingly helpful way. "Size medium, no label. Make out of it what you want, Artie, but I don't think they had a lady up there with them. That white splotch on the right cheek looks like bird shit."

Borachuk winked at me, sharing a conspiratorial joke about Knepp's apparent expertise in fecal forensics.

"They found some clotted white stuff on the crotch," Knepp added.

"Definitely looks like pecker tracks," Jettles said, demonstrating his own scientific specialty.

If this female undergarment were to analyze for semen discharge, I wouldn't be sure what to make of it, other than that Knepp and Jettles would have more ammunition for their graceless innuendos. *Roscoe asked me if they was acting perverted, like them homos.*

"Okay, next item," said Knepp. "It's my duty here to honestly disclose what we just got from the print examiners. Maybe you want to sit down."

I blanched as he showed me the report. Several matches for Gabriel's thumbs and fingers on the plastic panes in Mulligan's wallet. A thumbprint on the face of the watch. I did sit down.

My head was buzzing as Knepp carried on about how the fingerprints put Gabriel "right smack dab" at the murder scene. Surely there was an explanation for this. But why had Gabriel kept it from me?

Knepp was grinning – he could tell I was shaken. I tried to pull myself together as he opened the exhibits locker. Mulligan's fishing gear and clothes: jacket, shirt, undershirt, trousers, boots, hip waders. Assuming his lower undergarment was accounted for, all that was missing were socks. Mulligan wouldn't have gone sockless in those country boots.

The wallet was of worn leather, soft, like deerskin. Behind one plastic pane, a Kodacolor of Irene with shoulder-length auburn hair, smiling in an appealing way. On the back, this notation: *June 12, '57.* The year they married.

Knepp pointed to a 30-30 rifle, Gabriel's. "Oh, I forgot – ident also found a couple of 30-30 cartridges there. They test fired this baby and they're checking to see if we got a good match."

"They were found three days ago?" My voice cracked. "Where?"

He showed photographs, one shell lodged in weeds in a crack in a rock, the other beneath some ferns. They'd been planted there – that was my immediate assumption. I felt my chances for acquittal slipping away.

I said nothing more, tried to focus. Also seized from Gabriel were odds and sods of trifling significance: a chess set; a dented brass sports trophy; books, some from the Squamish library. Salary records, a pad with addresses, various handwritten notes. But also something unexpected – a carbon copy of Mulligan's unfinished memoir.

A greater volume of paper had been taken from Mulligan's cottage – the contents of his desk, I assumed – even his Remington upright. Among those bundled sheaves must be the original pages of his memoir. All too much to absorb right then. I was thinking about a stiff drink, thinking hard about it.

"I'd like to spend tomorrow looking through the papers."

"Be our guest. You want copies, we have a duplicator. You staying the night somewhere?"

"I'm camping."

"Keep your boots dry, pardner."

~~~

On returning, full of beer, to my tent I found my air mattress sitting in three inches of water. I looked balefully at a lean-to where dry split alder and hemlock were stacked. A brilliant woodsman might light a fire in this rain, but not a city lawyer with a skinful. I voided into the useless firepit, removed my wet clothes, and scrunched myself into my sleeping bag in the back seat of the vw. I couldn't sleep for a long time, worrying about those fingerprints, those 30-30 shells. Tormented, remembering how a jury had convicted the Truscott boy on circumstantial evidence.

SUNDAY, APRIL 29, 1962

T he threat of an exploding bladder propelled me naked from my car. As I watered a giant spruce, my head thick from drink, I took in the sylvan wonderland with its carolling thrushes, its pristine lake, the morning sun warming my bottom. The Squamish Hotel beer parlour where I'd been drowning my worries the night before had been much less pleasant. I had traded tales with railway workers and lumberjacks and had to swallow my distaste at their crude racist jokes about Natives, their mimicry of the Salish accent. I wondered how Swift could ever find a fair-minded jury from such a lot.

Finally I finished and turned around, to find my tent dismantled, spread on a slope in the sun, drying out. More confounding, the deflated air mattress was on a rope clothesline, steaming from the heat of a fire in the pit. A man in shorts and hiking boots – a man I felt I should know – was approaching from the lean-to with more wood, a motorbike leaning beside it.

"Better put some duds on. You're in a public park." The guy was grinning at me. Borachuk. Constable Gene Borachuk.

I blushingly dashed to the front of the car, got clean clothes from the trunk, and dressed while he fed the fire. About my age, and obviously an outdoorsman with his Thermos and coiled rope and sheathed knife and tanned, muscular legs. Mine were white, thin as cornstalks.

"I was planning a little hike up to Cheekye Falls. Don't suppose you'd like to come."

"Actually, no."

"I didn't think so." Looking at my scrawny chest.

"Thank you for this." I hung my damp clothes on the line and he passed me a tin cup, poured coffee from his Thermos. We squatted by the fire. "Good thing you didn't catch me driving up the 99 last night. I'd have needed a lawyer."

"Heard you were telling some tall tales in the Squamish beer parlour."

Meaning Knepp had eyes on me. But it didn't seem likely that Borachuk was here on his orders. There had to be a different reason. I said, "Can I ask a couple of questions?"

"Shoot."

"Last Sunday, Easter Sunday, after Gabriel led everyone to Mulligan's fishing hole, you and Grummond picked him up in a squad car. Why?"

"He hadn't been very forthcoming earlier. Roscoe asked us to check him out for an alibi." A shrug. "Seemed a fair thing to do."

"You were driving, Grummond was in the back with my client. Did you hear their conversation?"

"Yep. He said he was with his girlfriend all afternoon. I signed off on that."

"Okay. And then on Monday, Gene, you were on duty when my guy was brought to the station and charged, right?"

"I helped book him."

I quoted, reasonably verbatim, from the prologue to Gabriel's taped interview: "'Suspect looked like he'd been in a fight, because we observed facial bruising.'"

"That report I didn't sign off. Saw the bruises later, when I brought him some chow in the cells. Nasty welt on his side too."

"Kicking a man when he's down doesn't seem to be in the proud tradition of the force."

He winced. "This is an off-the-record meeting."

"I'm not sure if I can agree to that, Gene. I have an obligation to my client."

"Nothing I tell you can hurt his chances."

"I can promise discretion."

Borachuk rose and returned to his bike. From a saddle pack he pulled a thick bundle of documents. "Copies of everything."

Quite a gesture. I riffled the pages – about three hundred sheets, including the carbon of Mulligan's memoir. A bundle of photos too, mostly of Mulligan at various tasks. "You must have been up all night."

"Arthur, I got into this business hoping to make inspector one day, maybe superintendent. I'm not going to get there by condemning the men I work with; that's just the way the system works. But I'm not sure if I deserve to get there if I give false evidence in court. So if anyone asks me how your client got that whacking, I have problems. Roscoe's pissed off at me – he keeps saying we've got to sit down and talk about when I saw those bruises. Roscoe . . . well, he's got a honking big hard-on for Swift."

"I have received that loud and clear. He salted the scene with evidence, didn't he? Hid those 30-30 shells for the ID squad to find."

"Can't help you there, Arthur. Almost wish I could."

"What's his hold on Chief Joseph?"

"Roscoe calls him a good Indian. They share an attitude about Gabriel."

"Pretty obvious, isn't it, that he coerced Monique to say she wasn't with Gabriel last Saturday afternoon."

"He didn't take her statement, Arthur. Brad and I did. There was no coercion."

I wondered how true that was. "If not you, her father."

He shrugged. A deep breath. "Arthur, it doesn't make your client less guilty if a couple of cops pounded the shit out of him. The case doesn't turn on that. I'm taking a gamble that you're a sympathetic guy. I can't go through channels on this. There'd be a hearing, and I'd be exonerated and blacklisted at the same time."

I suggested he avoid channels by going directly to Smythe-Baldwin. The old fox was an honourable fellow, and we might work something out for Borachuk. That was the right thing to do, and maybe I could wrest some advantage from it. But my client's interests came first. I could not be party to hushing up the matter just to help an honest cop.

~~~

Fire extinguished, camp disassembled, Borachuk off to the falls, I headed to Brackendale for breakfast. Twiddling the radio dial,

I caught a fawning interrogator on CKNW asking Ophelia Moore about her triumph at Oakalla. Enjoying the attentions of the media, though I'd assigned her a full weekend of interviews with Gabriel. She was self-deprecating with her interviewer, casually basking in her fame while I struggled alone in the muddy trenches. (That, of course, is how I felt at the time; now I see the petulance of disappointment in it.)

The Big Chief Drive-in was busy but Doug Wall was not about. Several elders were sitting by the stove, with some children they were minding. The soft murmur of the Salish dialect. At another table sat a few of the Paul Bunyans I'd met the previous night.

I had no more entertaining stories to offer them, so I found an old newspaper and hid myself behind it. From the waitress who'd wished me good luck the day before I ordered the Sunday hang-over special – eggs, bacon, and hash browns.

She said her name was Mary. I asked if she knew Monique Joseph. She said they were in high school together.

"I need to talk to her, without her parents."

Mary flicked a look about. "Leave me your phone number." She strolled off and I went back to the paper. Ranger 4 had crashed into the moon; I felt a kinship to that rocket. Five thousand more American advisers heading to Vietnam. Castro selling prisoners from the Bay of Pigs botch-up back to the Yanks. And, locally, enhancing my hometown's stuffy reputation, a girl sent home from high school for wearing a back-combed bouffant.

When Mary returned with the food, she picked up my business card from under the salt shaker. "I'll see what I can do, Mr. Beauchamp."

After breakfast I wandered into the souvenir shop with its traditional cedar-root baskets, cattail mats, and carvings. There were several shawls and blankets tagged with the name Celia Swift – Gabriel's mother – and directions to her home outlet.

~~~

The small log house of Bill and Celia Swift was a couple of miles from Cheekye, just off the road, with an artisan sign out front and a workshop at the back. A DeSoto in the driveway on blocks, the hood open.

There was no doubt that the sour-looking long-haired man sitting on the stoop was Bill Swift – he had a stump leg. I parked behind the old car, hailed him, paused to pat a couple of snuffling dogs, and went up and introduced myself.

"Yep, I know who you are." He didn't offer his hand. He was working on a broken wheelbarrow, a scatter of bolts and nuts arrayed beside his crutch, a mickey of rye just visible beneath the stoop, as if secreted there. The front door was open, the interior tidy and clean, Native prints and masks on the wall, a crucifix.

I got down on my haunches, eye to eye with Bill. He was gaunt, with a full head of dark hair, and I could see traces of the handsomeness Gabriel had inherited.

I expressed the hope he and his wife were well on this unexpectedly fine day. No response. I told him I'd seen Gabriel two nights ago and that he was in good health and spirits. A shrug. I expressed a resolve to do everything in my power to get him out of this.

He snorted. "They're going to put a noose around his neck."

"I very much doubt that." With as much confidence as I could pretend.

"He'll be in a white man's court, with a white judge, white jury, white prosecutor, white cops at every door, and he'll have a white lawyer who don't look like he even shaves yet, and he'll get white man's justice. He'll hang." His voice rising with every word.

He reached back for his bottle, took a slug from it, made a face, and returned to the wheelbarrow.

"Juries may not convict where there's a reasonable doubt." That sounded lame even to my ears.

"White man's bullshit. Gabriel's been set up to go down, young fella. I been there, I done time, I know the white man's rules. I went to the white man's school; I fought in the war for the white man; I fished, I logged, I worked in the mill for the white man.

See this?" – gesturing at the leg that wasn't there – "Crushed by a tree. An Indian's leg ain't worth shit in the white man's gyppo camps – they gave me a two thousand lump settlement."

He took a swig from his bottle, then another, as if fuelling up for more rhetoric. Then he shouted, "Hey!" as the bottle was snatched away.

"He doesn't want to hear your cynical talk." Celia Swift was standing behind him, a stout, thick-shouldered woman wearing a smock daubed with paint. "Take that thing to the workshop, where you got some proper tools." He picked up his crutch and limped off, dragging the barrow.

"I don't know how we can help you, Mr. Beauchamp." She looked stiff, anxious. "Gabriel is in the Lord's hands."

I thought of saying it was my job to be his saviour and that Jesus, for all his worthiness, had not trained in Canadian criminal law. But I retreated to safety, asking if I might see some of the traditional weaving for which she was known.

She took me to the back entrance of the workshop, where we stepped around Bill, sitting on the steps and once more working morosely at his barrow. He spoke without looking up. "Wasting your time. They already decided he's guilty. It's all fixed."

Celia led me past an array of tools, then into a workspace featuring a rugged old loom, a wooden work chair, a hand-woven basket filled with wool. Photos of elder women on the walls, working traditional two-bar looms. A lamp, a barrel stove wasting its heat, the back door wide open. Near the main entrance was a show area for customers. A dozen garments, of finer quality than those displayed at the Big Chief Drive-in, were hung up for viewing: elaborate dresses, woollen robes and blankets. Long shavings of yellow cedar bark woven with red cedar strips in zigzag patterns, a colourful medley of natural dyes from roots, leaves, and berries. Her main customers, she said, were agents of well-to-do collectors of aboriginal artifacts.

"Highway robbers," Bill called out. "They squeeze you, buy on the cheap, and jack the price up ten times."

She continued to ignore him while letting me try on a replica nobility robe, traditionally worn, she said, by those of high rank. I was taken by it; its fur trim gave it a look of majesty. Celia was proud of her work, and she finally relaxed enough to talk about Gabriel.

I asked her where his cabin was, and she walked me outside to an overlook.

"Way back in there. You have to hike half a mile." A twin track descended to a creek and gushing cataracts, a motorbike trail going up the other side.

"Did you see him that day, a week ago Saturday?"

"No one saw him but maybe Doug Wall, and he's a lying man. I didn't see Monique neither, though she was always sneaking up there on weekends. I caught them once, sinning."

She could not imagine Gabriel committing the substantially more horrible sin of murder, especially of a man so admired. I expected some grief over her son's plight, but she was composed, dry-eyed. *They definitely lost the ability to love.*

As we returned to the workshop there came a moment of bitterness. "Top of his class. Then he took up with atheists." She didn't expand on that.

Bill finally had his barrow assembled and was at the woodshed, filling it. "That professor fella's still alive," he called. "He faked his death to get out of some kind of shit he was in."

That seemed as far-fetched as any theory I'd heard. The Dermot Mulligan I knew wouldn't stand by and let Gabriel be tried for murder.

From "Where the Squamish River Flows," *A Thirst for Justice*, © W. Chance

LET US EXAMINE BEAUCHAMP'S CLAIM, oft articulated, that he harboured no prejudice against the First Nations peoples, or against those of colour generally. That would be to deny his parents' influence, and while he masked his internalized conservatism by rebelling against their stodgy, almost Victorian value set, surely many of their biases remained at least skin deep, like warts and moles.

Dr. Thomas Beauchamp, head of the UBC Library, was the lesser of the parental evils: a dour, critical man whose favourite pastime was to correct others' grammar – often rudely – or their literary quotes and historical references. Thomas boasted that he'd never voted in his life, never encountered a politician who wasn't a self-serving fool.

Dr. Mavis Beauchamp was one of those obsessive anti-communists who began to take control of the political debate in the 1950s, a decade infamous for America's spy trials and congressional hearings. She was rare among academics in supporting the Social Credit Party, a right-wing outfit born of a discredited economics theory. She decried "socialist tyrants" such as T.C. Douglas, who in her view sought to impose universal health care against the will of the people.

So let us not pretend that our subject had somehow undergone some holy cleansing of illiberal views. The record says otherwise. In the election of 1958, at twenty-one, Beauchamp actively campaigned for the Progressive Conservatives, and his sympathies for the forces of the status quo remained with him through 1962 and for many years after. As a criminal lawyer, Beauchamp was committed to prevailing concepts of civil liberties, but it was only in the mid-nineties, after he fell helplessly into the orbit of Margaret Blake, that the socio-political reformation of Arthur Beauchamp began.*

---

* See chapters seven *et seq*.

Though the sun was creeping westward, it was unseasonably warm at seven-thirty, and folks were out for Sunday evening strolls in shorts and sun tops. My Bug wove through the West End's vast thicket of low-rise apartments and rooming houses, up Haro Street, and into the alley. I hadn't eaten since my hangover special and was looking forward to a meaty feed at a nearby Greek restaurant. I had earned that, and a flagon of retsina, after a weekend of unstinting effort and far more loss than profit.

As I pulled in, Crazy Craznik was on his back porch twiddling the dials of a shortwave radio. Ira Lavitch appeared at an upstairs window, then came racing down.

"You look ready to rack out, man." He helped me unload my gear. "Where you been, the upper Amazon?"

I was an unshaven, unshowered mess, and no doubt smelled.

"I hate to ask, Stretch, but can I borrow your jitney? I slept in, I'm broke for cab fare, and it's hootenanny night. Lawonda's holding the fort."

"I'm not going anywhere." I tossed him the keys, then displayed the nobility robe I'd bought from Celia Swift.

"Out of sight," Ira said.

"What?"

"Means gorgeous."

"A traditional Salish garment, my good man, reserved for those of the highest rank." I hung it loosely over my shoulders, and indeed I felt distinctive in it with its colourful rectangular patterns and trim of tiny seashells and animal fur. It smelled of the forest.

Craznik was watching me with suspicion. A voice was blaring from his radio, a Slavic language.

"He's receiving coded instructions from the Serbian Christian Patriotic Guard," Ira said. "Plans proceed apace to assassinate the Jew Lavitch. Thanks, man, for the loaner."

I waved off his offer to help me haul my things upstairs. As I lugged them past Craznik he turned down his radio. "What is it you wear?"

"A traditional robe of the Coast Salish peoples."

"You don't look good as Indian. No more phone – I am not message boy."

"Who called?"

"Your mother, two times."

At the door to my suite I dropped my things and searched vainly for my keys. It came to my overburdened mind that the key to the flat was on the ring I'd given Ira. I wasn't sure if I could brave pulling the landlord away from his shortwave. Why was Mother calling so insistently?

Then I remembered. Dinner. Professor Winkle . . .

~~~

After paying off my taxi driver, I raced up the stone walkway to the colonnaded veranda, then braked to take a peek between the dining room curtains. Four persons and one empty chair around the table, on which the cook was setting a platter of roast beef. Mother was looking aggrieved but Professor Winkle was expounding, being jolly, well into the wine. Attire, as always at a Beauchamp dinner, was semi-formal.

For some reason – maybe boredom – Winnifred Winkle chose that moment to glance out the window. Presumably jarred by the sight of a tall, bedraggled man in an Indian robe, she shrieked wildly and pointed. Three shocked expressions quickly mutated into smiling embarrassment, a searing look from Mother.

I calmed myself with steady breathing as I shrugged off my pack, slipped out of my dirty boots, and entered. My old slippers were in the foyer – my parents continued to keep traces of me, like talismans. Past the hallway antiques I went, toward the dining room with its faux Tudor arches and art, nearly bumping into the exiting cook.

Winkle, an unpleasantly plump expert in what Canadians used to call the Old Country, was picking up where he'd left off before my apparition at the window: a mirthful treatise about the role of roast beef as a culinary unifying symbol in seventeenth-century England. He trailed off on seeing me enter.

Father put on his glasses to inspect me. "We seem to have a visitant."

"This is utterly unbearable," said Mother.

I spread my arms wide in supplication. "I am the victim of an act of God. A landslide on the 99. Worst tie-up imaginable. I am devastated." My alibi might ultimately be proven false when un-mentioned in the morning *Province,* but at least I'd get through the night.

"Dr. Winkle, Mrs. Winkle, I am so delighted to see you. I came straight here from a weekend in the wilds, haven't had a chance to clean up. Ah, roast beef and roast potatoes . . . I have the combined appetites of Charybdis and Scylla."

I assumed Father would find fault with that mythical allusion, but he contented himself with, "Roast beef, yes, as past participle, but never roast potatoes. Roasted potatoes."

"I'll be back in a jiff."

"A slangy abomination, young man."

"Oh, we're dying to hear about your adventures." Winnifred Winkle, a saccharine woman in a beehive.

In the bathroom I assessed my clothing options: one clean sweatshirt, one rumpled outdoors shirt and the mud-caked trou-sers I was wearing. The nobility robe would have to stay on.

Wine alone was not going to get me through this evening, so I poured myself a whisky before taking my place beside Mrs. Winkle. She entreated me again: "Oh, do tell all. You absolutely must let us in on the secret of that garment you're wearing. It's quite . . . magical."

I felt bound to win them over, so I downed my whisky, poured another, and demanded the floor. I had discovered in my col-lege years that alcohol set loose the Great Entertainer, a far more fascinating me than the earnest stumblebum anyone may read about in *A Thirst for Justice.*

So we dined on roast beef and roasted potatoes to the merry accompaniment of sketches of meddlesome Thelma and smarmy Roscoe and cynical Bill Swift. I could tell I was doing well because of Father's darkening expression as he waited in vain to pounce on an unsustained metaphor or irrelevant allusion.

Though Mother had warned me not to talk about the "sordid details" to Winkle, Dermot's apparent death had obviously been endlessly chewed over at the university. The Winkles, after appropriate comments about how aghast and sorrowful they felt, kept pumping me for more. Mother seemed mollified – I was, after all, carrying the evening, rescuing it. The conversation was not for the ears of the cook, so she sent her away, and I laid out as much of the case as was appropriate. Not the pink panties, though – that was a little too rich a sauce for the overdone beef.

Irvine Winkle had a claim, much touted by himself, to Dermot Mulligan's friendship. I had promised myself not to mention the scurrilous talk about his relations with Gabriel, but my resolve weakened with a second glass of robust Medoc.

Winkle, who was quite pickled, laughed and shook his head at the preposterous thought that his pal had homosexual tendencies. "If a guy didn't know him, he might think he was bordering on queer, but Dermot, he was a horndog. He was getting nookie right and left."

"Irvine!"

"He had the pick of the grad school girls. They lined up."

"Irvine, tales out of school. Dermot was your friend."

"Not denying. He was a good guy. Out of the mould a little, but a real good guy." He raised his glass to Dermot's memory and we all followed suit but Father, whose frown suggested he regretted having the Winkles over.

Winnifred took up the cudgels for Irene, whom she had met once at a faculty wives cocktail party. "She's very sweet. Okay, she's no Ava Gardner, but she *adores* him."

"So why wasn't she at commencement last year when he got his honorary D.Phil.? I've never seen him once with her, wouldn't know her from Princess Margaret." And Irvine wasn't through with Dermot. "He had something going with the wife of Toby Schumacher, in Medieval Studies."

"Now just stop that!"

"Come on, darling, it's all over the department. Rita Schumacher – you met her – the high-beam headlights?" He raised his glass to mine. "Maybe I've given you something to work with here, Arthur. A red herring you can throw in – your traditional jealous husband. I even heard Schumie was threatening to sue for divorce and alien–What do you call it?"

"Alienation of affections. I'm not finding it easy, Dr. Winkle, to picture the head of Medieval Studies pitching Mulligan's naked dead body into the Squamish River."

I asked myself if the revelation of Mulligan's infidelity surprised me. Poor Irene was drab, and shared few of her husband's interests aside from his research and writing. I wasn't shocked that Dermot would be tempted but was repelled by this new perception of him, an academic bed-hopper.

The conversation eroded, as these things do, into academic gossip: a suspected homosexual ring in the Faculty Club, the scramble to cover up a faculty advisor's liaison with a prostitute, an indecent assault by a visiting Welsh poet. Over cake and coffee, Mother changed the tone with a polemic against our political leaders: Lester Pearson, with his suspect pacifist tendencies; Diefenbaker and his jettisoning of the Avro Arrow. Either would leave Canada defenceless against the hordes. Both believed in big government, and neither subscribed to the brave and serenely simple solutions of Ayn Rand.

Father was fighting sleep but interrupted her over a linguistic misuse. "We cannot be in a dilemma if we face a myriad of bad choices." Then his eyelids drooped again, signalling the end to the evening. I sneezed – that woke him up. The Winkles dutifully rose.

I escorted them outside to their sedan while my parents waved goodbye at the door. Irvine insisted on pausing for a cigarette, a luxury not allowed within because of Mother's asthma. Winnifred took the keys from him – "We don't want to be statistics, do we?" – and got in behind the wheel.

Leaning close, Irvine offered a final boozy confidence. "Irene let him have his affairs. That was their deal – he practically said as much. She'd cook for him and wash his underwear, type for him and do his editing, but he could fuck anyone he wanted."

I prodded him. "This wasn't just some kind of midlife crisis?"

"More like chronic; it was like there was some kind of deep-seated need to get laid. One time over a few, we got on the subject of a memoir he hoped to write, and he mentioned how his childhood was troubled. It sounded pretty damn bad – he was seeing a priest a few times a week for counselling. That was after his sister's death. Genevieve, she was his angel. Maybe that ties in."

"Darling, I'm *waiting*."

After they drove off I paced awhile, updating my mental bio of Dermot Mulligan. I don't know how much of what Winkle said was speculation or exaggeration; I'd seen no approaches by Dermot to female students, heard no rumours. Dr. Schumacher of Medieval Studies ought to be contacted – a task for my junior, Ophelia Moore, alienator of my own affections.

Upstairs in the split-level a bedroom light went off: Father's room. Mother's was down the hall. Mine was lower level at the back, and since I didn't have cab fare to get home, that's where I'd hibernate.

Undressing, I looked about my old, loathed room. The single bed upon which Mother caught me at thirteen, masturbating over the Eaton's catalogue lingerie pages (an episode not discussed then or mentioned thereafter). The framed certificates, the academic rings and trophies. The wall map of the ancient lands of Alexander, of Caesar. Five shelves of books, mostly texts. A desk and chair, a chess game set out for play. And something recently added, presumably brought out from storage: an array of 1940s Tinker Toys to remind me I was once and forever their child.

An old television set had been moved in as well. I turned it on and watched *Car 54, Where Are You?* until sleep came.

Gertrude looked on, concerned, as I detonated more snot into my handkerchief. "Holy macaroni, boss, maybe you should go back to bed."

I continued packing my briefcase. "Squamish court this morning. Can't be late." My schnozz was flowing like a firehose, my throat inflamed. I had not clocked in yesterday after heating up to 102 degrees. Aspirins were barely keeping me upright, but however ill, I had to persuade a jeweller I had a common-law right to interview witnesses unimpaired. I wasn't ready for battle, not against Cyrus Smythe-Baldwin, Q.C.

Ophelia appeared in the doorway. "My sessions with Gabriel are being typed."

"Did he explain how his prints got into Mulligan's wallet?"

She looked shocked. "We didn't talk about the crime scene."

"The news is bad." I told her about the fingerprints and cartridges. "Also, for some reason, he had a carbon copy of Mulligan's unfinished opus."

"Gabriel mentioned that. Dermot gave it to him to read and comment on. You're sure you'll be able to handle this remand in your condition?"

"Absolutely. And finally, this." I showed her the photos of panties snagged on a root.

"Whose are they?"

"Possibly Rita Schumacher's."

I told her about Winkle's claim of an affair between Mulligan and Rita.

"Well, maybe that makes Irene a suspect too."

"She follows him to his fishing hole? Orders him to take off his clothes or she'll pump him full of lead? Where would she have got a gun? They never owned one. And anyway, she's Gabriel's biggest booster."

"Out of sorts, are we?"

I blew my nose and sniffled an apology, then assigned her to check out the Schumie rumour and to read through the paperwork Borachuk had given me. She disappeared, looking miffed. I took two more Aspirins, then headed out to my car.

~~~

I arrived late, with no time to brief Gabriel. The Squamish court was up the stairs from Yarwood's Drugstore, a made-over apartment with folding chairs. I slipped inside and sat in the back. A smattering of locals, a dozen reporters squeezed behind a table. No sign of Smythe-Baldwin, but Celia Swift was near the front with a few friends.

The traffic infractions being heard didn't merit the services of a real prosecutor, so Roscoe Knepp was playing that role, calling folks up to plead guilty or have their trial dates set. The jeweller – the acting magistrate – whose name was Yaeger, nodded a lot and spoke little.

"Usual fine for failing to signal is fifteen dollars."

Yaeger nodded. "So ordered."

The accused complained, "How was I supposed to know my signal light was burned out?"

Knepp: "I thought you were pleading guilty, sir."

"I ain't guilty."

I was distracted by movement at the press table. Smythe-Baldwin had just popped in, hale and portly, a version of Colonel Sanders with his manicured goatee. He looked about, spotted me, and came over.

"I have had you investigated, young man, and the reports are in your favour. Your pro bono work speaks equally as well of you as your many successes."

"Better not come too close, Mr. Smythe-Baldwin. I have a rotten cold."

"I never catch colds, though medical science cannot explain why. It's not healthy living, I can assure you of that. Let us not interrupt these vital proceedings."

I followed him outside into the cool but dry morning air. I declined his offered cigar; he snipped the end off his, rolled it in his mouth, withdrew it, studied it, studied me. "I talked to Gene Borachuk. Sticky business, I must say."

"A dilemma for him."

"I am persuaded to give you an advantage. I shall not lead evidence of that interview with Knepp and Jettles. However, your chap made an earlier claim to have been with Miss Joseph all day. That, and her contradiction of it, will remain an important part of Her Majesty's case."

That earlier claim had occurred during a strained conversation with Borachuk and Grummond in a patrol car. "There was no caution, no warning about his rights of any kind, Mr. Smythe-Baldwin."

"Smitty – my friends call me Smitty. No warning was necessary. Your fellow wasn't a suspect at the time." He planted the cigar in his mouth and lit up.

I blew my nose. "Bollocks, Smitty."

"Then let us deal with that when the time comes. Motive remains a problem. A lover's quarrel has been widely suggested. Very tasty, and we shall be working that one up."

That, I suspected, would be time wasted. He obviously wasn't aware that Mulligan had achieved some minor fame in academia as a ladies' man.

"One wonders why, after the dirty was done, he played about with Mulligan's wallet. Robbery? Unlikely. The theory I favour is that he was seeking to find and remove any evidence of their secret relationship. A love poem? A full-frontal naked photo?"

He studied me for reaction but I was giving nothing away. At any rate it would have been hard to see anything in my red and puffy eyes.

"I shall be submitting Mulligan's incomplete memoir. Not a hint of suicidal depression. It's all rather gay, in fact. We're still awaiting the forensics from the serums and firearms chaps, but the pink panties are a little gay too, don't you think? Now, what else can we help you with?" He exhaled a massive plume of smoke and sighed happily. "I have them sent up from Havana by diplomatic bag. It is worthwhile being a friend of Mr. Green." The external affairs minister, presumably.

"Where are Mulligan's socks?"

"Someone must have walked off with them." His belly bounced as he chuckled.

"Knepp is hiding critical witnesses from me."

"An issue I am prepared to argue. A word of friendly advice, young Arthur. It would be unwise to raise your complaint, however legitimate, in front of a seller of rings and brooches. Your cold will only worsen if you spray yourself whilst pissing against the wind. I have appeared before this man, and he has the brains of a flea. Save your protests for a real magistrate."

"Okay, let's bump it a week."

He patted my shoulder. "We're transferring this entire shivaree down to Vancouver. We may get Orr or Scott – they have minds."

A venue change was – finally – good news. For the week or so of the preliminary, the witnesses would be removed from hometown influences, and from Roscoe Knepp.

On our return to the court, the clerk, taking pity, passed me a box of tissues. Gabriel was brought in through a side door in cuffs and shackles. He waved to his mother, but she seemed worried about the proprieties and returned only a nervous smile.

I was given a few minutes to confer with him by the railing of the prisoner's dock, and warned him not to get too close. "Your prints are all over Mulligan's wallet. When I next see you, I will want an explanation of that."

"I can give you one now."

"You can think about it."

"I was looking for a suicide note."

I was confused, until he explained that he'd been ten minutes ahead of Jettles's posse. He'd made a quick descent to Mulligan's fishing spot, searched wallet and pockets, found no clue to the mystery, and scrambled back up in time to meet his pursuers.

The jeweller coughed, letting me know that the day was getting on. Smitty, though, was sitting back comfortably, his hands clasped over his waistcoat.

"You mention this to Ophelia?"

A long hesitation. "She didn't ask."

"They also claim to have found two 30-30 shells there."

"They're lying."

"Okay. We'll talk more when I'm feeling better."

"Our elders know some good medicines. Speak to my mother."

We adjourned the matter to Vancouver to set a date for the preliminary inquiry. Smitty wished me well. The reporters filed out unhappily, snapping shut their empty writing pads. Knepp followed me to the door, but at a distance.

"Get better quick, Artie. That son of a bitch Jettles, eh? I warned him to take sick leave right away, but no."

Outside I was taken into custody by Celia Swift and a few women elders and taken away to be treated with Sitka spruce pitch, boiled fir needles, and bracken rhizomes with fish eggs.

D isappointingly, the glutinous tea didn't provide the immediate cure demanded by my fantasies. I was still sweating out my fever at home the next afternoon when I heard Ophelia and Craznik outside my door, he demanding identification, she offering rude advice relating to his rear orifice. She charged into my flat just as I was about to drag myself out of the bed in which we'd rutted and floundered.

As I subsided back onto it, she studied me from the bedroom doorway with a thorough lack of sympathy, then set on my table the documents from the Squamish RCMP, sorted and in labelled files. She chose one of them and airmailed it to the foot of my bed. "Covering memo and the copy of the memoir found in Gabriel's cabin, plus a letter from Schumacher's lawyer warning the deceased to stop fucking his wife."

"Be good if you could talk to Professor Schumacher."

"I've arranged to see him on the weekend."

"Very enterprising," I croaked. "Who's his lawyer?"

She aimed a manicured forefinger down her throat. Harvey Frinkell, obviously. With a quick exit line wishing me improved health, she departed.

I looked at Frinkell's letter, ominously dated Friday, April 13, eight days before Mulligan vanished. Addressed not to his Vancouver residence but to Squamish Valley Road. The standard cease-and-desist language of a lawyer's demand letter: a warning of severe consequences in the courts of law, a reference to incontrovertible proof of adultery, a claim for unstated general damages for alienation of wifely affections.

Ophelia's memo indicated that it had been found in a basket on Mulligan's desk, among other correspondence less volatile: a bank statement, an invitation to a faculty meeting, a note from his publisher about a reissue of *Myth and Morality.* Odd that he hadn't secreted Frinkell's intimidating letter, or at least hidden it from Irene. No sign of its envelope.

I had to get dressed because the river was calling, but I was naked and had no idea where I'd put my clothes. Scrambling through dresser drawers, I found only female garments – panties, slips, blouses. A woman was crying somewhere but I couldn't see her. Bells were tolling, telling me to wake up . . .

It was the phone. Alex Pappas, with a noticeable lack of tender concern. "Given that it's half past nine, should we assume you're still flat on your ass, Beauchamp?"

"A minute ago I was." I had raced naked into the main room. To my surprise I was no longer sweating.

"We don't want you spreading germs. Take off tomorrow too. I'll kick your burglary over a week to fix."

I wrapped a towel about me and stepped carefully down to the shared shower, testing my state of health. So far, so good. No fever, no runny nose, no cough. I was lightheaded, though – a sense I was floating at peace, as if opiated. As I slid under the shower I gave thanks to the Squamish elders and the power of their medicines.

Having floated through my morning routines, I found myself suited up and heading off in the Bug. I was wending my way east on the Number 1 to Burnaby, to that institution of incorrection that housed Gabriel Swift. I felt impelled to that place, to him, by a force then ill comprehended, though I have since realized it was a need to believe I was on the side of the gods. This was, wonderfully, the kind of trial honest lawyers yearn for – defence of the wronged, the truly innocent, a man framed. And I needed to put to rest those niggling hints that Gabriel hadn't been wholly candid. Why, during Ophelia's extensive debriefing, hadn't he mentioned probing through Mulligan's things by the river?

I asked him that right off, as we sat facing each other in Oakie's visiting hall.

Gabriel shrugged. "*Mea culpa.* An unintended lapse. It was logical, since I was searching for Dermot, that I would haul my ass down there. Obviously, on seeing his clothing, I would look for a note, some clue. I am not so stupid as to be unaware I would leave fingerprints."

Still enjoying the pleasant after-effects of my recovery, I needed little convincing of Gabriel's sincerity. The fact that he left prints actually counted in his favour. An assassin would not be so careless.

"Let's move along to matters of greater moment. As you see, I am restored to robust health. Those wise women of the Squamish band ought to patent that curative potion of theirs."

"Spoken like a true capitalist." A slight jab, but he added, "I'm glad you're well." He seemed well too, no sign of ill temper, and he seemed pleased with my tribute to Native medicine.

When I told him about the nobility robe, he smiled broadly. "If you dress Indian and take Indian medicine, maybe you will begin to think Indian."

"How does one think Indian?"

"With your soul."

Too enigmatic. Gabriel remained intent, focused, occasionally making a note, as I delivered a travelogue of the past weekend's tour of the Squamish Valley. He smiled as I recounted Thelma McLean's references to the red Indian next door and her missing clothes. He frowned as I told him about Knepp and Jettles walling off the Joseph family from me. He showed surprise that Mulligan had been accused of adultery. "I never knew."

I asked him when Dermot gave him the carbon of the memoir.

"The week previous. It was a burden. I was supposed to discuss it with him but never did. Who was I to critique it? I felt incapable of that, or of helping Dermot resolve his writer's block."

"Out of interest, what did you think of the completed six chapters?"

"I picked up a struggle, not always successful, to be open, intimate – as I assume memoirs are expected to be. There was humour, some sadness. He'd never talked to me about the early death of his sister, and I was moved by that. I was trying to find the courage to express those thoughts. I never got the chance."

Genevieve. Professor Winkle had called her Dermot's angel, had intimated her death had been a source of childhood trauma. I was keen to read those six early chapters.

I didn't press Gabriel about the 30-30 shells found at the site. I had no doubt that Knepp and Jettles planted them. They'd conspired, after all, to lie about the beating they'd given Gabriel. I kept to myself Gene Borachuk's affirmation of that; I had promised the constable discretion. I did mention, however, the pink unmentionables.

Gabriel responded carefully. "Okay, I occasionally got a glimpse of . . . that sort of thing. Like on a sunny day, when he'd change into shorts. Maybe it was just some kind of whimsy or impulse – silky underwear – maybe it felt good. I never asked about it and he never explained."

I might have pursued the matter but felt uncomfortable about getting into a discussion of fetishes, afraid of where it might go. Some people liked fur, some leather, some silk. I liked armpit hair. Nothing sinful about that. A semi-erotic *divertissement.*

I lingered long with Gabriel that day, going well off topic, jousting with him. I told him I wanted to know him better, wanted to know how such a bright rebel had turned communist, loyal to such a monolithic, unbending ideal. I wasn't happy about his political views; it would be to his great prejudice to be identified as a communist. They were regarded by most as marginal, likely subversive, possibly dangerous.

He was not to be deflected from his beliefs. Capitalism, I was instructed, would collapse in the next century and be replaced either by socialism or fascism. "There will be a fierce struggle and no middle ground, so where will you stand?"

I could picture him as the leader of a college debating team. He was a natural, deflecting Stalin's excesses, the purges, the camps ("Revolution is not a perfect art"), throwing statistics at me, quotes from Hegel and Marx, confident in the unshakable logic of dialectical materialism. He had been taught well. Jim Brady, I supposed.

We each stood our ground with all the sureness and arrogance of youth, but he had the last word. "At least there's something I believe in. What do you have?"

Touché – there wasn't much. A belief in justice, maybe.

As he was being led away for his lunch call, he added, "And after Rome fell, what was left for Dermot to believe in?"

I t was a sunny afternoon, and Ira Lavitch and I were at the backyard picnic table playing cards – klaberjass, a game he'd taught me. Craznik was hovering not far away.

"Poetry night at the Beanery, so there'll be lots of empty seats. I got a cat on the bill named Cohen, from Montreal. Maybe you want to catch him before he's famous."

I said the only famous poets I knew were dead, and so was the poetry of most modernists. Anyway, I had other plans. This was National Secretaries Week, I had phoned Gertrude Isbister to honour my promise, and dinner was reserved for this evening at Trader Vic's in the Bayshore Inn, a swank new waterfront hotel.

"Klaberjass. It's an old Jewish game," Ira told Craznik, who was standing over us.

"You a Jew?"

"Yeah, but I cut off my curls. So is Arthur – you can tell by the nose."

"No more loud music, you. And pay rent for May, overdue, or I throw you out."

"The cheque is in the mail," said Ira to Craznik's departing backside. I suspected Ira was broke; the Beanery was on its last legs. He mimicked, "No Jews! No ladies! Good thing he doesn't know I'm gay."

I was shocked. Not just by the admission, but by the use of such a pejorative word. "You are?"

"Relax, I'm in the closet."

"What's that mean?"

"That I'm not as obvious as Liberace."

I guess I'd not read the clues, particularly Ira's lack of interest in women. But he didn't seem, to put it awkwardly, the type. Maybe I didn't know the type; maybe I'd lived too sheltered a life.

"Screw the May rent. Let's evacuate this shithole."

We had talked about that. Our flats were cheap, with a choice location near Stanley Park, but there was the obvious downside.

"Jass, menel, and a run of fifty." Ira totalled up his winning points, then left to ready himself for work. Gay? He seemed so normal.

I pulled Mulligan's memoir from my briefcase for another go at it. Smythe-Baldwin was right that it bore no hint Dermot had been depressed while writing it – though his upbeat language did seem forced – but clearly he had been severely distressed in his early years.

I leafed again through his brief account of his provenance. Born in 1912 in Montreal, his parents Irish immigrants, the father a print shop operator who died at the Somme. His mother, a devoted Catholic, scraped together a living as a seamstress while raising a girl and a boy. Sensitive, studious Dermot doted on his older sister until she died at fourteen of leukemia. He was ten.

There followed a wretched time – years, it seemed – when I ached for the smiles and hugs and words of comfort that Genevieve had unsparingly bestowed on me. I suspect I spent as much time in a detention room or talking to the counselling priest, an uncharitable oaf, as I did in the classroom.

But all turned sunny in his teens.

Somehow a force had come into me, whether from God or the old gentleman below, I shall never know. I had made up two lost years of school and skipped two more, and suddenly I was in McGill's hallowed halls majoring in the great myths, a triumphant and arrogant eighteen-year-old.

It was a chronological history, no flash-forwards to the roiling Squamish River, no Irene, no Gabriel. No sex either, but much self-deprecating humour of the kind I recalled from his lectures, his brittle metallic voice: *Still in fervent contemplation of the priesthood,*

I was determined to get a jump on my vows, and retained my chastity at some cost to both my sanity and my bed sheets (a brave admission from a man whose writings shied from any form of ribald humour).

Dermot had never mentioned he'd been an amateur entertainer, so I was beguiled to learn he'd starred in varsity shows.

For some reason I found myself specializing in such nautical naughtinesses as HMS Pinafore, The Pirates of Penzance, *and* Show Boat. *I was fairly talented, I am not ashamed to admit, cutting quite a figure in my sailor suits, with a tenor voice that lacked Enrico Caruso's range but wobbled rather prettily through the higher registers.*

Several few pages on he described how, as a newly minted D.Th., he'd scorned offers of academic posts to serve as principal of Pius XI Residential School in Torch River, Saskatchewan – locally called Pie Eleven. Though he'd served as such from 1940 to 1942, his autobiography went silent upon his arrival there.

I believed, as did every Canadian, that the Native schooling system had been a wondrous gift to our aboriginal brethren. I had watched the documentaries: china dolls in their starched uniforms, boys with their prickly haircuts, at prayer, at play, at their cute little desks. "The best years of their lives," trumpeted the Catholic, Anglican, and United Church hierarchies, affording these youngsters a "free and equal chance" at education.

And all seemed true and good as, on my first day as headmaster (I preferred that to principal*), I walked into the auditorium of Pius XI School and was greeted by three hundred young voices in off-key choir, praising the coming of the Lord.*

It ended there, midway through Chapter Six. When did disillusionment come? And how?

~~~

My evening with my lovely young secretary was strained, maybe because the surroundings were too garish for comfort. Trader Vic's was a kitschy ad for the islands blessed by Paul Gauguin, and Gertrude seemed not to know what to make of it all – tiki masks and tapa cloth, an outrigger hanging from the ceiling. She was a small-town girl from Kelowna, where waiters didn't dress like tourists just back from Hawaii. Her eyes widened with shock as she looked at the menu prices. "Five dollars for steak and lobster!"

Those eyes were having a hard time making contact with mine. I supposed she was finding our out-of-office get-together novel and awkward. She seemed to have gone to the expense of buying a new outfit for the occasion, a tasteful pleated skirt of the style of the time. (Later, over the course of several decades, Gertrude would dress me, marching me off to the tailor's whenever I started to look hopelessly out of fashion.)

I in turn avoided looking at her bobbing breasts beneath her ruffled blouse. They heaved as she squirmed or as her hands dis-appeared for another tug at her nylons. They heaved as I entertained with my visits to Squamish, my miracle cure by boiled fir needles and bracken rhizomes. "Apparently," said I, "the preparation also has uses as an aphrodisiac." I almost slapped my forehead – what a stupid thing to say.

When I would look away, or deal with the waiter, I'd notice her staring at me, then quickly turning to study a hanging puffer fish. My suggestive remark must have frightened her.

She'd hardly touched her mai tai by the time I finished my Big Kahuna; I switched to Scotch. Seafood salad for the lady, and for her escort, rib-eye steak. Somehow I'd have to screw up the courage to submit the tab to the office expense account, past pinchy Bullingham.

I was probably over the legal limit as I drove her to her little East End suite. Certainly tipsy enough to give Lord Byron loud voice: "She walks in beauty, like the night / Of cloudless climes and starry skies."

At her door she kissed me on the cheek and hurried inside with just a breathless, "Thank you."

From "Where the Squamish River Flows," *A Thirst for Justice*, © W. Chance

BEAUCHAMP SEEMED UNAWARE Gertrude Isbister was suffering from one of those crushes nineteen-year-olds are prone to, and it speaks poorly of him that he never picked up her signals. It's easy to assume he was preoccupied with the Swift case, but the fact is that our self-doubting, self-belittling hero has little facility for reading those close to him, as this author can attest. All of which contrasts startlingly with his unparalleled skill at sizing up strangers, at picking up cues from lying witnesses.

"I don't know how many times I flashed him some leg," Isbister told me. She would have "walked to the moon and back" for him, and she hung in for the first few years, spurning the advances of many worthy men, while retaining hopes for this tall, awkward, Roman-nosed barrister who remained excruciatingly unromanced and unattached. Secretly, she confessed, she was relieved that his relationship with Ophelia Moore took such a "wrong turn."

It was in Isbister's living room that I interviewed her over a few glasses of wine. I pray she'll forgive me for suggesting she was feeling little pain, but when I asked what she meant by a wrong turn, she began laughing uproariously, recalling a comment by Ophelia Moore about a "great underarm deodorant" she'd discovered. Then she clapped her hand over her mouth and, despite entreaties, nothing more was forthcoming. Do I dare conclude Moore had told her about some awkward, relationship-ending event involving a can of deodorant?

After five years Isbister finally gave up on Beauchamp and found a husband. During her boss's interregnum on skid road (see "The Wet Years") she took leave of absence from

Tragger, Inglis to raise her two children, returning to the firm when Beauchamp did. This handsome woman is now fully retired, a widow and devoted grandmother of three.

As for Beauchamp, erotic opportunities were regularly opened up to him by his playboy friend Hubbell Meyerson, who had family wealth and claimed to know every blind pig and cathouse in town (or, as he put it, "the boils on the bum of staid Vancouver"). Beauchamp has admitted jocularly to a phobia about women of easy virtue – it's probably just old-fashioned moral fear – and insists that during such sojourns he didn't partake in any pleasures more earthly than drink. Knowing Beauchamp as we do, that's undoubtedly true.

He spent the first weekend of May with Meyerson at the family ranch in the Skagit Valley – the senior Meyersons were in Paris – where they took long, healthy treks, swam laps in the pool, and sampled rare vintages from the cellar while the cook grilled beef ribs. A womanless weekend, un-threatening, a chance for Beauchamp to unload his romantic woes on his trusted friend (who, as he confided to me, sought to discourage Beauchamp's pursuit of Ms. Moore: "It was typically guileless of the poor sod to get tangled up with a fox like her. He wasn't ready for a modern woman").

In any event, Beauchamp felt in fit form for his return to the office on Monday.

I walked to work that morning along Coal Harbour and the inlet side of the CPR tracks, a lovely, sunny day, mists rising from the sea, the North Shore mountains still capped with snow. One of Hubbell's reminiscences had stirred a memory of my own, long buried, and I couldn't stop playing with it.

"Remember back during law school?" he'd said. "It was your birthday. I took the one that looked like Grace Kelly with tits."

My memory jogged, I saw myself as in an old, shadowy movie, a scrawny eighteen-year-old at a makeshift bar in a cathouse, drinking hard, terrified by the offerings of the several women for hire.

"Couldn't drag you out of there!" Hubbell's raucous laughter as he raised his cognac in salute.

I remembered a slender young Native woman, so gentle, so hungry for my feed of poetry . . .

I got off the elevator at the Sweatshop floor, intending to pop in on Ophelia and hear about her visit with the medieval studies scholar Toby Schumacher – Schumie. He was well published and I'd read a few of his works: solid research, insightful, but marred by the prolix, unrhythmic prose typical of academic writing.

Several women were in the waiting room, all there to see Ophelia. Two were likely of ill repute, to use the Victorian term: tarty in attire, little heart tattoos, net stockings. Two were older, one with a black eye. My junior's practice had burgeoned since her coup at the women's prison. She was attracting not just a criminal clientele but, it would seem, abused wives who, until Ophelia made the news, were unaware our town had any woman lawyers to turn to.

Her door was closed but I saw through the glass partition that Gertrude was with her. They were laughing. *I never had a worse date. He wouldn't shut up.* I was spotted, so had no recourse but to go in. Gertrude blushed deep red but Ophelia didn't even try to stifle her smile. I had a sinking sense she'd just recounted the armpit episode.

"So what's with the fir needles, spruce pitch, and fish eggs? I hear they bestow stud-like powers."

Gertrude fled and I slumped into an armchair. Barely able to meet Ophelia's eyes, I took refuge in testiness. "It seems you've become the champion of ladies used and abused."

Ophelia looked at me with either dismay or disgust. "I have a woman out there whose husband was acquitted of assault by a prick of a judge who told her to go home and be a compliant wife. She got beaten again for making her complaint. What's it feel like being a man in a man's world, Arthur? Pretty good?"

"Why am I being treated like a symbol of what's wrong with the world?"

"Because you have a typical ego-testicle mindset." She softened. "Also, I guess because you're handy. I'm sorry. Schumacher set me off with his patronizing; he's very smug now that he's got his wife back. He didn't hedge much on his dislike for Mulligan – a few crocodile tears. He'd like to believe his threats of legal action drove him to suicide."

That was worth developing. "What was his proof of adultery?"

"A private eye caught them *in flagrante delicto* in Schumacher's bedroom. Guess who? Your pal Jimmy 'Fingers' O'Houlihan." She added, "There's some bad news on your desk."

"They matched the shells to Gabriel's rifle? I'm not surprised. This is the biggest railway job since the Great Train Robbery."

En route to my office, I slipped quickly past Gertrude so we wouldn't have to look at each other. The firearms report was on my desk, with photos from a microscope camera; the grooving, the impact dimple, everything matched. The serologist's report was there too – they had indeed found "pecker tracks" on the pink panties. There was no way to prove the semen's authorship, but I hazarded it was more likely spillage from masturbation than from coitus.

Gertrude had put a few phone messages on top of Ophelia's dictated notes. The first was from Mary, the waitress at the Big Chief. She would phone again in half an hour.

Mother had reported in, complaining of having caught my "beastly" cold. Gertrude's note: *She wonders if you're trying to kill her.*

Jim Brady again. Our meeting was overdue.

My return call was answered with a bold, "Communist Party campaign office." Upon being fetched to the phone, Brady was relaxed and jocular, not dour and obsessive as befitted a proper Marxist. Gabriel had told him of his high regard for me. I was an "up-and-comer." The Party was hoping to run a handful of candidates in B.C. Would I be interested in Vancouver Centre?

Then he laughed. "That's for my comrades in the Red Squad – this ain't exactly a private line." Nonetheless, he had to be near his phone all day. He gladly accepted my offer to come by with Chinese takeout.

My in-basket offered up a letter from Magdalen College instructing me either to take up their scholarship offer or lose it. I set it aside as a call came in from Mary in Squamish. She was hesitant, shy. She bore bad news: she had mentioned to Monique Joseph my interest in seeing her, and word of that had got out. Chief Joseph had sent his daughter off to Washington State, exact location unknown, to stay with distant relatives.

I was thinking seriously of handing the Swift file back to Pappas with thanks and regrets, then catching a flight to England, bowing to that ultimatum from Cambridge. I told Mary she had done well.

"I'm sorry," she whispered.

~~~

The Communist Party campaign office was on the second floor of an old brick building in the Gastown area, a slum in those years, though it was once the city's beating heart after the great fire of 1886. Today, of course, the old town is preserved, though blighted with tchotchke shops, galleries selling cheap art, and junkies doing up in back alleys.

A gabbing group surrounded a Gestetner that was pumping out leaflets. Posters on the wall loudly exhorted the working class to seize the day. A photo of their scrawny old leader, Tim Buck. A banner: "Hands off Cuba." In my suit I felt awkward among the Party workers in their patched overalls and hand-me-down dresses. Volunteers from among the unemployed, I assumed.

Jim Brady greeted me with a self-deprecating joke about his being an ordinary party hack, but he seemed to be in charge there, likely on loan from Mine, Mill to run the federal campaign. He looked to be in his early forties, copper-skinned, burly, healthy. Though self-taught he was well-read, according to my back-grounder, and a fine orator.

He led me to his inner office and cleared the pamphlets and periodicals from his desk to make room for our Number Three takeout. As we set to, he told me how he'd met Gabriel. Three years ago Brady was business agent for copper miners at Britannia, near Squamish. On his time off he visited the reserves and lectured about Native rights. Gabriel, then seventeen and just out of high school, went to a couple of those gatherings. Brady was impressed by the young man, invited him to "a small discussion group." Soon after, Gabriel arrived in Vancouver, stayed two weeks with him and his wife, Grace, and joined the CPC's youth wing.

Brady and Gabriel had been in regular contact ever since. They both enjoyed chess – Gabriel, he said, had the skills of an aspiring master. But most of the time they talked politics, economic theory, Native rights. Grace, a Party member, would often join in.

He talked between mouthfuls. "He admired me because I broke free from the white man's prison. He admired me for my ideals. But he admired Mulligan in a different way – intellectually. I may be smart but I ain't brilliant, and Gabriel was moving away from me."

I picked up a sadness. Both he and Mulligan had discerned something unusual in young Swift. Not just brains and drive but hints of future renown, even greatness. I had a similar sense of him, one that had grown with each meeting, and that weighed on me, to the point I'd had gallows nightmares.

I told Brady about the difficulties of the case: Doug Wall, the rumours of homosexuality flying about, the fingerprints, the cartridges. He showed no surprise at the machinations of the Squamish RCMP. He knew Knepp, knew Gabriel had thumped him.

"Gabriel has a volatile temper, that's for damn sure. I like that – the passion – no one's gonna turn this system on its ass unless they're passionate, even angry. But maybe there was too much anger; sometimes it just erupted. Working for a union, you learn how to deal with anger, and I spent a lot of time teaching him to channel it, to convert them thunderclouds into political action."

When he asked about Gabriel's chances, I answered with care. "They have no body. No credible motive. No eyewitness, just that weasel of an informer. But they've built up a trove of circumstantial evidence. Juries are fickle. Gabriel will face twelve people, almost certainly all white, most of whom will pretend they aren't racists. They will not be swayed by radical calls to action by a renegade who would like to turn this into a trial against the evils of capitalism. I'm not sure if I have his ear in that regard. But he will listen to you, Jim."

Brady became guarded. "Is that what you see as my role? To censor him? I read somewhere, maybe Lenin, that fear of consequences merely perpetuates the system."

"I won't aid in his martyrdom."

"What kind of justice is ever won on bended knee?"

"No competent lawyer will play by his client's rules. I assume Harry Rankin refused to."

"What does it matter what Gabriel's politics are? The charge is bullshit." He grew animated. "The homosexual stuff is bullshit. Fascists like Knepp will try to silence the resistance one way or another. Read some history, learn how they try to buy you, then bend you, and if that don't work, bury you. They're setting him up *because* he's a red. Why ain't that a good defence?"

I told him, weakly, that was not the direction I hoped to go.

Brady went back to his sweet-and-sour ribs, then sighed. "I'll talk to him."

~~~

Jimmy Fingers' office was nearby, at Victory Square, a stroll through the seamy side of town. But I had police protection, so to speak: a tail from the RCMP's Red Squad. I paused at a shop window, then retraced my steps to its doorway, crossing paths with a man under an umbrella, though it was barely sprinkling. By happenstance the business I entered was the People's Co-op Bookstore, added proof I was a tool of Moscow. I stared up at a row of thick, forbidding texts. *Read some history.*

As the follower took up his pursuit again, I scripted a comic scene of officers informing Mavis Beauchamp that her son had been offered the Communist candidacy for Vancouver Centre. Thus, finally, I might be disowned, made free.

A creaky elevator in a creaky old building hoisted me to the fifth floor and a hallway of shady businesses: a loan advisor, a theatrical agent, an escort service, and, at the end of the hall, "Private Investigations, Discreet Service" – Jimmy "Fingers" O'Houlihan. He had a tendency during his brief career as a beat cop to finger the innocent, thus his nickname. One such case, involving a prominent businessman, blew up in his face. He quit, went private. His services were mostly on behalf of the cuckolded. In those days adultery was the only well-trodden ground for divorce, and Fingers had a knack for coming up with the goods, not always legitimately.

His secretary paused from blowing on her freshly painted nails to tell me her boss was finishing with a client. I could see him behind a windowed partition: a handsome, roguish brush-cut blond in his early thirties, with an Irish gift of gab. Soon he led out a weeping well-dressed woman.

"That shit," she said.

"My heart goes out, ma'am. Harvey Frinkell is expecting you. Not cheap, but the best aren't."

He helped her into her cashmere sweater, let her out, then embraced me. "My man Beauchamp! My hero, my saviour!" He propelled me toward his office, instructing his secretary to phone Frinkell. "Tell him there's some heavy sugar coming his way."

He accepted my bottle of Jameson with a snort of pleasure and poured two doubles. "Never too early in the day. Can't say I wasn't expecting you."

"Toby Schumacher seems pleased with your work."

"That so? Then why did he balk at my fee? I had Mulligan all set up. He was my chocolate Easter bunny – I was going to serve the writ on Good Friday so he could share Jesus's pain. Then he ruins everything by pegging out. All the work I put into that job, it ain't fair." Chuckling.

I entertained him awhile with tidbits from *Regina v. Swift*, deflecting a few questions about matters delicate or confidential. Finally he went to his filing cabinet, looked through what he called his dead files. "Here we are." He pulled some eight-by-tens from a folder, along with his surveillance notes.

"They had this routine, Mulligan and Rita Schumacher. They wouldn't lower themselves to check into motels, so she'd sneak him into the house and they'd go at it in the bedroom upstairs." Checking his notes. "Tuesdays and Thursdays, when Schumie had a late seminar. He gave me a spare key and I found a perch on the bedroom balcony, but I was two hours up there. It was March, it was fucking cold."

He topped up both up. I was feeling a niggling discomfort as I tried to picture my mentor as a reckless roué.

"Four thirty-three, Rita parks her Chev Corsair in the driveway, enters house. Nine minutes later, Mulligan shows up in his Buick wagon, parks around the corner, slips down the alley, and she lets him in through the back. At four fifty-five they're in the bedroom, shedding, at four fifty-six he's sucking on her titties, and at five-oh-one he's between her legs."

The photos were all black-and-whites. The first showed a mussed bed, Mulligan in a naked romp with Rita Schumacher. No flash had been used, of course, so the scene was grainy and dark; one could hardly be expected to identify the rear end as the icon's. But with the interior lights turned on, other pictures were clearer, including a post-coital shot that showed him sitting up and putting on his horn-rims: short, thin but with a pot, bald of scalp and groin, a thick, stubby penis.

"So eventually she goes off for a quick shower, and Mulligan, he just hangs around in his underwear, as if he's got all the time in the world."

A shot of Rita in slip and bra at a mirror, doing her makeup. Then Mulligan helping her into a back-buttoned blouse. Yet another photo had her slipping into a dress, again being assisted by Dermot, barefoot, still wearing only his underpants – white Stanfields or similar. A bulge down there, his erection seemingly resurrected. Almost fifty, and indefatigable.

"Schumie and his lady had a dinner engagement that night, okay? But he told her he was gonna be late picking her up, so he'd drive up and honk and wait for her. Understand, this was a set-up; I scripted it for him. All that effort and the pinchy bastard stiffs me for half the bill because I didn't have to go to court."

I raised my glass in sympathy. Odd that the demand letter from Frinkell had not been remarked on in the police particulars. Because it didn't tie in with their theory of a homosexual affair? I would have to sit down with Irene and discuss it – an awkward prospect I'd been avoiding.

"So it's six-thirty and Schumie drives up in his old Packard and hits the horn. She says to Mulligan, 'He's here. I have to run, darling.' Exact words, because she opened the balcony door to look out and wave. I had to make myself small – Jesus, that was a close call, but it was dark. Then she tells Mulligan to go out the back way after they drive off."

He packed away all the photos, including some he seemed reluctant to show me. "Missed out on a financial opportunity." I didn't get his meaning. "You think Schumie did Mulligan in, counsellor?"

"What's your view?"

"You ever seen a man sick with jealousy? Schumie was sitting right where you are, ranting like a loony."

"Did Mulligan ever find out you had these photos?"

"Not from me, anyway." Jimmy Fingers shrugged, almost too nonchalantly. "Harvey Frinkell has a set."

~~~

I had planned to spend a few hours preparing for Gabriel's appearance the next day at remand court, where I would condemn the injustice of witnesses being concealed from counsel. An early night was in order.

But after sharing a final glass with Fingers, I went on a pub crawl, maybe to drown a sense of revulsion. Something to do with having seen Dermot naked, his thick, unsatiated cock. More to do with my disappointment in him, and in myself, my own failure to see that side of him. As consolation, the affair – and Dermot's notoriety as a campus skirt-chaser – knocked the stuffing out of the Crown's theory of a male lovers' quarrel.

At nightfall I was in a beer parlour by the Granville Bridge: the Cecil Hotel, full of rowdy anarchists and poets. I remember having a merry time spouting Byron. *On with the dance! Let joy be unconfined . . .*

I affected a false air of sobriety and confidence as I strolled into the remand court at 312 Main, all the while struggling to remember the night. I hazily recalled stumbling from the Cecil, the beatniks and I, with a couple of cases of off-sale, then finding our way to a flat under the Granville Bridge. A "pad," its resident poet called it, a scrawny chap who called himself, poetically, Newlove. Somehow I'd staggered home and remembered to set the alarm.

I settled on the counsel bench, hoping the Listerine and cherry breath mints would be potent enough to mask my beery exhalations. There was a full house: witnesses, complainants, miscreants on bail, and the usual lot of retired regulars enjoying the humiliations being dealt out to life's losers.

Vancouver abounded with news outlets in those pre-Internet days, and the press table was overflowing. *Regina v. Swift* was the menu's main course, so in a sense they were there for me, Arthur Ramsgate Beauchamp, Esq., the alleged up-and-comer.

A sentencing was in progress. Hugh McGivern was in fine form, seeking forgiveness for a collector of protection money from neighbourhood mom-and-pop shops. Magistrate Oscar Orr, a wise old hand, surprised me by letting the extortionist off with two years less a day. It bode well that he was in a good mood; I'd been wise to bypass the jeweller.

Smitty finally made his smiling entrance. Heads turned, elbows nudged ribs, and voices churred his praises. Orr immediately put him at the top of the list – seniority prevailed in remand court, especially when it came to the old fox.

"An unusual role for you, Mr. Smythe-Baldwin, representing Her Majesty."

"I shall have to fight the impulse to make light of the Crown's case. I call Gabriel Swift."

I hastened to the defence table as magistrate and prosecutor continued their to-and-fro, Orr letting Smitty know he was honoured by his presence in any guise. The prisoner's door opened and Gabriel was led into the dock, rubbing a wrist recently cuffed. The nod he gave me was curt; he looked out of sorts. He was something of a Janus, Gabriel – a brittle, bitter face and then frequently an affable one, as when he relaxed in debate.

"To business at hand," Smitty said, "the setting of a preliminary inquiry date. I suspect we may need three or four days."

Orr conferred with his clerk, flipped through a datebook. After a few exchanges with Smitty the hearing was set to begin Monday, July 30. I was not called upon, merely nodded my assent. I had already warned Gabriel that the dockets were crowded, but he seemed displeased at this long delay, his arms crossed defiantly.

"And now my learned friend wishes to be heard on a matter regarding certain witnesses."

On observing me standing there, Orr started, in the manner of one who'd suddenly noticed an intruder in his bedroom. But he settled in to listen to my complaint that the police had erected a no-go zone around the Josephs and may have contrived to spirit Monique across an international boundary. My right to a fair defence was being grossly compromised. This was a capital case; denial of access to witnesses could have irreversible consequences.

Orr was nodding. I'd done well, overcoming the pain, the thrumming in my head. My pitch made, I sat, then twisted around to the counsel bench to see Alex Pappas lowering his ample bottom onto it. I'd seen Hugo Schlott's name on the docket, the woman-batterer Pappas had foisted on me – he was due for sentencing.

Smitty was velvety in reply: he was powerless to countermand the Joseph family's wishes, even though their fears of intimidation by his honourable and learned friend were surely baseless. They were decent folk but naïve in the ways of the law, unsophisticated. At preliminary inquiry his able friend would have full and untrammelled right to cross-examine these guileless, unworldly, God-fearing Indians.

Gabriel took this in with a growing expression of incredulity. He seemed about to say something but swallowed his words.

Orr had the apologetic look of one fearing for his soul if he defied the Almighty's commandment. "I'm sorry, Mr. Beauchamp, I deny your motion. You will have your chance at the preliminary. Were these people educated Caucasians I might have a different view –"

My sinking heart sank further into my tender, gassy gut when Gabriel called out, "That is insulting, patronizing, sanctimonious bunk!"

Astonished whispers and murmurs in the gallery. Orr was nonplussed for the moment. "Order," he called. Court security officers were on the move.

"It's one law for the educated so-called Caucasian, another for the rest of us dumb, unsophisticated, thieving Indians." Gabriel's voice carried to the far wall, the room going silent for him. "What law punishes the thief who steals our land and language? Where is that law written in your books of justice?"

As a trio of burly constables dragged him off, he continued to declaim. Ours was a legal system that "thrives on bigotry and is structured to maintain class interests." This actually encouraged a smattering of applause, a hurrah from someone at the back. The rest went unheard, except dimly from behind the lockup door. Orr was crimson-faced. The only lawyer in the room who hadn't gone rigid was Smitty, who gave me a pitying smile.

Orr: "Call the next case."

"Hugo Schlott, assault causing bodily harm."

As Pappas exchanged places with me, he whispered, "You better get that fucking loudmouth under control, pal."

I waited until Schlott got four years, one for each of the teeth he'd knocked out, then headed past his wailing mother on my way up to the cells. Yes, I was less than pleased with my short-fused client, yet struggling against an impermissible pride in him for saying the unsayable truth.

I met Gabriel in a dark locked room, a guard glaring at us though metal-wire glass. Gabriel looked fiercely at me. "Okay, I lost it."

"I hope it's out of your system, but I bet it felt good."

"It felt right."

I wasn't aware I was smiling until I saw him staring oddly at me. "The look on Oscar Orr's face . . ." I couldn't help myself, and let go. Gabriel joined in. It felt good and it felt right to share that moment with him. Laughter is such a catalyst for friendship, and we were easing ourselves in that direction.

"You letting me off the hook, Arthur? I was sure you were going to fire me as your client."

"Just promise it won't happen at your trial."

"It won't." He shrugged, put on a serious face. "They found another way to screw me."

"Please explain."

"They put a rat in my cell."

From "Where the Squamish River Flows," *A Thirst for Justice*, © W. Chance

THE REPERCUSSIONS FROM SWIFT'S OUTBURST were unexpected and contentious, for on the following day Attorney General Robert Bonner signed a rare direct indictment, sending the case to jury trial without a preliminary hearing. It was widely known that Smythe-Baldwin had not been consulted and there'd been a flap over that. But the press already had the story; there was no backing down.

In his column in the *Sun,* Jack Scott wrote acerbically: "It seems Mr. Bonner jumped to the impetuous conclusion that the defendant planned to use the preliminary as a pulpit for expressing incendiary views that are not in accord with Social Credit philosophy. Apparently the smattering of applause in court spooked the Cabinet into thinking the revolution was at hand."

The direct indictment had the effect of accelerating the onset of the trial, which had been expected to take place in late fall. So now the prosecution had to scramble to ensure that defence lawyers had reasonable access to Chief Joseph and his family. Otherwise Beauchamp would have a telling ground for appeal.

In those days the press was allowed to report on a preliminary, and Beauchamp had hoped to use it not just to prepare his defence but to alert all of Vancouver there was something rotten going on in the Squamish RCMP. The pool of citizens from which a jury would be selected would already have a taste of the defence and come armed with skepticism about police assertions. But Beauchamp was persuaded there were also advantages to foregoing a preliminary . . .

G rab it and run with it," Alex Pappas instructed me, confusingly. "Do not stop at Go. Go directly to trial."

He had called me into his office to give me his counsel about the advantages of bypassing a prelim. "It's just a free dry run for the Crown, Stretch. Gives them a chance to correct their fuckups, rehearse their witnesses. You ever noticed on a second go-round how witnesses always sound more credible? Especially the cops."

That wasn't quite my experience, but he had more of it. At least Gabriel would be cheered by the prospect of an earlier date.

Smitty, when he'd called that day, had been as close to apoplectic as was possible for the old smoothie. I gathered he'd almost resigned his retainer. This rancour against the Attorney General seemed a blessing from the Fates, those mischievous sprites, because I suspected – he implied as much – that he was no longer interested in putting that much oomph into the case. "Do not, Sir Arthur, expect any rabid pursuit of your client. Justice is all I aspire to. A fair trial and a friendly glass or two at the end."

"Another big advantage," Pappas continued, "is you'll get extra leeway because you'll be constantly on your feet, complaining they robbed you of the right to a prelim and you need absolute full disclosure, extra time with the witnesses. Your judge will have to pamper you, give you free rein. Smitty ain't gonna be ready he'll be too busy plugging all the holes. I don't even think he's got a junior yet to do all the dog work."

Pappas didn't know the particulars of the case beyond what was in the papers, but he was a pretty good tactician, and he made sense. But I had to tell him that Smitty had just been assigned an assistant counsel: Leroy Lukey, from the Crown counsel office.

"That dumb fuck? You're in even better shape. I think he took too many hits to the head in his football days."

Lukey had been a college all-star, even had a couple of tryouts with the Edmonton Eskimos. I'd been lined up against him several times, found him abrasive, lacking a firm handle on ethics. Smitty had charged him with getting us face time with Monique Joseph and her parents, Benjamin and Anna. Ophelia, with her finely tuned social skills, would do the interviews.

Smitty had dropped a hint he'd like to set the trial for the week already put aside for the prelim. His fall calendar was filled to "catastrophic proportions." We agreed he'd have to use all his wiles to persuade the Chief Justice to order a special summer assize.

I thanked Pappas for his insights and wisdom and headed off to Oakie to compare notes with Gabriel about the rat in his cell.

~~~

One could never predict the moods of Gabriel Swift. He seemed uncommonly relaxed as he was ushered into the interview room, and shook my hand with some enthusiasm. I brought him up to speed and asked him how he felt about a July 30 start to his trial.

"Thanks for asking. I'm okay with whatever you advise." That was a new and helpful tone.

"I've checked out your cellmate." A longshoreman, Burt Snyder, who sold an undercover cop an ounce of uncut heroin from a freighter out of Hong Kong. "I can't find a record, so he's a first-timer, but he's still looking at five and up." I told Gabriel he was right to be suspicious of him; it was a hallowed Crown tactic to offer deals to prospective snitches – a minimum sentence, even probation, witness protection.

"He's so obvious it's pathetic. A union guy, a brother, a fucking comrade. Claims he's part Native. Give me a break."

Gabriel knew to keep his own counsel but I warned him anyway. His vocabulary in that cell should be limited to grunts and grumbles. He assured me he was ignoring Snyder in favour of books, currently working through Frantz Fanon's *The Wretched of the Earth*, in French, aided by a *dictionnaire* Larousse. (During later visits, as I recall, he even conversed with me in that liquid tongue, with growing ease.)

We spent another hour together and didn't speak about the case. We argued about Fanon – the anti-colonialist psychiatrist had died only a few months earlier – and his alleged calls to violence. I, who had read the reviews but not the book, got badly mauled. I had to award Gabriel the day; for our next debate, I would pick the topic.

I arrived out of breath at the riverbank. Below me a naked corpse floated down the blood-red Lethe, river of forgetfulness and oblivion. I suddenly realized I too was naked, I was next, I felt the pull of the river, I wanted to jump into the river and drown . . .

I awoke sluggishly from this dark dream, variations of which had been proliferating. Each time I would be hurrying to the river, I needed to be there. Sometimes Gabriel was there, sometimes Mulligan, sometimes his bloodied body. Soundtrack by Huddie Leadbelly.

I have always been prone to vivid dreams and, unlike more balanced people, have a hard time shaking them off. A common nightmare involved a trapdoor swinging open, the snap of a neck. Such dreams would often awake me. I was sleeping poorly, and sensed I had gotten too close to my client. Bad practice, not done. One ought to keep a safe and proper distance.

In the nearly three weeks since his outburst in court, we'd met half a dozen times, debating the books he'd challenged me to read: Fanon's *Black Skin, White Masks,* Durkheim, Sartre, all in French, all about collective behaviour, rebellion, revolution. Not Marxist dogma, though – he correctly sensed that would be pushing too hard.

I listened to the eight a.m. news as I dressed and coffeed up. Scott Carpenter had just orbited Earth three times, a feat that made me dizzy. It was confirmed that Arthur Ellis, Canada's pseudonymous hangman, was under contract for two executions scheduled for December. In local news, the Gabriel Swift murder trial had been set for one week beginning Monday, July 30, at the Vancouver courthouse.

~~~

As I stepped from the cage at the unlucky missing thirteenth floor, Pappas was behind the desk of the receptionist, looking at her appointment book while also looking down her dress. Mister Hands caught sight of me, stubbed out a cigarette, and led me to a private corner.

"I don't know what you been up to, cowboy, but the fat man is in an uproar." Senior partner Tom Inglis. "He sent me to fetch you, so you better come clean with me – we only got a minute."

I released my elbow from his grip. "I have no idea what you're talking about, Alex."

"Well, I don't neither, but I guess we're going to find out."

He escorted me like an arrested felon into Inglis's roomy, gloomy office. Bullingham was there too. Neither rose. Pappas stood nervously by the door, ready to bolt, fearful of Inglis's temper.

"How's the Swift case shaping up?" This, from Inglis, was less a question than a bark. He was slouched behind his desk, hands clasped over the farthest reaches of his abdomen. Important political connections, a Diefenbaker crony and bagman.

"I think I'm on top of it."

Inglis scowled. "Nasty little outburst in court a few weeks ago. Unscripted, we assume."

"I am not in the habit of encouraging clients to denounce the legal system."

"Bit of a Bolshevik, is he, this Swift?"

"He holds some strong views."

"I suppose the two of you, ah, engage in political conversations?"

"What's this about, sir?"

"Let's say we're concerned about whether you two share beliefs that might not only compromise your defence but cause embarrassment to this office."

"I don't know whether to find that insulting, Mr. Inglis, or merely confusing."

A flush rose from neck to jowls and he seemed about to erupt. Bully intervened. "I'm sure that wasn't meant as an accusation, Arthur. We have some concerns, that's all."

Inglis struggled to rein himself in, adjusted his bifocals, peered at some records on his desk. "You hold a PC membership. Friends tell me you followed John into the party in 1958. Good, if that be true. But sometimes people slip through and play the double agent. One has to be careful. These are dangerous times."

Pappas was seated by this time, trying to make himself small. He'd recommended me as Gabriel's defender – he too might be seen as a tool of the Kremlin.

"You may relax, Mr. Inglis. I have not infiltrated the firm, nor do I seek to overthrow it."

Bully seemed to be stifling a smile; I sensed he admired me for showing spine. Inglis fingered his watch chain, trying to look affronted but, I suspected, sensing the imbecility of his mission. "Let us get to the point. You know a Mr. Jim Brady?"

"I was in the campaign office of the Communist Party several weeks ago. I spent an interesting hour with Mr. Brady, after which I was followed by an underskilled undercover officer. Who then reported to his seniors, who obviously have confided in you. Notes of my session with Brady have been transcribed in triplicate in the Gabriel Swift file, should you care to see them."

Inglis harrumphed, looked for support from Bully, then Pappas. "One should be careful whom one meets. You were observed packing Chinese food in there to feed their campaign workers. Something was overheard about your running in Vancouver Centre."

"That was said in jest, for God's sake," I erupted. "This is absurd. Mr. Brady is a central figure in this case who can be of help to a man facing the death penalty. I am bound by ethics to represent Gabriel Swift to the best of my ability and without fear of being red-smeared by the senior members of this firm."

Inglis looked pretty red himself by then. "I detect impertinence, Mr. Beauchamp." He again looked about for help, didn't get any. Another harrumph. "I want that file put on my desk s.a.p." He slowly heaved himself up to show us out. At the door he said, "Young man, I fully expect to see you at our reception for the Prime Minister next week."

The firm had booked the Hotel Vancouver penthouse, with appetizers and a free bar for a selected list of the wealthy and worthy, to kick off a rally that night at the Forum. "I intend to be there and to wish Mr. Diefenbaker well," I said. I had campaigned for the Chief in 1958, and I still admired him despite his reliance on friends like Inglis.

Pappas hustled me out, down to my office, shutting the door. "Let's see that file."

"On my desk."

He began shuffling through it, talking the while. "You just blew any chance you had of rising in this firm, pal. I was grooming you for associate, but lipping off to the fat man that way, you screwed yourself in the ass."

I tried to imagine the contortions required by such an act. "You can kowtow to the bosses all you want, Alex, but I've had it with being treated like a schoolboy around here." Where was this newfound spunk coming from? Gabriel. Jim Brady. *Fear of consequences merely perpetuates the system.*

Pappas ignored that; he was groaning over the police reports. "Jesus H. Christ. Matching cartridges. This sucks."

I shuffled through several new files, referrals from satisfied clients. The world hadn't stopped because I was defending a capital murder. I was juggling half a dozen new clients, paying ones, including that day's trial – an eighteen-year-old jewel thief, Nick Faloon – another up-and-comer. I didn't need Tragger, Inglis; I could do quite well on my own.

"For crying out loud, your guy is spotted on the way to the kill? And then a false alibi?" He lit a cigarette, took a deep drag. "Okay, what we obviously got here is a couple of closet fags who spent their idle hours shagging each other in the woods. Maybe Swift got tired of being on the bottom, or being the professor's plaything. There was a confrontation and Gabriel whacked him. Maybe you better start thinking of cutting a deal."

"There's not a Crown witness who isn't a liar. No one's fished out a body. They can't discount suicide. I can beat it."

"You want to get back on the good side of the fat man, maybe you don't want to beat it. Cop a plea to non-capital – a lovers' quarrel, an impetuous act, not planned. Put a little effort into Smitty, he'll go with that. I'll talk to him if you like; I got his respect. Count it a victory – life behind bars, maybe even parole after a few decades. But if he wants to martyr himself, fuck him, no one's going to remember a lippy redskin buck who got his neck stretched at the New West pen."

"I'll handle it my way."

With an exasperated grunt, Pappas picked up the file and headed back to Inglis's office.

~~~

I bought a bottle of tequila on the way home, looking forward to celebrating something, even if it was just the day's easy win. No one actually saw young Faloon snaffle the diamond ring from the jewellery store counter, so I never had to put the skinny booster on the stand. The arresting officer took it in stride, shook Faloon's hand. "Catch you later, Nick."

As I pulled into my backyard parking spot, Ira was sitting on the outer staircase looking weary, trying to relight the butt of a cigarette while being harassed by Craznik.

"For last time, pay rent owing or I take execution."

Ira yawned. "So shoot me."

"What do you owe?" I asked, joining them. "Maybe we can busk for it."

Craznik scowled at me. "Seventy bucks including late penalty. Canadian dollars. Not Russian rubles."

"Russian what?"

"Hah. Why do police ask am I harbouring communists? You a communist? In my country we shoot communists. No communists here, no Indians, no deadbeats who don't pay rent." He stomped off.

"I'm out of this stalag," Ira said, groaning. "I've got a cot at the Beanery . . . shit" – remembering the Beanery was going broke, its lease up in five days – "I'll stay at the Nowhere Hotel if I have to. The YMHA. The Sally Ann. Shit."

I washed out a couple of cups with the garden hose and poured from the Don Julio Reserva. "To your health."

Ira knocked his back, poured another. "There's no future in coffee bars." A sigh. "I'm an impresario. I got no other talents."

I could hear the phone ringing in my room. "Finish your drink," I said, "then I'll drive you to work."

Despite a presentiment that my mother was calling, I failed to take evasive action. It might have been Ophelia, eager for amends. Or a reporter with news that Dermot Mulligan had been pulled over at the Blaine border crossing, in a car with Rita Schumacher.

"This will kill your father. *And* me. Is that what you want?"

"You have nothing to lose but your chains."

A pause, recovery. "You're playing some kind of silly game, aren't you?"

"The game is called smear the lawyer. Some overzealous cops have been defaming me high and low, to my mother, my boss, and my landlord."

I reeled off a stern defence of the role of criminal counsel, and she finally let me go, petulant and unforgiving. I felt oppressed. The Mounties had ganged up on me – not only Knepp and Jettles, but the infamous Red Squad as well. In collaboration with senior members of Tragger, Inglis.

Cop a plea to non-capital. I felt a gun at my head.

~~~

Lawonda and I could make out Ira's voice over the shuffling of chairs and the chatter of departing customers. "Mark it on your calendar, folks: Thursday, end of the month, our last night. No coffee, just cheap wine, two bits a glass. We're jamming – everyone bring an instrument."

I was in the back helping Lawonda clean up, scraping plates and bowls, steel-woolling the pans. We were both fairly tight – we'd shared my tequila while Sonny Terry and Brownie McGhee were "laying out their cool blues," as Lawonda put it. She was again wearing something African, brightly coloured but slinky. The kitchen alcove was so cramped that our bodies brushed in passing, breasts against ribs, hips grazing buttocks. The contact was electrifying, at least for me. She was talking all the while, candid, nonchalant.

This black Aphrodite, like Ira, was soon to be jobless, but her reaction was a gay indifference. She had Third World survival skills, had travelled the world doing jobs like this. She also had some borderline trades, as she casually confessed, including two years in London as a call girl. "I didn't come cheap."

I was more titillated than shocked, then became flustered as she leaned over to wipe the counter and her bottom nudged my groin, the swelling there. "That why they call you Stretch?" she said.

I backed away, tight to the wall, knocking a pan from its hook. I thought she might laugh, but she frowned, studying me: a clumsy oaf with an undisciplined cock. Reject. Return to sender.

"Glad you could come" – Ira, still doing his goodbyes – "Hey, anyone got any good contacts in the music industry, leave me your card. I do all aspects of entertainment. Weddings, grad parties, bar mitzvahs, your kids' birthdays."

Lawonda and I retreated to an equally cramped annex with a desk, a cot, a Barcalounger, a couple of easy chairs. I was still rigid with embarrassment as we sat and finished the tail end of the tequila. Meanwhile, Ira was arguing with the entertainers over their fee. "Half the take, guys, that's the deal."

"No, brother, you take the bigger end. You in need."

Ira nobly rejected that. After letting them out, he strolled toward us, peeling a rubber band off a packet, spilling its contents on the desk blotter: leaf bits, stems, seeds. "They wished me happy bankruptcy and made this here donation of Mexican tea to help cure my woes."

"Mexican tea?" I observed it came with a packet of Zig-Zag papers.

"Reefer, my man. Mary Jane. Maria Juanita."

Lawonda took over, picking out the stems, expertly shaking out the seeds. I looked on, nervous, unsure about this enterprise, yet intrigued. This was the infamous source of reefer madness that the films and tabloids had warned about. A narcotic – illegal, like heroin. I'd witnessed Judge Hume jail a college student for a year for a lesser quantity than this. I wandered off, affecting insouciance, checked to ensure front and back doors were locked.

Another drink might ease my anxiety, but a peek into the refrigerator offered no relief, not even a beer. I would watch Ira and Lawonda, see how they reacted, maybe do a little taste, no more than that.

I don't know how many sticks of Mary Jane we smoked that night, but I was having trouble seeing the point of it. I was feeling nothing. If it had any effect on me, it was merely to make me sad as I listened to Ira's woes. Where was he going to live? *How* was he going to live? Ultimately he retreated to the cot and I was glad to see him nod off – he'd been sleeping poorly.

Lawonda did the talking then. Confessions of a sinful life: nude modelling for French artists, hustling dukes and earls in England, hanging about with jazz artists in New Orleans. As much as I was dazzled by her, I was mystified by how anyone could pack so much into her thirty-plus years. She finished a story about her last, unreliable lover, a man of means who'd met her in London, escorted her to Canada, then jilted her for the wife he'd promised to divorce. She then went silent, contemplative, and there was only the sound of Ira's gentle snoring. After a while she said, "So how's *your* love life?"

An easy answer eluded me. Finally: "Non-existent." A blurt of unbridled honesty that for some unfathomable reason triggered a cannonade; suddenly I was on a flight without a pilot. Ophelia Moore was the theme of this self-pitying discourse, and my clowning attempts to romance her. Lawonda chimed in occasionally with a question, prodding me into ever more shameful confession. Within the cloud of memory, certain words stick and stay, words like *ineptitude* and *disaster* and *armpit*. Yes, my unhinged tongue described my entry into that inviting false orifice.

And I guess that's what started her on that laughing fit. It continued until she had to leave the room so as not to wake Ira. She beckoned me to follow her, and soon we found ourselves outside the Beanery with our jackets on. She still couldn't suppress laughter. "When a lady offers you head, man, you supposed to take it, not go off in the armpit."

"What are we doing out here?"

"For starters, you gonna walk me home, honey."

As she took my arm, a sudden dizziness came upon me, followed by a panicky cold sweat.

From "Where the Squamish River Flows," *A Thirst for Justice*, © W. Chance

WE MUST VIGOROUSLY DISCOUNT RUMOURS of an alleged sexual encounter between Beauchamp and the mysterious woman known as Lawonda. The author of such rumours, Ira Lavitch, the well-known impresario,[*] sought to convince me that Beauchamp, as he vulgarly put it, "got himself royally fucked" on the night of Friday, May 25, in her illegal ground-floor suite in Kitsilano.

Beauchamp (typically) denied all. My interview notes read: "Interesting woman. From Ghana. Worked at the Beanery."

He had no idea then, but will be aware on reading this, that "Lawonda" was a false name, that she was not from Ghana but New Orleans, and that she had never been outside North America. She had plied various illegitimate trades in her home country before jumping bail and arriving in Canada with a false passport. Her real name is Katherine Irvine. All this is revealed in a confessional blog[†] that Irvine has maintained during her senior years. The blog is replete with erotic anecdotes but she has wisely censored the names of her multitude of lovers. There is no hint of her coming together with a lanky, big-nosed young barrister who achieved fame in later life.

Irvine did not respond to my emailed entreaties to put to rest the canard that she'd seduced Beauchamp, royally or otherwise, so this writer considers such scandal mere smoke.

---

[*]   He lives in Toronto now, with a partner. Semi-retired, he still "agents" some surviving rock bands from the sixties and seventies.

[†]   2AllMyLovers@blogspot.com

At any rate, one doesn't see our awkward hero as having the romantic wherewithal to sexually engage a woman of such experience, especially given his unavailing pursuit of Ophelia Moore, for whom he continued to endure feelings that lay somewhere between puppy love and infatuation. It is interesting to note that both these women were much older than him. We have already explored his lack of normal nurturing – enough said.

Beauchamp felt sorely oppressed at having been maligned by senior partner Tom Inglis, with his near-paranoid concern about communists under the bed. In this connection I can't resist an anecdote – which comes with well-documented proof – of how that suddenly turned around, thanks to a handshake with the Prime Minister of Canada.

That occurred at the reception for Diefenbaker sponsored by Tragger, Inglis at the Hotel Vancouver's famed Panorama Roof, which the firm had booked for the afternoon of May 30. Inglis and Bullingham were escorting the Prime Minister, working the packed room, focusing on the wealthy donors. On reaching Beauchamp, Inglis began introducing him (as caught on film by a campaign worker) as "one of our able young trial lawyers."

The Prime Minister interrupted: "Arthur Beauchamp, of course, aspiring criminal lawyer. We met in fifty-eight – the Quadra campaign office, wasn't it?"

"I'm astonished that you remember, sir."

"Young man, I have an excellent memory for flattery. You had the audacity to claim I inspired you to enter criminal law."

There is a photograph of this moment in the Law Society's journal *The Advocate*. Diefenbaker's right hand is glued to Beauchamp's, the other arm around his shoulders, posing with him as flashbulbs pop. Inglis's protuberant belly can be seen in profile, the rest of him lopped off . . .

I've got my eye on you, young fellow," the Chief had said. Rumours of his phenomenal memory were confirmed: he'd even pronounced my name correctly.

The episode gained me unbounded respect within our little huddle of counsel. Hubbell put on a show of bowing and scraping, begging to be allowed to touch the hem of my suit jacket. Ophelia asked for my autograph.

Pappas was in an unusually good humour as he watched Inglis waddle off with the Chief. "Did you see the look on the fat man's face? Went so white I thought he was having a stroke. Congratulations, you almost killed him."

At the end of the evening, Inglis and Bully competed to be the first to shake my hand. I decided I might give the firm another chance.

I wasn't able to feel too cocky about myself, though, not after my unmanly exhibition of cold feet on the previous Friday night. I may as well deal with it, get it over with, and in so doing persevere in my campaign to debunk Wentworth Chance's exaggerations and innuendos. I shall admit he got me with his scoop about Lawonda's secret life, though it ought not to have surprised me – I had heard little of Ghana or London in her accent. But the gall of the man to revel in such shameful gossip on the published page, then dismiss it as smoke!

My mood on reading the advance copy of *Thirst for Justice* was not lightened when I called Ira in Toronto to complain he'd betrayed a friend of five decades. "You didn't even score a goodnight kiss? What a schmendrick. Guys were lined up around the block to get close to that dame."

A goodnight kiss might have been the final, shattering blow. By the time I'd reached the doorstep of her flat I was ready for the psychiatric ward, alternating between hot and cold, torn between mindless desire and abject fear of this artful professional seductress. But fear of what consequences? Exposure? Failure? Another show of virginal ineptitude? Maybe (as I later, callowly, consoled myself) of disease.

She'd invited me in. I stammered an excuse about feeling ill, which, from my manner and agonized expression, she might not have doubted. Then I bolted.

The vast majority of heterosexual men with at least a modicum of libido would not have spurned the opportunity. I accept that. I am guilty. I suffered in my youth from neurotic responses to sexual invitation. Maybe it has a name – situational erotic aversion disorder. Translation: incurable shyness.

Later, in my bed, I masturbated away my disgust at myself.

Now let us bury that and return to the Panorama Roof. Pappas and Hubbell were at the bar, refilling, so our group had dwindled to the tricky twosome of Ophelia and me. She was zipped into a smart tight, calf-length dress that showed off her Rubenesque figure, and she was getting looks. I was dying to ask her why Jordan Geraldson hadn't shown up, but we avoided tender ground, restricting ourselves to wry comments on what Ophelia called an "orgy of suckholing."

There was an air of tension in the room. The election was only nineteen days away, and the polls predicted a close race. I felt guilty about not having time to campaign for the Chief.

Ophelia's nemesis, Harvey Frinkell, came skulking into view. The shyster was uninvited, of course, but could usually be counted on to gate-crash such functions to cadge some quality booze. "Fuck you," Ophelia said as he came into hearing distance.

"Any time, gorgeous," Frinkell said, carrying on to the bar, plucking a martini.

I waited as she delivered some hoarse, low, and obscene opinions of the man. Finally she shrugged it off. "Honestly, I'm not obsessed with that prick."

We laughed, played with the prospect of summoning Frinkell to court, cross-examining him about his threatening letter, accusing him of driving Mulligan to suicide.

She had interviewed Chief Joseph and his wife the week before, in less than relaxed circumstances: in the Squamish detachment at the back of the squad room, where she had to keep the volume low so as not to be overheard. Benjamin and Anna were nervous, hesitant, but both insisted Monique had been home at all critical times. They made no bones about opposing her relationship with Gabriel. The Crown claimed to be having problems coaxing Monique back from Washington, and Ophelia suspected stalling tactics.

Ophelia had then visited Gabriel, just the day before, to brief him. I asked her how that went. I was keeping this cocktail conversation neutral, avoiding the personal, the risky.

"We've become fairly palsy since he decided I'm not a dumb blonde. Anyway, he didn't seem perturbed that the Josephs were sticking by their guns. Monique, he insisted, will have something else to say. I doubt he was much in love with her, by the way. I think he feels love is somehow irrelevant to the grand missions of his life, maybe even a hindrance."

"And she? Monique?"

"She had a crush, he says. Whatever that is."

I didn't offer to explain what a crush felt like. I asked how Gabriel was getting along with the supposed rat, Snyder.

"They chitchat. I told him not to, but he thinks it's a game. They do play games – chess and cribbage. It's hard to tell Gabriel to stick to himself; it gets lonely in those cells."

"Darn him. I warned him." But not strenuously enough. Too much talk about Fanon and Durkheim when I visited, not enough about prison safety.

Ophelia moved a little closer to me, a scent of perfume and a hint of warmth intimating a thaw was setting in. So I was emboldened to ask, "And where's Jordan this afternoon?"

"I'm taking a little vacation from him."

I suppressed a smirk of triumph. Perhaps she had punished me enough for fraternizing with Frinkell. Geraldson had been a stopgap; she'd merely used him to demonstrate to me her value.

Hubbell took that inopportune moment to return clutching three doubles on the rocks. "Mr. Johnny Black here is going to help us through this terrible time. How are you two getting along?" He put an arm around Ophelia. "Unlike Pappas, I wouldn't mind if you squeezed my nuts. Just not too hard."

She shrugged away. "You're getting a little smashed, Hub. And we have company."

Advancing was Cyrus Smythe-Baldwin, and in tow was Leroy Lukey, a beefy fellow, still in his twenties. "May I take advantage of this august occasion," said Smitty, "to present my aide-de-camp, Mr. Lukey – whom I believe you know, Arthur – and to make acquaintance with the young lady at your side, whom I take to be your own junior, Mrs. Moore."

He kissed her hand, commended her for quelling the Oakalla revolt, and complimented me on my taste in juniors. I agreed, looking at Lukey, that I had the better deal. Smitty laughed and went off to talk to Pappas.

"Heard this one?" Lukey got close. "What did Tonto say when the Lone Ranger tied his cock in a knot?" He waited. "'How come?'"

Out of some warped sense of politeness I affected a smile, as if finding this vaguely humorous. Ophelia pinched me in the side hard enough to raise a welt.

Lukey raised his glass. "To equal injustice for all. The offence will be scoring fast and early." He assumed the stance of a running back waiting for the snap.

"The race goes to the swift, Leroy."

He took a moment to get it. "Like the archbishop said to the choirboy, up yours, my son."

He'd been sizing up Ophelia, smarting over my claim to have gotten the better deal. "First criminal trial? Maybe you want to add a learning curve to the others on display."

"What I lack in experience I make up for with an instinct for bullshit." She smiled graciously and sipped her Scotch.

"Sister, you are going to be a distracting influence in court. First female lawyer I've met who doesn't look like a dyke."

"And I wish I could say you don't look like a dick." She took my arm, about to lead me away.

Lukey persisted. "You guys like surprises?" He pulled an envelope from a pocket, handed it to Ophelia with a bow. "Read what Walt Lorenzo says. Then maybe we can talk about your guilty plea."

He wandered off. Ophelia took the envelope as I slugged back my Scotch. When I looked around, she'd gone somewhere with her own drink, presumably to find privacy to read about Walt Lorenzo, whoever he was.

Frinkell came wandering past again, this time wiping his face and shirtfront with a handful of napkins. He didn't return any of the curious looks, just headed straight to the washroom.

A second later Ophelia hove into view, her glass empty, even of ice cubes. Her other hand held the envelope from Lukey and several sheets of wet stationery. "Let's get out of here," she said.

~~~

All the firm's able-bodied lawyers had been expected to continue on, drunk or sober, to the Conservative rally in the Forum, so the fourteenth floor was unoccupied but for cleaning staff.

Meanwhile, Ophelia was draped over an armchair, looking wan. "I thought the plan was to shy away from this idiot."

"That's why this stinks."

The idiot in question was Corporal Walt Lorenzo. This astonishingly inept actor – stage name Burt Snyder — had been brought in from Winnipeg RCMP to share a cell with Gabriel at Oakalla.

I smoothed out the drying papers and read them again – Lorenzo's brief of evidence. The first page described the set-up: his instructions, his cover as a longshoreman and heroin peddler, his attempted insinuation, over several days, into Gabriel's confidence. Glaringly displayed was an undeserved sense of self-importance.

Subject and I had little conversation at first, as I pretended to want to keep to myself. There was no mention of the crimes he and I were "charged with" until Day Four, when he asked what I was in for. I related the cover story, and asked the same question of him. He said he was being "framed for murder."

Verbatim notes of the aforementioned and following conversations were made daily by me, when I was taken from the cell to see my "lawyer" or a visiting "relative" or to make a court "appearance."

The verbatim notes, a dozen Photostatted scraps of paper, were stapled to his quotation-mark-riddled brief. He and Gabriel had been together three weeks, from May 6 to 28, an unusually long time for an operation of this kind, giving rise to a suspicion this operative had been too proud to admit failure and cooked up a stew of lies.

On May 12 (Day Six) I broached the subject of politics, and he was pleased that I "supported" the aims of the Communist Party, whose programs and philosophy I studied in my training for this assignment. I also mentioned in passing that I was part Ojibwa, on my mother's side, which I believe caused him to relax his guard further.

Those patent lies had done just the reverse. Gabriel had told me the man betrayed only a rudimentary knowledge of politics, let alone the history of class struggle. I'd chided him for even passing the time of day with him. "I was only feeling him out," he said.

Lorenzo continued to try to engage him, claiming a tentative but growing friendship. He prided himself on his skill at chess, but "I made sure I lost most of the games." Eventually he affected curiosity about Gabriel's crime, claiming he'd heard "scuttlebutt about it in the joint."

Gabriel had politely declined to respond, returning to a biography of Louis Riel. Thereafter, Lorenzo seemed not to have made similar blunt overtures, confining himself to denunciations of the rich. He tried to interest Gabriel in an "escape plan," but he didn't bite on that, either.

I sensed he was weakening. We had developed a bonding, especially as we agreed politically, and he took me to be a "comrade." I didn't have the impression he was a real "bad" person, and it's my experience that people like him eventually have to get it off their chest.

Finally, on Day Nineteen, the previous Saturday, the frustrated spy must have realized his chances for promotion would dry up if he didn't produce. Over the cribbage board that evening, he tearfully regurgitated to Gabriel a crime he claimed he'd bottled up. He had once killed a man, broken his neck in a back-alley fight, but escaped detection.

I told him my secret was torturing me and he was the first person I'd ever told this, because he was like a brother, and I felt deeply in my heart I could trust him. I said, "It was me or him, I had to kill him."

Swift heaved a big sigh, and I could sense him giving way. Then he said, "I had to kill too." He said he had no choice, Professor Mulligan had to pay for his crimes. He got very choked up so I didn't get his full meaning, but he went on about children being strapped and beaten, sexually assaulted, at some Indian school in Saskatchewan. He told me he'd planned to confront the deceased at his fishing hole, and make him take his clothes off so he could fake a suicide, but the deceased tried to grab his rifle and there was a tussle and he hurled him down over the rocks, into the river, where he shot him as he flailed.

That was faithfully copied from one of his stapled notes, word for word. Signed and dated: *27-05-62, at 0910 hours.*

I was of course floored by this unexpected, yet almost credible, scenario – credible at least to those who might see Gabriel as obsessively vengeful – but I couldn't remotely see my client blurting out a full, quick, unadorned confession. Apparently nothing else was said, other than Lorenzo swearing he would never repeat those words. Gabriel was, to employ his cellmate's compositional bad habit, "emotional."

It seemed hardly plausible that on Ophelia's visit two days later there'd been not a whisper of this. "Gabriel was just like . . . normal," she said. "Anger-free, talkative in his cynical way – he'd actually been getting his hopes up." She stood, put on her jacket. "This is going to be hard."

"I'll bet the farm that Roscoe Knepp knows Lorenzo, that they served together. Maybe Lorenzo owes him one."

"Maybe Knepp saved his life? This is so sick. Could a jury possibly believe anything so obviously cooked up?"

I wasn't sure.

~~~

Gabriel was slumped in his chair, looking up at the walls of the tiny interview room as if wondering why they seemed to be closing in on him. I had waited for an explosion, tensed myself for it, but he'd just gone small, arms crossed, shoulders curled in. "Does Knepp know this guy?" he asked.

"We're working on it."

He must have wondered how hard we were working, Ophelia in her tight designer dress, I in a conservative dark suit. I was too embarrassed to explain we'd been at a Conservative Party function.

"He'll be laughed out of court," Ophelia said.

A wan smile from Gabriel. "I live in the real world."

"What world is that?" she asked.

"Tell me how many Natives will be sitting on the jury."

"I doubt there'll be any."

"That's the real world."

He seemed less despairing than resigned, settled, accepting of the worst. It's never easy getting one's hopes up, risking them being dashed; it even strips you of anger. If anything, he seemed more relaxed now that he was back in the real world.

"It's crap, a transparent farce." I tried to sound enthusiastic. "Let's do a rerun. Everything that passed between you and Lorenzo on Saturday."

He looked at his hands, sighed, straightened up. "Okay, I didn't say a fucking thing to him all day, until maybe half an hour before lights out. Then we sat down to play some crib. And he went into this malarkey about killing someone. It was pathetic. I told him so."

Ophelia was startled. "Why didn't you say that when I saw you?"

Gabriel looked down again. "I didn't want you to climb all over me about it. I just told him he wasn't going to win an Oscar, that he was a lousy ham actor. That was all, and he went red and shut up. I honestly never thought he was a cop – he was too dumb."

Ophelia made notes as I drew from Gabriel a detailed account of all his dealings with Lorenzo. He seemed contrite, as he ought to have been; humiliating Lorenzo may have incited him to devise that extravagantly false confession. My client's quick tongue had again caused a self-inflicted wound.

I had him look again at Lorenzo's statement. "He says you 'went on about children being strapped and beaten, sexually assaulted, at some Indian school in Saskatchewan.' So let me ask: did Dermot tell you his writing block had to do with Pie Eleven?"

"No, but I sensed it. I think he'd uncovered some abuse situation there. Maybe the Church told him to take no action and keep his mouth shut. Maybe that's why Rome fell. I hope I won't be asked in court if that motivated me to kill him. I would die laughing."

I told him to make inquiries through the prison grapevine; another inmate might have encountered Lorenzo. I intended to seek out other sources.

"I guess I shouldn't have belted Roscoe in the chops." A cynical smile.

"Don't give in to him," I said.

"He wins. I hang."

Ophelia: "Don't even dream it."

"*Je n'ai pas l'espoir.* Except to hope I have his courage. Riel's."

~~~

Ophelia and I had done well to miss the Diefenbaker rally. It was a circus, according to the news on my car radio, the Chief thrown off script as he contended in vain with heckling from infiltrating socialists. There'd been scuffling and, to top everything off, a baring of bodies by protesting Freedomites.

Silence reigned in the Volkswagen after I turned off the radio. We were too depressed over Operation Lorenzo to utter anything but the occasional expletive.

"Pricks," she said. "They're pricks."

With all the honest cops on the federal force, how had we managed to find ourselves tangled up with a clubby little ring of the debased and unscrupulous? Two senior officers, with that born follower Constable Jettles surely in the thick of it. I constructed a daydream of exposing them, disgracing them, hauling them into court in shackles.

Professor Mulligan had to pay for his crime. That was the theme they'd chosen, apparently casting aside their cockamamie theory of a homosexual affair gone crosswise, knowing they couldn't sell it to a jury. And besides, such an approach would leave open a lesser verdict: non-capital murder, even manslaughter, a death caused in the heat of passion. That wasn't enough for Roscoe Knepp. Capital murder required proof of planning and deliberation, and Lorenzo had supplied that.

"They're all pricks."

Maybe she meant men in general. Maybe not, but the comment dissuaded me from making even a subtle approach to her. I could have told her that she looked stunning that night. I could have asked what had transpired between her and Geraldson. I kept my mouth shut.

As I pulled up at her place, she kissed me lightly on that mouth. But she didn't invite me in.

I ra and I returned to our lodging at one a.m. after rescuing his movie posters and other memorabilia from the Beanery. Closing night had been a lugubrious affair at which locals of middling talent took turns playing sad songs and getting drunk on the Andres we'd provided.

I had to help out; Ira told me Lawonda had "split from town." Just as well, as I would have been ill at ease with her. She'd taken off for the South. "Memphis or New Orleans, where she has friends. Where they still have music."

There was yet more to pack into my little car: Ira's clothes and keepsakes, his stereo and record collection. We worked in silence, avoiding the creaky third-from-the-bottom step, sneaking past the window of the snoring landlord.

Craznik had had one of his fits that day over the rent. "Due and payable one month before month just ending!" Ira had apologized for not making it to the bank on time. I paid my rent to date, and that mollified Craznik enough to enjoy an uninterrupted sleep while we smuggled out Ira's seizables.

We pushed the car down the alley until we were well away from the house, then started the engine and headed off to Lawonda's "pad," as Ira called it. He was taking possession of it.

"She paid a month ahead. It's an illegal suite, so the landlords won't complain."

"Why did she leave so fast?"

"Maybe because you broke her heart."

"By not sleeping with her?"

"Bullshit. Give me the scoop – how was it?"

"All I did was walk her home."

"Man, I've seen your tongue lolling. She has her pick of lovers and she picked you. Feel honoured. How was it?"

I gave up, and eventually we pulled into the driveway near her side door and hauled his stuff into the suite I hadn't dared enter the week before. Kitchenette, bath, a small bedroom and a little sunroom, and a gorgeously decorated central parlour. Expressive African masks and brightly patterned tapestries on the walls. A sofa and armchairs covered with similar motifs. A seemingly authentic zebra rug. Sliding glass doors to a terrace and a bowered rose garden. No linoleum.

Lawonda had left it all untouched, hadn't even made the bed. Ira bounced on it. A waterbed – it sloshed. "This where you guys made out? Man, a guy could get seasick." He chuckled at my discomfiture. "Listen, there's a cot in the sunroom if you want to crash here."

"Crash?"

"Spend the night. Hell, you could move out of the internment camp and batch here. Don't worry, I'll stay in the closet."

I demurred, feeling awkward, self-conscious. I tried to imagine Mother's reaction to my rooming with a homosexual.

"Hey, a glimmer of hope: I met a former sideman to Ronnie Hawkins. The Hawk can't keep his band together; he's looking for a manager, my name came up." Then a sour face. "Rockabilly . . . it's come to that. Toronto."

A silence.

"I'm sorry to rib you, man. You seem depressed."

"My murder case. Do we have any of that wine left?"

Horseshoe Bay is a pretty little outpost on the road to Squamish. I was in a small café there that offered a take-it-or-leave-it choice of all-day breakfasts or fish and chips. But I was without appetite, nursing a coffee. It was shortly after seven, the sun sucking the mists off the strait, a colourful clutter of boats in the harbour, a ferry grunting away from the dock for the run to Nanaimo, gulls gliding and squawking behind.

This altogether pleasant day failed to penetrate my gloom. Forty days before the trial, and Minerva, the goddess of justice, had done nothing to intercede with the malicious Gorgons who had conspired to hang an innocent man. Gabriel told Lorenzo he was being framed for murder. That, I would tell the jury, is the only essential fact the officer didn't make up.

I had no recourse but to make an all-out assault on the little clique of corrupt cops. But what jury was going to disbelieve senior officers of the world's only police force that was a proud tourist attraction? Even to make a dent, I would need the skills of a Branca or a Walsh.

I distracted myself by leafing through the morning *Province:* news from Monday's election. With all polls counted, the Progressive Conservatives were still in power, but with a minority. Dief the Chief, my chum, was bravely carrying on.

Today's oddball item: a right foot had washed up on Gambier Island, just north of Horseshoe Bay, torn off at the ankle but otherwise whole, within a size-eight running shoe. A woman, apparently, with remnants of polish on a toenail. Police were mulling over the missing persons lists.

Gene Borachuk came walking by the window and glanced at me. Hiking boots, a rucksack. He walked in, past me, taking a table in a windowless alcove. I joined him there with my coffee.

"If anyone sees me with you, I'm dead; they'll call it a hunting accident. We have a deal?"

I'd been talking to him by pay phone to avoid a trace to Tragger, Inglis. The deal: I would cross-examine him at the trial with gloves on, not compromise him in any way, not ask about the beating of Gabriel, from whom I'd got reluctant consent for these negotiations.

"Yes, we have a deal."

"No loopholes, no backing down?"

"Of course." I was impatient; this was the second time I'd sought to rescue this honest cop from his dilemma.

"Walt Lorenzo. Sixteen years on the force, the last seven with various city drug squads. Not too brilliant, I guess – still hasn't got a third stripe. Lots of commendations, though. Undercover specialist, pretty good at pretending to be a bad guy; he can talk the talk. Nothing smelly on his record. A complaint in Winnipeg two years ago about roughing up an Indian kid. It didn't proceed. Cops get that sort of hassle all the time."

"What about the connection with Knepp?"

"He and Lorenzo are tight. Lorenzo did a tour with him in Grande Prairie, forty-seven through fifty. Kept in close touch since. Hooked up with Roscoe again last year – an undercover job in Squamish. I was part of it; we busted some swingmen running a heroin backend. Roscoe and Walt and their wives took a holiday in Reno after that." He rose. "I'm hiking up Cypress. We never saw each other."

"Hang on. Where's Monique Joseph?"

"Can't help you. Roscoe has stopped sharing."

"I want you to tell me this whole thing is a fix."

"What do you think?" He walked off.

THURSDAY, JUNE 21, 1962

I had talked with Irene Mulligan on the phone a few times but had put off the distressful task of spending extensive time with her, preparing her for the courtroom. I dreaded the awkwardness of discussing Frinkell's letter and its claim of adultery. But Irene was key to launching a successful defence, the only Crown witness I could count on to speak glowingly of Gabriel. And so we arranged to meet at her home late on the day of the summer solstice, after she got back from her bridge club.

As I approached the old Point Grey two-storey, a well-timbered structure faced with stone, I saw a curtain move behind a bay window – Dermot's studio. Irene opened the door before I could ring the bell.

A powerful scent of perfume. Her face made up, a bounteous head of hair, some grey in it now. A black dress that would seem funereal except for the sparkles above her ample breasts. I supposed that's what one wore to duplicate bridge. The hallway through which she led me was dim, unlit, and so was the small salon where she bade me sit while she brought tea. She apologized for her cough: she was enduring the tail end of a cold. She said she hadn't been sleeping well, understandably.

I sat near a window so I could see to make notes. As she returned with tea and oatmeal cookies, she apologized for not having anything more elegant on hand. "I don't get many callers." A little bout of coughing. I imagined she was lonely. Probably her friends, such as they were, had tired of soothing her way into widowhood.

After a few pleasantries, I gave her a rundown on what to expect in court, then spent an hour rehearsing her for the witness stand. She answered my questions directly, and even fed me some ammunition against Doug Wall and some useful observations as to how Dermot and Gabriel related. But I felt tension from her throughout, or at least discomfort. I saved the hardest part for last.

"Irene, when you were first questioned by the police – Constable Borachuk, I think – you said Dermot hadn't seemed depressed. I'm sure Mr. Smythe-Baldwin will remind you of that. It does complicate the defence of suicide, I'm afraid."

Gabriel, too honest for his own good, had agreed that his employer didn't appear depressed. However, it would seem Mulligan hid his feelings well. He certainly hid his personal life – Gabriel had been as shocked as I to learn of Professor Schumacher's threatened court action.

"I'm sorry, it's what I said. I didn't know then that Gabriel would be a suspect."

"You had no reason to think Dermot was facing an awkward situation?"

Even in the dimness of the room I could see her eyes widen. "What do you mean?"

I showed her Frinkell's letter. She studied it, read it twice, in a seeming state of shock. Then she broke down and wailed, "That's why he did it, isn't it?" Suicide, I supposed she meant. "I didn't know, I didn't know . . ." She went into a coughing fit, and was in such a disconsolate state that I offered to adjourn the interview.

She merely said, "Please," and swept from the room.

"Good Night, Irene" was in my head again as I drove off in search of the nearest bar. *Now me and my wife have parted.*

I'd been in the Crypt for an hour, doing little but brood. I could not possibly have handled matters with Irene more clumsily. I ought to have led up to the letter, prepared her for it with some sympathy and dignity. I was shocked by the surprise she'd shown. Hadn't she been aware of Dermot's many liaisons?

Irene let him have his affairs, Professor Winkle had asserted. *That was their deal.* Maybe he was just mouthing off; he was drunk. Or maybe that was the story Dermot told himself to assuage his guilt. I hadn't mentioned to Irene my session with Jimmy "Fingers" O'Houlihan, the photos showing Dermot *in flagrante delicto.* I saw absolutely no reason why I should, even if I could bear to do so.

I jumped when the phone rang. Gertrude told me Mrs. Mulligan was on the line.

I composed an apology before taking the call, but Irene seemed uninterested in hearing it. It was she who apologized. "I can't blame you for thinking I was aware of Mr. Frinkell's letter. It came as a shock. The police never said anything, or the prosecutors."

I explained to her where it was found: the in-basket.

"Truly? Why didn't he confide in me?" Distress in her voice, but she regained control. "Arthur, I've had . . . well, time to think, and I've decided I haven't been entirely honest with myself, or with the police, or you. The truth is, Dermot was becoming increasingly moody as Easter approached. Maybe not depressed, but distracted, thoughtful. It was so unlike him . . ."

We discussed how she might phrase those observations in court. Though her second thoughts smacked of invention, she was clearly onside with the suicide defence. I suspected she hadn't yet abandoned hope that Dermot was still alive, but that it had receded. More important, her faith in Gabriel's innocence had deepened.

It was early evening, and Ira was packing his clothes and toiletries as he prepared to leave Lawonda's former flat after only three weeks. He had landed the job of jumpstarting Ronnie Hawkins, and was heading off to Toronto on TCA's midnight express.

"Don't stack them flat – they'll warp." He gently eased an LP into its sleeve, then paused to kiss Harry Belafonte on his cardboard lips before placing him on the shelf, alphabetically, beside Chuck Berry. "I'll be coming back for them in a limousine." He settled the needle on another album. "Early Bo Diddley sessions. You will die an ugly death if this goes missing."

It was heart-warming to see him so ebullient. My cash loan had paid for his ticket, and as a reward I had inherited the Kitsilano suite – decor by Lawonda, music by Lavitch.

My escape from Craznik, just an hour earlier, had been less challenging than Ira's. Some books were left behind, but everything else fitted into two bulging suitcases and a suit bag that were roped down from a side window. My faithful Beetle loaded, Ira and I loudly sang a chorus of the "Internationale" as we drove off, but I don't think Craznik heard; he was doubtless plugged into his shortwave.

As I emptied my suitcases, Ira, the perpetual borrower, filled them while reciting household tips. "The bathtub hot runs cold, and vice versa. You'll never see the landlord and lady except for fussing about the garden. I never got around to switching the phone into my name, so you may get some heavy breathers."

I carefully hung up my nobility robe, then splashed some gin into two glasses filled with ice. The fridge worked, its freezer worked – this was paradise. Roses were in full bloom in the garden, the glass doors open to their perfume. A small Magnavox TV and a countertop radio for the CBC news, weather, and to feed my addiction to Max Ferguson's Marvin Mellowbell and J. Philip Buster.

Ira squatted on the zebra rug with his drink and a packet of Drum, rolling a cigarette. I looked out the sunroom windows at roses in bloom in the fading sunset, thinking of Ophelia, that last soft, hope-restoring kiss on the mouth. She would approve of these digs. *She will tease me, will coyly suggest moving in with me . . .*

Ira snapped me out of it. "I better make that flight, Arturo."

We took Fourth Avenue, past the former Beanery, now neon-lit and called Café à Go-Go. At eleven it was busy, a happy throng hanging around outside. Ira insisted he didn't care – his sights were set higher.

I sn't this super?" Gertrude said, enjoying the view: our bustling downtown, Stanley Park beyond. I was out of the Crypt. Either as an apology or a reward for being chummy with the Chief, the partners had promoted me to posher quarters.

"Too bad the Marine Building is in the way."

"Well, that's a lovely building too." The perpetually sunny Gertrude Isbister.

"You can leave early if you want." It was four-thirty.

"Oh, no, I've got oodles to do."

Pappas wandered in unannounced, as he was wont to do – the one drawback to the new digs was they were next to his. "I want you to free up a month in the fall. You're doing the Palmer prelim. They liked what they saw at the bail hearing. You continue to perform, maybe I'll give you the trial. They're quality clients, and they expect quality service."

"Deservedly so."

Gertrude gave me a helpless, almost pleading look as Mister Hands led her from the office to fetch the file. The Palmer brothers, accused of breaking the arms of four would-be competitors, controlled the East End heroin market. I'd persuaded Magistrate Scott to free them on a twenty-thousand-dollar property bond.

I suspected I was getting these meatier cases because Pappas, who was human after all, felt guilty about saddling me with a losing capital murder. He'd read over Ophelia's brief of evidence and put a consoling hand on my shoulder. "Well, pal, you can't win them all."

I didn't want to win them all. But I fiercely wanted to win this one.

Jim Brady had finally, at my urging, counselled his young disciple not to fashion political theatre from the trial, but I worried that the advice might not have sunk in deeply. Now Gabriel was constantly on about Riel, Dumont, the Red River Rebellion, the

Battle of Batoche. The Métis leader had replaced Fanon as his hero. I worried that he was developing a fixation, was seeing parallels. Maybe he wanted his hanging as well to be remembered as a monstrous disgrace on the white man's record. It smacked of a hubristic death wish.

Gabriel would morbidly remind me how Riel had renounced the insanity defence his lawyer advanced, how he'd bravely faced the hangman. *Je suis content de quitter ce monde,* Riel had said. *Every day on which I neglect to prepare myself to die is a day of mental alienation.*

I had brought Gabriel writing tools – he'd moved beyond reading to composition. He was just putting down random thoughts, he said. "Something may come out of it."

I could hardly bear the depression that came after these visits, the frustration. I'd had a reprieve from despair after my meeting with Borachuk, but it hadn't lasted. Who was I kidding? Knepp and Jettles had done a masterful job of setting Gabriel up. I didn't believe that even Irene's new "memory" of her husband's distraction would really help.

Other than quaffing a few after work, my evenings for the past week had been taken up mainly by reading in my exotic rooms. I hadn't seen much of Ophelia, whose practice was still burgeoning, but I expected her presently, after a family court case. It was just after five when she showed up. "I beat the shit out of *that* asshole." Another errant husband bites the dust.

She leaned back on my office settee, kicking off her shoes, and related the high points of her trial. I dutifully applauded but was distracted by her liberal show of thigh as she stretched her legs. I wondered at this body language. A seductive message or just a tease? Or did she no longer even register me as a possible lover?

I turned quickly to business, asked her the latest on Monique Joseph. Her parents were now with her in Seattle, where they were entertaining their distraught daughter at the World's Fair. Then it would be on to an extended summer holiday in Navaho country, Arizona, the Grand Canyon. Lukey claimed to be doing his best.

I asked if Ophelia had got anything on Mulligan's wartime stint as principal at Pie Eleven. We assumed the Church would deny any abusive behaviour there and help us deflate the Crown's case.

"I must have made a dozen calls, went all the way up to the top holy father in Prince Albert – Pie Eleven is run by his diocese. They were defensive to a man, perplexed that anyone would suggest all was not sweetness and light. Oh, no, their priests, nuns, and teachers had proudly served God by raising their sweet angels from ignorance and poverty. The Church gave them the love that had failed them at home."

Flagrant denial. Dermot Mulligan had written widely about that tendency on Rome's part.

"But they won't cooperate, won't give me teachers' names or student lists. They're afraid we'll harass them. I'll keep working on it." A pause. "How's your new joint working out?"

"Lush African decor, yet cozy, smells of roses, and it's three blocks from Kits Beach. You have to come and visit."

"Sounds perfect."

"A bit of a stroll to the office, but worth it." I was having trouble looking at her, my eyes fixed outside, on the phallus-shaped Marine Building.

She seemed about to rise. "Well . . . is there something else?"

"I was wondering . . ." – I cleared my throat – "if maybe you had some free time this weekend. I was thinking of toodling down to the Seattle Fair." *Toodling* – did I really say that? "I just thought you might like to join me."

She looked contemplatively at me.

"The tower, the monorail. They say some of the exhibits are amazing. Futuristic."

"The weekend . . . You mean, overnight?" She sat straighter, adjusted her dress.

"Well, to see everything. I haven't looked into the hotel situation."

"I think accommodation might be pretty tight."

I flushed. "Christ. Let me be blunt. We got an awkward start. I thought we should make amends. You'd be insensate, Ophelia, not to know I am extremely attracted to you." God, how stilted that sounded.

She rose, joined me at the window. "It's nice out now, but I heard the forecast. I think it may be raining all weekend."

It was at least a subtle rejection. "Good point. Some other time, maybe."

She took my arm, turned me toward her. My eyes felt fuzzy but I met her gaze.

"Arthur, this is a conversation we need to have, and I'm sorry it's come so late. I'm too old for you and I've been damaged in marriage – it left scars. And I can be lousy company, mean sometimes, caustic . . . whatever. There's a whole lot of shit you shouldn't have to deal with. I wouldn't be good for you."

Then silence, still looking at each other. I was expected to recite a few lines of sorrowful acceptance of our disengagement, but I couldn't get my tongue in gear.

She straightened my tie. "You need someone to look after you. I'm not it. Sometimes I feel like your mother. I have to fight the need to pick up after you."

I found a smile. "It's not the sort of thing my mother often did."

"Arthur, we're sharing a very important case. I know it's eating at you. I know you admire Gabriel; you like him and believe in him, as I do. I just think we'll work more efficiently if we put aside any feelings we may have for each other."

"You're absolutely right."

I found myself soon thereafter on a barstool at the Devonshire. I don't remember the later hours but have been reliably told I recited the entire first book of *The Aeneid. O passi graviora, dabit deus his quoque finem. Have you not known hard hours before this? You sailed by Scylla's rage, her booming crags. You saw the Cyclops' boulders. Now remember your courage, and have done with fear and sorrow.*

PART TWO

———

THE TRIAL

After a slow and grunting ascent, my ancient Fargo attains the sloping mesa at the crown of Breadloaf Hill and wheezes to a stop near the Garibaldi Island Community Hall. The engine won't die; it rattles and coughs for thirty seconds, like an old man gasping his last. Though I suspect my revered truck needs a valve job – the mechanical equivalent of heart surgery – I dread rendering it unto the slothful mercies of Bob Stonewell Motors. The last operation, a transmission transplant, took Stoney five months.

Alighting by the Fall Fair registration table, I check my cargo: fifteen varieties of fruit and vegetables, from the humble (carrots, cukes, corn) to the locally esoteric (okra and rutabaga), with nuts and berries lined up like gleaming marbles on their trays. Prime produce of the globally warmed summer of 2011, a historic year, a comeback year. Gone are the days when my multi-talented agronomist spouse, before she retired from competition, would walk off with enough blue ribbons to tailor an evening gown – veggies, breads, eggs, preserves, livestock – walking off with Most Points in Fair half a dozen times.

I haven't dared set my sights so high, focusing instead on my strengths: the yield from my cluttered deer-fenced garden, where I have toiled daily from spring through fruiting season. I have vowed that the Mabel Orfmeister Trophy for Most Points in Fruits and Vegetables will once again grace the fireplace mantle at Blunder Bay Farm – if "grace" is the right word. It's a lingam-like bronze corncob.

I pay my fee: seventy-five cents per entry. A volunteer passes me a fistful of exhibit slips as she peeks into the bed of my truck. "Looks like you're going for the Mabel Orfmeister this year. Again."

A cruel adverb, a cutting reference to my history of failure. Three years ago I came in a dismal fourth; with redoubled effort, I won silver in the past two. But each time it was Doc Dooley's name that was engraved on the base of the muscular metal phallus. Five straight years, five straight Orfmeisters. A further source of envy: Doc Dooley's roadside stand flourishes while mine, near a dead end on Potters Road, is rarely visited.

There he is, the spindly semi-retired M.D., lining up his entries at one of the prep tables, popping a rejected loganberry into his mouth. His carrot tops seem trimmed too short, his pickling onions of uneven size. *Amat victoria curam.* Victory favours those who take pains.

I take my turn at a table, double-checking the Standards of Perfection guide, realigning nuts and berries and baby potatoes. With calculating eye I watch as the Sproules lug a misshapen monster to a table bowed with entries for best pumpkin. Sixty pounds at least, heftier than my own pampered beauty but lacking its richness of colour, its plump symmetry. Best pumpkin, not biggest – that's the qualification for this special category.

Volunteers start removing my trays into the hall, where the judges wait. A long career as a barrister has inured me to the imperfections of judges. I'm still peeved that they gave me only a third-place ribbon last year for my faultless leeks.

I wince with every step as I return to my Fargo and park it out of the way. The pain is in my left heel. I have recently turned seventy-four, and the debilities of age are mounting: rheumatism in the lower joints, a creaky back. I'm not sure about my brain, but I have noted alarming signs. I struggle to remember people's names, people I know. I am forgetful about dates, tasks, obligations. ("But you always were," says Margaret.)

Perhaps this mushrooming state of senescence – am I to become a vegetable myself? – has led me mindlessly back to the law courts. It's a deeply personal case, one that I and no other can argue, one that still evokes dreams of being naked where the Squamish River flows, of feeling its pull, its remorseless, lethal pull. This will definitely be my last role in the *theatrum lex.* I mean it. This time I mean it.

How many times have I made that vow? Since fleeing to the island from Vancouver a dozen years ago, intending to retire to book-lined den and garden patch, Arthur Ramsgate Beauchamp,

Queen's Counsel, has been dragged back multiple times to do battle, usually at the wheedling insistence of Roy Bullingham, my flint-eyed ancient partner at Tragger, Inglis. This re-entry, though, is my own risky, ineluctable choice.

I wait for Dooley to finish up, then limp toward him for our traditional exchange of insincere well wishes. He reads my slow progress and confidently announces his diagnosis: "Plantar fasciitis."

"Yes, I've been to a foot specialist." Something to do with inflamed heel tendons. "He told me to get fitted with orthotics."

"For that advice he goes to some fancy city specialist." Dooley shakes his head. "Smoke a little pot. Works wonders for my arthritis."

"I am shocked."

"Get with the changing times, Arthur."

I take a moment to assimilate this new information: Doc Dooley, eighty-nine, a decade and a half my senior, lithe, sharp, everything still working, has taken to soothing his aches and pains with pot. I am leery about cannabis; I experimented with it years ago and found it pleasurable and therefore dangerous, like alcohol. But it's as available as gumdrops on this island, especially now – high season, harvest time.

Dooley glances at my offerings with shrugging indifference. "Nice collection. The kohlrabi ought to win."

"I always like to throw in a few oddballs for the A.O.V." Any other vegetable. "Not in it for the competition, of course."

"Of course not, Arthur."

"Answering the call of the community, that's what it's all about, isn't it? Sharing this fine island tradition with our neighbours in relaxed conviviality."

"As I see it, we're educators. Grow local, buy local, eat local."

A noble cause that discredits my platitudinous twaddle. "Absolutely. Encourage others to grow their own healthy food."

"I'm not one to count ribbons," Doc says. "Educate, spread the organic word."

I nod vigorously. "Amen." The Mabel Orfmeister is the last thing on my mind.

From "Where the Squamish River Flows," *A Thirst for Justice*, © W. Chance

BEAUCHAMP WENT INTO TRAINING in the final weeks before the trial, much as a young contender might in preparing for a match against the heavyweight champ. Having traded the many temptations of downtown for the relaxed ambience of Kitsilano (a neighbourhood soon to become an international hub of the psychedelic sixties), he spent his free time taking long beach walks and swimming and rowing, toning up his body while seeking to relax so he would not come into court tight and mentally stressed.

He even managed to abstain from drink during that time, and consequently was seeing less of his cocktail companion Hubbell Meyerson. With Ira Lavitch gone and Beauchamp's romance (if we dare call it that) with Ms. Moore having collapsed under the weight of sheer implausibility, he felt almost friendless. Frequent visits to Oakalla Prison Farm helped make up that deficit: long sessions with his client, lively debates about art, history – especially the heroic, tragic life of Louis Riel – current politics, and even occasionally about the case.

Worries constantly broke through during Beauchamp's training regime, a sense he wasn't competent for the task ahead. The elaborate effort to frame Swift had gone forward, he believed, because Knepp and his intimates regarded the young counsel as green, naïve, credulous. They wouldn't have dared such a game against Harry Rankin.

Legal historians have already noted the case's significance as a clash between the reigning champ, Smythe-Baldwin, and the young upstart who would one day wear his mantle.[*]

---

[*] Clausen and Shortt, *Take No Prisoners: The Life of Cyrus Smythe-Baldwin* (1989).

There has been much written as well about the controversial role played by the judge, Anthony Montague Hammersmith, the former city prosecutor, a man of acerbic temper and caustic tongue.

It is fortunate indeed that a transcript of the trial survived Beauchamp's efforts (often alcohol-fuelled) to turf out many of his early records. For some reason he kept his copy – indeed, the entire file – papers that ultimately made their way to the UBC Law Library's archives. (The cross of Doug Wall is now regarded as a classic and is recommended reading in criminal practice seminars.)

Very well. The deck has been stacked and the cards have been played, so let us move smartly toward the scene of combat, up the main steps between the impassive stone lions that guard the doors of 800 West Georgia Street . . .

I'd hesitate to say how many thousands of times in my fifty-plus years of practice I've walked up those hundred-year-old steps. Once, before Vancouver took off skyward, you could see outlined against the horizon the crouching lions of the North Shore that inspired their stone-faced brethren. The courthouse had the stolid British Empire look that was expected of Francis Rattenbury's designs, but it served its purposes perfectly well, its high-ceilinged carpeted corridors and oak-panelled rooms providing a proper gravitas, a sense that justice is serious business. (Sadly, a glass and concrete greenhouse has since replaced it – Arthur Erickson's flighty view of a house of justice – and the Vancouver Art Gallery now occupies the old building, awkwardly, unsuited to its ponderous ambience. But don't let me go on . . .)

Ophelia was already in the rotunda when I entered, beckoning me as she joined a few others studying the posted dockets. Until now the name of the judge seconded to this trial had been a secret of the registrar and the Chief Justice. I was praying for a liberal.

"Justice Hammersmith," Ophelia said, as I drew up behind her. "Isn't he the one they call The Hammer?"

I groaned. The former city prosecutor was an acid-tongued conservative and, worse, gifted with an intelligence rare on the bench, at least among the many failed politicians awarded judgeships as consolation prizes. At least he wasn't one of the dullards who barely listened to the evidence and convicted blindly. His charges to the jury were constructed to survive the Appeal Court, and most did.

I went directly to the gentlemen's changing room and gowned up, shrugging into a robe that gave evidence of previous sweaty battles, old stains, and repairs – it was a hand-me-down from a retiring barrister. This was Long Vacation, as the midsummer months were called, and only a few lawyers were at their lockers, mostly doing continuations. I exited through the barristers' lounge, earned good-luck wishes from a few colleagues working out a plea deal.

I smilingly greeted the many standing in the hall outside the assize court. They were on the jury panel, dutiful citizens summoned from the voters' list, waiting to be escorted into the courtroom. I didn't see many non-Caucasian faces there.

The court was a high-ceilinged chamber with stained glass doors and windows and cascading daises in darkly varnished oak. The judge overlooked the court clerk and official reporter and, a few steps below, Crown and defence lawyers at their adjoining tables. A raised prisoner's dock was the room's centrepiece. For the spectators, rows of seats at the back and a gallery above. To the right was the witness box; behind it, the press table. To the left was the jury box, with its twelve uncomfortable chairs.

As I headed up the centre aisle I was aware of a hushed tension, reporters nudging each other. The clerk, a straight-backed old boy, seemed about to take flight; his elbows were out like vestigial wings, but he remained glued to his chair. Smitty and Lukey were watching him struggle, glancing occasionally at Ophelia.

I saw what the problem was. Ophelia was wearing trousers. Black, sedate, formal, but trousers nonetheless – unheard of in those days. I felt a little aggrieved that she'd chosen this ticklish murder case to push the boundaries.

Alerted to the emergence of his Lordship from his chambers, the clerk was propelled upwards as if on a pogo stick. "Order in court!" Anthony Montague Hammersmith in his crimson-enhanced robe stepped stiff-legged from the chambers door and mounted the steps. A halo of russet hair around a bald dome, manicured moustache, half-moon reading glasses that made him look four-eyed.

"I have a sense, Mr. Clerk, that someone is missing." Sardonic off the bat.

The clerk looked confused and glanced again at Ophelia, as if she might in some sense be the one missing. Then he realized that the centrepiece of this arraignment was absent.

"Bring up the prisoner," he bawled, and a pair of uniformed court officers led Gabriel from the well below the prisoner's dock.

More flustered than ever, the clerk had trouble with his lines. "Oyez, oyez, oyez. All persons having business at this Court of Oyez and Terminator and General Gaol Delivery holden here this day in, ah, Vancouver, draw near and give your names when called. God save the Queen!"

He meant *Oyez and Terminer,* to hear and determine. More orotund in Latin: *audiendo et terminando.* Such lovely though arcane jargon – calling for prisoners to be brought before the assizes – is meaningless even to most lawyers, a throwback to England's Dark Ages.

"You may release him," said Hammersmith, and Gabriel's cuffs were removed. He sat, looking about, rubbing his wrists, taking in this grand and sombre court. He caught my eye, nodded, then looked behind him, spotting his mother and several friends from the Cheakamus Reserve. A nod and smile for them.

He was in better shape than his lawyer: clear-eyed, unafraid, finding strength from his Métis hero. On my last visit, two days ago, I had explained that the Prince Albert diocese had taken a cowardly stance, and he said, "Why are you surprised?" His cynicism hinted he was almost looking forward to a pronouncement of guilt, a chance at martyrdom, noble defeat. He often quoted Riel's simple, stirring words at Batoche: *In a little while it will be over. We may fail. But the rights for which we contend will not die.*

"Are we ready, gentlemen?" Ignoring the gentle lady beside me, at whom the clerk was still looking with steely disapproval.

As Smitty and I put our appearances on record, Hammersmith nodded at me and bowed slightly, which I took as a salute to my successful appeal against the most recent of his wrongful convictions. He did not remark on Ophelia's attire but looked at her with discomfort: an unknown quantity, a courtroom *rara avis,* in pants but unmistakeably female.

I applied to have my client join me at counsel table. "I would appreciate having him at hand to seek his counsel during jury selection."

Hammersmith studied Gabriel coolly. Here was the insolent young Native who'd blown up in the Chief Magistrate's court. A troublemaker. "I would imagine, Mr. Beauchamp, that he needs your counsel more than you his. Mr. Smythe-Baldwin?"

"I make no objection."

His reaction displeased Hammersmith. "It is not my practice to let prisoners stray from their historic and proper station, and I cannot see how I can countenance it in a capital case."

Smitty raised his eyebrows at this lack of appropriate servility. Hammersmith clearly distrusted the old Q.C. – he was defence-oriented, not a real Crown. They'd fought many bruising battles when the judge was senior prosecutor, so there were likely un-healed wounds.

Leroy Lukey caught my eye and winked. I wouldn't have put it past him to have gone judge-shopping. However else could we have ended up with The Hammer?

~~~

Jury selection, as was typical in those days, was a speedy process; members of the panel remained mute, not subject to questioning. I had names, addresses, occupations, and the right to challenge up to twenty without cause. I weeded out whom I could: the lugubri-ous dog trainer (probably worked with the police a lot), the red-faced hausfrau (imagined as a scold), the red-necked steelworker (who scowled at my client), the banker, the lumber executive, the prim vice-principal, the retired army officer.

The ones who got seated looked only marginally better: six of each sex, a range of ages, occupations varying from waitress to electrician to antique dealer to pumphouse operator. Two jurors got on after I ran out of challenges, a grumpy-looking customs agent and a hockey coach and former minor league workhorse, Ozzie Cooper. He had enough of a reputation among his peers to get himself elected foreman. This was the Vancouver jury I had expected and feared – not a person of colour aboard.

Hammersmith ordered them sequestered, which meant that a block of hotel rooms would be provided. No radio, no newspapers. None looked too happy as they returned to court after setting their immediate affairs in order.

"Call your first witness, Mr. Smythe-Baldwin."

That was an identification officer, custodian of the exhibits. After taking the oath, he kissed the Bible. This unsanitary practice was a custom that pervaded the lower courts in the sixties. It was adopted by police officers in high court in an effort to give their testimony credence, though it's now a curious relic.

The ID officer began the dreary process of describing and labelling the Crown's sixty-seven exhibits. Diagrams, maps, garments, fingerprints, serum samples, cartridges, documents. Frinkell's letter. Dermot's memoir. Several innocuous photographs taken from Mulligan's desk, mostly of him: feeding his horse; astride his horse; riding his horse, playfully doffing a hat to reveal his bald top; Irene in their city home, hair piled up, dressed as if for a party. None showing them together.

Smitty called Irene next. Like all subpoenaed witnesses, including policemen, she had been excluded from the room. It took so long to fetch her that I feared she'd run off, but finally she came, walking unsteadily up the aisle in high heels. Pleated skirt, elaborately buttoned sleeves, tight collar, something puffy and flowerlike adorning her blouse. Over-powdered, with glossy lipstick exaggerating a thin mouth. Even through the half-veil attached to her rather shapeless hat I could see the dark circles under her eyes.

"Ghastly," Ophelia whispered.

"Madam, I expect this is distressing to you," Smitty said, "so we shall try to keep it as brief as possible."

He led Irene quickly through undisputed terrain: age, residence, year of marriage, husband's achievements and station in the academic community, date of purchase of the Squamish Valley farm, and, with the aid of survey maps and photos, the layout of that property. She described their general run of activities there. She conceded she found the hobby farm lonely and hadn't been looking forward to spending her husband's sabbatical there.

Irene spoke in a breathless voice, no weight to her syllables, and Hammersmith twice asked her to speak up. His war service, with the Royal Canadian Horse Artillery, had dulled his hearing.

Smitty's first task was to discredit the suicide hypothesis, and he drew from her that Mulligan had been in good health, diligently working on his memoirs, planning a time out to visit the Seattle fair. Then she added, "But in his last days he seemed to be brooding over something. Worried."

Smitty hid well his displeasure at that excursus, and proceeded cautiously in asking about Gabriel and his role as caretaker/house-sitter. He'd had the run of the house before Irene showed up the week before Easter, but thereafter declined invitations to come in to warm himself after chores. He even brought his own lunch, so she had negligible contact with him. His mornings were often spent with Dermot, sharing yard and barn chores, talking, debating. In the afternoons, from three to six, Dermot would usually closet himself in his study and Gabriel would disappear.

"Dermot was very fond of him," she added.

Smitty had no interest in asking whether Gabriel shared that fondness, and moved on quickly: "Dermot was fond of him, but what were your feelings?" A tricky question, but Smitty had obviously interviewed her carefully and may have been expecting something noncommittal.

"I regret I never got to know Gabriel better, but he was unfailingly polite and helpful. A very nice young man. Very intelligent and well-spoken."

Hammersmith: "I'm sorry, very what? Intelligent and soft-spoken?"

"Well-spoken," Smitty said.

"Unfailingly polite and helpful," I added.

"Please be seen and not heard, Mr. Beauchamp. Your time will come."

(A verbatim transcript that Wentworth Chance found in the law school archives and copied to me serves as an *aide-mémoire,* so to bring back specifics like these I don't have to rely on old memory cells, with all their smudges, erasures, and flaws.)

Smitty moved Irene quickly to the Saturday of Easter weekend. Mulligan had spent the morning at his desk and after lunch gathered up his fishing gear, promising to be back by supper.

"And he went off to his fishing hole?"

"That was his intention."

"Do you know where it is?"

"I don't think anyone did."

"Except Gabriel Swift."

"Well, yes."

"And your husband never returned."

"He didn't."

"Let us leave it there. Other witnesses will fill out the rest more than handsomely." And Smitty turned her over to me.

I began by expressing appropriate words about her husband's disappearance, reminded her to try to keep her voice up, then made what hay I could from Gabriel's role as Mulligan's diligent hired man, omnivorous student, and faithful outdoors companion.

"He never showed hostility to your husband?"

"I never heard a cross word."

Hammersmith cupped an ear. "He never did a crossword?"

I could see that the jury was having trouble hearing her too, and I repeated her answer. "And did the accused show any lessening of affection in the days just prior to your husband's disappearance?"

"No."

"In fact, on the previous day, Good Friday, they hiked together to the top of the Stawamus Chief?"

"Yes."

Hammersmith asked, "Who or what is the Stawamus Chief, madam?" Irene looked at me for help.

Ophelia retrieved an article from a travel magazine with graphic, dizzying photos of the mountain, and passed it around while I educated his Lordship. "A fifteen-hundred-foot sheer rock face just south of Squamish. It is accessed by back trails, and the cliff face descends almost perpendicularly to its base. Certain death for anyone who might slip over the edge."

Hammersmith looked up from the photos, stared at the Crown table, saw no one stirring. "I hear no objection to counsel's travel-ogue. The article will be the next exhibit."

I returned to Irene. "And they seemed to be getting along well that day? No problems between them?"

"Not at all. I saw them go off together; they were chatting amiably." Her voice was stronger now, though still husky. Much throat-clearing.

"There'd been no quarrels on this trek?"

From the bench: "How could she know? Unless she had some-how transported herself there."

"Let me rephrase. Your husband didn't seem distressed on his return?"

"Just exhausted."

"Now in answer to my learned friend, you said that in the days before Easter Dr. Mulligan seemed to be worried. He was brood-ing. Did you find that strange?"

"It wasn't normal for him."

"Did you know what was distressing him?"

"Not at the time, no."

I let it go at that. "Two decades ago, Professor Mulligan served two years as principal of an Indian residential school in Saskatchewan. You're aware of that?"

"Yes."

"Did he ever talk about it?"

"Very little."

I picked up restlessness from the bench and hurried on. "As far as you were aware, he served there honourably?"

"Where is this going, Mr. Beauchamp?"

"To the heart of the Crown's case, milord."

"The question – if it is a question and not mere rhetoric – calls for both speculation and hearsay. It probably fails the relevance test too, but I shall suspend judgment while I try to figure out where you're going."

I looked him squarely in the eye. "As always, milord, I appreciate your helpful instructions." Hammersmith awarded me a little smile – he relished combat.

Back to Irene. "Let me ask you this, then. Dr. Mulligan made many public pronouncements, did he not, about his opposition to the residential school system?"

"Yes, he believed they were obliterating Native culture and should be shut down."

Hammersmith was glaring at Smythe-Baldwin, challenging him to object. But Smitty was focused on me, maybe intrigued a little. Maybe he hadn't expected much from me.

"Your husband hired Gabriel some two and a half years ago?"

"October of 1959."

"Let's talk about the circumstances of that. The accused was on probation at the time?"

"Yes."

"He'd received a six-month suspended sentence for assaulting a police officer in Squamish?"

"Yes."

The judge stopped making notes, taken aback by this rare instance of a defence counsel putting his client's criminal record in issue. Lukey too looked confused – I was doing the Crown's work.

Reporters were scribbling; they'd caught a scent of something, maybe today's lead item. I wanted this story shouted over the radio, printed in boldface: how a vengeful cop falsely incriminated a lippy Indian.

"Gabriel had felled the officer with a single blow?"

"Yes, it was in the papers."

"And the man he put on the ground so unceremoniously was Sergeant Roscoe Knepp, the chief investigating officer in this case?"

"I believe so, yes."

"And that incident occurred after the accused intervened to protect his father from harassment and false arrest—"

That brought Smitty to his feet, but not fast enough for Hammersmith: "The objection you are about to make is sustained."

I bulled ahead, talking loudly over him. "Whereupon Sergeant Knepp taunted my client by calling him a lippy Indian shit –"

"This court is adjourned!" Hammersmith rose, paused, gathered himself. "You will have ten minutes, Mr. Beauchamp, to compose your plea for clemency. I shall expect an appropriately cowering apology."

The jury filed out, looking bewildered. I headed directly to the men's for an urgent piss – I'd been imbibing gallons of coffee since going off the sauce. Maybe I was over-caffeinated. I'd shocked myself by letting loose like that, though was pleased I'd found the courage. The press had enjoyed it. So had Gabriel, who awarded me a half-hidden thumbs-up.

Ophelia and I had spent many hours briefing him on his testimony, preparing him for cross, how to relate to the jury. His evidence would expand on Irene's: his innocent and caring relationship with Mulligan, his total lack of motive. There would be forceful refutation of Lorenzo's claim of a gushing confession. But much would depend in the end on whether the alibi about being with Monique would hold up. We still hadn't achieved access to her, though she was under subpoena. Lukey had guaranteed us a full hour with her before putting her on the stand.

I was still emptying when Smitty came in and eased his generous patrician belly into position at the adjoining urinal. "Nice bit of work, old chap."

"I don't know what got into me."

"Bollocks. You have both jury and press titillated." There'd been a race for the bank of pay phones.

Smitty finished, washed, brought out a cigar, sniffed it, snipped it, rolled it between his fingers, tasted it, put his Ronson to it – a long, silent cameo while I zipped my fly.

"You were distraught, of course." He blew a plume of smoke. "Pressure of a capital case. The first one can be a highly emotional experience. The formidable burden of defending when the penalty is death. Retain your dignity – don't grovel."

I thanked him, and we hurried off.

Leroy Lukey impeded my progress to counsel table. "You're putting Roscoe on trial? That's your best shot?"

"Along with whoever invented the phony confession."

I slipped past him and joined Ophelia, who looked at me as if at a stranger. "What got into you? Who was that masked man?"

"The Lone Ranger. *How come.*" I was still learning, but I'd watched the courtroom masters: Branca, Bert Oliver, Smythe-Baldwin himself. They understood the theatrics of law. "This is not a big deal. Irene never got a chance to answer the question."

"It wasn't a question, it was a speech. Then you drowned out The Hammer when he was calling you to order."

"I did?"

~~~

Court was called and I treated Hammersmith to a penitent face as we waited for the rumble to cease, reporters hurrying in, bottoms meeting benches. The jury remained out.

"In a couple of recent trials, Mr. Beauchamp, I have observed a tendency to deliberately ignore both the rules and your duty of courtesy to the court. I say 'deliberately' because you are not at the intellectual level of some of the cretins currently being pumped out by the law schools. I am encouraged to believe you knew what you were doing. Please persuade me that I am wrong."

"I am informed, milord, that I talked over you as you were admonishing me. I am distraught about that. I had allowed my voice to rise and my attention was elsewhere."

"On yourself, no doubt."

His little sally hinted that his anger had dissipated. I spoke of the formidable burden of defending when the penalty was death, and built on that in ways I hoped Smitty would approve of. I had been too consumed by the case, I'd got carried away. It had been wrong to adduce evidence by hearsay. No harm was intended, or done. Sergeant Knepp would have his chance to tell his side.

"Let me make clear, counsel, that without a firm evidentiary basis this court will not permit the maligning of peace officers. It smacks of gutter tactics, and there will be a price to pay if it happens again."

"We will build that firm evidentiary basis, brick by brick." Said with a confidence I didn't feel.

Nothing was said to the jury when they returned. They seemed surprised to see me still in action. Irene was back on the stand, maybe less apprehensive but still under a strain. I had her relate her practice of taking walks on Squamish Valley Road in the afternoon, and asked if she'd followed that routine on Saturday, April 21.

"I did."

"What time did you leave for that walk?"

"About three-thirty or four."

"In the course of it, did you happen on anyone or see anyone?"

"A delivery truck. And one of the neighbours from the upper valley drove by and waved."

"Do you know Doug Wall?"

"Not really. You showed me a photograph of him."

"You're right, I did. A mug shot." A sharp look from the judge, and I hurried on. "Did you see him that day, or a small red car, a Nash Metro?"

"Not during my walk, but in the morning, yes. Around eleven a car like that drove by."

"What were you doing at the time?"

"I went out to get the weekend *Province* from the mailbox."

A little bonus earned during our interview, and it had Lukey tugging at Smitty's sleeve. This seemed a good point at which to quit, but I checked first with Ophelia.

"Are you going to show her Frinkell's letter?" she whispered.

It hadn't been mentioned here so far, just filed as Exhibit Thirty-Seven, *Letter dated April 13, 1962*. "I'm going to save it for when we need it most."

Irene again wobbled on her way out; I imagined she was unused to wearing high heels. An older couple joined her at the door, maybe bridge club friends.

Taking the stand next was Thelma McLean, hair in a beehive, wearing a flowery print dress with ruffles, something one might wear to a square dance. I'd expected her to seize this chance to make the news again, and she didn't disappoint, answering Smitty's questions at great length – homey, colloquial, discursive, with occasional glances at the press.

"Me and Buck moved to the Squamish Valley in fifty-two, after our kids grew up and left the nest. We're just plain folks, living a simple, honest life logging and farming, raising a few chickens."

Thus positioned as guileless and upright, she told of meeting Dermot Mulligan three years earlier, without his wife, as he was closing the deal on the nearby ten acres. "We were his only neighbour for half a mile, so Buck and me did our best to help. Passed on some tips about flood season, about how the reservation's real close and you get thieves, also the occasional cougar, that sort of thing. Buck connected him to a reliable builder for an addition to that old A-frame."

Smitty cut in. "I see, and did you form a friendship with Dr. Mulligan?"

"I wouldn't say we ever got real close. He was . . . I'd like to think shy, but if I'm honest, it was more like standoffish. He wasn't much for small talk, anyway. I'd deliver a dozen eggs and it would be thanks, keep the change, goodbye. We never met Irene till the next year. She only visited off and on, like on a nice weekend, but we got along pretty well. Obvious she was lonely; the Squamish Valley wasn't her thing."

As to Gabriel Swift, he "just suddenly showed up one day, unannounced – this was back in fifty-nine, soon after they bought – and started taking down some brush. I went over and asked him what he thought he was doing and he said he was clearing the site for the addition, and I asked . . ."

"To cut it short, madam, he'd been hired by Dr. Mulligan as a live-in caretaker. Did you seek to befriend him?"

"Well, to be honest, Buck and me tried. We took every opportunity. We'd wander across the road and try to get him talking, just chitchat about the weather or Buck's bad back, whatever . . . Well, he'd kind of look right past you. Like he couldn't be less interested."

Snotty, she wanted to say. The cigar-store Indian, aloof, superior. She carried on relentlessly, describing her many sightings of Gabriel at his labours, how he had the run of the house, his unusual way of relaxing – with books.

Clearly she'd been ordered not to rebroadcast her opinion that Mulligan and Gabriel were lovers, limiting herself to this confusing peregrination: "We hardly ever saw Dermot with his wife. He spent more time with Gabriel than he did with her; they were like glue, if you want my honest opinion. We wondered maybe if he missed not having a son and he was almost fifty and making up the time. Whatever, I wasn't sure what was going on."

Smitty gave up on her and sat. I feared a lengthy cross-examination might do more harm than good. I didn't want her rambling on about missing chickens and underwear or declaring that Gabriel was a book-reading subversive.

"Mrs. McLean, we've heard that on Good Friday, the day before Dr. Mulligan disappeared, he and the accused went hiking up the Stawamus Chief."

"I heard that too." Unprompted, she added that she'd been up there once with her husband and darn well wasn't going to try that again. There were no guardrails.

"Yes, and if an evildoer wanted to push some poor soul over the edge, no one would be the wiser, right?" Quoting her very words to me. "One would never know if it was an accident."

"Well, unless there was other people up there watching, people from the city, like you get on long weekends."

Having already asked one question too many, I dug myself in deeper, suggesting that someone with murder in mind would wait until there was no one about. Her response: she didn't know; she wasn't there. Surely, I urged, she would agree the trail to the Chief attracted little traffic except in summer. No, she wouldn't agree.

I retreated to safety. "You know Doug Wall?"

"We're on chatting terms. He stops by. He has a cabin up north there, by the old Indian graveyard. Does little fix-it jobs."

"Yes, but his main occupation is selling bootleg whisky and rum, mostly on the reserves, isn't that so?"

"I heard he does a little trade in that, but it's more like he offers a convenience. A lot of the Natives don't have vehicles. I don't think no one complains."

"Especially the RCMP, right?"

"Mr. Beauchamp . . ."

"Sorry, milord, we'll get into that later. Now, on one of his visits to you and Buck, the three of you sat around and fantasized about how the deceased might have been done in."

"I don't know about fantasized."

"Speculated. There was talk of a homosexual love affair, a lovers' quarrel."

"Everybody in the valley was talking about it. It's not against the law to sit around over a beer and speculate about a murder in your backyard."

Leroy was grinning like a jackal – he'd prepared her well.

The witness had devoured the morning; I wanted to get her off the stand before the noon break. In a last desperate bid to end on a high note, I reminded her that Knepp had called Gabriel a communist troublemaker.

She hesitated. "Not exactly."

"Then what, exactly?"

"Actually, he said communist shit-disturber, if you'll pardon my French."

"He also sought to know if Gabriel had demonstrated any, quote, 'sexual problems or unusual perversions.'"

She affected confusion, and I showed her those phrases from Knepp's interview notes. She attempted to hedge – "Well, I'm not an expert in that sort of thing" – then finally conceded. "To be perfectly honest, nobody ever saw or heard anything like . . . like sexually unusual."

"But Sergeant Knepp seemed very interested in that kind of nonsense, didn't he? He was keen on coming up with some kind of motive, any motive – spurious, mendacious, ridiculous, it didn't matter –"

I was at full volume, but the last words were buried beneath the louder uproar of prosecutorial protest, Lukey joining his master's voice, barking and baying.

"No more questions," I said, ducking down into my seat.

"We'll adjourn until two o'clock." Hammersmith studied me with a little whorl of a smile. He was savouring the prospect of putting leather to the repeat offender's bared bottom. "Enjoy your lunch, Mr. Beauchamp."

~~~

We ate in the Georgia lounge. Across the way was Leroy Lukey, deserted by his senior, a connoisseur of finer dining than the plain fare offered there. But joining him, just back from the men's, was Roscoe Knepp, who must have been briefed on my courtroom exploits. He sent me a look of great sadness and confusion, as if he'd been betrayed by his dearest friend. Lukey did not stoop to such artifice; I got the exhilarated smile one might see from the cheering Roman *vulgus* as they anticipated the crucifixion of a rebellious slave.

The Hammer had offered me a second chance. I had spurned it and must be taught a lesson. A contempt citation, a fine, a spell in the clink? Over weak coffee, a ham on white, and a pickled egg, I urged Ophelia to believe I hadn't planned to go off the rails again

"Arthur Beauchamp, passionate young barrister, as played by Laurence Olivier."

I think I had gotten over the worst of my physical longing for Ophelia by then, though a glimpse of bared knee would still cause a flaring of desire. But since she'd announced the new ground rules, one source of tension had gone: the tension of not knowing where we stood. Now we stood as friends, *simpliciter.*

"You should take a fling at the legitimate stage."

"It's Roscoe." We both looked his way. "The mere thought of him causes me to spin out. All I see is red."

"So fuck it – it was effective. You were good."

"Not with Thelma. I was bloody awful."

"She came across as a hypocrite and a racist. She doesn't matter, Arthur. Save your energy for the real players: the cops."

She was right. I would have to be in better control when their turns came. Knepp was glib, would enjoy the protection of this law-and-order judge. Ultimately his hearty, back-slapping style could impress a jury.

"You going to kiss the judge's toes this time?"

"If he jails me you'll have to take over."

"Absolutely fucking not."

"Then you'd better get me out fast on appeal bail." I watched thirstily as a waiter swung past our table with a tray laden with cold, sweating bottles of ale.

Ophelia grabbed my arm before I could signal him. "I don't think so, Arthur."

I was astonished. "I beg your pardon?"

"We have a trial to worry about."

"Do you think I have a problem? I haven't had a drink for a week."

"Great. Keep it up. I dare you." She insisted on leaving it at that. I felt insulted.

~~~

The wall clock had just ticked off the tenth minute past two o'clock. The court clerk was biting his fingernails. The room was hot, smelled of the sweat of impatient spectators and fussing re-porters. Adding his own peculiar odour was the former fullback, staring at the door that never seemed to want to open upon Cyrus Smythe-Baldwin, Q.C.

The jurors were still in their room but Lukey had already sat bull-like Buck McLean in the witness box, as if by that act he would magically cause his senior to appear. Buck looked like a patient in a dentist's waiting room, tense and rigid after hearing from Thelma, over their free government lunch, how that legal aid attorney had badgered and shouted at her.

Smitty's unforeseen lateness gave me more time to come up with an abject apology, but the words weren't coming. I truly hadn't the faintest idea what to say . . .

I deeply regret, milord, that I lost control again. I am possessed by this case; my nights are sleepless, filled with gallows nightmares. I am distracted by the closeness of my junior, who dumped me after a one-night stand. The RCMP'*s Red Squad is following me wherever I go. My mother hates me. 'Spurious, mendacious, ridiculous'? That wasn't me talking, milord, it was Satan – he visits me during psychotic episodes that frequently come just before lunch. Gutter tactics? No one admires our gallant upholders of the law more than Arthur Beauchamp.*

In fact, I have always had a high regard for the police. Theirs is the most over-romanticized job on the planet, tedious with routine and detail, endless paperwork, pounding the pavement, passing out tickets, listening to citizens' woes. Dangerous to boot? Maybe, but every cop I know enjoys a shot of risk: their antidote to boredom. Bad apples were probably no more common than in my own line of work. But a statistical fluke had me facing off against three such apples. *This court will not permit the maligning of peace officers.* What defence did that leave me with?

Ophelia lifted her nose from a magazine article by her latest feminist hero, a Mrs. Friedan. "Why are you mumbling?"

"I'm doing my prayers."

"Do you actually believe in God?"

"I'm going to find out soon."

Soon might have been overstating it. The clerk had been on the line with Hammersmith, and now was consulting Lukey over a telephone book opened to the Yellow Pages under "Restaurants."

Efforts to reach Smitty at the Timber Club and other of his known venues bore no fruit. At twenty after two the chambers door squeaked open and Hammersmith peered out, surveyed this unsatisfactory scene, then strode stiffly to his chair and sat.

The clerk called, "Order in court!" but too late – almost everyone had already got up, except for Lukey, who was focusing all his energy toward the back, trying to beam Smitty through that door. He looked over his shoulder to see Hammersmith glowering at him.

"If I might interrupt your meditations for a moment, Mr. Lukey . . ."

He shot to his feet. "Yes, sir."

"Given that Mr. Smythe-Baldwin declines to honour us with his presence, I assume you are ready to proceed with the next witness. Because I see he's already on the stand, raring to go."

"Ah, no, I didn't want to leave that impression. I can't . . . I'm sorry, milord, I haven't prepared the civilian witnesses. I'm doing the police. Mr. Smythe-Baldwin may have thought we were resuming at two-thirty. Or maybe he became ill."

"When I prosecuted, young man, counsel were prepared for all exigencies."

"Well, yes, but I don't have instructions, I wasn't expecting –"

"Never mind, just stop babbling. Has anyone checked the hospitals? That is the only excuse I will accept – he had better be on a stretcher. I don't care if it's Cyrus Smythe-Baldwin or the prime minister or the Duke of Edinburgh, no one delays this court for nearly half an hour unless he can satisfy me he's just survived a near-death experience. I will not be treated like some minor functionary –"

He ended it there abruptly. Who knows what heights he might have reached had not a Falstaffian form suddenly entered. Smitty bowed and advanced at a calm, leisurely pace, affecting an insouciance that added to Hammersmith's irritation. "I'm so pleased that Your Royal Lateness has deigned to visit," he snapped.

"Horrible table mix-up at Chez Antoine, milord, quite embarrassing. I was with Chief Justice Harry McRory and his granddaughter, celebrating her eighteenth. Add to that an inordinate wait for the bill and an awkward struggle over it with Harry, then my taxi getting bogged down in Chinatown. I'm immeasurably sorry for discommoding the court, but the time will be made up as I go full speed through the day's remaining witnesses."

Hammersmith had no choice but to hastily rethink his position. The emphatic dropping of the name of the chief of the Appeal Court had altered the rules of combat, effectively stripping The Hammer even of the weapon of his tongue. Meanwhile, the jury had been hurriedly summoned.

"I call Mr. Buck McLean."

Hammersmith made a late try at saving face. "Just a second. Mr. Smythe-Baldwin, that was such an utterly flimsy excuse that I almost want to applaud it. To save you from a failing grade, I have given you marks for honesty. Full speed, then."

Miraculously, I had performed the scientifically impossible feat of making myself invisible. The Hammer never even glanced at me. And what could he do to me now? My minor transgressions of the morning were dwarfed by His Lateness's brazen dawdling, and he'd got off with a jocular scolding.

I caught Smitty's eye as Buck was being sworn in. His expression was almost blank but I read, *You owe me one, son.*

Smitty led Buck through his skimpy résumé as tree-falling husband of Thelma, and his equally meagre dealings with the professor next door. "I wouldn't exactly say we was friends, eh. I don't think we was anything." One couldn't escape the sense he'd felt put down by Mulligan's courtly patronizing. "*Hobby* farmers," he called the couple, the adjective emphasized like a dirty word.

"How long have you known the accused?"

Buck just sat there as if waiting for the rest of the question. "The accused what?"

"The accused person." Indicating Gabriel, who gave Buck a nod of greeting.

"Oh, yeah, Gabriel. Well, I seen him around a lot as a kid. His dad used to work for my outfit. Gabriel did some cash work for us sometimes, cleaning up the sites."

"What were your reactions on hearing he'd been hired by Dr. Mulligan?"

"I didn't figure him for a bad Indian. He took a swing once at Roscoe Knepp, and his dad is a lush, but Gabriel's a hard worker. Smart too. Thelma and me never had no problems with him. Never expected to. We didn't talk much, but he was always polite, never asked no favours."

Gabriel gave me a speculative look as Buck completed this clean bill of health. I was sorry I hadn't interviewed him, assuming he would parrot his spouse. (I continued to be baffled by Buck's unexpectedly benign assessment until, days later, I learned he'd told some drinking mates that if the fruity professor had come on to him that way, all buck naked with a hard-on, he'd have chucked him in the river too.)

Smitty went quickly to Easter weekend and brought out that Buck was among the posse that pursued Gabriel to the fishing spot. "We lost sight of him real soon; we couldn't keep up."

"He was that fast?"

"Well, we was slowed because Brad Jettles had to stop and catch his breath. He wasn't in the best of shape." A chuckle from one of the jurors.

They lost sight of Gabriel for ten minutes, he figured.

"No more questions."

I wanted to ask Buck if he was aware that Gabriel had already come upon the clothes, but that's the kind of question, when wrongly answered, we lawyers call an exploding cigar. I helped Smitty speed through the day by asking nothing.

"Call Mr. Doug Wall."

The greying bootlegger looked around casually as he came forward – he was an old hand in the courtroom. With a recent cut and a beard trim for this occasion, he no longer looked so bear-like, except in girth.

Smythe-Baldwin stripped his testimony to the bone. At about two o'clock Wall was driving south on Squamish Valley Road, intending to meet some friends for a beer in Squamish. Half a mile below the Mulligan gate, he saw Gabriel cross the road with his rifle and enter the bush on the river side. He identified his signed statement, Exhibit Fifteen.

"My learned friend may have some questions." The dry tone suggested Smitty was well aware of my threat to come hard after Wall.

I began by asking about his means of income, and had to pry out the truth. "I do it as a courtesy to friends" became "I just run a delivery service," then "I never sell to minors." That proved a lie when I put his record to him: he'd been fined for that very offence. There were eight other convictions on his sheet, and I decided to run them all. Two bootleggings, two assaults, two thefts under fifty dollars, one possession of stolen goods over fifty, and one arson of a warehouse. For that, in 1957, he'd got four years in the penitentiary but was paroled in 1959.

"Quite an enviable record, Mr. Wall."

"There ain't been nothing recent." A surly demeanour. I had expected misunderstood, wounded.

"Yes, they're all at least three years old."

"I been clean ever since."

An implausible claim, given his continued flouting of the Liquor Act, and it produced a sound from the bench, something like a snort. The Hammer's long career as prosecutor had bred in him a hearty dislike of the criminal class.

The way seemed open to safely add Roscoe Knepp to the mix, and I brought out that they were well acquainted. Wall added lamely, "I like to be friends with everyone." He agreed that everyone included the entire RCMP detachment.

"When was Sergeant Knepp posted to Squamish?"

"Ah, three years ago, 1959, I think."

"Just about the time you got out on parole for torching that warehouse?"

"Around there."

"He kept a good eye on you?"

"Yeah, he checked in on me."

"Had a bit of a hold on you, didn't he. A parolee plying an illegal trade."

"I kept my nose clean. I was always okay with him."

"That's because you became his informer, correct?"

"No, I never done that."

"You would call him from time to time with information, wouldn't you?"

"I don't remember calling him about anything."

"Do you deny calling him right after you and I met in Brackendale last spring?"

"I'm not sure."

"You informed him I was in the area taking witness statements." I got a blank look. "Come now, Sergeant Knepp told me as much."

"Okay, yeah, I did. Now I remember."

"That was your deal with him. 'Anything interesting comes up, you call me' – that's what the sergeant told you, am I right?"

"I ain't sure what you're getting at."

"Let's be plain. The fact is that the local RCMP knows you traffic in alcohol. They let you do it, they turn a blind eye to it, and that's why your slate has been clean for three years. In return, you reward them with information."

"There was no deal like that."

"Come now, be honest. You're their faithful informant."

"I don't fink on my friends."

"But you don't regard Gabriel Swift as a friend, do you?"

He'd set a trap for himself. "I guess not. But I ain't a snitch."

My accusation wasn't good for either his business or his safety, so he was not going to back down. Still, every juror with a brain must have put two and two together. No one was objecting, and the judge was giving me room. A couple of approbative looks from Gabriel, who was otherwise intent, jotting notes.

"Okay, tell us when you first heard about Dr. Mulligan's disappearance."

"It was all around the valley by the next morning. I heard there was a call for a search party, then heard about them finding his clothes and stuff."

"That was Easter Sunday. And what were you doing that day?"

"I would of helped search, but it was a long weekend. I had a lot of friends to see."

"Did you talk to the police that day?"

"I had no chance. They was busy."

"When did you hear Gabriel Swift had been arrested and charged?"

"My memory ain't that good, but maybe Monday."

"And what were you doing that day?"

"The same, I guess. Seeing friends."

"Customers."

"Whatever you like." He'd been making eye contact earlier but was faltering now, looking past me, at the wall, at the Queen, as if hoping for royal support.

"What about the next day, Tuesday?"

"I had a day off. Drove down to Vancouver to see my ex and help her out a little financially."

"And it was not until the following day, Wednesday, that you talked to the police?"

"I kind of bumped into Brad Jettles."

"After which you gave him this skimpy statement." I displayed my copy.

"That's right."

"For three days you withheld this critical information. Why?"

"I was busy. The cops was busy. They already nicked Swift, so I didn't think there was no emergency."

"Dr. Mulligan's disappearance and Mr. Swift's arrest were the talk of the town, right?"

"Lots of people was carrying on about it."

"Including all those friends you were seeing."

"I guess."

I came close enough to Wall to pick up a boozy scent. "So no doubt you regaled them about seeing the accused cross the road with a rifle near the Mulligan farm at two o'clock on the day Dr. Mulligan vanished."

"I can't remember what I said."

"Really?"

"Maybe I was drinking too much."

"But surely you told many people about having seen him?"

"I guess naturally it would of come up, yeah."

"Okay, give me the names of all the people you told this to."

Again he was looking away from me, at the gallery this time – Celia Swift and her group of stalwarts. The bear retreated to the safety of his den. "I don't remember."

"You kind of bumped into Brad Jettles. How did that come about?"

"I was out at the sports grounds and he came up to me."

"What was going on at the sports grounds?"

"Nothing. It was getting dark, around seven."

"So no one was there but you and Constable Jettles?"

"I don't remember seeing no one."

"Okay, let's not play games. Not only was this meeting pre-arranged, it was instigated by the RCMP. Brad Jettles phoned you to meet at the usual place, isn't that right?"

That caused Wall to pause. "That was a few months ago. Maybe he did . . . No, I must've called him. I'd been meaning to, so I must've."

I took him back to Saturday the twenty-first. He was hazy about when he'd got up and about what he'd done that morning. He was "pretty sure" he'd slept in till noon, because he'd been up late with pals.

"You were hungover?"

"You could say."

"And of course you took a couple of drinks to relieve the pain?" An assumption based on my own expertise.

"I may have added something to the coffee."

"Okay, so we have you recovering from one hangover and getting a good start on another as you take off in your Nash Metro. When did you set out?"

"Just before two."

"You weren't wearing a watch."

"No, it got stole."

"And though you were drinking and had no watch, you maintain you saw Gabriel Swift at around two o'clock."

"I seen him walk across the road with a gun."

"Was that where the road cuts through the Cheakamus Reserve?"

"No, sir, it was nowhere near the reserve. Where I seen him was four or five telephone poles from the Mulligan driveway."

"And what did you think he was doing with that gun?"

"Deer hunting, like everybody does illegally up there."

"Did he cross the road in front of you or behind you?"

"In front."

"How far in front?"

"Maybe fifty yards."

"So obviously he must have seen you. Or at least your Nash Metro."

"Yeah, he waved –" Cancel that thought. "No, that had to be another time. No, he wouldn't of seen me, I was too far back of him." The image of a friendly wave from a man on a murder mission was unhelpful to his patrons on the force. Skepticism was writ large on the face of the foreman, hockey coach Ozzie Cooper.

"How many times that day did you drive down to Squamish?"

"Just that once."

"Did you see anyone else while you were on the road?"

"I don't recollect no one in particular."

"Irene Mulligan?"

"I seen her sometimes having her walk, but later in the day."

"Did you see her at her mailbox that Saturday?"

Long pause. "I can't remember."

I had the court reporter read back to him Irene's testimony: *Around eleven a car like that drove by.*

"A red Nash Metro, Mr. Wall."

The struggle to keep his flimsy structure from collapsing was too much for him; I saw surrender in his sagging shoulders. "Like I said, this stuff all happened over three months ago."

Ophelia cheered me on with a smile. *Yes, my love, there is something I'm good at.*

"Mr. Wall, you're not sure whether you saw my client in the afternoon or the morning, or a day earlier, or in another week, right?"

"I guess anything's possible." Total surrender.

"It's hard to tell the days and weeks apart when you're half in the bag from sampling your own merchandise."

"Was that intended as a question, Mr. Beauchamp, or are you merely chopping wood?"

"I think I was chopping wood, milord."

That produced a faint smile. "You have probably covered all the bases with this witness."

Code for *Stop beating a dead horse.* "No more questions."

Hammersmith beamed at me; we were on the same side for the moment. We all followed his gaze to the clock. "Nearly four-thirty, Mr. Smythe-Baldwin. Are we on time?"

"Most assuredly so." And that was the end of Day One.

Ophelia and I didn't join the race for the door. "That was almost cruel," she said, bringing out her pack of Players. "Smitty had the look of someone enjoying live theatre. He likes you – I think it's an avuncular thing."

The clerk caught her lighting up and exiled us to the hallway, where we followed the trail of cigar fumes to the Law Library. He was flipping the pages of a thick reference tome, apparently looking for a quote source. "Ah, yes, Quintilianus. 'A liar needs a good memory.'"

"*Mendacem memorem esse oportet,*" I said.

He looked up. "*Ipsissima verba.* You are no unfledged student of the great tongue."

"Six years of it. Smitty, it was very generous of you to absorb the wrath of The Hammer. I hope I can repay you. Sounds like you had a great lunch with his Lordship."

"And his granddaughter, whom he's pressing to go to law school. More and more of you lovely creatures seem to be doing that, Mrs. Moore."

"Yes, we intend to desegregate the profession, infiltrate the judiciary, and ultimately take over the Supreme Court of Canada."

Smitty and I laughed heartily. I asked, "Who won the battle for the bill?"

He stroked his Colonel Sanders goatee. "In such matters, my friend, as in most matters, I invariably win."

~~~

Among those changing into civvies in the gentlemen barristers' room was one who'd not been returning my calls: Harvey Frinkell, who had just wrapped up a divorce. He'd heard about my day's efforts.

"Congrats, Artie. You just made number one on the all-time coppers' hit list. Stick to the back roads or they'll bury you in tickets."

I told him I hadn't even started – wait till his cuckolded client was revealed as the killer. He reacted to that with excessive merriment.

I reminded him he'd yet to respond to my requests for copies of the photos showing Mulligan and Rita Schumacher at play.

"I only got one set. Ask Jimmy Fingers."

"I don't want to have to subpoena you guys."

"Tell your bitch associate to lay off of me and I'll think about it."

In fact I didn't feel driven to seek a subpoena. That Mulligan had received Frinkell's letter threatening a suit was enough to make my point that suicide was a valid hypothesis. The Crown was no longer relying on the scandalous theories of a homosexual affair gone wrong. There was no point in needlessly embarrassing Irene,

~~~

Ophelia and I had a good time later, at the Green Door in Chinatown, a BYOB restaurant entered by a back lane. In those days there were a few such unlicensed restaurants behind the neon streets, known not by name but door colour: green, orange, red. Those crowded little joints offered astonishingly good food.

We were at an oilcloth-covered table in a space no bigger than most kitchens. In fact it was a kitchen, plus annex, full of steam and pungent smells and loud Cantonese. We drank only tea, but we celebrated a good day in court just the same, over mussels and squid and garlic ribs. We replayed the day's highlights many times, and after lightening my wallet by six dollars with tip, I suggested a drive to Second Beach to catch the sunset. I wanted this day to continue; I was feeling great about it – clearly Hammersmith had found Wall's testimony palpably false.

"Sounds swell, Arthur, but another night. I've got a date with Lenny Bruce at Isy's." The supper club – the bawdy comedian was there for a run of several days. I wondered who her real date was. I told myself I really didn't care.

I dropped her off on Georgia, near Isy's, and went directly home, where I put on Ira's old Leadbelly disk that I'd been playing in my head. *Sometimes I take a great notion to jump in the river and drown* . . . Suddenly exhausted, I flopped onto the bed.

The next morning in court was painful, too painful to recreate here, and so I defer to Wentworth Chance.

From "Where the Squamish River Flows," *A Thirst for Justice*, © W. Chance

NO JOURNEY TO GREATNESS IS WITHOUT its stumbles, its snares and pitfalls, and the Swift trial, which I regard as a major turning point in Beauchamp's career, was to offer them in abundance.

He was too young, some said, too green to take on a murder case, and this author reluctantly shares that view. Criminal counsel, like opera singers, generally don't peak until their senior years – there are countless lessons and tricks to learn along the way. "But one has to start somewhere," Beauchamp said musingly during our March 2009 sessions.

It was with Smythe-Baldwin's prophetic remark – "in most matters, I invariably win" – that things started going downhill, and with a speed that surprised Beauchamp, for he'd been riding high after the first day, inflated by glowing press reviews. He had underestimated the guile and adroitness of the enemy. A more seasoned counsel would not have faltered when the going got tough. That is my view, based on reading the transcript, and Beauchamp didn't argue with it.

Leroy Lukey, who took over the reins on Tuesday, was determined not to be as relaxed as Smythe-Baldwin about advancing the Crown's case. It would be altogether too easy not to give Lukey his due* – he had obviously spent long hours rehearsing the Squamish police, and the first test of his efforts came with Constable Brad Jettles, who reeled off answers that were crisp and confident.

Beauchamp was flabbergasted at how this officer, regarded heretofore as a lightweight, held up coolly under

---

* He was later to become senior Crown counsel, then a judge of the B.C. Supreme Court, but he ultimately met with scandal and drank himself to death.

his fire. Though an air of self-flattery pervaded Jettles's incident reports, on the stand he was jokingly modest, confessing to having been the out-of-breath butt of his posse's humour. The jury quickly warmed to him.

Jettles didn't remember the accused saying anything when they caught up to him, and Beauchamp was content with that. Those seven fingerprints were a key concern, and he wanted the way open to persuade a jury that Gabriel had raced down there and, in a state of shock upon finding Mulligan's clothes, frisked them for a suicide note.

But why hadn't he made that explanation to Jettles? Why had he been so late offering it to his own lawyers? These were questions that had begun to plague Beauchamp, to infiltrate his stubborn faith in his intriguing client. Had Swift truly been looking for a suicide note or (a not so attractive possibility) something incriminating? Is that why he'd bolted from Jettles, raced off like a deer? Had he been telling his lawyers nothing but the truth or fudging it?

Jettles had been the lead officer in the questioning of Chief Joseph, wife Anna, and daughter Monique. Beauchamp had hoped to show the officer bullied them into making false statements, but he heard a candour that caused him to sense, as he put it, "a distant tolling of alarm bells."

Ben and Anna had told Jettles that Monique was home all Saturday afternoon, helping to prepare for an Easter Sunday banquet. Fetched from her room, Monique had concurred with that, absent any parental prompting. The Josephs had explained they wanted to protect their daughter from all the turmoil; thus they sent her down to the States. Neither Crown nor court objected to this hearsay, "presumably because I was doing such a masterly job of damaging my own case," said Beauchamp in his self-disparaging way.*

* The complete 2009 sessions with Beauchamp about the Swift trial, recorded in his Garibaldi Island parlour, are to be found on the website ThirstForJustice.com.

Jettles may have sensed, from the broken rhythms of that self-destructive cross-examination, that Beauchamp was floundering, and he became bold. Accused of joining Sergeant Knepp in a campaign of retribution against Swift, the witness explained, in tired but patient tones, that the Squamish RCMP did not go around framing people. That brought on a murmur of agreement in the jury box that caused Beauchamp to feel, as he put it, "that I was melting into my shoes."

Jettles didn't appear offended by Beauchamp's accusation that he and Knepp assaulted his client in the cells: "When somebody told me that's what Gabriel was putting out, I just laughed." Justice Hammersmith, who had been showing increasing irritation, warned Beauchamp again about maligning the police. But he pressed on, directing Jettles's attention to the report of prison doctor Guy Richmond and the photographs taken of Swift at Oakalla.

When asked, "Where did you suppose he got these bruises from?" Jettles said: "My best guess would be from a fist-fight the previous night in a bar in Squamish. You see that sort of thing all the time." Beauchamp got snarky. "When you look at this one closely, can you make out a standard-issue RCMP boot print?" That had Smythe-Baldwin rising in umbrage. Hammersmith again scolded Beauchamp for a vexatious cross-examination.

"And that, Wentworth, is when I realized the folly of having promised not to ask Borachuk if Gabriel was bruise-free when brought in." He added: "I was stuck with the deal, and at trial it would be the word of two white cops against one red hothead." That deal would long continue to haunt him.

Jettles vigorously denied he'd initiated the rendezvous with Wall at the sports grounds: "He came to us." As for Lorenzo, Jettles did not know him well, had never met him until two weeks earlier, had never talked to him for more than five minutes.

At this critical juncture Beauchamp felt as if he were pedalling backwards. As he put it, he went off the road, with a sarcasm-laden final cannonade at Jettles and much irrelevant sniping at the remaining police witnesses. During this he was constantly skirmishing with Hammersmith.*

The jury was removed for a voir dire to test the admissibility of Swift's curt alibi after he was picked up by Constables Grummond and Borachuk on Easter Sunday afternoon (he'd said: *I was with my girlfriend all afternoon. Anything else?*). Beauchamp put up a strong argument that the officers' failure to advise Swift of his rights poisoned the statement, and the jury ought not to hear it.

It was half past eleven. Hammersmith reserved on it until two o'clock.

---

* Beauchamp tussled with him many times in ensuing years, notably in the infamous cult mass-killing trial in 1985, the Om Bay Massacre. See Chapter Sixteen, "The Dance of Shiva."

I was sweating as I fled the court, thinking of a frosty glass of ale, scheming a way to sneak one past Ophelia. But Gabriel had asked to see me, so I told her to run ahead to the Georgia and find a table for lunch while I detoured to the little holding jail.

I was taken right into his cell, as was the practice there. I was still in black robe and vest and wing collar; it's a funereal look at best, and he stared at me darkly, as if I were the messenger of death. I would not have been surprised to hear him announce that my services were no longer required, that he'd revived his plan to defend himself – better having a fool for a client than a fool as a lawyer – but he merely said, "I guess Jettles is one of those born liars. Nice talent to have if you're a cop."

"I was frustrated and angry. I lost it."

"I've been there. Congratulations, Arthur, you have normal human feelings and frailties. I knew they'd show eventually." A biting comment – I wasn't used to that from him. "Why is it so important to keep that statement out?"

"So no one can accuse you of inventing an alibi."

He grimaced, seemed troubled, perhaps by something else he hadn't been forward about. "Who's up next?"

"Crime lab people. Ident officers. The fingerprint guy, firearms guy, serologist."

"What about Benjamin and Anna?"

"Tomorrow morning."

"What are you going to do to them?"

"I have to take them on. They're lying about their daughter being home."

"And Monique?"

"An hour has been set aside tomorrow for us to interview her. I may need to shake her up in court. It could be unpleasant."

He nodded, wandered off in thought, wandered back. "Food here's better than at Oakie. They send out – Chinese, Greek, steak sandwiches Deluxe."

I read his lack of eye contact as bad news. "Was there something you wanted to tell me?"

"The cartridge shells they found." He finally looked at me. "They could have been mine from a few months earlier. A bear was hanging around while we were fishing. I shot in the air a couple of times to warn it off."

"Did you just remember this?"

"Well, I usually took my rifle along on those trips, so my folks could lay in a little venison. Yeah, I just remembered about the bear. I remember Dermot being pissed off; he hated guns, wouldn't own one."

"So he was with you?"

"Yeah, it was Christmas break."

I had warned Gabriel it would be a hard slog to convince a jury that Knepp planted the shells, so this was a boon, but also, I suspected, a convenient falsehood. "Okay, that will be our defence. We'll fill in the details well before you testify." I held myself back from a sharper reaction. I was nagged by a feeling he was playing with me, doling out information when it suited him. Ophelia's remark continued to rankle: *He knows he can't manipulate a top counsel.*

As I readied to leave, he said, "I may want to see you at the end of the day."

"What about?"

He spread his hands, palms up, as if offering them for the teacher's strap. "I need time to work through something."

~~~

Outside it had turned hot, the pavement of Georgia Street shimmering with summer heat. A day for the beach, not an overheated courtroom. I was starting to reproach myself for having been so swellheaded in taking the case on, believing I had the moxie to win.

In the Georgia lounge I was irritated to find that Lukey had taken my intended chair at Ophelia's table. "How about that Brad Jettles?" he said. "Bullets bounce off."

I dragged in another chair and situated it between them, forcing him to shift over. Ophelia had already ordered; she passed me my coffee, now lukewarm. She was nursing a white wine, Leroy attacking a cold Calgary Ale.

Jettles was enjoying a beer too, celebrating at a far table with Knepp and another cop – red of face, thick of neck and shoulder, balding in front – fairly fitting Gabriel's description of Walt Lorenzo.

"So I'm wondering, how do you guys explain why your boy's dabs are all over the dead guy's wallet and clock?"

"How should we explain it, Leroy?" I signalled the waiter, pointing to the beer taps. That brought a frown from Ophelia.

"Okay, your Indian's got some jets. While the laughingstock puffs along behind, he goes whooping off, has time to check out the scene, decides to rummage around, maybe collect his week's pay out of the dead man's poke. Have I got it right so far?"

He had, sort of, but I wasn't about to say so.

"That scenario starts to sound almost rational, except why does he go running off there in the first place? Trying to lose everyone? Answers?" He smiles at me, then Ophelia. "Because he suddenly remembers: *Jeez, I got my prints all over the pervert's wallet after I snuffed him yesterday. So I better run off and lay down some more prints, so there's no way to pick out the day-old ones. And I'll say I was looking for, say, a suicide note.*"

I wondered if he had a spy at Tragger, Inglis, or if the Oakalla interview room was bugged. He craned his neck, either to look down Ophelia's dress or at the magazine article open in front of her.

"Friedan," she said. "A psychological critique of Freud, according to whom I'm supposed to be envious of your penis."

"Sigmund got it wrong, my love. Only the guys envy my penis. Girls swoon."

"Do they have to bring their own microscopes, or do you supply?"

Lukey leaned toward me. A stage whisper: "I hear she likes guys to sit on her face and fart in her mouth." He downed his beer and trotted off toward his RCMP team.

"Fuck yourself," she called. Those nearby were staring.

I took a deep swill from the mug of ale newly set before me, felt that first ease of false escape. "How was Lenny Bruce?"

"Not as filthy as Leroy, and a lot funnier. Just that one, okay?"

Two Denver sandwiches arrived. I had little appetite. "Now I know what it's like to feel Jettles's boot. And he's the local dimwit. Knepp will pulverize me."

Ophelia dug into her sandwich, not even a smile to shore me up, and I sensed a slipping of respect, of confidence. She greeted Gabriel's eleventh-hour disclosure with cynicism. "Scaring off a bear, was he? Fair enough. At least he's playing the game right. I guess he's decided not to be a martyr after all."

I caught Lukey and the triad of cops appraising me. The scouting report was in: Beauchamp has a good tongue but lousy hands, fumbles a lot.

As I sought to signal the waiter for a refill, Ophelia grabbed my arm and tugged me to my feet. "Get yourself together, for God's sake. Let's go back to work." She marched me back to Court One, a schoolmistress with an errant child.

~~~

Hammersmith's reasons on the voir dire were not exactly bullet-proof but predictably framed to aid the prosecution, were they to be attacked on appeal. To ward off any suggestion that he held any animus toward defence counsel, he began by thanking me for my "able and eloquent submission" before dismembering it.

Let me quote salient passages from the transcript:

Mr. Beauchamp argues that the accused's statements in the police vehicle are inadmissible because he wasn't warned of his right to be silent. To me, that incorrectly frames the question, which should be:

Were the officers required to issue any warning at all? If a questioned person is regarded as a suspect, yes, the usual caution is highly desirable. But if such person is merely regarded as a possible witness, an information-giver, the authorities face no such obligation. Can one imagine the chaotic situation that would occur if all prospective witnesses in all criminal cases had to be told they could remain silent?

Mr. Beauchamp argued that the accused was indeed seen as a suspect by the two officers, and he made the point that ordinary witnesses "are not picked up on a rural road, and given a third-degree in the back seat of a cruiser." The evidence on voir dire is far less clear than that. Constable Grummond made it abundantly clear to the accused that they had no reason to suspect him, and that they just needed, and I quote, "the whole picture from someone who knew the deceased so we can figure out what happened." The fact that they drove him a few miles to his reserve is to their credit.

Lukey then brought the jury back to hear Grummond and Borachuk recite Gabriel's alibi about being with his girlfriend. Grummond and Gene Borachuk were not this drama's culprits, and my cross-examinations were brief, restricted to implying this was all part of a set-up by others to pin a murder on my client. More flack from the bench.

Smitty had little to do that afternoon – he'd sluffed off to Lukey the tedium of leading the expert witnesses – and for much of the time reclined in his chair with eyes closed, as if enjoying a nap after an appetizing meal.

I'd already read the reports of the crime lab people, all of whom I knew from previous cases, and asked few questions. I had nothing for the fingerprint examiner. The ballistics man accommodated me by agreeing there was no way to tell how long the 30-30 cartridges had lain on the ground. Could have been months, years? Possibly.

The prissy Victorian clerk kept glancing at Ophelia with disapproval. She was in a dress that day, but too short – one could see her calves and ankles. He seemed doubly offended that she smothered mirth when the pair of frilly panties was displayed to judge and jury, or at least remnants of same with swatches cut from them. One of the Eaton's brands, described in its catalogue as "flare-leg nylon tricot, $1.99."

These, the serologist found, contained excrement from an unknown bird as well as semen from an unknown male. No traces of blood were found on site; however, one's blood type can be determined from semen. That was type A. Mulligan was type A. So are forty per cent of humans.

The Crown's version seemed in conflict with an onanistic dalliance such as masturbation. According to Lorenzo, *he'd planned to confront the deceased at his fishing hole and make him take his clothes off so he could fake a suicide.* That seemed a dubious way to inspire arousal and orgasm.

The expert was unable to say how long the panties had been tangled in that tree root. Maybe weeks? Not likely, given that rain hadn't washed away the stains.

I checked my watch frequently, checked the wall clock, urging them to hurry up, to get to four-thirty. My entire effort for the afternoon had been desultory. I had no spark. I had, instead, a terrible sense I was blowing this case.

Finally Day Two was done. "I have to dash off," I told Ophelia, but didn't say why.

I just didn't want to depress her. I didn't want to deal with anyone, including the insistent reporter and cameraman I had to outrun.

~~~

I'd like to think I was iron-willed in not pulling into a bar or liquor store, but more likely it was cowardice that drove me straight home, fear of Ophelia's censure – I wouldn't have been able to lie to her. *I dare you.* I did pause at a drive-in, then made quickly to my suite with a double patty, fries, and shake.

I dined in front of the TV, the local news. There I was, a camera having trouble catching up to me as I fled to my car. In contrast, Smythe-Baldwin was shown easing himself into a taxi, serene, confident, declining to comment on the case. "The Crown is driven by only one goal, and it is called justice."

Hammersmith's hostility to my theory of a conspiracy to frame the accused had made an impact on the jury, which I fear was seeing it as a wildly swinging mud-casting effort. But I wondered if Smitty, the seasoned defence counsel, was getting a whiff of what Hamlet smelled in Denmark. How could he not be riven with doubt about Lorenzo?

From Lawonda's lovely oak desk – a gift from a suitor, I presumed – I had a view out back of tall conifers, evening rays weaving through their branches. I thought of a walk to the beach but sighed and spread out my notes from the hearing, Crown particulars, exhibits. I began to work on my cross of the Joseph family. I couldn't conceive how I was to go after those folks without seeming a bully.

Something was bothering me, something I hadn't done. The phone began an insistent ringing. I played awhile with ignoring it, then gave in. A male, a repeater. "I was hoping Lawonda was back."

"Once again, let me explain she has moved to the States."

"If she calls, tell her it's Otto. I'm in a pretty bad way."

Possibly suicidal. There'd been others, less plaintive, men with husky, panting voices.

It was then I remembered Gabriel had asked to see me after court. Surely, I decided, nothing was so vital that it couldn't await the morning, before we resumed.

I still recall the dream that awakened me briefly that night: its protagonist unbearably frustrated as he tried to sort out shape-shifting figures, Ophelia pressing me to her ample bosom, then becoming Gabriel, who, as I retreated in shame, took on Dermot's form, who became Irene, and they were nakedly writhing, making love with Rita Schumacher in her second-floor bedroom. I was running through the snow about to cry "Eureka" because I had the answer . . . and suddenly I was sitting up in bed and couldn't even remember the question.

It was excitement that woke me, I suppose. Though I struggled, no divine afflatus came; whatever had arisen from my subconscious was erased. The dream seemed portentous as well as phantasmagorical, and for hours I stared out at the moonlight-dappled garden, trying to tie its threads together.

It was still in my mind as I took a last swig of instant coffee and a couple of Tums, gathered my papers, knotted my tie, and strode off toward the Burrard Bridge, planning to get my mind together by briskly walking downtown. This healthy notion dissipated by the time I puffed over the busy art deco bridge and gained the downtown peninsula. I considered pausing at St. Paul's Hospital for oxygen, but instead waved down a taxi.

I borrowed the driver's newspaper. A fanfare piece about the Trans-Canada Highway's ribbon cutting. The Wasserman column, a gasping, puritanical report on Lenny Bruce's show at Isy's. On the third page: "Sparks Fly as Lawyer Flays RCMP." Another bad review, the flayer coming across as desperate.

On my being let into Gabriel's cell, I quickly saw he was in distress. He didn't ask after my well-being, didn't even say hello, just sat and stared at his hands. My premonition of a calamitous turning point in this case was soon realized.

"I want you to leave Monique alone."

"I beg your pardon?"

"Her parents too."

"Impossible. The Josephs have been hidden from me, Monique squirreled away in the States. It's my only chance to have a go at them before trial." I was met with silence. "Gabriel, I warned you I would not let you commandeer this defence."

"Monique's . . . her statement was the truth. I lied to the police. I have lied to you."

I was taken over by a sense of tremendous emptiness, of loss. It is still hard to describe it, but it was as if I'd been overcome by a failure of faith. My stunned gaze wandered from his tightly clasped hands to the wall beside him, and settled on a few words of protest inked onto the wall: *Burn in hell, Scheister.* Who was Scheister?

While in this fugue, I heard but couldn't quite get a grip on the phrases tumbling from Gabriel, an explanation, a *mea culpa.* I raised a hand to silence him. When he finally looked up, I saw his eyes were raw. Then it was my turn to avert my gaze, back to the graffiti. *Shyster,* misspelled as Scheister, inscribed by a dissatisfied client. Possibly German.

"Let's back up, Gabriel. Do I have this right? You urged Monique to tell the police she was with you. All afternoon. In your cabin."

"I begged her."

"And she agreed."

"I don't know. She didn't promise; she was confused. We didn't have much time together, she was already late for church."

"Where was this?"

"Just around the corner from her place. I'd just got back from the river, from finding Dermot's stuff."

"And you hoped this pious young woman would lie for you."

"I hoped."

I slowly regained equilibrium. "And you are telling me now that you were home alone."

"I felt I needed an alibi, Arthur. Knepp would be going hell for leather to lay a murder beef on me. I got frantic – I'd left my prints on Dermot's stuff. They'd have nabbed me anyway. He was white,

215

well-off, my boss, and I'm a fucking barely employed Indian who hates the system and punched out a cop. That's all they needed; they'd invent a motive as they went along."

I would have stormed at him if others weren't in earshot. *You lied to me;* that's what I wanted to scream. You nearly had me attacking an innocent sixteen-year-old, her mom, her dad.

I looked at my watch. Nearly start time. "And what the hell were you doing all afternoon in your cabin?"

"I was reading Dermot's memoir."

~~~

Our trial was held up while Hammersmith listened to a vigorous but incomprehensible submission by Harry Fan on sentencing. In the dock, with hands clasped as if in prayer, was a middle-aged man charged with gross indecency at the English Bay bathhouses.

Ophelia gave me a critical once-over as I joined her on the counsel bench. "Bad night?"

"Bad morning."

Hammersmith and Fan were tangling over the pre-sentence report, so I had time to brief her *sotto voce.*

"He was reading the fucking *memoir?*" Ophelia looked heavenward, as if for salvation. "You sure he's not lying about lying? He saw you rip Doug Wall apart and wants to protect Monique from similar."

I shook my head. "I believe him; he wasn't acting."

"There's nothing in her statement about Gabriel asking her to lie."

"Let's hope she withheld that."

"Well, we'd better find out. Lukey has her waiting for us in the witness room."

"You talk to her. I'm too depressed."

Hammersmith sentenced the fellow in the dock to two years less a day, expressing the hope that such a jail term would help him correct his devious tendencies. The man went down to the cells sobbing, and Gabriel replaced him.

Mounting the stand as the jury returned was Chief Benjamin Joseph, a short, stout fellow with an easygoing way of talking. He had presided over a tribal council meeting on the Saturday afternoon and returned home at four, expecting to watch the final game of the Stanley Cup, only to find it was set for Sunday. Monique was with her mother in the kitchen, helping prepare a "big old ham that with the Lord's help was gonna get us through the Easter weekend."

This casual jocularity cast serious doubt on Knepp's anthropological expertise: *You're dealing with people who are withdrawn. It's in their nature.* I'd not bought that, though I had believed Benjamin was a corrupt truckler to authority. That came from Gabriel, his feelings coloured by his resentment of a protective dad.

Benjamin's opinion of Gabriel, on the other hand, was unexpectedly neutral, even slightly approving. "Known Gabby since he was a kid. We called him that because there was times he wouldn't stop talking." But as he grew up, "he got on the wrong side of every issue, talking up revolutionary socialism, he called it." Monique, he implied, was too young to commit to a relationship with this beater of war drums.

I put myself in Benjamin's place. Were I the father, I might also have put my foot down; here was a sixteen-year-old involved with a militant who'd slugged a cop. (In fact, decades later, when my own daughter was sixteen, I railed at her for bedding a pot smoking draft dodger from Duluth.)

I was sorely depressed by how our case was crumbling, chunk by chunk, at an accelerating pace, and couldn't imagine what I could seek from this unpretentious gentleman that might slow the decay. Ought I to portray him as too palsy-walsy with the uniformed thugs at the local detachment? I looked over at the jury, the six and six, fathers and mothers.

"Your witness," Smitty said.

"No questions," said I.

As Benjamin walked past the dock, he gave Gabriel a closed fist of support, hidden from the judge. I had trouble working through my surprise at that. Gabriel, who seemed relieved and contrite, struggled to find a smile for me.

Ophelia returned from her session with Monique, looking grave. "Bad. She did tell Knepp – and Lukey – that Gabriel asked her to alibi for him." Morosely I read her scribbled notes.

But now I had to concentrate on Anna Joseph, who spoke in a voice softer even than Irene Mulligan's, and with a gently slurring Salish accent. Hammersmith repeatedly urged her to up the volume, then finally sat back and resigned himself to waiting for the next batch of pages from the court reporters – he had them working in shifts, pumping out a running transcript.

Anna was younger than her common-law spouse (or as we say today, no less awkwardly, partner), church-going, and lacking in guile. She was firm in her recall of that Saturday afternoon: she and her daughter sharing kitchen duties, Monique preparing a fish soup, Anna worrying over the logistics of an Easter Sunday banquet "with a whole army of relatives."

As to Monique's mid-teen romance? "I says to her, finish high school before you get serious. If he loves you he'll wait for you." I sensed she felt Gabriel Swift was bound for trouble, and she didn't want Monique along for the ride.

"No questions," I said. However belated, Gabriel's warning to expect the truth from these folks had avoided grief to his cause. Stern cross-examinations of the Josephs would have been a kamikaze mission, sinking not the enemy's ship but mine.

Anna looked quickly at Gabriel – a quarter-second – then cast her eyes down at the aisle carpet and joined Benjamin outside as Monique came in. She was a pretty cherub, short and perky, striving hard not to show nervousness. Smitty placed her statement before her and asked her if it was true.

"Yes." Quietly, lips quivering.

She was brief in response throughout. Had she seen him at all that Saturday? No. Had she planned to? Yes. What changed her mind? She couldn't get away from the house. Why was that? There was too much to do. Had she seen him the following day?

A long pause. She began to tremble. She looked at Gabriel, then quickly away, and her eyes filled.

"Near your house? Perhaps just before Easter Mass?"

Smitty must have felt guilty about playing the prompter so blatantly. He was trying to rush her through this, get her safely off the stand, but his efforts were failing. Monique was weeping into a handkerchief, unable to express herself.

Lukey appeared to be suppressing a smirk. He had not disclosed this conversational tidbit from Sunday, hoping to lay a trap. It might have worked if Gabriel hadn't finally owned up.

"Young lady, I must urge you to compose yourself." The Hammer.

She wept all the harder. Gabriel was in distress, his mother and her entourage looking uncomfortable. *Someone should go to this girl,* I thought, *give her comfort, assuage her pain.*

I stood. "The defence will admit that the accused had a brief conversation with Miss Joseph at midmorning on that Sunday, in which he told her he was scared the police would falsely accuse him of being involved in Dr. Mulligan's disappearance. The defence will further admit that Mr. Swift asked her to tell the police that they were together the previous afternoon."

Smitty gave me a tired wave as if to say, *It's a deal,* and he sat. Lukey made a pained face, displeased that I'd grasped what advantage I could from the situation.

"Defence has no questions."

Hammersmith: "No, I'm not satisfied. I want to hear from the witness about this conversation."

Smitty grunted back to his feet. "I have accepted my friend's admissions of fact. That, with respect, should be an end to the matter. May Miss Joseph be excused?"

"No. I expect this young lady to testify from her own memory, not as coloured by Mr. Beauchamp's second-hand version."

"Ours is an adversarial, not inquisitive system, the judge an arbiter, not an interrogator." Smitty then added, straight-faced, "I say that, of course, with the greatest respect."

I had learned a lot watching Smitty over many trials. This was a lesson in not giving in, a lesson in heroism. And decency – protecting the girl from courtroom trauma. But I was keeping right out of this, scrunched down, the flak passing overhead. Monique had stopped crying but still looked frightened and confused.

"Witness, please look at me."

"With the greatest of conceivable respect –"

"Sit down!"

Smitty did so, but with contemptuous sluggishness, as Hammersmith, still flushed with anger, a fist curled as if ready to pound on something, turned again to Monique. "What did the accused tell you on that Easter Sunday morning?"

Monique cried out in unexpected defiance, "Just what his lawyer said! Just that! That's all!"

Hammersmith winced, in the manner of someone suffering heartburn. "We'll take the morning break."

Smitty gave me a wink as he made for the exit, drawing his morning cigar from a waistcoat pocket. Not for the first time, I got the sense he regretted his role there, was uncomfortable with prosecuting, couldn't shake off old habits like the baiting of judges.

But his junior was in charge of the key witnesses, the conspiring police. Ophelia was at Lukey's table, giving him hell for not giving us full disclosure, but he was cracking right back in his rude, mocking way.

Roscoe Knepp was up next. I wasn't prepared for him; I was still overcome by blows recently taken, exhausted. Nor was I positive any longer that Knepp was manufacturing a completely false case against Gabriel. I had a niggling sense of having been betrayed by my rebel client.

Ophelia returned to my side, muttering. "An oversight. My royal Canadian ass it was."

~~~

When court resumed, Smitty was still off somewhere lingering over a particularly tasty Havana, a gesture of disdain – no one shouts "Sit down!" to the dean of the criminal bar. But Lukey wasn't waiting for him this time. With a vocal flourish he called upon RCMP Staff Sergeant Roscoe Knepp to take the stand.

The square-chinned witness, in iron-crisp RCMP tunic, strode with confident step to the stand and accepted the oath as if posing tall in the saddle, the Bible aloft in his right hand. "So help me, God," he said, and planted a kiss on a page somewhere in the Book of Job or Psalms.

Lukey then announced he had no questions, was tendering the witness as a courtesy for cross-examination. He sat, beaming at me, knowing I would have to adjust on the fly – no witness is harder to cross than one yet unheard. I couldn't immediately find the cross-examination notes I'd spent many hours preparing, and I went at it blindly. Pick a topic, any topic. Doug Wall.

Knepp approached his task with disarming candour, sharing my view that Wall was less than reliable, agreeing he drank too much, that he curried favour with the law. But what could the Squamish RCMP do? Wall had approached them, however late; they'd had no choice but to take his statement.

Hammersmith, who had already written off Wall as a dubious party, a felon, nodded with appreciation at this earnest apologia from an officer just doing his job – it wasn't up to him to suppress evidence, however fishy. The jury, too, seemed appreciative.

Knepp calmly dismissed my allegation that he'd sought out Wall in desperation to bolster an alarmingly weak case. "I wouldn't rely on Doug Wall to bolster a parking offence." Chuckles from the gallery. Lukey grinning. *That's your best shot?*

Rattled, desperate to recoup, I retreated three years to the summer of 1959, Knepp's faceoff with Gabriel outside the Squamish Hotel beer parlour. Bill Swift had been drunk, said Knepp, and was causing a scene. And yes, he admitted sorrowfully, he may have used inappropriate language in ordering Gabriel not to intervene. On being assaulted, Knepp stumbled and fell. He and his partner "proceeded to arrest both individuals." He said it was part of police training "to keep a cool head under such circumstances."

A disbelieving guffaw from the back of the room. Hammersmith looked about but was unable to pinpoint the offender. He couldn't resist a little drollery: "That rude objection is not sustained. In my view, the sergeant showed admirable restraint."

"I'm sure the witness appreciates being cheered on by the bench," I said.

"Do I take it your purpose is to discredit him, Mr. Beauchamp?"

"I gather I haven't made that plain to your Lordship."

Tempers might have flared had not Smitty chosen that moment to enter. All went silent as he bowed to the judge almost theatrically, then took his seat in the anticipatory manner of one settling in to watch the Friday-night fights on TV.

I reminded myself my real opponent was not Hammersmith but Knepp. While he was dancing and jabbing, I was missing with my punches. I was embarrassed that the great barrister had returned to see me at my worst.

I put it to Knepp that he'd been furious when the local magistrate rewarded Gabriel with a suspended sentence.

"Not at all," Roscoe said, affecting shock, finally overacting. "As a police officer my duty is to gather the evidence, not to question what the courts do with it."

Another snort from the back of the room. Hammersmith looked up sharply, this time zeroing in on a familiar face. Jim Brady in the back row, covering up by applying a handkerchief to his nose.

I hurried on. "Thelma McLean said you described my client as a shit-disturbing commie. You don't dispute that?"

"I don't think I used that exact language, but your client never made a secret of his radical sympathies. If there was any kind of demonstration, he'd be there."

He continued to bob and weave as I flailed about, trying to egg him on, prodding him to admit to his vendetta, his racism, his slanders about Gabriel. My cross finally deteriorated to its low point when I accused him of fetching his old pal Walt Lorenzo from Winnipeg to play the role of lying jailhouse informer.

His response: Lorenzo was indeed a good friend, but more importantly a fine undercover officer. They had worked together as constables in a small detachment in Alberta, and years later had joined in breaking up a heroin ring that Lorenzo had expertly infiltrated. "I put out a special request to have Walt brought in for the Swift case. He was someone I could trust to do a professional job." He put on a mask of confusion and hurt as he denied there was anything improper about a trip with their wives to Reno to celebrate smashing that heroin ring.

Eventually my efforts to discredit Knepp proved tiresome, and Hammersmith interrupted wearily. "Am I to understand your defence involves a conspiracy among police officers to perjure themselves in an effort to frame the accused for murder? Do I have that right?"

I didn't know what to say. It seemed a preposterous defence the way he'd framed it. The gutter tactics that he'd earlier inveighed against.

"A conspiracy theory." Hammersmith shook his head, smiling as if in pity. "Good luck with that one, Mr. Beauchamp."

That earned laughter, led by the hockey coach, Cooper. I was piling up the penalties and he was clearly against me. Most of the jurors, if I read them right, were of similar mind, appalled by my desperate measures.

I think I was suffering at that moment what actors call flop sweat, the clammy sense that one has so badly flubbed his role that the audience is about ready to boo the bum offstage. I'd been going after Knepp for an hour; nothing was working. Smitty was watching me with growing disappointment, if not concern.

In short, I choked. I actually seized up, unable to frame a next question. I no longer knew what to ask. I played for time by shuffling through my notes.

"Harvey Frinkell," Ophelia whispered.

I had no idea what she meant.

"His letter." She scribbled in big letters on her pad: *Exhibit 37.*

"Time passes, counsel."

"Excuse me, milord. Ah, yes, Exhibit Thirty-Seven – may I have that?"

The clerk passed me Frinkell's letter, the one found on Mulligan's desk, his threat of a messy suit. I'd let the suicide defence gather dust while trying to put a shine on an unsalable conspiracy theory.

Knepp said he'd found the letter in what he called an in-basket. He hadn't shown it to Irene or contacted its author, Frinkell. "I didn't think it was my business to stir up an unhappy marital situation."

That seemed rather puerile. "Put yourself in Dr. Mulligan's shoes, Sergeant. Had you received a letter like this, you would be fairly distraught, wouldn't you?"

"I wouldn't be happy, I guess."

"A distinguished scholar, a world-renowned ethicist – and suddenly he's looking at a scandalous trial, at becoming a laughing-stock, at his world falling in. Enough to make you want to end it all, isn't it?"

"Well, I'm not Dr. Mulligan. I wouldn't say."

I'd finally got the jury interested. Maybe they'd forgive the hapless ninety per cent of my cross-examination. "No more questions."

All eyes followed Hammersmith's to the wall clock. "I see the noon hour is upon us. Let us break for lunch."

I told Ophelia I wasn't hungry; I needed to be by myself. I escaped out into the hot summer air, found my way across the CPR tracks to the industrial docks, and stood on a pier for a long, long time, staring into the slurping waters of the inlet, trying to form a picture of Mulligan similarly gazing down at the thickly flowing Squamish River. Naked but for socks, perhaps, as he flung away that soiled gaudy undergarment.

Maybe he intended it to be found. A clue. *There it is. Now find my murderer.*

~~~

Bull-like, thick-necked Walt Lorenzo embraced the Bible with even more ardour than his comrades-in-arms, an audible smooch on the spine. There seemed a corollary there: the more flagrant the intended perjury, the more showy the reverence.

He was methodical in answering Lukey's questions, describing in monotonic detail his laborious campaign to bond with the accused. The pridefulness that was so apparent in his written statement had been coached away; he'd been told to stick tightly to a script.

He seemed less than razor sharp – certainly duller of mind than Knepp – so I expected him to be not as good a counterpuncher. I hoped he would reveal himself in cross as the lousy ham actor Gabriel had made so bold as to call him to his face.

Smitty again wandered in late after another successful dining experience, and upon settling into his chair he closed his eyes, seemingly lulled to sleep by the witness's emotionless recounting of how he infiltrated the enemy camp.

Finally Lorenzo slogged his way to Day Nineteen – confession day – when he'd shared with Gabriel his tale of dealing a death blow in an alley scuffle. "I told the accused it was him or me; I had to kill him."

"Give us that in your own words," Lukey said.

Lorenzo seemed unable to elaborate. "I said, 'It was him or me. I had to kill him.'"

"Just for the record," said Lukey, "was there any truth to that story?"

"It was my invention, sir."

Supposedly overcome with a burning need to share, the accused had described how he'd planned to waylay Mulligan at the fishing hole and send him to his reward for having mistreated children at "some kind of Indian school in Saskatchewan." Lorenzo's account of this alleged conversation was remarkably similar in wording and sequence to his written version, right to the end: "He shot him as he flailed."

"Your witness."

I drew a half-chewed pencil from my mouth as I gained my feet.

"I understand you've earned quite a reputation as an undercover performance artist."

He didn't hear the sarcasm. "Thank you, sir. It's something I'm often asked to do." Warming to the topic: "I've been told I have a way with people."

"A talent for the stage."

"Maybe."

"Ever had any training as an actor?"

"No, sir. I just have whatever talent God gave me."

"Is this your specialty – posing as a prisoner?"

"Not really. Mostly it's drug purchases. I guess I've done the jail thing five, six times, different places across the country. Ontario, the Maritimes. Even Iowa, on loan to the U.S. Bureau of Narcotics." His hubris finally showing.

"Typically you would play the role for how long?"

"That varies. I got one confession after three hours. On average, I'm at it maybe a few days."

"But this operation took nineteen. Ever heard of anything similar, outside the USSR? An undercover officer sharing a suspect's cell for three weeks?"

"No, I guess that wouldn't be the usual experience."

"Unheard of, in fact. There were times, I'll bet, when you wanted to give up."

"Well, that wasn't my decision, totally."

"Whose decision was it?"

"The officer in charge."

"Your good friend Roscoe Knepp."

"I've known him for some years, yes."

"And he said, 'Keep at it, Walt. Give it another week, another few days' – that sort of thing?"

"He encouraged me."

"Throughout your twenty-one-day tenure at Oakalla Prison Farm, you met with him privately at least a few times a week?"

"Yes, in an interview room there. When I was supposed to be seeing, like, a lawyer, maybe, or the visiting priest."

"You'd consult, plan tactics."

"And I'd write out my notes from the previous day or two."

"And he'd coach you."

"No, sir, he'd ask questions. Debrief me."

"You've known Roscoe since you were young constables in Grande Prairie, Alberta – 1947 to 1950, is that correct?"

"Yes, sir."

"Kept in contact over the years?"

"Sure. Our wives too. We'd call each other. Exchange Christmas cards."

"Visit each other on holidays?"

"Sometimes. Camping with our trailers, that sort of thing. Cookouts."

"You'd go off to places together too. Reno, where else?"

"Fishing lodges. Disneyland with our kids."

"You consider him one of your very best friends."

"One of many, sir."

I wasn't getting much traction. "Okay, back to your efforts as a jailhouse informer. Despite your persistence, the accused declined to talk about the case for twenty straight days, yes? Except to say he was being framed for murder."

"As I explained, he was a little slow to warm up to me."

"He was quiet, uncommunicative, right? You'd play some cards, some chess, but he hardly ever talked."

"That's . . . Yeah, well, Natives are like that, I found."

There came another sound from the back, like a half-smothered expletive – Brady, of course – and I pressed on quickly, "When you told him you supported the Communist Party, what was his reaction?"

"He kind of nodded and smiled. I took that as approval."

"And when you said you were part Indian, how did he react?"

"Pretty much the same. I think he appreciated my sharing that."

"It was a lie, of course."

"Yes, sir."

"Another approach you made was to suggest an escape plan. What did you propose exactly?"

"I never got into details. He didn't seem interested."

"Did the accused strike you as slow on the uptake?"

"No, he was pretty smart, actually. A reader. He was learning French."

"Beat you regularly at chess."

"I wasn't really trying."

"And you didn't think this smart fellow had guessed what your real game was?"

"Apparently not."

"Come now, Corporal, from the outset it was clear, was it not, that he distrusted you?"

"I can't say what was in his mind."

"So on Saturday, the twenty-sixth of May, you tearfully regurgitated to him some nonsense about a murder you claimed to have bottled up."

"You could put it that way, I guess."

"Over a game of cribbage?"

"Yes, sir."

I read to him from his notes: *I told him my secret was torturing me and he was the first person I'd ever told this, because he was like a brother.* "Suddenly he's like a brother? Where did that come from?"

"I considered it important to let him know how close I felt to him."

"And so when you told your tale of a back-alley brawl, breaking a man's neck, you felt this intelligent young fellow fell for that hook, line, and sinker?"

"Yes, sir."

"In fact, witness, he said you were a lousy actor who wouldn't be winning any Oscars with that pitiful performance." Commotion at the press table.

"He didn't say that. He told me how he planned to kill Professor Mulligan."

"What exactly do you claim he said?"

"He told me he planned to confront the deceased at his fishing hole and make him take his clothes off so he could fake a suicide, but the deceased tried to grab his rifle and there was a tussle and he, ah, threw him down over the rocks, into the river, where he shot him . . ." – a pause as he fought to get it exactly right – " . . . as he flailed."

Again, almost word-perfect from his original notes. The only difference: *he hurled him* became *he threw him*. Those notes were signed and dated *27-05-62, at 0910 hours.* In more relaxed format, May 27, at nine-ten in the morning. Sunday, not Saturday.

"Give us that in your own words," I said, mimicking Lukey.

"Exactly?"

"Yes, the words the accused spoke to you. Each and every one. I don't want to be surprised later on to find you've added or amended something."

"Okay, well, the accused said, 'My plan was to confront' . . . no, 'meet the deceased' . . . or he would have said 'Dr. Mulligan' . . . I didn't write down his exact words, just a summary."

"Why not the exact words?"

"I memorized the substance. It was some time later before I could put things on paper."

"How much later?"

"Well, I had to wait for the morning – that would be around nine o'clock. A meeting with my lawyer was scheduled." He put *lawyer* in wiggling finger quotes.

"That doesn't register on the transcript, Corporal." Hammersmith's tone seemed almost apologetic. Throughout, he had been treating this poseur with the benevolence owed a favourite son-in-law.

"Sorry, milord. The lawyer, unquote, was actually my case officer."

"Sergeant Knepp," I said.

"Yes, sir."

Smitty's eyes were still closed but I knew he was listening. Was that a smile? Did he feel I was finally making some limping progress?

"So something like twelve or thirteen hours after this allegedly teary cribbage game, you sat down with Roscoe to write this up?"

"I recorded my conversation with the accused to the best of my memory."

"I see, and did Roscoe try to jog your memory with little additions here and there?"

"No, sir."

I waited, staring hard at him, daring him to break the silence, expand on his simple answer. It was a technique I'd seen Smitty use many times to good effect – encouraging witnesses to go off script.

Finally he said, "I know what you're implying."

"What am I implying, Corporal?"

"That my memory isn't perfect."

"I'm implying a lot more than that, but surely you agree that your memory in fact isn't perfect?"

He had to think about that. "I guess not. No one but God is perfect, I guess." Then, earnestly: "Mr. Beauchamp, I would never lie about something like this. I would never lie in a courtroom."

Said like a polished, seasoned liar, but others not so cynical – most of those who packed that courtroom, the jurors – likely heard sincerity. I'd expected Lorenzo to come across as shallow and vainglorious, had prepared poorly for him.

"So here we have the two of you in a cell, confessing to your crimes. The accused was emotional, choked up. Surely to goodness the whole wing of cells could hear your wailing and sobbing."

"I didn't say we were loud. Nobody was wailing."

"So my client spoke in a low voice? Hard to hear him?"

"I got most of it."

"You said, and I quote, 'He got very choked up so I didn't get his full meaning."

"He was talking about the deceased presiding over an Indian school in Saskatchewan, and he'd committed or been involved in some physical or sexual assaults – that's the gist of what I heard. He was clear about pretty well everything else."

"Come on, now, Corporal, let's be fair. If all this transpired as you claim it did – a major cathartic scene, emotions running high – the accused's words could easily have been misconstrued. Correct? Is that fair?"

"I always recorded to the best of my ability what he said, so help me God." (Only later, on reading the transcript, did I become mindful of his tendency toward extraneous pieties. One assumes he saw Gabriel, an atheistic communist, as an enemy of the Church. More motivation for him to lie, though it may seem unchristian to say so.)

"According to your version, there was some kind of struggle for the rifle. During that, the deceased fell over some rocks into the river. He could have stumbled, right?"

"I have in my notes, sir, that the accused hurled him down over the rocks."

"Gabriel could easily have said, *I heard him go down over the rocks.*"

"That's not what he said. Because he added, 'I shot him as he flailed.'"

"But you're not sure those were his exact words. He was talking in a low voice, you said, sobbing and gasping, so he was hardly distinct. He could have said, *I shouted at him as he flailed.*"

"That's definitely not what I heard."

It was nearing four-thirty. The last witness, the last day of this hearing. I couldn't allow it to end on such a contrary note; I sought a rhetorical flourish: "What you did hear correctly, Corporal, was a calm affirmation on Day Four, when you asked him what he was in jail for. In his exact words, his answer was . . . ?"

He looked from me to Lukey, to the judge, but got no help. "He said, 'I'm being framed for murder.'"

I resisted the urge to punch that home. Why spoil the moment with overkill? I sat.

Hammersmith remained stone-faced. "Ten o'clock tomorrow."

From "Where the Squamish River Flows," *A Thirst for Justice*, © W. Chance

DESPITE THAT LOVELY LITTLE TOUCH at the end, Beauchamp was clearly disappointed with the day's effort. A loss to Knepp, a draw with Lorenzo, when he had needed to deliver each a shattering blow.

The bits of cross-examination reproduced above show the best and the worst of him, and the worst of him was sad indeed. Note how often he telegraphed his punches. Be it remembered, however, that at twenty-five he was far from attaining the form of his prime years, when he could disarm a witness with a smile while slitting his throat.

Nor had he learned to make full use of his large, commanding voice or imbue it with emotion. (In subsequent years he got over inhibitions about doing so by fortifying the defence table's water pitcher with gin.)

It should surprise no one that the troika of Knepp, Lorenzo, and Jettles defended so well against our young challenger. These were not rookies; all had been in court many times, the two senior officers battle-hardened veterans, all led expertly by their commanding officer, Leroy Lukey, who had drilled them relentlessly. (This was confirmed to me by Gene Borachuk.)

Significantly, in the final stages of that critical last cross, Beauchamp took a cautious approach. Instead of attacking Lorenzo as a shameless perjurer, he sought to blur the words of Swift's alleged confession, thus seeming to accept that Swift had made some sort of inculpatory statement.

I asked Beauchamp if that meant he'd decided to open up a manslaughter defence, based on an unintended homicide, as the safest route to save his client's life.

"I don't know what was in my mind," he said. "I guess I was looking for any port in the storm."

Whatever the reason, that decision made manifest his loss of confidence – in his client, in himself. As Ophelia Moore confided, he was so "obsessively depressing" it was a chore to be around him.

Ophelia and I supped that evening in a popular but culturally confusing all-you-can-eatery called the Marco Polo Chinese Smorgasbord. Over my tong shui and shrimp I continued to be bugged by a question a reporter had asked as we fled 312: "What's your theory about the pink panties, sir?" First of all, it bugged me that he was no longer calling me "Arthur" but "sir" – more proof the press was distancing itself from me, seeing as more inept than brave my defence of an underdog.

It also bugged me that this newsman followed Ophelia and me halfway to Chinatown without once daring me to repeat my insinuations that Knepp and Lorenzo lied under oath. If politely asked, I would have done so, bluntly, and dared them to sue for slander.

Also vexing me, as I admitted to Ophelia, was the pink panties puzzle. "Maybe something *was* going on between them."

"Dermot and Gabriel?" Ophelia spooned up some egg drop soup, sat back. "Get realistic. Dermot was fucking faculty wives and grad students at a pace right out of Ripley's 'Believe It or Not.' And Gabriel . . . well, if it's not obvious to you, it sure is to me. He's pure, unadulterated hetero. He gives me all the looks, the signals."

"He does?"

"Under normal circumstances I'd be climbing all over him." Said as if she meant it.

"Well, maybe his unadulterated hetero hormones triggered some kind of wild outburst. What if it wasn't suicide? What if –"

"Bullshit. Mulligan was about to be exposed by a cuckolded colleague. That threatened his totally utilitarian relationship with Irene, a woman invaluable if not loved – his cook, secretary, washerwoman, fuck-who-you-want freedom-giver, full-time serf, and, presumably, donor of the pink unmentionables. More importantly, an illustrious reputation was about to be reshaped as a source of side-splitting humour. Abject with despair but always neat, never wasteful, he lays out his clothes, conjures up Rita Schumacher as a masturbatory last wish, then kicks off his sticky bloomers and jumps."

I applauded her by clicking chopsticks.

Still ill-tempered after Gabriel's eleventh-hour disclosures, I'd been unable to face him after court, so Ophelia had attended to him while I brooded on the courthouse lawn. He too was massively depressed, she said, blaming himself for not being on the level about so many things. He assured her there were no more secrets.

But I'd heard that song from other clients. I felt I could no longer trust anything, even my instincts. "What if Lorenzo was actually telling the truth?"

"How unlikely." She had finally located a retired nun, Sister Beatrice, who'd been at Pius Eleven Residential School in 1942. Affecting a cloying voice: "Principal Mulligan was such a *kind* young man, so *spiritual.* We all just *loved* him."

"Well, what would you expect Sister Beatrice to say? Stay with me on this. What if Lorenzo isn't lying? What if it's our guy who's lying? About everything."

"Yeah? About being punched and kicked by Knepp and Jettles? Do you think your pal Borachuk was lying?"

On taking the stand, Gabriel would offer his own version about that, and the many other facets of the case that, he'd bluntly say, the police lied about. The defence was to open on Friday, after argument on motions Thursday. Gabriel would be the sole witness and, I feared, would miscarry in that role, despite all our coaching. It would be clear to the jury that he'd never graduated from charm school. He would decline not only to kiss the Bible but to swear on it. He wouldn't be recanting any revolutionary views – of that I was painfully certain. Smitty would snipe at him artfully, create confusion, contradictions, expose his irritable side, his disdain for bourgeois justice. The Hammer would rattle him, infuriate him. Gabriel had been a sleeping volcano, and an eruption was due.

Ophelia fumbled for her smokes, tried to switch topics. "The bylaw inspector shut down Isy's. Did you hear about that? 'Lewd and immoral performance.' This is such a hick town. Lenny Bruce called it the last outpost of puritanical hypocrisy. We're going to be on an entertainers' blacklist; we'll be down to Liberace, the Happy Gang, and Paul Anka."

I wasn't to be distracted. "No, I've got it. This is what happened: Gabriel did confess to that clown, but he lied. Gabby, the locals call him. Gabby lied. He didn't really kill Mulligan but he wanted Lorenzo and Knepp to believe he did."

"You're losing it, Arthur."

I batted away her smoke. "Don't you get it? This is a carefully crafted plot by Gabriel to get himself falsely charged with a murder so he can be hanged, feeding a martyr complex inspired by Louis Riel and somehow advancing Native rights through an upswelling of our notorious national guilt."

"Yeah, and he beat off into some pink panties to titillate the press and get even more publicity for his cause. Hey, maybe Hammersmith's part of the plot, and the entire trial is a fake."

"There's something we're missing."

"*You're* missing something."

"Bill Swift claims he's alive. That Mulligan faked his own death, disappeared."

"And he's manning the gas pumps at a BA station in Upper Spodunk."

Afterwards she herded me into a taxi. "The sun will rise in the morning, Arthur. It's not over. Get a good night's sleep."

~~~

As I slipped into my suite, I hummed, *I'll see you in my dreams.* The phone began nagging me. It had to be another of Lawonda's former suitors; I'd given the number to nobody but Ophelia and Gertrude.

I tucked away the mickey I'd bought, laid out my writing tools, centred my typewriter. I had to organize a pitch to The Hammer, what we call a no-evidence motion: a motion to direct the jury to acquit. I pictured him smirking. *You can talk till the cows come home, counsel.* He'd enjoyed watching me drown in a sea of damning evidence. I had been a bad boy with my aggravating outbursts.

Manfully I ignored the whining demon on my shoulder (*Why bring home a mickey of rye if you're not going to partake, Arthur?*). I submitted to the phone instead.

"I know you've been intending to call, Arthur, but the thought struck me that you'd forgotten our number."

"How did you get *my* number?"

"I went up to your office and dragged it out of that stubborn young thing who runs interference for you. I had to hint that your father was ill, though I regret to tell you he's quite hale and hearty. I assured her you would never dream of breaking contact with your devoted parents."

"Excuse me, I have something on the stove." I reached up, uncapped the rye, took a big, quick slug, gathered strength. "As doubtless you're aware, Mother, I'm at the tail end of a rather complex murder matter. It has been with me day and night for the past several weeks. I apologize for not having been the dutiful son."

"Dutiful? Is that how you see our relationship? As one of duty?"

"When this is over, let's the three of us go out for dinner."

"Not if you look the way you did on CTV – like a tramp, in that wrinkled suit. Please do something with your hair."

"I am really up against it right now, Mother. Overwhelmed."

"Goodbye, then, *Vale, jurisconsulte.*"

The call ended on that abrupt note, and I punctuated it with another shot of rye, grimacing from its sharp bite, then rolled a sheet into my Smith-Corona.

Again the phone. "I need to speak to Lawonda." A new one, a gruff voice.

"She doesn't live here anymore."

"You better not be covering for her, pal, or I'll take it out of your skin."

"Take what out?"

"She owes me five grand." He disconnected. I used to wonder how Lawonda could afford her fine clothes and furnishings. Not from tips at the Beanery, it seemed.

I worked for an hour on my motion. Its basis: there was no evidence of an essential ingredient of the charge of murder, i.e., an actual death. My fingers kept getting stuck between the keys, their hammers jamming on the page. I was tired, that was the problem. Then I saw with surprise that the mickey was almost empty. I ripped my speech from the typewriter. It was stiff, over-prepared. I'd be better off winging it after a sound sleep.

The phone was ringing. It must have been for Lawonda, because there she was, a swirl of colour as she disrobed. Bubble-gum-pink panties slipped down her ebony legs. The phone wouldn't stop ringing. Her hand grasped my cock . . .

But it was my own hand holding that stiff instrument as I stumbled to the phone. It was barely seven o'clock. Lawonda's castasides never called that early, so it had to be important. I croaked a hello, my throat clogged by night phlegm.

"Tell her I am standink here with Luger pointed at ze right temple."

"Lawonda isn't here."

"You bring her to phone or I having twenty seconds to live." Obscure accent, maybe Slavic.

"Lawonda moved out two months ago! Who is this?"

"Time is wasting. Soon you having my blood on your hands."

A spurned lover's empty threat? I dared not take that chance. "Give me your phone number. I have some contacts. I'll get right back to you." After I called police emergency.

"Ten seconds, you Bolshevik scum."

"Craznik? Is that you?"

"Three, two, one – I die!"

The bang that came wasn't quite the sound of a gun firing, more like a serving spoon hitting a pot.

"Ira?"

"How's it hanging, Stretch?"

"It wasn't, until you woke me up."

"Aw, man, the time difference – I keep forgetting. You had a boner on?"

"Lawonda was here a while ago."

"In your dreams, Studley. She's in Loosiana. I'd give you her number but then you'd just be one of the loonies bugging her with calls. Guess one night with that hot hammer didn't satisfy. She's more addicting than shmeck, man – you're gonna have to sweat her out of your system. How you holding out otherwise? Trial-wise?"

Fine, I told him, adding that I expected to die later that morning under the judge's withering fusillades. Otherwise I didn't need to bring Ira up to speed – the case had been fully reported in Toronto.

"You're going to have to turn your Marilyn Monroe calendar to the wall. It wouldn't be right to use it as a wanging-off aid given she's got a new boyfriend who just happens to be the President of the US of A. I have the inside dope, schnookie – she's just had an abortion, and Kennedy provided the spawn. Expect the CIA to shove her off to keep it covered up. After that, they'll be going after JFK himself. I'm setting up some dates for Ronnie and the Hawks. I'll call you if we do the Coast. Give your hard-on a hug for me."

~~~

"The charge is wholly misconceived, milord." That was me walking to the office, slightly hungover. "It has proceeded on the assumption that Professor Mulligan is not alive, yet he hasn't been formally pronounced dead. If he is dead, where are his remains?"

I was mumbling so loudly that two boys giggled as our paths crossed, repeating, "Where are his remains?"

A grey day, and from the heights of the Burrard Bridge I was denied one of my frequent pleasures on a summer's walk, a view of pretty girls in bathing suits on Sunset Beach. I was actually feeling refreshed that morning by a sleep of unexpected soundness. With the Crown evidence in, no surprises waiting, my brain had turned off its engines for eight hours. I expected my motion to be quickly disposed of, then to be granted the rest of the day to prepare my defence: a final run-through with Gabriel, a tough pretend cross-examination à la Cyrus Smythe-Baldwin.

But what chance would we have with twelve dutiful middle-class strivers brought up to be respectful to police, distrustful of

240

extremists, and chary of minorities, particularly our First Peoples? How could they possibly find the courage to believe veteran officers would perjure themselves so wantonly?

I thought again of Steven Truscott. Aged fourteen and sentenced to hang. A white kid, never in trouble. By the time I got to my building I was in the pits once more.

Pappas was just outside my office by the secretarial pool, propositioning a summer temp, a task he set aside to follow me in. I supposed he intended to lecture me again on how I was handling Hammersmith (*An old-timer might get away with it, not a cocky young punk like you; you got to learn to suck a little*).

He unfolded the *Province*. "At least you're getting some ink off this sucker. 'Cops Conspired to Lie' – that'll make the Palmer brothers happy. Shows them you got a healthy attitude. Guys like the Palmers, they respect a man who goes down fighting. Unless, of course, he goes down for the big count. That they don't respect."

"My guy isn't going down."

"Is there anyone in this town believes that? Including you, hotshot? Way I read it, your chances of bringing this stinker home are next to zero. I could've maybe got you a deal for non-capital, but that's slipping away."

He turned to leave and met Ophelia coming in. They did a little dance in the doorway, Ophelia finally manoeuvring past him. She mimed washing her hands and shaking them dry.

"Smythe-Baldwin's office called. Case is being put down for an hour or so. Mysteriously, they want to meet us at the Coroner's Court."

Now what? I affected nonchalance. "Gee, maybe they're conducting an inquest into their case."

~~~

The Coroner's Court, a deco heritage building near the police station, is now a police museum, but in those days it also housed the city analyst's laboratory, the morgue, and autopsy facilities.

As our cab pulled up, we saw Lukey holding its ornate carved door for Irene Mulligan, who exited grief-stricken. She brushed off his attempts to comfort her and approached us, signalling our driver to wait. "It's his." She daubed at her runny mascara. "I'm sorry. Oh, God, my Dermot . . ."

I couldn't form the words to ask her to complete her sentence, left it to Ophelia. "What do you mean, Irene?"

"His toe."

Lukey barrelled toward us. "Come on, guys, she's in a pretty bad way."

He held the cab door for Irene, who hissed, "Leave me alone. You didn't have to be so cruel."

Leroy pulled a look of repentance as the taxi sped off. "Maybe we should've showed her a photo instead. Now we got to apply to recall her to the stand, making everything even messier, tougher on her."

"What the fuck are you talking about?" Ophelia said as he piloted us to the door.

"Goodness, deary, wash your mouth. That foot that washed up on Gambier Island a couple months ago? We got a match."

We took the stairs, but to the morgue, not the courtroom. Smitty was there, along with Dr. Brenner, the city pathologist.

Smitty got right to business. "Please explain to our guests the process of ocean decomposition on the human body."

"Sharks get most of the blame, but seals, crabs, and other sea creatures also feast upon a corpse. As well, limbs commonly detach as a body decomposes. Over several weeks and months, feet in particular undergo adipocere formation, the fleshy parts turning into a waxy substance no animal will eat. Feet do not normally float, but the shoe has been determined to be buoyant enough to be carried by whatever currents carry flotsam to the shores of Howe Sound."

"Can you help our dumbfounded friends with an estimate of how long the body – or at least the foot – had been in the ocean?"

"I would hesitate to say on oath, but given the limited extent of adipocere formation, I would suggest a range of several weeks to several months. Some more biochemical testing could be done."

Lukey took over. "The runner is a men's size-eight Puma, right foot, which Irene confirmed he had a pair like this, but she couldn't identify the sock; there are only remnants left. Mulligan's boots, the pair found with his clothes, were eight and a half – close enough, I guess, given with boots he'd need thicker socks. Missing Persons wasn't interested in men because they thought it was a lady's foot – there was a speck of fingernail polish on the big toenail. Hey, who knows what secrets lie in the hearts of men? 'The professor wore panties.' Sounds like an Ellery Queen title."

He gave me a friendly poke, and to keep my balance I had to grab the stack of body drawers. One of them was open. A wrinkled white foot, on its side.

"So I'm thinking about those panties, and I figure what's there to lose – let's show Irene the foot. Okay, I handled it badly with her. Maybe I was a little flip . . ."

"Facetious, Leroy," Smitty said.

"I make no defence. I couldn't stop cracking up when she said the baby toe was his. So look at the little toenail. Just a wee, hard pebble of a toenail – that's how she id'd it. They're vestigial anyway – right, Doc? – our toenails, given we no longer hang from trees."

Dr. Brenner kept out of it. The nubbin was the size of a small mole. I wasn't about to touch that cold, wizened foot. I was feeling nauseated.

"Definitely Dermot's right foot, says her affidavit." Lukey extended a carbon. "Forgive my typing – I was in a hurry, she was kind of stressed out."

Eight lines, concluding with "sworn by me this second day of August, 1962." Her signature and that of a justice of the peace. All my rehearsing, all to naught. *If he is dead, where are his remains?* The last loophole filled.

Even the lack of socks on the riverbank site was explained. Presumably Mulligan brought extra footwear in case his boots got damp.

"Well," said Smitty, "shall we carry on to court?" A solemn look my way. "Must we really put her through this?"

From "Where the Squamish River Flows," *A Thirst for Justice*, © W. Chance

A SIDE NOTE: Those who prefer their humour black may be amused to learn that after the case concluded the foot was returned to Irene Mulligan, at her request, for burial at Mountain View Cemetery. There was even a small private funeral. Eric Nicol had a morbid take on it in his column in the *Province*. Would there be a second funeral if the rest of the body washed up? Would each part of Professor Mulligan merit its own burial ceremony?

Mercifully those questions have never had to be answered. The size-eight foot with the nubbly little toenail is all that has ever been found of Dermot Mulligan, D.Th., Ph.D.

Ophelia and I searched for reaction from Gabriel as we related the latest downturn in fortunes. Nothing. Not a flicker. All emotion swallowed, denied.

"Best for Irene that she finally knows," Ophelia said. "She can get on with her life."

I chimed in with another uplifting viewpoint. "Doesn't affect our main line of defence. Suicide. Enhances it, really; let's us focus on it."

"Spare the bullshit, Arthur." Gabriel's voice was low, monotonic. "It's another door closed, isn't it? So my dad was wrong. He was telling me last week Dermot went on the run because he'd done something evil, light years worse than screwing a faculty wife. Dad met him a couple of times, didn't like him."

We said we were pleased to hear his father had visited.

"He came with Mom. Finally."

Then his feelings betrayed him, a glistening in the eye. An awareness, maybe, that his dad, that cynical victim of white connivery, might not have lost the ability to love.

I looked away, at the wall. *Burn in hell, Scheister.* That complaint seemed somehow, arcanely, directed at me. The wet-behind-the-ears shyster who wanted this murder case for its supposed glory. Who didn't have the experience for it, the wisdom, the judgment.

I checked my watch – they'd be waiting for us in Assize Court. I called for the jailers to release us from the cell, which seemed to be closing in on me, a Lewis Carroll event.

Gabriel collected himself. "The truth will emerge decades after I'm gone." Soft, toneless again. "There will be official expressions of regret. Unfortunately, they will say, the system sometimes fails. And then the system will just carry on failing for years, a century maybe, until it collapses under all its dead weight." Another Riel quote: "*A century is only a spoke in the wheel of everlasting time.*"

This was not a case of his martyr complex finding new life from an invigorated prospect of death. After our many swings of fortune, it sounded, finally, of the extinction of hope.

~~~

We would be seen by the jury as the bad guys if Irene was dragged back into court (*I'm sorry, Mrs. Mulligan, but they insisted*). In any event, Gabriel felt concerned enough about her emotional health to instruct me to dispense with her viva voce evidence regarding the toe and its highly evolved toenail. In court, as Smitty solemnly filed her affidavit as the final exhibit, I watched the jury, imagined their minds snapping shut now that they had proof of death. Cooper, the foreman, turned to look at a juror behind him. An exchange of nods.

"That completes the case for the Crown."

The jury went out and Hammersmith puckered his lips, as if offering me a sarcastic good-luck kiss. "You have the floor, Mr. Beauchamp. You may now seek to persuade me, with your usual eloquent oratory, that I ought to direct the jury to acquit. Explain to me, if that's your position, why you think the Crown's case is full of holes."

"There is no evidence whatsoever aside from the lies of Corporal Lorenzo that the accused was at the alleged murder scene. Otherwise, the evidence is entirely consistent with suicide. It is the most rational conclusion available. On that basis, the defence moves for a directed verdict of acquittal." There was no point wasting more breath.

"Judgment. I have heard ample evidence that if believed by a jury would almost inevitably lead to conviction. I need not review it. The case will go to the jury. Tomorrow you will open for the defence. If that involves a continued attempt to malign our enforcers of the law, so be it. Adjourned till tomorrow."

"White man's justice!" Shouted not by my client but his father, his crutch raised like a war club. Celia Swift was weeping beside him. Hammersmith looked coldly their way, then retreated to his chambers.

~~~

Smitty motioned me to join him at the gentlemen barristers' urinals, and over a joint piss he offered to treat me to lunch. "Just the two of us? Mrs. Moore's close presence would cause me an irregular heartbeat, and Leroy can be hard on the digestion."

We agreed to meet at Chez Antoine, and I told Ophelia to get a head start tuning up Gabriel for the witness stand. We didn't want him over-rehearsed, but on a loose leash, one that could be tightened if he became too discursive or belligerent or wandered onto perilous political terrain. I had little confidence that he wouldn't pull something. I felt him incapable of tact. The one thing he'd been doing right with the jury was making eye contact, though in a challenging way that might have unnerved them.

Antoine's was a new restaurant on Robson Street (known widely as Robsonstrasse back then, when it had a vaguely German flavour). But this was French, new, tricked out with Lautrec posters but otherwise attractive, with an upper outer terrace overlooking the sidewalk, a next-door flower shop, and, across the street, Danceland, proudly offering "The Best Twisting in Town."

Smitty was on the terrace under a patio umbrella, fondling one of his Cubans as he engaged with a sour-looking elf in chef's whites. "This, Antoine, is the young talent you have heard me praise so unreservedly, Arthur Beauchamp. Treat him like Charles de Gaulle."

"I spit on de Gaulle." He didn't offer me his hand, and swept away.

Smitty explained that Antoine had run a starred restaurant in Algiers popular with the *pieds noirs* and the OAS. "A fascist bunch, really. Terrorists. He had to flee after independence. Marvellous chef, however. Good food *ne sait rien de la politique,* however liberal may be one's appetite."

He put out his cigar as an *amuse-bouche* appeared – escargots in tiny pots of garlic butter. A waiter joined us, rattling off the day's specials.

"While we consider the entrées, François," said Smitty, "I think we might be interested in *salades vertes et huîtres Balzac,* and may we double up on the escargots?"

I hadn't expected this to be a quick lunch anyway. I wondered if Smitty had more on his plate than the shells of his escargots. Probably he was just doing me a courtesy, entertaining the prospective loser.

"But our immediate, overriding need is for a matched pair of martinis, François, and they must be dry enough to burn the throat. Sliver of peel with mine. Would that satisfy you, Arthur?"

"*Exactement la même chose, merci.*"

"A simple table wine . . . let's say the fifty-seven Château Tour Haut Vignoble, which you might open early to let it sniff these lovely summer breezes."

Nor was it going to be a dry lunch. Those vital items of business attended to, we moved on to the more mundane matter of murder, which Smitty opened by raising his martini. "To justice, wherever she may be hiding." We clinked, drank. That delicious tickle of juniper on the tongue.

The starters arrived and I nibbled mine while Smitty attacked his, eating, swallowing, talking, eating.

"I have assessed you, young Arthur, as uncommonly perceptive, so you are likely aware that you are dead."

I choked on my martini.

"I have also assessed the jury – I am rather a hand at this – and they all seem to defer to the foreman, Mr. Ozzie Cooper. He played three games with the Boston Bruins one season, enough to give him godlike status in this idolatrous dominion. And I have learned he has a brother on the federal force. He has made up his mind. Mind you, out of twelve persons good and true, there's always the chance of a resister – some fierce libertarian distrustful of authority – or a nincompoop nursing a grievance over a speeding ticket. But the eleven other good Canadian burghers, who respect our famed Royal Mounties above politicians, journalists, lawyers, and maybe even Gordie Howe and Tim Horton, will bully the poor fellow into submission. No question of that, old boy."

Smitty was playing with his cigar, threatening to reignite it. "Another pair of these – what do you say?" He held up his near-empty glass. Mine, I saw, had been drained.

"How much of this is bluff, Smitty?"

"Look here, old chap, I think you deserve better than to lose your client to the hangman. You will not be able to live with yourself. These are still your salad days – well short of your thirties, are you not?"

"Twenty-six in a few months."

"Truly? All the more remarkable. As I have observed, you have a keen instinct for what we do, and skills rare among many who have toiled for decades in the trenches. You may yet strop those skills to razor sharpness. Or you may not. A death sentence can be particularly devastating to a young counsel, can destroy pride and confidence, and even one's career – especially, if I may be so bold, if he is haunted by his own irreversible errors."

Irreversible errors? My hand shook as I lowered my glass. My lamb tenderloin arrived like a reprieve. We tucked into our food in silence but for a few appreciative exchanges about the fare. The empty Haut Vignoble was removed and replaced by a fresh one. Finally Smitty struck a match and cranked up his cigar with a few quick puffs, their exhaust catching the breeze, whipping past my nose. His sigh was either of sadness or contentment, I couldn't tell.

"Something happened between Dermot Mulligan and Gabriel Swift on the banks of the Squamish. I believe a homicide was the end result of a confrontation. I am not comfortable with Lorenzo's testimony, but I won't say he lied. My duty was to proceed without qualm or question to put forward his evidence as it was presented to me."

"Your case fails if the jury disbelieves him."

"To do so they will have to disbelieve Knepp as well, who pummelled you quite hard. Part of the game – it happens to all of us.

But he's a polished witness whose square-chinned looks and boyish smile have captivated the ladies of our jury. Miss Kempthorne, the travel agent, was virtually swooning. You lack even a molecule of corroborative proof that he is a liar. Or any of them. And you did it to yourself."

I had to admit guilt. "I made an unwise deal with Gene Borachuk."

He nodded; Borachuk had obviously told him about it. My promise not to cross Borachuk about the assault in the Squamish cells had been a bad trade. The backgrounder on Lorenzo had paid off poorly.

The wind corralled more cigar fumes and spun them toward me, causing my eyes to water. I played with a twig of mint on my plate, unable to look at Smitty for fear he'd think I was crying.

"Had you been able to trap Knepp and Jettles in that one grievous lie – and let's assume it was a lie – you'd have cast a pall on their entire testimony. Your undertaking to Borachuk has queered that line of defence. It's now Swift's word against theirs."

That's what he meant by my being haunted by irreversible errors. Even if unwritten, a lawyer's undertaking is like God's writ; I could no more break or bend it than I could a steel rail. I'd face disbarment for even attempting to renege.

"Okay, thanks for the report card, Smitty. What does all this come down to?"

"It's already a nasty trial, Arthur. With nasty repercussions. Innuendo, exaggeration, gossip. An internationally celebrated writer/scholar – one of the few we cultural outlanders can boast of. His legacy at risk, his name shamed in death, his lucid, provocative critiques of our moral dilemmas buried in the compost of slander. The abusive ex-principal, the panties-wearing adulterer – all grist for the spiteful flesh-eaters of academia. Eight honorary degrees, had he not? And such a writer."

I felt a little overpowered by that speech. Weakly: "You've read him."

"Of course. But who am I to speak of our distinguished late friend with any familiarity? You were his student, I believe."

"I had that honour. In short, Smitty, what are we talking about here?"

"A plea to non-capital murder. Saving the posthumous reputation of a major thinker and writer. Saving the life of a bright but troubled young man. A sentence of life imprisonment, yes, but parole will be available after twenty years. Your fellow can walk out of there in his early forties if he impresses the parole board. Meanwhile, he could take correspondence courses; the penitentiary has excellent programs – he'd easily earn a degree."

Smitty carried on, a long, hypnotic flow: not only would a life and a reputation be rescued, but also the career of a praiseworthy young talent. Then he evoked the black-robed spectre of The Hammer, who would persuade any doubters on the jury to convict, and would weep no crocodile tears as he imposed the mandatory death sentence.

"I can assure you, Smitty, unequivocally, that Gabriel Swift will never plead guilty to murdering Dr. Mulligan. He would rather die."

"Ah, well, that is too bad. I lost a client to the rope many years ago."

"I'm aware." The notorious Emily McCubbin, who poisoned her husband as a reward for his many adulteries. "I studied the transcript."

"What it does not show is that I'd wangled a life sentence for non-capital. She declined it. Only hanging I've ever attended. They do rather depress one."

It's your turn, was what I was hearing. *Make me an offer.*

"Maybe . . ." I had trouble saying it. "Manslaughter."

Smitty's response was to sit back, eyes closed, pondering perhaps, or simply enjoying his cigar.

I repeated to myself that complex word. *Manslaughter.* Killing without intention, without malice aforethought. The maximum sentence, life imprisonment, was reserved for the most grievous cases. Death by drunken brawl might merit five. Death of a renowned thinker would be more costly. Then I tried to picture myself recommending it to Gabriel, and I flinched. "Possible, not likely."

Smitty set the cigar in his ashtray, giving it a rest, as the waitress collected plates. "The *profiteroles au chocolat* are made not here but in heaven. You may find the berries gratin healthier, though that seems such an irrelevancy."

I said I'd pass. He chose the profiteroles and insisted I join him in a snifter of VSOP Hennessy. I asked for a coffee as well – I was fairly woozy with drink. Smitty, in contrast, seemed perfectly lucid. I wondered what the Attorney General was paying him that he could afford such lunches; this would run to at least forty dollars.

"Manslaughter," he said, swirling his cognac. "A tough sell." To his employer, I assumed – Robert Bonner, the Attorney General. "But I must say you showed some very deft footwork with Lorenzo in setting it up. *I shot him as he flailed* becomes *I shouted at him.* I rather liked that." Another swirl, a sip. "Bob would want a substantial sentence, I warn you. Not life, but up there. Twenty, twenty-five years."

This was Smitty's backup position, obviously. I resisted a powerful urge to offer my hand on it. Done – twenty years. Depression relaxes its grip, worries scatter to the winds. It's on to further challenges, the Palmer brothers, organized crime, trials featuring the immoral and the simply evil, clients I wouldn't care a hoot about . . .

I pictured Gabriel looking at me with astonishment and disillusion as I put such a plea deal to him. I did care a hoot about him, that was the whole damn problem with this case. I found him stimulating, challenging, *homo sui generis.* I wanted a friendship that would survive this case, survive his imprisonment, survive our stressful roles as counsel and client.

I explained I'd set the afternoon aside to confer with the accused. Smitty had François bring over the phone. He called the Criminal Registry, asked them to pass word to his Lordship that "counsel were in discussions" – code for settlement negotiations. A similar message went to Leroy Lukey, who undertook to advise Ophelia. Word soon came back that Hammersmith proposed returning the jury to their hotel until Monday. We agreed.

Smitty and I were able to relax then and enjoy several more cognacs while I peppered him, Wentworth-like, with questions about his many notable cases.

~~~

After parting from Smitty at around half past three, I found myself in front of the flower shop, literally scratching my head – as if that would somehow jump-start memory. I had no idea where I'd parked the Bug that morning. A two-hour zone, that's all that came back; now I would have to shell out yet another buck for a ticket.

It didn't strike me that I ought not to be driving anyway until, twisting to look at a pair of ankles, I almost sat on a tray of peonies. The ankles belonged to the flower shop saleslady, who asked if she could help me. Odd what one remembers – often the trivial – and what one doesn't. I have no recall of ordering roses for my mother (where did that impulse come from?), but the next day she called Gertrude to thank me.

The first lounge I hit was The Library in the Hotel Vancouver, whose bookish decor I felt might help me analyze that altogether too cordial plea-bargain session. I felt I should level off, so I had a coffee with my shot of rye.

Twenty to twenty-five – a final position, or had Smitty got the nod to negotiate down? How far? Ten, twelve, thirteen years, less parole, less a year and a half for good behaviour . . . *The time will go by in a blink, Gabriel. What do you say, old buddy, old pal?*

Manslaughter: snap it in two and it's either *man slaughter* or *man's laughter* – which is what I keep hearing in my head. *Your laughter, Gabriel, your mocking laughter, you with your martyr complex, with all your nobility and arrogance . . . You will see a jail sentence as the worst of outcomes, the only ones you will countenance being acquittal or hanging.*

Damn you, Gabriel, you dissembled and equivocated with me about matters so critical as to disentitle you from choosing your preferred outcome. Surely a mind as penetrating as yours can see the elegant logic of manslaughter. You were reading the memoir; you had Dermot on your mind the day he died. You're prone to fits of temper and aggression – anything could have sparked it off.

Did Dermot confess he'd covered up crimes against children at Pie Eleven? Did that inflame you, Gabriel – the hypocrisy of it? You'd been proud of him, hadn't you, for taking a tough, unpopular stand against the residential school system. And you exploded, didn't you? You didn't mean to kill him. That's why it's only manslaughter.

And if that's what happened, I can forgive you for it, Gabriel. I still want to be your friend. Please make it easy on yourself. Make it easy for me . . .

From "Where the Squamish River Flows," *A Thirst for Justice*, © W. Chance

CERTAIN REPORTS SUGGEST Beauchamp received with relief and enthusiasm Smythe-Baldwin's openness to manslaughter, but he claims to have been hesitant, fearful that an injustice might be done, all the while fearing Swift rejection (as it were). Ophelia Moore thinks Beauchamp advanced such a deal because he'd suffered a massive loss of confidence. In himself more than in his client. In his ability to pull a victory from the ashes of a trial that on the whole had gone badly for him. "Old Smitty reeled him in like a fish," she said, adding that he saw in Arthur someone who hungered for his approval, so he played the avuncular game. "Poor Arthur built up so much trust and respect that he got conned. He forgot why they called him The Fox."

That theory seems less cynical when we remind ourselves that Beauchamp had a yawning need for the love he never felt from his father. He had long been a fan of the old Q.C.,* and though not as obsessive as those who lurk outside the mansions of rock stars, he'd been copying him for years. The cozy rapport with jurors. The shark-like circles swum around witnesses before striking. A tongue that spared neither opposing counsel nor judge. The oratorical flourishes and overblown mannerisms that became more common in Beauchamp's fustian years.†

With all due respect to former Madam Justice Moore, I hold a less acerbic view of Smythe-Baldwin's willingness to consider manslaughter. The veteran defender was famously

---

* Smythe-Baldwin passed away in 1981, predictably of a heart attack, though some called it heartbreak after his failed defence of the serial killer Dr. Au, known as The Surgeon.
† See Chapter Eighteen, "The Fustian Years."

warm-hearted and helpful to young colleagues of the defence bar, and though he believed that a homicide occurred by the Squamish River, he also felt that Beauchamp had got a raw deal. I was not surprised that my biographee became touchy when I put to him Moore's view he had been under Smythe-Baldwin's spell. Clearly, forty-eight years later, it remains a raw issue between him and Moore.

At any rate, he went home that night to brood over the matter. It must have tormented him, for Moore recalls him looking drained the next morning.

On entering Ophelia's office, I fell prostrate on her little sofa. The excesses of the previous day had produced a thundering headache.

"I suppose you blame Smitty." She stared pitilessly at me from behind her desk.

"I couldn't keep up with him. Anyway, we're trying to work something out. I told him bluntly there was no chance of Swift's copping a plea to non-capital. But he might go for manslaughter." I held up a hand to forestall loud response. "I'm going to discuss it with Pappas, but you first. Quietly."

"I guessed something like that was happening. I tried to phone you at home." She had more bad news, from the Prince Albert diocese. "The bishop has been following this in the news. His chief flunky says the Church wants nothing to do with it. They're putting the clamps on everyone who ever worked at Pie Eleven, especially Sister Beatrice." Whom Ophelia had just phoned. A falsetto imitation: "I'm not going to talk about it. I don't know anything."

Ophelia told reception to hold her calls, opened her window, and smoked her way through my recitation of Smitty's spiel – the whole thing – the critique of my performance, the broad hint that Attorney General Bonner wanted this nasty matter settled quietly to stop the hemorrhaging of reputation of a famous local, the pitch about Gabriel earning a college degree in a minimum security facility, early parole, the dangers of leaving the case with Ozzie Cooper and his fans on the jury.

She butted out with an air of decisiveness. "Smitty must have decided he's got a shitty case."

I ought to have expected as much from her. Clearly (as my thinking went back then, prior to my supposed liberation from false assumptions) women didn't have sharp instincts for criminal litigation, an understanding of how we play the game. Ophelia might have been scoring well in family court, but this was the big time.

"He's got a cinch." I tried to tell myself I wasn't exaggerating, but now, in 2011, I'm not sure if Ophelia was wrong to slam me in her talks with Wentworth. That massive lack of confidence . . .

"Something has gone haywire; that's my bet," she said. "Maybe Doug Wall got tongue-loose in a bar, told everyone he was paid off by Roscoe. Maybe Lorenzo had an attack of conscience and flipped out. Whatever, they're hiding it from us."

"Okay, Ophelia, we take that chance, and it turns out Smitty was playing us fair and we end up killing our client. You'd feel okay about that?"

I gained a sitting position and tendered her my theory, the one I'd worked at so assiduously while earning my hangover. I reminded her of Gabriel's words to me: *Something happened there, I think, in Pius Eleven Res School. He left the Church soon after.* Gabriel had forgiven Mulligan for sins committed on his watch – or so I'd believed.

"Dermot was complaining of writer's block. So naturally, during one of their daily discussions, they explore the reasons for it. Finally Gabriel wrests from him the dark and terrible secret Dermot hadn't been able to put to paper. A secret so shocking that it prompted in Gabriel a sense of betrayal – his god had failed – and ignited a fierce anger, a murderous rage."

Ophelia applauded. "Bravo, well-rehearsed. So he sits down, plans it out, and coolly arranges a suicide tableau before chucking Dermot in the drink. Right. Both essentials of capital murder are there: planning and deliberation. Congratulations, Arthur. You figured it out, now you can let them hang Gabriel in peace."

Her scorn stunned me. She didn't let up. "Oh, yeah, and somewhere along the way, Gabriel prevails upon him to jerk off in his panties. Arthur, you can't do this thing with a loser's attitude. Do you or do you not believe Gabriel did in Dermot Mulligan?"

Hesitation. "I can't answer that."

"Try."

I accepted a cigarette – I needed a nicotine lift. "I'm not certain I can separate what I believe from what I want to believe."

"You're going to advise him to accept twenty years? Even if he's innocent?"

"That's their opener. I'll bargain them way down."

"Okay, sixteen years. Is that about right for a guy framed for punching a racist cop in the mouth? You're really underestimating Gabriel. He's bright – brilliant in his way, he's capable of being a very persuasive witness for himself." She was unrelenting. "Damn it, you have it in you to pull this one out. Smitty sees that; it's why he likes your manslaughter."

I abandoned the cigarette and rose. "I'm going to put it to Gabriel. If he shows interest, I think we can assume he did it."

"Sorry if I don't join you. The whole thing makes me sick."

~~~

However base as a human being, Alex Pappas was a crafty court-room veteran whose reaction I welcomed after that frigid exchange.

"Boy oh boy, you got to count that as a win – a big win. What did you agree to do, marry his ugly daughter? Was he drunk? You want to grab it before he returns to his senses."

He got on the blower to Bullingham and gaily relayed the news. "Give me some credit, Roy. I mentored him, the firm's golden boy."

He handed me the receiver. Bully told me we must pop open some champagne when it wrapped up and have a little talk.

They all seemed to assume the golden boy would have no trouble bringing the accused around.

~~~

Old Jethro expressed disappointment, as I signed in, that I was alone. "Where's your female associate? She's some doll. Real smart cookie, Miss Moore, real persuasive."

Maybe that's why I hadn't insisted she come. I didn't want her persuading Gabriel to make the wrong choice. I didn't want him to commit himself, not yet.

He'd been moved to the Protective Custody Unit. PCU. "He got into a fight at breakfast, and now we got a death threat against him. It's what happens when you get famous."

A scrap. I found that distressing; it wasn't how one earned time off for good behaviour. The threat had come from the White Clansmen, a few of whose members were guests at Oakie. Seventeen years since Hitler's end, and people like that were still floating around.

Gabriel was playing chess in the common area of the segregation wing, and he signalled me to wait while he checkmated his opponent. There were other visitors: a probation officer, a clergyman, an assortment of glum relatives. The poor fellow Hammersmith had jailed for having been indiscreet at the bathhouses.

The ambience was less repressive than in the main cellblocks, mostly because PCU housed not the dangerous but the endangered – informers, misfits, sex offenders, the occasional corrupt cop or politician. It was unusual for one who'd merely been in a fight to be sent there rather than isolation. The warden's real motive might have been to limit Gabriel's effectiveness as an organizer and advocate for his fellow inmates.

By now I had enough Aspirins in me to mask my pain, but Gabriel gave me a frowning once-over as he joined me, probably guessing that I'd tied one on. He was astute that way, a good reader of people, so I confessed. "I relaxed a little too hard yesterday." I chose not to say celebrated.

"As long as you weren't drowning your sorrows."

"Why did those characters threaten you?"

"Because I called one of them a racist piece of shit. He came at me and he got his thumb broken."

His casual attitude rankled me. "Dying with a shiv between your ribs is even more ridiculous and bathetic than dying at the end of a rope."

He shrugged; he wasn't worried, he had friends in there. That was true – he was widely admired on the inside. Not by Corrections, though, to whom he represented trouble: he was too vocal, an agitator, demanding of rights. He'd initiated several complaints, caused an annoying lot of paperwork. (I had an awful premonition of guards turning their back on him in the yard.)

"How's the writing going?"

"The atmosphere in here isn't conducive to the arts. I'm doing a Dermot – I'm blocked. What's up?"

"I want you to sit quietly and listen to this. Afterwards, ask any questions you want, then take a few days to absorb it all. The Crown may be willing to accept a guilty plea to manslaughter – homicide without intent, in the heat of the moment."

He didn't storm off. Remained quite still, in fact, eyes large as if in surprise – or a surge of relief?

I felt encouraged. I parroted Smitty's pitch: our bleak outlook, the expected hanging address from the judge, a jury in thrall to a foreman whose brother was a Mountie. I tried to describe the negotiations in as neutral a way as possible, though I delicately left out the bits about the emasculation of my promising career. I told him the Crown could get soft on the twenty years. In any event, such a stiff sentence could be appealed. Early parole could be sought.

A flicker of annoyance – I was trying too hard to sell this. "What about the truth, Arthur? What about my right to take the stand and tell the truth?"

"Okay, there's an enormous amount to explain. How your prints got in Dermot's wallet. Why you begged Monique to alibi for you. We can't corroborate your account of being in your cabin all afternoon. That you were absorbed in Dermot's memoir has unfortunate connotations, given the prosecution's vengeance theory."

"What is your estimate of my chances?"

"Not in our favour."

"Spell it out bluntly."

My spelling out was sterile, formal. "A verdict of capital murder is more likely than an acquittal. Hammersmith will likely curtail the options of non-capital murder or manslaughter, based on your testimony that you weren't present. Your word against Lorenzo's on that issue. If they believe him, they will believe you killed with intent and will convict you of capital murder." Gabriel's searing gaze didn't falter. "If I can get them down substantially from twenty, I will likely recommend this deal. It's your right to seek another opinion. I could ask Harry Rankin to see you."

"I didn't level with you about a couple of things. Is that why you're giving up on me, for not being straight with you?"

"I am bloody well *not* giving up on you." That was so vehement it sounded false.

Gabriel contemplated one of the barred windows, as if assessing his chances – Deer Lake was out there, a swim to freedom. Or maybe he didn't want me to see his struggle to control himself. "What would I admit to?"

"You would say nothing. Simply plead to the manslaughter indictment."

"The judge has to know what I did. He doesn't sentence in a vacuum."

"A sufficiently ambiguous recital of facts will have to be filed. It remains to be worked out,"

"How about . . . when I caught Dermot masturbating, I kicked him into the fucking river. How does that sound? Would you like me to admit to something like that?" The sarcasm suggested the fuse had been lit. "Is that recital of facts ambiguous enough, Arthur?" He was half out of his chair. "For Christ's sake, do *you* think I killed Dermot Mulligan?"

Instead of hedging with the standard disclaimer (*what I think doesn't matter*), I simply asked, "*Did* you kill Dermot Mulligan?"

He didn't explode but visibly deflated, as if he'd taken a punch. Wearily he shook his head several times. He wasn't just expressing denial, I think now, forty-nine years later. There was also bafflement, disillusion. Shock at my betrayal.

From "Where the Squamish River Flows," *A Thirst for Justice*, © W. Chance

WE MUST CREDIT BEAUCHAMP for staying relatively sober that week, despite the crushing pressures on him, despite the sense of timidity and guilt he must have felt. Most of the pressure came from his bosses, who believed he'd engineered the plea bargain of the decade and were dismayed that he'd told the client not to make a rush decision.

I believe Beauchamp when he says their cajolery had no effect on him. I believe it because he needed no help in pursuing a course he'd committed himself to, after what he claimed was a nebulous reaction from Swift. (Beauchamp wouldn't relate this privileged conversation, but a note dictated to his file reads: *G to think over, 2 days.*)

Moore could sense the pain he felt, and was somewhat forgiving. "I may have unfairly accused him of not having the *cojones* to go all the way," she told me. "Arthur persuaded himself – and finally me as well, I guess – that he was ethically bound to put the best interests of an innocent client ahead of any duty to defend when execution was a plausible outcome. It is a touchy issue, with ethical considerations."

Beauchamp had to battle his own conscience, of course, and swallow the bile that rose whenever he thought of Knepp, Jettles, and Lorenzo swigging beers around the barbecue pit, congratulating themselves for putting that lippy Indian where he belonged. But our hero also sought refuge in doubt – maybe Swift did do it, maybe manslaughter was indeed a victory – and he even indulged in the fantasy of Swift pumping his hand in thanks when it was all over.

Much of Beauchamp's difficulty arose from the bond he'd allowed to develop with his client. Even as he speculated about his innocence, he admired him, envied him for qualities he himself lacked: the passion, the rebel spirit, the pride in who he was. Beauchamp couldn't live with the thought of losing him to another Arthur, Canada's pseudonymous hangman.

So he didn't sit by idly as Swift thought it over: he began a diligent campaign to sway him. His primary strategy was to make the deal more palatable. He was repeatedly on the phone with Smythe-Baldwin, begging for something to show his client he was actually working for him, seeking to bargain him down from eighteen years – the Crown's alleged final offer – to less than half of that.

The second leg of his campaign was to recruit allies. He sent a Tragger, Inglis driver up to the Cheakamus Reserve to fetch Bill and Celia Swift to his office. One must assume he was at his most eloquent, because later they spent ninety minutes with their son at Oakalla. Beauchamp also got a letter from the grieving widow urging leniency, a powerful and emotional appeal that can be read on my website.

But the key to getting the client aboard was Jim Brady, the young man's other mentor and father figure. Beauchamp spent a long Saturday evening with Brady and his wife at their home . . .

An old frame house in the heart of working-class Vancouver, not far from the CN yards. Jim had been unavailable earlier – feuding with raiding Steelworkers – but insisted I come for a dinner of fresh sockeye. He and his wife, Grace, were outside, slow-smoking the fish in a pit of cedar chips, when I arrived with a dozen each of Pilsner and roses. The three of us gathered by a backyard picnic table.

I had them laughing over my red-baiting episodes, but when Grace said, "Now you're one of us," I felt a chill. *Us* was the Communist Party, and I had a sense of it, even in those post-Stalin years, as a disciplined secret religion, a persecuted sect. Grace was the CP's provincial treasurer. She and Jim had met at a Party convention back East. She was Montreal Jewish.

I was hiding my anxiety. Gabriel seemed not in a compromising mood; he'd been threatened with a stay in isolation after his loud and scathing lecture to a visiting priest about the res schools. He knew he must decide by Sunday at noon to either gamble with his life or take a plea. Fifteen years, less parole, less time off for good behaviour – that was Smitty's most recent final offer. I'd begged him to go down to nine, but he was constrained by the Attorney General's concern over political implications. Had Mr. Bonner read the gracious, forgiving letter penned by Irene Mulligan? Smitty assured me it would be on the AG's desk in the morning.

The mosquitoes were out, so Jim, Grace, and I retreated to their kitchen table – their small home lacked a dining room – with our salmon and fixings and beers. I'd had a couple, just enough to embolden me to make my pitch, and I did that with clarity and reason, but also with the unflappability of a claims adjustor weighing the risks for Mutual of Omaha. But I was too cool and detached for the Bradys, too unimpassioned. Their body language told me I wasn't making much headway.

I'd seen similarly unreadable faces on Bill and Celia earlier that day, but both ultimately let their masks drop. Celia's eyes went damp with relief and she crossed herself; she'd been sure they were going to put her son in the grave. Bill weighed in with the usual refrain: "He's alive, that slick professor. He faked his death." Gabriel listened in silence, did not commit himself.

My dissertation in the Bradys' little kitchen was followed by an awkward silence, broken by a haunting train whistle. Grace got up to make tea. Jim played with his empty long-neck Pilsner bottle, casually spinning it on the oilcloth-covered table. When it came to a rest, its mouth pointed accusingly at me.

"What are the chances he will be hanged?" he asked.

"Too high. You saw them in court – Knepp and Lorenzo."

"It was obvious they were colluding in a lie."

"That wasn't so obvious to the judge and jury."

"But it's obvious to you, Arthur." He sat back, frowning. "Or is it?"

"I'm certain they were lying. But Gabriel lied as well. That is a matter of record. Also – I measure my words – his accounts to his own lawyers have not always been consistent."

Grace was staring at the kettle, urging it to boil, but she picked up that her husband was watching her for a reaction, and returned him a troubled look. I had a sense they much valued each other's advice.

"So you're not entirely sure he's innocent."

"I'm not sure if that's the point."

"Do you believe he's not guilty?" Not letting up. He'd done many labour arbitrations, knew something about cross-examining.

I spoke honestly. "He may well be innocent. I expect he is. A great crime may have been committed against him"

"And if he rejects the plea bargain?"

"I will continue to defend him as best I can. I will put him on the stand. But there will be no political theatre. I will not let him portray himself as a brave communist martyr taking on the fascist state."

Jim winced. I had the cynical thought that was a scenario the CP might prefer: Gabriel expendable, a tactical sacrifice to advance more significant goals. The organizational hallmark of communist parties the world over was their discipline. And that's actually what I was counting on.

"If they convict, he can appeal," Jim said. "Right up to the Supreme Court of Canada."

I sighed. "And after years of appeals, a fresh trial, more appeals, he could be out on parole." I slapped a hand on the table, spoke with emotion. "Damn it, I'm fond of Gabriel. I admire him, I am *awed* by him. I see something of genius in him. I want him to live. He will survive jail. He has an unbounded future after that." Abandoning caution, I added, "He will be of immeasurably less value to the Party as a dead martyr than as a great leader and thinker."

Jim brooded, flushed as if ashamed. As Grace brought the tea, he rose and mumbled something about duties elsewhere. I took that to mean bathroom duties, but he closed the door to the living room and I heard him talking, presumably on the telephone.

Grace took over. "Even if he loses all his appeals, they could commute a death sentence. Like young Truscott."

"And he'd spend his life in jail."

"Can you appeal a conviction based on a guilty plea?"

"No, not really."

I hadn't mentioned the attack on him by the White Clansmen. That would distract from the main issue. I didn't want them thinking a long jail term would be fraught with danger.

Jim's voice became louder, more animated.

I sipped my tea. Grace sipped hers. There came a sudden silence from the living room. That seemed to serve as a cue for Grace to grasp my hand. "Thank you for saying what you did." Finally smiling.

"What do you mean?"

"There are some who feel it's necessary to sacrifice our bravest sons and daughters."

Jim took a few moments to return, as if composing himself after winning an argument. He went directly to the fridge, snapped the cap off a Pilsner. He gave Grace a weary smile before turning to me. "We expect Gabriel to take the deal," he said.

After reading Irene's note, Attorney General Bonner had satisfied himself there was little danger of a media uproar if Crown and defence consented to a twelve-year sentence. I told Smitty I was sorry, I couldn't possibly go above ten and a half. A few hours later we telephonically shook on eleven years and four months.

A few hours after that I was staring at Oakalla Prison, a sullen, brooding monster staring back at me through the softly falling rain, a monster with multiple barred eyes. I'd been waiting almost an hour in my Volkswagen, in the visitors' parking lot, for Jim Brady to return from his visit.

When he finally emerged through the gloom and rain, he went straight to his old Ford coupe without pausing to chat. Just a nod of his head signifying the work was done – Gabriel would take the eleven and four.

Despite his hurling of calumnies at the prison padre, Gabriel was still in the relatively relaxed confines of PCU, safe from the White Clansmen. There was an AA meeting going on, led by a Salvation Army volunteer, so we met in his cell. I took a chair, he the cot, both of us alert to the hazards of looking squarely at each other, of reading each other's faces. I brought out some paper and we began to work through the rough statement of facts I'd proposed to Smitty. A final version would be filed with the court before sentencing.

We were calm and businesslike on that rainy Sunday afternoon. No chagrin from me, no apologies or expressions of shame. No regrets voiced by him, no faulting the evil capitalist system. We were formal, cautious, purposeful, a typical solicitor and typical client going over the contract, deliberating, suggesting a change of wording here and there. In the aural background, men confessed their woes to each other.

"I won't say anything that will denigrate Dermot Mulligan."
Denigrate: a word not often heard in that old and ugly building.

"Everyone's in accord with that. The government would like to stem all the odious speculation."

We worked on it until we were satisfied. Time and location. A quarrel. A push. The deceased sent plunging onto sharp rocks and then swept away by the river, apparently dead. That was enough.

"All neat and clean," Gabriel said. "Whitewashed." It was not a complaint but something accepted, not to be quarrelled with. He lay back on the cot, stared at the ceiling. "As my counsel, can you make the plea for me?"

"Hammersmith will want to hear it from you."

"Is he bound by this agreement?"

"Practically."

"What does that mean?"

"If he goes off half-cocked, the Appeal Court will almost surely reverse him."

"*Almost surely.*"

I heard skepticism, felt an edge of tension.

"He hates what I represent; he's itching to put me away. But not you, Arthur. You're with me, getting me the best deal possible – a decade plus, even though Jim told me you think I'm innocent."

Gabriel turned his head toward me and squinted, as if trying to fathom the depths of my betrayal. "The word is going around the joint, Arthur. You're the new white hope around here. Take a bow. Your first murder case – huge success."

"I told you to get another opinion if you had doubts."

"You have the silver tongue, Arthur, no question. Worked Mom and Dad like a sideshow magician, got them wondering if I really did it. But the *pièce de résistance* was with Jim and Grace – using them, using the Party. *Take the eleven-year fall, you're more useful alive than dead.* That's practically what he said." His voice rising. "Meanwhile, you admire me, you're fond of me. In return for such brotherly feelings, I guess it's not too much to ask that I subtract a decade from my life."

I was on my feet. "Christ, Gabriel, let's do the trial then! Take the stand, take your chances! It's your fucking life!" I can't remember ever having spoken that ignoble word before, one I despise for its immoderate use, but I was irate.

"And it's your fucking system!" Sitting up again. The AA meeting had gone silent; he lowered his voice, but it was hard and cutting. "Your fucking liberal, democratic, egalitarian justice system that you so blindly cherish – thanks to it, I'll do eleven and four for a crime I didn't commit. I wasn't *there!*"

We were both standing by then, two feet apart, and he was inching closer. I wasn't going to back up.

He grabbed me by the shoulders. "I loved Dermot, goddamnit, as I ought to have loved my father. And you, my white, polite, bourgeois brother, you worshipped him too. Dermot told me about your absurd parents. Dermot was the father we both hungered for."

If Dr. Mulligan was your god, what do you think he was to me? His fierce challenge at our first meeting.

I felt consumed by his dark, intense, knowing eyes. Paramount among my bag of mixed emotions was an astonishing impulse to embrace my passionate, radical aboriginal brother, and I nearly did that.

But he let go, stepped back against the bars, shuddered, caught his breath. "He killed himself, Arthur. I don't know why. Whatever his atrocity, whatever his guilt, I can't believe I would not have forgiven him."

S o, after four days, we were again in the grand court of the Vancouver assizes, and for that occasion we had a little play to enact, a farce: the dance of the barristers. Smitty had his patter, I mine. The reporters at their overflowing table already had wind of the plea deal, and their expressions were sour and cynical. They had wanted to see Smitty work Gabriel over, wanted conflict, titillation, revelations about pink panties. But none of that was in the script. Gabriel would have only one line, one word: *guilty*.

In the lower gallery, behind the prisoners' dock, were Bill and Celia and their supporters from Squamish, a dozen that day. In the balcony, in uniform, were Knepp and Jettles. They knew about the deal, of course, and looked smug. Manslaughter would do. The guilty plea would mean their villainy would never be discovered.

Leroy Lukey was leaning back, affecting an interest in the carved ceiling patterns. He would have wanted the case to go the whole route – conviction, sentence, a proper Canadian hanging – but I doubted he had much say, or if Smitty even consulted him. On the courthouse steps he'd called me a lucky cocksucker, slapping my shoulder in false camaraderie.

Ophelia had managed to sit as far from me as possible without ending up in the aisle. It was not that I stank – the whole deal stank. She had stopped opposing me but remained disgusted at our criminal justice system for having produced this miscarriage, this monster. I, on the other hand, was not bothering with such thoughts. They were too negative, too irksome, too distracting. *Alea jacta est.* Only by numbing myself would I survive the day.

Ophelia's form of protest was to wear pants again, teasing the Dickensian clerk. He was like a man with a phobia, fidgeting at his desk. But he remembered to bring Gabriel from the cells. After his cuffs came off he remained standing, at ease, a captured enemy soldier.

As Anthony Montague Hammersmith took the bench, he frowned at me, a slight arching of eyebrows above his half-moon glasses. He'd been briefed on the plea bargain but refused to meet counsel in his chambers. "It wouldn't seem right," said the clerk. "His Lordship doesn't want to be seen as in on the deal."

"Proceed, Mr. Smythe-Baldwin."

Smitty explained that the Crown had filed a new indictment, for manslaughter. The record would include a transcript of the trial, an admission of fact by the accused as accepted by the Crown, and a letter from Irene Mulligan.

"And this is the admission of fact?" Hammersmith pushed his half-moons up the bridge of his nose and perused it with a frown. "Time, date, place; then we have a quarrel, which is not explained, 'as the result of which the accused sent the deceased plunging onto sharp rocks and then into the river, in an apparent unconscious state.'" Down slid the glasses. "That's the total admission?"

Smitty glanced at me. He had not quarrelled with my final edit. "The matter cries out for brevity, milord. Reputations have already been unfairly maligned. In any event, there's nothing more we *can* say. We, the Crown, don't know the details. Only the accused does."

"Mr. Beauchamp?"

"The defendant's signed admission is enough to make out the crime of manslaughter. My client accepts responsibility but disputes the testimony of Corporal Lorenzo as to an alleged conversation with the accused relating to motive and intent. There has been an enormous amount of malicious talk about this incident, and neither the Crown nor defence wishes to escalate that."

There was a rumbling from the press corps. Hammersmith looked their way, but instead of reproving them he grimaced, as if to let them know he felt their pain. He had the jury brought in and thanked them, assuring them they hadn't served in vain. They had no role to play in sentencing, and they bore the expressions of loyal workers fired without cause.

There was an oddly supernal moment when Gabriel was asked

to plead to the new indictment. He seemed to be pondering the alternatives while looking up at the shafts of tinted sunlight streaming through the stained glass. Necks stretched as all followed his gaze. Then the sun was swallowed by clouds and the windows lost colour. Gabriel looked down at the empty jury box, then the judge, and said, "Guilty."

Smitty and I recited our scripted lines and filed the admission of facts and Irene's letter. Smitty proposed that a fair term of incarceration "under all the circumstances" would be eleven years, four months. I did not oppose but threw in ten minutes' worth of encomia about Gabriel and read aloud Irene's letter, all for the edification of the sulky press and the disappointed jurors.

Again Hammersmith looked hard at me, as if to let me know he hadn't forgiven me for my insolent theatrics. Then he turned to Gabriel. "Sentencing. The young man standing before me took the life of an esteemed professor and writer who rescued him from the poverty of the Native reservation where he was born and raised and in which, without Dr. Mulligan's intervention, he would likely have been mired for his remaining years."

He carried on portraying Gabriel as a thankless malcontent. I saw what was going on. He was taunting Gabriel, trying to incite rebellion from my stone-faced client. The Hammer's mean streak was showing, glaringly. He, like the jury, had been robbed of a more dramatic role – he'd longed to intone those final words of the ultimate sentence: "May God have mercy on your soul."

Getting no reaction from Gabriel, his Lordship took a turn at the madly scribbling press. "I have heard in this court concerns about reputations being maligned. Indeed they have, and I speak not of the reputations of the dead. Unmentioned among those slandered is a senior officer of the RCMP who was accused of shamelessly rigging his case out of malice. Given that his good name and those of other veteran officers have been so sorely impugned, I feel obliged to put on record that the victims of those verbal assaults impressed me to a man as dutiful, fair, and even-handed."

"You fucking asshole."

Whether that was loud enough to be heard by Hammersmith's artillery-weakened ears I wasn't sure, but he at least knew it was a slur. To this day I'm not sure where it came from. I didn't see Gabriel's lips move, and unless he threw his voice like a ventriloquist, the author had to be a spectator near the dock. Bill Swift was a candidate, but it didn't seem his voice.

"I will pretend I didn't hear that." A toss of his russet tuft as he glared at me again, as if I were the suspected heckler. More likely he was blaming me for wheedling the Crown into granting such a benign sentence. "I shan't speculate by what legerdemain the proposed eleven years and four months was arrived at, but counsel know well enough that the court is not bound by any such agreement. I am firmly of the view that the term proposed cheapens the offence. The appropriate sentence in my opinion is twenty years. However, with some misgiving, I will impose a sentence of sixteen years and four months in Her Majesty's penitentiary. The jury is excused. This court is adjourned."

From "Where the Squamish River Flows," *A Thirst for Justice*, © W. Chance

THE FOLLOWING DELICIOUS BIT comes from a retired city policeman who was operating a prowl car in the small hours of Tuesday, August 7, 1962, on the unit block Powell Street. He at first thought a drunk was being rolled, but when he pulled over, he saw that a homeless man, known to the officer, merely had an affectionate arm over the shoulder of a tall gentleman in a suit. The latter was in a very bad emotional state, choking back sobs. Both were drunk.

My confidant, who prefers not to be named, recognized the distraught man as a barrister currently in the news, our own Arthur Beauchamp, and while he had every right to throw him in the drunk tank, this uniformed Samaritan broke with protocol to drive him home and even assisted him into his suite. (As an inopportune consequence, Beauchamp later found himself defending his landlords under the illegal suites bylaw. That case he won.)

Beauchamp's drunken crying jag was more evidence to support Moore's view he was in agony over not having fought the Swift case to the bitter end. "He'd rationalized that to the extreme. Once the gates of denial were sundered, he gave in to a sense of incalculable failure." Powerfully said. Of course, Justice Hammersmith's unexpected slap – the additional five years – added prodigiously to his mortification.

(Some observers and bloggers have tried – and failed – to make something of the fact that another communist of even greater fame was arrested only ten days later, on a charge of incitement to rebellion. His name: Nelson Mandela. He served out his term. Swift, as we shall see, did not.)

It is difficult to analyze Swift's reasoning in copping a

plea, to use the argot, given his unavailability to this (or any other) author. It seemed entirely out of character. Maybe an appetite for martyrdom had given way to that most fundamental drive of animate beings: for life to go on. But one also suspects the stuffing had been beaten out of him by the many reversals during the trial. As he lost hope, he lost his feistiness, disappointing the press with his failure to erupt. Yet that does not explain the rift that ensued between him and Beauchamp.

That began when Swift mailed Beauchamp a formal letter severing their relationship. He declined visits from him. He undertook his own appeal of the sentence, during which he subjected three Appeal Court justices to a hectoring sermon about their historic false roles and assailed the guardians of law and order, particularly the Squamish RCMP. It was a grand speech, hearers said, however inflammatory. The court upheld the sentence.

Ironically, to the bar and to much of the public, Beauchamp was still seen as a winner, despite the extra five years that were tagged on. That wasn't seen as his fault; he was a smart bargainer who'd got a killer off with sixteen and a bit. The Swift case may have spurred in him, as if in penance, a powerful drive to excel in the courts, to never fall down again, to never lose. But in all his remaining years at the bar he was to remain bitterly disappointed with himself over the case. He bore his pain openly, visibly, like a scar. "Ophelia was right," he told me. "It was an act of cowering gutlessness, pleading him guilty."

The "sense of incalculable failure" Moore spoke of seems a significant determinant in his growing drinking problem. Not to mince words, the Swift case was undoubtedly the *causa sine qua non* of his alcoholism, and may have caused enduring psychological damage. Certainly it exacerbated the sense of inadequacy and self-doubt trained into him by his coldly critical parents.

He lived almost monastically after that trial, working eighty hours a week, winning cases, building his reputation, and restricting his bacchanals to weekends – these were invariably celebrations of hard-fought victories. (The most impressive, the controversial 1965 defence of fraud artist Tony d'Anglio, entangled the mayor and several veteran city councillors.)[*]

Many are deceased who were witnesses or otherwise involved in the Swift case, and some who survived were unwilling or unable to share their memories with me. Shortly after her husband's death, Irene Mulligan sold the Squamish Valley hobby farm to the University of British Columbia, and its residence has remained as a grant-funded writers' retreat. At the time of this writing she was close to a hundred years old, living in the small coastal town of Fanny Bay under the care of a full-time nurse, who rebuffed my attempts to talk with her elderly charge.

The neighbours across the way have gone to their reward, and Doug Wall to his, when an over-liquored hunting companion mistook him for a bear. Swift's former girlfriend, Monique Joseph, remains alive, though her parents do not; she refused to meet with me.

Among the police, Sergeant (later Inspector) Roscoe Knepp, in his late eighties at the time of this writing, lives in a retirement community in Arizona. Brad Jettles, in his mid-seventies, is a victim of advanced Alzheimer's. Gene Borachuk remains hale and hearty at seventy-three, owner of a successful trekking and outback equipment business in Whistler. A notorious event (and controversial, because theories abound) brought a sudden end to the life of Walt Lorenzo: he died in an unsolved drive-by shooting shortly after retiring in 1983.

---

[*] See next chapter.

As to Swift, no one could have predicted what would befall him in the penitentiary in 1967, or the unexpected events that followed.* These would reignite in profound ways Beauchamp's sense that he'd failed his client's trust.

---

* See postscript to Chapter Five.

PART THREE

———

THE PUNISHMENT

Competitors are barred from the community hall while the Fall Fair judges sniff, snip, finger, and taste, so I limp about the booths, sharing with friends the blessings of a sunny summer day, hiding my tension with strained exuberance. I stop awhile to enjoy the Fensom Family Singers on the open-air stage. I watch demonstrations by spinners, weavers, and quilters.

A quilt designed as a map of Garibaldi Island is being raffled for the Build-a-Library campaign. Among its points of interest, in stitched black lettering, is the farm I have shared with Margaret Blake for the past dozen years: Blunder Bay, named after home-steader Jeremiah Blunder, who met his end in 1895 when, overcome with drink, he fell headfirst into his well. His ghost still haunts the island, it is said.

A supporter of folk arts, I invest heavily in tickets for the quilt. Margaret has a taste for the exotic; should I win, I'll gift it to her, another gesture of amends for my flaccid failures of the marital bed. My partner, younger by nearly two decades, sublimates, finding release in the frenzied heat of politics. For the past four years she has been the Green Party's lone voice in the House of Commons. Though Parliament is in summer recess, the member for Cowichan and the Islands is forever bustling off to do her political work: green events, weddings, civic celebrations. Shared moments of intimacy have become sporadic and rare.

I have had nightmares in which Margaret fades from me into the distance, into the arms of another. Different settings, different supporting casts, same plot. She will be returning to Ottawa in eight days for the fall session, to which she's been looking forward with unsettling eagerness. Politics, that delusive art, has become her world. I have given up trying to keep pace. I tested a couple of Ottawa winters, found the weather unforgiving, apartment life unbearable, and retreated to the full-time lonely comforts of my West Coast home.

I linger awhile at the sheep-shearing, then join Margaret at the animal pens, where she has been all morning, giving pointers to two young Japanese women who will be showing five of Blunder Bay's less rambunctious goats, three snarling geese, and a rooster and hen, our entries for the livestock prize. Yoki and Niko are enrolled in Willing Workers on Organic Farms – known familiarly as woofers – youthful rovers who trade half a day's labour for room and board. They come, they go, but these two have been around for two months, living in the refurbished house of Ms. Blake – former neighbour, present spouse.

As I slip an arm around her waist, she says, "Did you see that quilt with the misshapen island map? Beyond ugly."

My arm tightens and I stop breathing for a moment. I must now pray that my twenty tickets will be buried deep in the raffle box.

"Arthur, you're squeezing too hard."

"Sorry." I remove the offending hand, stick it in my pocket.

Our attention is diverted by Rosencrantz the rooster, who has somehow escaped his pen and is desperately trying to take wing. Yoki, one of the woofers, calls out, "Sorry!" – one of the few English words she's mastered – and charges off in pursuit.

A few judges emerge from the hall, two of them slightly wobbly: arbiters of the homemade wine and beer. The children's art judge joins them, fumbling for her cigarettes. Only minutes remain before the doors are opened and the winners announced. My tension isn't allayed when I spy Doc Dooley sprawled on a grassy knoll, smiling, too composed. I wonder if he's stoned.

There will be no avoiding Stan Caliginis, now done with his wine-judging duties, who is inexorably approaching. Chair of the Newcomers Club, one of the well-fixed parvenus who've begun to infest the Gulf Islands. Retired investor, instant farmer, self-proclaimed *cognoscente* of fine wines, he's been resuscitating the Bulbaconi vineyard on the Centre Road bypass, which went broke a decade ago. His other less than admirable qualities include being trimly handsome (though half a foot shorter than me) and recently divorced.

He plants himself in front of me with extended hand. "Been reading your biography, Mr. Beauchamp. Totally absorbed in it." *Bo-chom.* Caliginis could not have been totally absorbed in its preface, which instructs readers in the anglicized pronunciation. "Amazing stuff." With that apparent compliment, Caliginis turns on his bright smile for Margaret. "Dying for a chance to consult with you, Ms. Blake. Professionally, of course. Not in the market for free advice." A man of incomplete sentences.

I'm shocked she would give ear to this poseur. Intends to go organic with his grapes. Delighted to pay for a day's consultation. Margaret regretfully declines; she no longer practises as a professional agronomist. But, he implores, she must come anyway, and bring her equally illustrious husband, enjoy an afternoon at the heated pool. Share a glass of a delightful Mendocino Pinot Gris he's discovered – silky texture, very pleasant finish. Debate the pressing issues of the day.

Such issues as the woeful state of the planet, climate change, species loss – yes, Caliginis has an interest in all things green. He even manages to turn the topic to the sad state of Canadian politics, the urgent need for electoral reform. I find myself irritated that he unerringly hits so many of Margaret's buttons.

I wait until he wanders off. "Were you actually buying the guff from that sheep's-clothing environmentalist? I heard he was gaming the market. Derivatives. Sub-prime mortgages."

"Well, he's out of it now, isn't he? Some people change."

I'm not sure if she's taking a poke, so I don't say – though I want to bellow it – that no one has changed more than the emotionally bulldozed son of Mavis and Thomas Beauchamp (*requiescant in pace,* side by side, in the same cemetery as the recently disinterred foot).

Margaret has to judge the scarecrow contest, so I'm left alone with Gretchen, the blue-ribbon nanny, feeding her alfalfa over the enclosure. Down by the stage, a throng has gathered about the Fensom Family Singers, who are going full tilt, building on their success at the Fulford Harbour Folk Festival.

At the rim of the crowd, I am astounded to see Professor Dermot Mulligan – slightly shorter than I remember, and balder, but with his trademark black horn-rims – and he's tapping his feet to "Oh! Susanna." Reason quickly rebels. Mulligan would be almost a hundred years old were he alive today. In the time it takes me to find my glasses, the doppelganger has vanished into the crowd.

A mirage brought on by my brooding over the Gabriel Swift appeal, which is less than a month away. I'd learned Gabriel was in La Paz, Bolivia, on a project to conserve the language of a remote aboriginal community. Several calls went unanswered before I finally received an email from him, terse, almost curt, granting me permission to file the appeal. It concluded, "Good luck," which I read (wrongly, I hope) as grudging and sardonic.

It's a rare appeal – of a conviction founded on a guilty plea – and will involve two days of contention with three appeal justices crankily poring through evidence half a century old. I have new proofs, but even to my biased eye they seem inconclusive. My chances of reversing an ancient guilty plea are scant, the effort a cause for cynical snickering among lawyers; it will be a dismal way to make my final exit from the bar. But I will do all I'm capable of for my Squamish brother. My counterpart, *my white, polite, bourgeois brother, you worshipped him too.*

This is a debt that has eaten away at me for five decades. I will not be released from it even if I win.

The fellow in horn-rims appears again. Doesn't look at all like Mulligan. But the *trompe l'oeil* has me tangled once again in the mystery of his disappearance. Though my mind struggles with recent memory, long-ago events regularly intrude in high definition. Constable Jettles, with his excellent eye for pecker tracks on pink panties. Thelma McLean, whose own underwear was thieved from the clothesline. Was it you, Dermot; were you the panty pincher?

The Fensoms have finally run out of repertoire, and now the public address system squawks. "Arthur Beauchamp, you're wanted on the main stage. Arthur Beauchamp."

I fear I have won the raffle, the beyond-ugly quilt.

"Arthur Beauchamp. Come on up here, old fella." The booming imperatives of Scotty Phillips, master of ceremonies, fetch me to the stage, where I see a blue ribbon clutched in Scotty's hand. Hope soars.

"Here's Arthur now." A full-throated roar into a microphone, speakers at full volume. "One of our best-loved seniors, Arthur Beauchamp." Scotty drags me before the mike. "Okay, we're starting off here with a novelty category – best pumpkin. And it goes to old Arthur Beauchamp!"

I manage to spout some words of thanks and tribute to the losers, then shuffle offstage, still smarting from Phillips's impertinent introduction. Ageism. Taking my place is the women's softball team – Nine Easy Pieces, they call themselves – unbeaten champs of the inter-island league. Up there with them, on behalf of their sponsors, the Newcomers Club, is Stan Caliginis. He and Scotty lead a round of hip-hip-hoorays.

Reverend Al Noggins, the handicrafts convenor, exits the hall and shares a few pleasantries with Doc Dooley, then strolls over and puts an arm around me as if in consolation.

"Out with it," I say. "Who got the Orfmeister?"

"I have no idea."

"Then what were you talking to Dooley about?"

"The weather, old boy, the fine weather. Relax, for Christ's sake." He tugs at my sleeve. "Let's wander over to the dunk tank. Could be worth a chuckle. Nelson Forbish has volunteered to go first."

I find myself squeezed among the jostling mob in front of the dunk tank, a re-engineered cedar hot tub. Above it is a banner that shouts "Fun Raiser for the Library!" Forbish, the three-hundred-pound editor of the island weekly, *The Bleat*, ventures up the creaking steps to the catbird seat. He is shirtless and shoeless, a pair of cut-offs belted somewhere among the multiple folds of his belly. Gasps from onlookers as he settles into place, turning to cheers when the seat holds.

A young lad picks up an old, much-abused softball and rears back to lob it at a target that, if tripped, will release the ejection seat. The throw goes awry, as do two further tries, and Forbish raises an arm in triumph. Baldy Johansson is next, but he's had a few in the beer garden and his throws are wildly off the mark. Tension mounts as two more contenders fail.

Into this picaresque scene comes Stan Caliginis, this time with Tildy Seares, star chucker of the Pieces. The crowd chants, "Tildy, Tildy." She hefts the lumpy ball, tosses it in the air, getting its weight. Her arm whirls like a propeller and she fires a strike down the middle of the plate. A squeak of terror from Forbish as he begins his fall. As he hits the water a tsunami rises, swamping me and several unlucky others.

From the stage a squawk of microphone: Scotty Phillips demanding attention. "This is a big one, folks, the Mabel Orfmeister. And the winner is . . . pass me the envelope, please . . . for the sixth straight year, Doc Dooley – ninety years young and still the champ! Jump on up here, young fella."

~~~

Sunk deep in my club chair by the western window, I am practising my thousand-mile stare, seeing but refusing to enjoy the taunting beauty of Apollo's chariot in fiery descent toward the sea.

"We should do that, Arthur." Margaret, in an apron, at the kitchen doorway. "Check out Stan Caliginis's pad. Heated pool."

"I did not come to Garibaldi Island to hang around some finance mogul's pool listening to him go on about his bloody silky-textured Pinot Gris."

"Oh, dear. That sounds sardonic."

"Sorry, what means 'sardonic'?" Niko, the woofer.

"Sour. Like a lemon." Margaret wins laughter from Niko and Yoki.

"Rich guy, not too old, look good," says Niko. "Maybe I visit too." Loud giggles.

I am left alone to mope for a few minutes, then Margaret reappears with a basket of peas for me to shell. My peas, from my second-place garden. They're making a special dinner in honour of my narrow loss. Three points. Three points!

"He's someone we may want to get to know." Stan, she means, Stan Caliginis of the silky texture. "I got the impression he's coming out of the closet politically. He intends to rehabilitate that mess of a vineyard organically, and we ought to encourage that."

"I can't imagine it's escaped your notice the vineyard was returning to forest. Alders twenty feet tall. Baby cedars. All being ploughed up – even the producing old vines."

"Darling, they're mostly Cabernets and Merlots, and they don't produce in this climate, as the Bulbaconis learned too late. The whole area's overgrown with broom, ragwort, and thistles – if it's on the invasive list, it's there. I'd prefer to see healthy vines and a natural groundcover. I know you try, Arthur, but you are hardly a frontline fighter for the environment."

"Unlike a certain handsome male divorcé, I don't pretend to be."

"I'm not interested in his looks." Said sharply, but she smiles. "Kind of interested in his money, though."

Which the Green Party is constantly, profoundly short of. Margaret spends half her waking hours fundraising. She hates it, and I can't blame her.

I apologize for my crotchety behaviour. She says she understands. She kisses me on the forehead and sets the basket on my lap.

I stare sadly at the fat green jewels filling my bowl. I massacred Dooley with my twelve pods – got the blue – but he'd rebounded with his dills and pickling onions.

The phone rings. Seconds later, Margaret walks out of the kitchen with it, talking softly, and enters her study. Something political, private, not to be shared.

I must rise above disappointment, closet myself in my den awhile, read through the factum, the depositions, the written exhibits, the cases. Prepare myself to put up a sporting fight for the brilliant renegade I wrongly sent to jail.

Postscript from "Where the Squamish River Flows," *A Thirst for Justice*, © W. Chance

READERS CURIOUS TO DELVE INTO Gabriel Swift's history post-Beauchamp have various sources available to them.* A brief summary must suffice here.

It was his leadership of a three-day prison revolt in 1965 (*riot* was the word used by officialdom and the press) that condemned him to lose any hope for early release on parole. It has been calculated that, over his first few years, at least a quarter of his time was spent in the hole. Acts of defiance for which he was punished included the smuggling out of calls to action that found their way into the radical press – proposals, for instance, to occupy lands he deemed stolen from Native nations. A superb linguist, he regained full fluency in the tongue the residential schools had tried to erase. He took on an ancestral name meaning Thunderbird – he who throws bolts of lightning.

The festering contention between Swift and the White Clansmen came to a boil three years into Swift's sentence, when he was grabbed from behind by two men while another laid his left cheek open with a knife, from eyelid to chin, causing impaired vision in the left eye. On hearing about that attack, Beauchamp kept it together for one day – during which he tried to visit Swift in a guarded emergency ward and was rebuffed – then went on a bender that found him, a week later, phoning his office for funds to fly back from New Orleans.

Through his recovery, Swift continued to decline visits from Beauchamp as he had declined many times before, refusing to answer his letters, refusing even to speak his name. There has been no known contact between the two men since.

---

* See the appendix.

Swift's obduracy in this regard seemed excessive to Beauchamp until he reluctantly concluded that Swift believed he'd been persuaded to plead guilty by a green lawyer who had been inveigled by a cunning one. That is a scenario about which Beauchamp remained in denial for many years – maybe until this day, because he still waffles – and there can be little doubt it was one of the factors that catapulted him into his skid road phase.

As to Swift, at such times as he was not embroiled in prisoners' rights crusades, he pursued a UBC correspondence degree. As a reward for earning it, he was escorted under guard to attend commencement at the Point Grey campus. On that day, June 16, 1967, eleven years and six months before the expiration of his sentence, he vanished into a mob of mortarboard-throwing grads. Picture this: a gowned young man, scarred like a pirate, a black patch over his eye, a scroll under his arm certifying him with a degree in history with honours, magically disappears not just from a university campus but from the country of his birth. It's assumed he had confederates.

It may not be particularly useful but it is interesting nonetheless to compare the life paths of Beauchamp and Swift through the next two decades. Beauchamp may deny it now, but for the first half of the seventies he was busily buying into the North American dream – wife, family, attractive home in a posh neighbourhood – while earning prestige doing interesting, well-paid work. Deborah came along in 1973, and he was lovingly occupied with her. Annabelle was not yet having affairs openly. Those were years in which he found contentment, even happiness, to a degree that later eluded him, at least until he found peace on Garibaldi Island and the love of Margaret Blake.

Swift, however, while on the run found himself in the heady whirl of gun-toting guerrilla politics – the Weather Underground, the American Indian Movement in its early, militant years – then making his way to Mexico, to Cuba, and thence to East Berlin. There he attended Humboldt University and (if certain romantic modern European histories are correct) kept a safe house for the most radical of the seventies underground groups, the Rote Armee Fraktion, while sleeping with the anarchist cult figure Ulrike Meinhof.

A stay in Moscow followed, during which his bad eye was surgically repaired to eighty per cent of normal vision. Then a return to Berlin, to Prague, then Krakow. He was a hero of the Soviet bloc, of course, and much feted. At each stop he accumulated classes and credits and honours toward a doctorate in linguistics, finally conferred in 1979 by the Free University of Berlin. That's when he took up with the anarchist punk poet Bettje Kristoff and began writing. The Canadian government tried to extradite him from West Berlin, but that attempt bogged down and was abandoned.

It was while Dr. Swift was composing *Linguicide: The Death of Living Tongues* – which went on to win the 1984 Feversham Medal – that his estrangement from Soviet-style socialism became apparent, as confirmed in several articles he produced for the *New Statesman*. But he remained a proud radical, and in one of his rarely granted interviews (none came my way!), he claimed not to have deserted his cause but to have been deserted by it.

For Beauchamp, in comparison, the late seventies and early eighties were a blur of hard work and hard drink, getting criminals off by day, being the life of the party at night, suppressing the guilt associated with the Swift trial, suppressing the pain of cuckoldry – a man trapped by love. Finally, in 1985, after drunkenly falling though a skylight above his bedroom, he joined AA. Three weeks of forced sobriety in hospital, and some intense ruminations about his future, seem to have finally wrung him dry.

A carb job won't solve nothing," says Stoney from under the Fargo's hood as its engine coughs and wheezes. "Maybe you want to retire the old girl from active duty, eh? I got dibs on a eighty-seven F-250 I think I can wangle for three large, plus dealer's commission."

I have spent ten times as much on repairs to my bionic pickup: valves, front end, clutch, wiring, brakes, *omnia et omnia*. The alleged master mechanic sold her to me originally, and somehow I have never found the heart to service her elsewhere. And so the Fargo is here again outside Stoney's cluttered garage, sputtering, farting, finally expiring.

"I am not ready to give up on her. She's family." And Blunder Bay's sole vehicle, other than a light tractor. Margaret keeps her Prius in Ottawa.

Stoney emerges from under the hood, gazes across his two acres of skeletonized relics. "My inventory of used carburetors is currently depleted, so I'm gonna have to move heaven and earth to locate a transplant."

There follows the traditional ceremony: the haggling over fees and disbursements, the greasing of an already greasy palm. But I manage to secure a courtesy car.

"The Fargo is job one, and this here spiffy loaner is my guarantee of that." Stoney points to an aging muscle car in the garage: a Mustang convertible, circa early 1980s. It seems to have benefited, if that's the word, from a recent paint job: eggplant purple, with graffiti-esque designs of crackling lightning on the hood and on each door, a galloping horse with mane aflame. Hairy, testicular dingle balls. Black leather around the steering wheel.

"Picked up this here rag-roof cheap at a customs auction for my fleet of luxury rentals. It's not for around here, though. It's a city car – rides an inch off the ground; I already got a dent in the tran pan. Normally I would charge at least a token fee for such a high-test car, but not for the legendary Arthur Beauchamp."

It's dark in the garage but I make out rust spots at the back end, some hidden by decals. Stoney promises it will be serviced and brought around tonight. "By the way, I never had no chance to give my sincere commiserations over how you crapped out at the Fall Fair. I heard it was a crushing blow."

"Thank you," I say, inanely.

"Can I give you a ride somewhere, sire? On the house."

"I'll walk." I have mail to pick up. I am prepared: hiking boots, packsack, a walking stick. It's a sunny, laid-back Saturday afternoon on the Labour Day weekend, which I intend to enjoy at all costs. I wish Stoney well and limp off, my walking stick taking the burden of my left foot, still tender though newly fitted with orthotics. The discomfort is compounded by the wound reopened by the reminder of the lost Orfmeister.

I take the East Point cut-off, a steep trail but with a grand Pacific view. Below the escarpment, in Hopeless Bay, a pair of harbour seals is corralling a school of herring. Gulls spiral and dive for leftovers. A bald eagle awaits its turn on a tall low-bank fir. In backdrop to this wildlife display are the steep cliffs of neighbouring Ponsonby Island, where craggy arbutus and oak struggle from the cracks. Now, as I continue down to the store, the Salish Sea opens up to a view of the Olympic Massif in Washington, its white peaks.

The appeal is twenty days hence. In a few days I must cross the Salish Sea and isolate myself in the Tragger, Inglis library with old Riley, the research gnome, and somehow pull it all together – all the strands, the grounds. There are several.

First, Gene Borachuk. Now in his early seventies, healthier than most in their forties, he still hikes the mountains, skis the diamond runs at Whistler. Many years ago, after he retired from the RCMP – as an inspector – we had a chance meeting at which he expressed doubts about Gabriel's guilt. When I got the nod for an appeal, he waived that boneheaded undertaking I'd given him and signed an affidavit avowing Gabriel was unmarked when he booked him but battered after Knepp and Jettles left his cell.

In itself, not much to vacate the guilty plea. But it establishes that two central police witnesses could reasonably be suspected of other perjuries. At appeal, Her Majesty's emissaries will complain they're at a disadvantage. Knepp and Jettles are ill-equipped to defend themselves; the former, at ninety, is in a Tucson retirement home, and the latter in a care facility and can no longer recognize family or friends.

My second ground involves the foot that washed up on Gambier Island in its men's size-eight Puma. I got an order to exhume it – which of course attracted great public chatter – and to everyone's shock, including mine, two X chromosomes showed up in the skeletal tissue. The defence had been misled by the Crown, I will argue, encouraged to believe it was a male foot – Dermot's foot – a factor that led to the plea bargain.

That exhumation was also prompted by a dig through Dr. Mulligan's archives that turned up a kind of suicide note – more a meditation on suicide than a cry for understanding. It had been buried in his papers for almost five decades. But how could that be? Would not scores of thesis researchers have pored through them?

The discovery of that note inspired an appeal that, old Riley informs me, holds the Commonwealth post-trial lateness record. I'd got leave to appeal from Justice Bill Webb, a crony, a fellow AA. That was in May, after advance proofs of *Thirst for Justice* showed up in Blunder Bay's P.O. box. Though I read with dismay the personal calumnies in "Where the Squamish River Flows," I will not deny that Wentworth's dissection of my efforts helped propel me to action.

~~~

I finally clump my way to Hopeless Bay, the island's commercial hub. Overlooking the public wharf is Abraham Makepeace's General Store and Post Office, a venerable institution, and next to it his new licenced lounge. An architectural novelty thrown up by local tradespersons paying off their tabs in goods and labour, this sturdy post-and-beamer is several degrees out of plumb. It still smells of fresh-cut cedar – Makepeace couldn't afford kiln-dried – and walls are already warping. Its most notable feature: a deck dangerously cantilevered over rocks and tidal pools at the toe of Hopeless Bay. Ernst Pound's RCMP van is sitting among the beaters and rusting pickups parked out front, and he and his auxiliary, Kurt Zoller, are up there on that deck, lecturing several of the regulars.

Before tackling my shopping list, I head up the ramp to the deck, hoping to be a soothing presence. Pound has been testy of late, and Zoller, who runs the island's water taxi, is an odd fellow with his twitches, flinches, and hints of paranoia. Slightly built, buried in a uniform a couple of sizes too big. Right now he is acting the nuisance, getting into peoples' faces, smelling their breath.

"This one has definitely been smoking." Zoller jingles his handcuffs.

"Cool it, Kurt," Pound says. He is trying to ignore me, but my presence may be adding to his irritation. "None of you individuals are the required three point two metres from this building, so I'm gonna have to pull Abraham in for not enforcing the smoking bylaw."

A chorus of insincere apology – unnecessary, as the case fails for lack of evidence. No cigarettes are visible, nor an ashtray. Presumably all exhibits disappeared when the boys saw the cops driving up.

"None of us want Abraham doing hard time, so I'll let this infraction go if you gentlemen help us out about some of the local plantations." Pound is referring to Garibaldi's main agricultural export. It's harvest time. His pathetic ruse to extort information is greeted by grins and silence.

"Come on, guys, or they're going to transfer me off this rock." He's reduced to begging. "Don't want nobody's names, just locations. A couple of small grows. A hundred plants is all, just to show I'm doing my job."

Ernie Priposki, already in his cups, issues a challenge. "Hey, Ernst, instead of putting the squeeze on us lawful abiding citizens, why ain't you out lookin' for that runaway girl from . . . from . . ." He tries to get his tongue around it. "Skachewan."

Pound turns to me. "See what I'm up against? A wall of silence. Kurt, I'm gonna have a word with the counsellor here while you explain to these losers they can either do their duty as citizens or we'll be waiting around the next bend with a radar gun and a breath test kit."

He leads me inside, takes a stool. I pause by the bulletin board, study a missing persons notice. The girl from Saskatchewan, Kestrel Dubois: fourteen, pretty, dark, slight, staring sullenly at the camera. She went missing five days ago, was spotted on a B.C.-bound bus.

Emily LeMay, the voluptuous barkeep, sets down coffees, then chucks me under the chin. "You old sweetie. When I think what coulda been." A sigh. It disheartens me that Emily seems to have given up pursuing me, further proof I'm over the hill.

"Cut Priposki off," Pound tells her. "I see you serving intoxicated individuals, I'm filing charges."

"No wonder she gave you the heave-ho." She flounces off.

The island is abuzz over the open affair between the constable's wife and the telephone man. Unable to sustain the mellowing effect of two stints on Garibaldi, Pound has become a surly, snarling cuckold.

"I'm way down on my catches for this year. Unless I pull something off they're going to put me behind a desk." He looks at me in a needy way. "You're in the know around here, Arthur. Just a little tip – nobody'll guess it came from you."

I am offended by the presumption I would rat on fellow islanders. I intend a sharp response, but Pound is drawn away by Zoller, who has entered shaking his head, still jingling the cuffs, obviously having failed to break through the wall of silence. Finally the two officers drive off, whereupon the boys on the deck light up again.

The opening bars of the fourth Brandenburg have me grabbing my pack from under the barstool, fumbling for my cellphone. My hello is answered by the seductive, breathy voice of April Wu, the enigmatic Vancouver private eye. She is on a retainer to unearth long-buried evidence in the Swift case.

"Arthur, I have come across something very interesting."

"Do say."

"I would prefer not to. Not on a cellphone. How soon can we meet?"

The possibility of a breakthrough persuades me to cut the long weekend short. "I can come in on Monday." Margaret is leaving for Ottawa then to meet with her rump caucus, so a trip to Vancouver will allay the bout of loneliness that accompanies her every departure. "Surely you can give me a hint."

"Silence is a friend who never betrays."

April has a Confucian proverb for every occasion. My favourite: *If you don't want anyone to know, don't do it.* Quite the seductive beauty, this mystical young woman.

The afternoon is waning and I must attend to business, so I make my way down the ramp to the General Store, collecting oranges, pepper, allspice, figs, and pipe tobacco – foreign exotics not found amidst the bounty of our farm. Mint jelly too – Margaret is doing lamb; Al and Zoë Noggins are coming over for dinner tonight.

At checkout I engage with two fellow members of the Organic Garden Club, busty middle-aged back-to-the-landers whose tank-tops read, respectively, "Wellness" and "Wholeness." They're un-afraid to flaunt hairy armpits, messages of female earthiness that have always excited me. I'm not sure why, and I'm not sure if I care to know.

My final stop is at the mail counter, where Abraham Makepeace is sorting this morning's delivery. The postmaster lightly slaps my hand as I reach for a pile of envelopes addressed to Blunder Bay. "I haven't checked these yet for junk mail."

He pulls them away, tosses a couple of fliers into the waste along with a letter fat with coupons, then holds up an embossed envelope to the fluorescent light. "This seems legit. Invitation to speak at the Commonwealth Law Conference in Mumbai. Chance for you to get off this rock. When do I ever get a holiday? Here's your *Small Farm* magazine. Wentworth Chance copied you a bunch of reviews for *A Thirst for Justice*. I don't suppose my name ever gets mentioned, though I was a major contributor. And here's something you might be interested in: a postcard from Germany. 'Looks like François and I are quits.' Signed 'A.' That would be your first wife, I guess."

"Annabelle."

"That's right, Annabelle. Sent you a Christmas card last year with her picture on it. Society gal. Looked pretty good in that low-cut dress."

I have always envied the postmaster's sharpness of memory. Wentworth, an avid cyclist, spent many days pedalling up and down this island's byways, and many lucrative hours with this local archivist, recording mirth-provoking anecdotes: the time I showed up at the store unaware I'd sat on a wet sheep turd, the night the entire island was out searching for me when I got lost on Mount Norbert.

"Yep, Annabelle Beauchamp. She kept your name – I always found that odd." Makepeace finally forks over her card, which illustrates the Bayreuth Festspielhaus, site of her husband's many triumphs.

My dearest Arthur, it begins, disconcertingly, then goes on to apprise me of her pending divorce. No smudged teardrops, no sighs of regret or sorrow. Her marriage to that foppish conductor was bound to go under. She'd probably been outrageously disloyal to him too. *I'm quite well set up but I shall be taking up an offer from Opera Vancouver as sets manager, just to keep active. It would be lovely if we bumped into each other.*

I would prefer that a comet strike Earth and all life perish. But I will suppress mean thoughts. I have a moment of fellow feeling for the fop, the former wunderkind. Broken-hearted, no doubt, but generous in the divvying up. I have a loving wife now – preoccupied at times, yes, burdened with important duties, but caring and loyal. Growing more restless as she prepares to dive again into the parliamentary whirlpool.

Margaret has been so engrossed in her preparations that she's almost oblivious to me. Her hug last night, after her return from an off-island fundraiser, was perfunctory and cool. Lips failed to touch lips. I don't mind that she's more in love with politics than me. I'm honoured to be husband of a woman who calls for carbon taxes and massive spending to stave off ecological collapse; these concepts are a hard sell to the air-conditioned masses.

Makepeace bundles Margaret's thick pile of mail in an elastic band, hands it to me.

"Nothing interesting in here?" I say.

"It's not my role to discuss other people's private correspondence," he says.

~~~

Hoping I might cadge a ride to avoid the hike home, I relax with a pipeful on the steps outside the pub. Though *relax* is hardly the correct word: Annabelle's card, folded in my back pocket, feels somehow radioactive, hazardous.

I am finishing my pipe as Stan Caliginis pulls up in his Lexus and calls, startling me. "'Where the Squamish River Flows.' Must have read that part three times. Can't put the damn book down. Truly Boswellian, Mr. Beauchamp, amazingly candid."

"Arthur."

"Stan."

He exits the car with a thick bundle of mail-outs and passes me one. It promotes a public "planting party" next weekend at his vineyard. "Come in Your Best Western Garb." This is the kind of function I despise, and when he invites me to share in the food and wine and frolic, I politely demur.

Caliginis accurately assesses my situation – no vehicle, full pack, walking stick – and without my asking (and I wouldn't dream of doing so) insists on giving me a lift after he "hops up" to the post office. This fellow bores me with his pretentious wine-tasting jargon, but no intervening bids come in the several minutes it takes him to mail his flyers. He returns with a six-pack from his personal wine wholesaler. He wins a brief struggle for my rucksack, holds the passenger door for me.

"Good luck on reopening the Swift case, Arthur. Such a noble thing." He shakes his head as if in awe, and we drive off.

To stifle further discussion of the topic I make the mistake of seeming curious about his boxed set of fine wines. A New Zealand Sauvignon Blanc is on his favourites list, with its "incredible clarity and amazing tension." In contrast, a Napa Chardonnay promises to be "steely and crisp, with a majestic nose of hazelnuts and tropical fruits; very good length."

Half-listening to this mumbo-jumbo, I experience an itching sensation, under my skin, where I can't scratch it. The epicentre is in the region of my ass, my back pocket. *It would be lovely if we bumped into each other.* That feels like a threat. The card was mailed two weeks ago; she could already be in Vancouver.

From "Falling in Love, Failing in Love," *A Thirst for Justice*,
© W. Chance

BY THE AGE OF THIRTY-THREE Beauchamp had amassed
a sterling record; he was coming off eight straight wins
in headline cases such as Smutts and the Father's Day
Massacre. The senior partners had taken a liking to him,
had removed him from under Pappas's thumb, and let him
do his legal aid work while awarding him with the firm's
meatiest, and most lucrative, criminal cases.

The richest of these – the retainer was nearly a million
dollars – was the complex defence of several business-
men accused of running a pyramid scheme. The trial is
significant because it introduced Beauchamp to Annabelle
Maglione, then a young fine arts graduate, a set designer.
Relying on promises of ten per cent per month returns,
Ms. Maglione had put a hard-won arts award at the disposal
of these gentlemen, and was called upon by the prosecutor
to relate her heart-rending story. She looked stunning as
she took the stand: jet-black hair and magenta lips, mini-
skirt and high-heeled boots.

No transcripts are extant of Beauchamp's cross-
examination of Ms. Maglione, but several law students
were present – they later enjoyed successful practices –
and each remarked on the ease with which Beauchamp
brought the witness to stammering confusion. One brief
exchange was quoted in the evening paper. Witness:
"Excuse me, but am I making sense or am I sounding
totally incoherent?" Counsel: "The latter, Miss Maglione."

Her ordeal over, she sat spellbound through the rest of
the trial. During breaks she would boldly engage him in
the corridor. While the jury deliberated, the pair slipped
out to the Schnitzel House, where he entertained her

over dinner with stirring tales from the courtroom.

"I was wowed by him," Annabelle told me during our sessions in her Lucerne chalet. I reminded her that Beauchamp claims to have regarded her at first "with the fascination one might hold upon seeing an alien disembark from a spaceship."

She laughed. "That's so Arthur. But, yes, I was playing at being a hot, hip chick, Ms. Counterculture of 1969. My shtick worked – he was just as gone as I was, whatever he says. Two nights later, after the jury finally acquitted everyone, we got drunk and ended up in his high-rise apartment. The rest is . . . I'll leave you to finish the sentence."

Given Beauchamp's long lack of womanly companionship, one isn't surprised that he fell in love so suddenly and thunderously. This relationship remains – not to insult Margaret Blake – the most dramatic and life-altering experience of his adult years.

I lie stiffly awake, listening to the haunting whoops of a barred owl as I struggle to understand how I could have acted so badly. Old age has cursed me with yet another disability: an irascible temper. I am in danger of becoming the grumpy old fart of Blunder Bay. I accept the greater blame for last night, but surely the woman with whom I share this bed should share culpability. Maybe she does feel guilt, because hers seems a fussy, fitful sleep.

In brief, dinner with Reverend Al and Zoë was a disaster. I arrived late after refusing to let Caliginis take me down Potters Road – I didn't want Margaret to see him drop me off. Then, while trying to shortcut through the upper pasture, I managed to rip my pants on barbed wire.

"You're late and you look like shit," Margaret announced, herding me to the shower as our guests looked on with strained smiles. She was doubly irritated because she'd overdone the lamb while waiting for me. Meanwhile our hero was also in mean spirits, and during dinner went on a rant about the island changing, old ways dying, money pouring in, mini-mansions going up, new fences, private roads, you can't find a decent walking trail any more.

"It's all about Stan Caliginis," Margaret said. "Arthur thinks he's after my body. Or vice versa, I'm not sure." Right in front of company. It hardly matters they're our closest friends; it was impolite, embarrassing.

I turned to the Nogginses, seeking support. "He slavered all over her, invited her to drop by." I mimicked, imitated his leer: *"Dying to consult with you, Ms. Blake."*

"I'd be delighted to have you chaperon me, darling." Ice in her tone.

I seethed. When Margaret began talking Green strategies – Reverend Al is her Garibaldi ward boss – she took personally a comment that her party had lost all nobility with its constant money-grubbing. She threw her napkin at me, and on the way out slammed the door.

Al bustled Zoë out of there, pausing only to share a homily about storms soon blowing over. In the dim nine p.m. light I made out Margaret by the beach, receiving comfort from her staunch allies Homer, the border collie, and the cats, Shiftless and Underfoot.

As I was cleaning up and putting the dishes away, she came back and went straight to her little home office, not looking at me. Her apple pie was still in the oven, untouched. I cut her a piece, then approached her to seek amnesty. Without saying a word, she stopped typing an email and closed her laptop lid. I set down the pie, apologized for having spoiled the evening. She dismissed me with a weary wave.

The barred owl voices a long series of ghostly scornful rebukes. *Arthur, Arthur, you are a foo-ool.* Yes, it's the damn Orfmeister — that still galls — and it's Annabelle anxiety and Margaret anxiety. (What was that email all about? *Darling, you will not believe the hell that life with him has become.*)

But add up all those stressors and they're not the half of it. Most of it is Gabriel Swift. I'm seeing people who don't exist. The other day it was Thelma McLean, neighbour from hell, but when I stuck my glasses on, it was Martha Pebbleton coming from the hen-house with an apron full of eggs. These images are trying to tell me something, to remind me of feelings long suppressed. Feelings that go back to a moment in 1962, when Gabriel and I were preparing the guilty plea, when I wanted to embrace him and felt he wanted that too.

Maybe, just maybe, a breakthrough looms. *Something very interesting,* said April Wu. Maybe to do with Dr. Mulligan's musings about suicide that so mysteriously came to light. Maybe she'd found proof that he did indeed drown himself.

The owl's spooky lament gives way to a growl of engine. When I raise myself up, I see headlights advancing along the driveway. Instinctively I know it's Robert Stonewell — who else comes calling at the midnight hour? In my pyjamas I race downstairs and out, by

which time the entire barnyard has awakened: chickens squawking, geese honking, goats complaining, and lights going on in the
woofer house.

Homer barks greetings to Stoney as he cuts the engine, clam-
bers out, and extends the ignition key. "Your limousine, sire." My
discourtesy car, the three-decade-old ragtop muscle car.

Stoney's flatbed pulls up behind it. His henchman, Dog, a squat
little fellow built like a beer keg, erupts from it and lurches into the
bushes to relieve himself, simultaneously refilling his bladder from
a can of Coors.

Stoney doesn't seem as intoxicated but is on a jabbering high;
he smells of pot. "A few tips regarding this here vintage beauty.
If you gotta brake suddenly, yank her hard right, because she has
a tendency to drift left; the rubber don't have much grip there.
Emergency brake usually works but the fuel gauge exaggerates,
so tank up early and often. And if you take her to town, you also
might wanna have them tires looked at. Maybe stop at Quickie
Tire and Muffler; they got the best deals."

In the glow of the yard light I balefully eye this death machine
with its insignia of lightning and flaming horses' manes. Stoney
jumps into the truck, shouts to his companion to get a leg on. I
glance up to the bedroom window, where Margaret, silhouetted by
a light, stares wearily back at me.

Reverend Al is on a Sunday-morning rampage, sermonizing against "fast-food approaches to faith" and "charlatans and mountebanks selling salvation on the boob tube." He's going after the fundies, as he calls them – the fundraising fundamentalists – a sermon heard often by this congregation; he hauls it out when in a bad mood.

Margaret begged off from attending, complaining of, though not listing, the "thousand things" she must do before returning tomorrow to Ottawa. At least she was speaking to me, though obviously still simmering after last night's spat. I haven't found the right moment to mention Annabelle and her pending arrival. I have even destroyed evidence of that, furtively tucking her postcard between burning fireplace logs. *It would be lovely if we bumped into each other.* This unsubtle invitation threatens to feed the flames licking at the edges of my marriage.

Reverend Al concludes by asking everyone to join in a prayer for Kestrel Dubois, the young teen who disappeared six days ago.

After the service ends, I eavesdrop as Al shepherds his flock to their cars. "Nonsense, Mrs. Bixbicler, you look stunningly swan-like in that neck brace. And here's the indefatigable Winnie Gillicuddy." The island centenarian.

"Good sermon," pipes blunt Winnie. "Even better than the first ten times I heard it."

Once in the parking lot, the congregants can't seem to get out of there fast enough. Soon only the Jenkins sisters remain, who demand to know what Al is going to do about all the drugs on the island. He can't appease them, and they walk off sourly, grimacing as they pause to examine the rear end of the garish Mustang that got me to the church on time.

In my hurry I hadn't seen the lurid messages posted there, slogans that may have provoked several of the flock to flee in dread.

A bumper sticker: *Jesus loves you. Everyone else thinks you're an ass-hole.* Other stick-ons cover the rust spots: *O Canada, we stand on guard for weed; Bad cop – no doughnut.*

"Where'd you get that piece of shit?" Al demands.

The reverend normally enjoys a good joke but seems incapable of finding humour in my explanation. He leads me into the little brick annex that is his office. His door secured, he whips off his collar, pulls out a bottle of rum, and pours a liberal helping. "*This* is what I'm going to do about drugs, goddamnit."

~~~

I break away from the depressingly lovely sunset, stare sourly at my desk, the thick files and transcripts for the Swift appeal, then finally summon the strength to pull out a photocopy of the document that spurred me to reopen the case. It came to light only last March, in Ottawa's National Archives. I would not have known about it but for an anonymous tip, and I've been puzzled ever since why the caller didn't identify himself or herself; it was one of those in-between voices, sounding eerily like Dermot Mulligan himself.

He or she had also phoned the National Archives with the tip on the same day, Thursday, March 17. The two pages, on aged six-by-eight white paper, were found folded and tucked into a book. I could see how it might happen: a scholar who shares a popular feeling – at least among leftists – that Gabriel was framed, stumbles upon this helpful evidence, alerts Gabriel's old lawyer. But why hide his or her identity?

I click on a table lamp, stick on my glasses, and read once more Dr. Dermot Mulligan's brooding reflections on self-destruction – typewritten, unsigned, undated, discovered by happenstance ...

Albert Camus, who was unhappily taken from the world two years ago, wrote "there is but one truly serious philosophical problem and that is suicide." This is no flashy new notion. Sophocles argued that not to be born is the appropriate anticipatory solution to the burdens of life, and that the second best solution is for life, once it has appeared, to go swiftly whence it came. Yet he lived to ninety, a great age in that Great Age, "fortunate in death, as he had been fortunate in life," said his contemporary Phrynichus.

As I ponder the quality of existence, upon attaining slightly more than half of Sophocles' years, I find myself emboldened by other sages of millennia past, those Greek philosophers and Roman heroes who accepted suicide as the noble route to oblivion. I am emboldened too by more modern thinkers. Nietzsche: "Conversely, the compulsion to prolong life from day to day, and accepting the most painful, humiliating conditions, without the strength to come nearer the actual goal of one's life: that is far less worthy of respect."

And here is Dermot Mulligan, professor emeritus, author of no little repute, at the supposed peak of life and career, almost relishing being accused at graveside of committing suicide by leaping from the pinnacle of success.

Do I engage in such contemplation in defiance of God, who alone, we are taught, is life's giver and taker? Or have the sanctified popes and other twisters of Christian truth corrupted the Word? Did not Moses himself beg of his Creator: "Kill me at once, if I find favour in your sight, that I may not see my wretchedness"? And did not Christ himself choose to go to the Cross, not just inviting death but welcoming it with his unbending passion? And is not a self-willed death therefore at the heart of redemption?

After all, why ought we to assume God condemns us for self-inflicted death but not for abandoning Him? For having committed evil, unforgivable evil.

This is surely the loneliest moment, knowing that consciousness will presently be extinguished. This is surely the loneliest moment.

Take arms, Mulligan, take arms

And that's it – one and a half double-spaced pages with slightly raised o's and dotless i's. A few corrections, some words crossed out by overlaid X's, interlineations above. Not a mark by pen or pencil, but there can be no doubt this came from the same typewriter that produced his manuscripts. I have filed affidavits from two document examiners hired by the Archives, and the Crown will likely concede that this discursive declaration was produced on Dermot's old Remington upright, last seen by me in the Squamish RCMP exhibits locker.

Why had he so carefully edited and repaired this little dissertation, then somehow lost it in the shuffle of his papers? Is there another page somewhere, a lost confession of unforgiven sins? *Evil, unforgivable evil.*

The final sentence lacks a period. I visualize Mulligan rising from his desk, drawing *Hamlet* from the shelf, rereading that most famous of soliloquies. For surely that was the reference: *Take arms, Mulligan, take arms against a sea of troubles, and by opposing, end them. To die, to sleep no more.*

His *Dilemmas of Moral Behaviour*, I recall, contains a lively analysis of the soliloquy. It was not fear of the unknown that made cowards of us all, but moral guilt. But what was Dermot's dilemma, what was the unforgivable evil that would drive him to suicide? Something far more desperate than writer's block.

I feel warm breath behind my ear, a touch, Margaret's soft voice. "Let's go out to the point, darling, and catch the final rays."

I am in much finer fettle this morning, enjoying a bracing wind off the bow as I lean upon the railing of the *Queen of Prince George*, whose transsexual name still provokes humour after forty years on the Gulf Islands run. Known locally as the *Queen George*, this old tub brought me to Garibaldi twelve years ago, a refugee from the law and the wounds from a faithless spouse.

My concerns about Margaret, distorted to the point of near-illness by my febrile imagination, have eased. There were warm cuddles last night, and some activity that could almost pass as foreplay, though it soon wilted into sleep. How could I have allowed myself to sink into such a cesspool of doubt? My proud feminist partner scorns the cheap sexual games, the flirtations, the hushed-up bed-jumping practices of the many satyrs among her political peers.

I am Pavlov's dog, conditioned by years of marital torture to seek unfaithfulness in the remotest clues. At the end, Annabelle had finally admitted to twelve medium-to-long-range affairs over our quarter-century of marriage, the final one to the popinjay she's now divorcing. I had thought there'd been only four or five – the notorious ones. I'd blinded myself to the details of what everyone else knew.

Below me, awarded a prime spot at the bow by the ferry staff, is the Mustang with its ribald decals and motifs of lightning and fiery manes. I'd got taunts in the ferry lineup: "Lose a bet?" "You get this off of some Seattle pimp?" "Hey, Artie, ain't you too old to be having a mid-life crisis?" But despite its imperfections, the car seems reasonably street legal: the horn works, the lights work, as do the brakes, in their fashion.

Soon the wind is whipping my hair as I head north from the Tsawwassen terminal across the verdant Fraser Delta, the rising Pacific lapping at its dikes. Then I am in the dense grid of the world's most liveable city, or so the street banners proclaim. I get fist pumps from a carload of teens, and I salute them back.

~~~

The elevator disgorges me onto the forty-second floor of the BMO building, one of four occupied by Tragger, Inglis, Bullingham. Roy Bullingham is the threesome's sole survivor, still in harness at ninety-two, and reputed to be immortal.

The irascible tyrant usually pops in without warning on long weekends, and I don't want to see him, don't want to endure his digs. *Out of retirement so soon, Beauchamp?* He's irked that I have undertaken my pro bono appeal while rejecting a seven-figure fee from a tycoon who allegedly electrocuted his mother-in-law in the bathtub.

I enter by a medieval-looking pair of oak portals and return greetings from some Labour Day workaholics. A private elevator takes me to the partners' floor. There I move stealthily down a deep-carpeted corridor, past Bully's closed door to my own, and escape into the anteroom. Gertrude Isbister yelps with surprise at my quiet entry.

"Holy cow, don't do that."

I kiss her cheek "Thank you for being so unretiring, my dear."

"My other choice was to get hauled around by the grandkids at the PNE." She'd called me after *A Thirst* came out, hugely embarrassed that Wentworth would publicly repeat her confidence that she'd had a crush on me.

After sharing news, as older friends do, about our respective states of health – her arthritis, my foot – she asks, "Will you be staying at your club?"

"If they're not full. Otherwise, ask if the Hotel Vancouver has my favourite corner room."

"You have a bunch of messages."

"You know where they can go."

"Ms. Wu phoned to confirm she'll be here at one-thirty. Hubbell wants you to join him for lunch."

"Excellent." Hubbell Meyerson, also retired. I haven't seen him since Iris divorced him. It's been awkward – Margaret is fond of Iris.

"Also, this just arrived." On her desk near the wall, a stem vase with a single red rose, and beside it a copy of *A Thirst*. "It's from Annabelle – she's back. She'd like you to sign the book."

I was aghast. "Did you tell her I was coming in?"

"Arthur, it's hard. I've known her for ages – I couldn't cut her off cold. She has your direct line anyhow, so I had to pick up."

"Is she threatening to come by?"

"I warned her you'd be tied up."

I go to the door, peek out. "Explain to her I missed my ferry."

"Please don't ask me to lie."

"Call April Wu, tell her not to come here; I'll go to her office instead. Meanwhile, I'll be hiding in the library."

I close my ears to Gertrude's protests, pick up the Swift file, and scoot down the emergency staircase, a back channel to the vaulted, tiered imitation-Gothic library, where portraits of Tragger, Inglis, and other prominent dead glower from the heights.

I presume that's old Riley at his usual table, hidden behind a slag heap of casebooks. Most lawyers now use computerized research services, but Riley does it the old, familiar way. I approach quietly, lean over his scrawny shoulder, read a heading in *Wigmore on Evidence* – "Inadmissible Confessions." Other texts form a ring around him. Questioned documents. The forensics of DNA.

He must sense me hovering but doesn't turn, merely points to a pile of bookmarked cases. "Start there. Baron Parke, 1845, Exchequer Court, top of 321 to 323, a third of the way down to the paragraph ending 'makeshift analogy.'"

I'm not yet ready to swim the turbid waters of *stare decisis,* and in seeking diversion spot Hubbell Meyerson in a corner cubicle. He is absorbed in a book, smiling so lasciviously that I suspect it may be pornographic. He has grown a curly beard as amends for his baldness and has fattened his face with chipmunk cheeks. A wry smile as he sees me approaching.

"Hot stuff." His hand jumps from the book as if burnt.

I am dismayed on seeing the cover: a nose in profile to rival Cyrano's. My second sighting today.

Hubbell rises, grabs his hat. "You owe me lunch from two years ago. Chez Jean Genet?" He slips *A Thirst* into his valise, then gives me a friendly nudge. "Tell me honestly, old chum, did you really go groin to groin with Ophelia Moore?"

The question is too offensive to merit an answer. But it's a reminder to call her. She has retired to the Osoyoos desert for her asthma.

I lead him to the firm's row of reserved parking spaces, where a Land Rover, a BMW, and a Cadillac sit several stalls away from the Mustang, shunning the purple, topless, tattooed hoodlum.

"Join me for a spin, Hubbell. This baby burns."

"Burns what, oil?" He stares at my machine, suspicious. "Is everything all right between you and Margaret?"

I pretend I didn't hear that and take him on a breezy spin uptown to downtown, to the Jean Genet, a chi-chi bistro disarmingly located on Granville's rough half-mile. We take a window table, where I can watch my steed at a meter. Hubbell, smiling his cheeky smile, proffers his copy of *A Thirst* to be signed. "How could you be so stupid as to allow that fellow Chance such liberty? He had a bloody field day with you."

I scribble, half-heartedly, *To my close friend of fifty-five years.* Has it been that long since the college years? Were we really so close? Strait-laced Stretch and the Ladykiller – I'd been in awe of his amorous prowess. "I expected discretion from Wentworth. I trusted him."

"Nonsense. You might as well have been emptying your heart to some supermarket tabloid writer. He hustled you."

"I'd thought, until I read this, Wentworth was incapable of hustling anyone, let alone the prime object of his almost religious devotion. Somehow I must have embittered him toward me. *A Thirst* was his revenge." Had I been abrupt and unfeeling in persistently brushing off that fluttering moth?

"More likely he fell under the sway of those brigands he's partnered with. I can picture them, Macarthur and Brovak, working him over: *Juice it up, Wentworth. Let's see the real Arthur, warts and all, preferably with his dick hanging out.*"

As this bear-baiting continues over *naissains d'huîtres* and salade Niçoise, I decide Hubbell is getting back at me for my hesitant support during his difficult divorce. The marriage collapsed under the weight of his final, ridiculous affair, which also died on the vine. He's alone now at seventy-six, and I can see how forlorn he is behind the big laugh.

"The critical consensus," I say, "has it that I am portrayed as extraordinarily human – even, however tacky it sounds, lovable." The review that most frightened me began: *Expectations of a dry, pompous paean free of ribald anecdotes were quickly doused . . .*

Hubbell recites his favourite passage, the quote from Ophelia Moore: "*If Arthur doesn't want to say what went on, I shall not embarrass him.* Ho-ho. Yes, you'll get quite a ribbing from the Appeal Court this month. Not sure if they'll be able to take you seriously."

Wednesday, September 21, in Room Sixty of the Law Courts. Wentworth, who has boned up on the case, will surely be there, making notes for his revised edition with its heartbreaking conclusion of the Swift saga. *Oblivious of his fading powers, Beauchamp had clearly stayed in the ring too long.*

"You ought to thank me for keeping your Mr. Chance at bay. He pestered me, of course. I had to send him on a few innocent detours to nowhere. When I think of some of the yarns I could have told him . . . That cathouse in Grandview? Your birthday? You were making out with that tawny little knockout."

I nearly choke on a baby oyster, quickly change the subject. "Another fan has just popped up with a book to sign."

"Yes, I heard she was back."

"How?"

"Well, actually, from Annabelle herself. She phoned me." Hubbell tips back his glass of Chablis, dabs his lips – spinning it out, taking excessive comfort from my lack of it. "Her job at the VOA hasn't kicked in yet, so she's busy reconnecting with old friends. Mind you, we maintained contact while she was overseas. Her letters gave me quite a boost when things were at their bleakest. How goes it between you and Margaret these days?"

"Fine. And what did Annabelle have to say?"

"About you?"

"About anything, damn it." Hubbell has got under my skin.

"Oh, she felt she shouldn't bother you. I told her, 'Nonsense. Arthur doesn't retain awkward feelings. The past is past.'"

"And you suggested I wouldn't mind getting together."

"I assumed that, naturally. Good lord, you were married thirty years. You shared the raising of a wonderful daughter."

Deborah, a high school principal in Australia, cherished mother of my cherished grandchild, Nick. Deborah was a supporting angel during the stressful final years of that marriage.

I check my watch. "Time flies. I can't stay for coffee. You'll be fine with a taxi?"

I drop a credit card on the table but Hubbell returns it. "Not a chance – you're buying dinner instead. I've reserved at Hy's."

I am finding this a bit much. Has Hubbell no other friends?

"So everything is fine with you and Margaret?"

That is obviously what Annabelle is seeking, through Hubbell's agency, to squirrel out of me. "We are inconceivably happy."

Hubbell nods, skeptical. "Where are you staying? I've been stumbling around my condo like a ghoul in an echo chamber. There's a vacant room with an en suite Jacuzzi and a view over English Bay. I've even had the maid perfume the sheets for you."

"A handsome offer, but Gertrude has reserved other digs." A white lie. Hubbell seems needy for my friendship, but that may be a cover for his role as fifth columnist for the stalking divorcée.

I hesitate, then embrace him. As I hurry to my car, I call Gertrude on my cell. "If you've checked me into any of my preferred hotels, check me out." Annabelle knows all of them.

"Well, where am I supposed to put you?"

"You're not to worry, I'll find something. I may not be back today."

"Riley will have his brief on your desk by this evening."

"Buy him those chocolate-covered macadamias he likes. Annabelle?"

"Nothing."

~~~

I hurry off to the tarted-up part of Chinatown, East Pender. There, on the top floor of a low-rise near the Sun-Yat Sen Gardens, is the April Wu Detective Agency, established three years ago after she quit a major investigative service in Hong Kong, where she'd learned her trade. Most of her work entails following disloyal husbands, but she prefers the more dramatic assignments from the several criminal lawyers who conspire to keep her a secret from the rest of the bar.

April's burly male assistant escorts me to an inner office, where awaits the slender Oriental temptress. She is posing for me, framed in the sunshine from a tall window behind her desk. Normally she's a sun-avoider, a night person, and her face seems extraordinarily pale against the jet-black hair that frames it and the blue-black eye shadow. Early thirties, though it's hard to tell. I have always assumed that her air of witchy mystery is an elaborate masque. She knows lawyers love theatre.

She advances and busses me on the lips – just a bunt, but it startles me. I hadn't known we were that well acquainted.

"Everything is well in your life?" British accent with an underlay of Cantonese. She directs me to a well-padded rattan chair. The prints that adorn the walls are of terraced hills, ancient palaces, pagodas.

"Everything is not well. Margaret is off to Ottawa, my ex-wife is on the prowl, and I am back practising law when I should be selling goat cheese at the farmers' market. How are you, my dear?"

"Content. Choose a job you love and you will never have to work a day in your life."

"Who says?"

"Confucius."

I counter with something I'd read on a bumper sticker: "When you realize there is nowhere to go, you have arrived."

"Sounds New Agey. I want you to relax, Arthur." An ethereal smile as she draws the drapes across her windows. "I have just come back from a Cree reserve in Saskatchewan. I talked to a number of elders there, students at Pius Eleven in the early 1940s."

The room is in semi-darkness. April has paused, fully expecting me to beg for more. I give in. "What inspired you to go to there?"

"The Truth and Reconciliation Commission."

That body has had some engine problems but is soon to chug off on a coast-to-coast tour. The First Nations are preparing for it, gathering and publishing histories of those abused in residential schools. I've read Gabriel's critique of it in the *New Internationalist*. The "forgiveness game," he called it, a sly government effort to forestall heavy reparations and keep the churches solvent.

"I've been on the phone to various band councils." April clicks a remote and a wall screen lights up. "I finally had some luck with the Pelican Lake band. They're a people of the woods and lakes. This is from my camcorder."

A man at a microphone. A high school teacher, April explains, addressing some kind of forum: "Over many years, the children of Pelican Lake were regularly taken hundreds of kilometres away from their parents and their homes, to the town of Torch River, to the hell they still call Pie Eleven."

He recites a litany of injustices: children treated like herds of sheep; one-size-fits-all instruction; denial of free speech; kids with welts on arms and backsides, black and blue and bleeding, forced to sign happy letters home that they copied from blackboards. I've heard similar and worse from Gabriel Swift, and more recently in the press, so such accounts no longer shock. But I didn't want to believe that Dermot knew this was going on.

April pauses the tape and draws a chair close to me, her solemn eyes studying me for reaction. "They emailed me statements from three elders, all in their eighties, who remembered Dermot Mulligan from those years. Only one woman had a memory that was sharp.

Ethel Brière, who is eighty-three. It's she I went out to see. Are you comfortable, Arthur?"

"Becoming less so. Please don't tease – lay it out."

"She was fourteen in 1942. Her best friend was a girl named Caroline Snow, same age. In early June, in a whispered exchange in the girl's dormitory, Caroline told her . . . Well, you will hear."

She fast-forwards. Ethel Brière is sitting on a sofa, a sturdy, clear-eyed woman with a weathered face and flowing white hair. Around her neck, a silver chain and crucifix.

April's voice: "Who else have you told this to, Mrs. Brière?"

"Only the lady over there from the band office."

"You had kept it to yourself until then?"

"Caroline asked me to swear, and I did. In God's name. For years I kept that secret." A sigh. "She was such a pretty girl. The most beautiful, the smartest. So pious. But she is long gone, and times have changed." She sits up, a firm set to her chin.

"And she didn't report it?"

"She was ashamed. She was afraid. You would have been too, miss."

The image wobbles. "Oops, I almost lost you."

A third voice, off-screen: "Ethel, can we go back a bit?" The camera pans toward a young woman whom I presume to be a band counsellor. "Tell us what used to go on in the discipline room – isn't that what you called it?"

"Yes, in the basement. There was a table there. That's where the nuns used to strap us down to get whipped for speaking Indian. They used to force us bigger girls to hold a little girl on the table while they strapped her for , , , it might be bedwetting, or you got lickings for not doing the bed, not eating, being late. The boys who ran away got punished in front of everyone. You also got strapped for lying if you complained about the sex they forced on us."

"Thank you."

That was a kind of public service announcement, but far from irrelevant. April's voice again: "Did Caroline talk to you about this incident more than once?"

"A few times, when we were able to get alone. But earlier I saw what started it. We were on recess in the schoolyard and a monitor heard Caroline talking Cree, and she was reported to the principal and sent to his office after school."

I feel queasy as Ethel recounts Caroline's confidences. "It started off as a scolding for speaking Indian, and then Mr. Mulligan told her he didn't want to punish her if he could avoid it. And then he began touching her, and she didn't know what to do."

I am aghast, yet an emphatic inner voice tells me I should have expected something like this. *Evil*, he wrote. *Unforgivable evil.*

April's assistant enters with a tray and silently serves us tea as I listen in utter discomfort to a predictable tale of touches and fondling and the victim's frozen lack of response. All efforts to disbelieve this elder are bound to fail. I can see the truth in her eyes, her gestures, as she recalls Caroline Snow's account of standing rooted to the floor while Mulligan undid her buttons, bizarrely caressing in turn each item of clothing, playing with her brassiere and panties.

"And so the principal laid Caroline down on the rug, and that's where he did it to her."

April presses pause, and the image holds on the doughty Mrs. Brière snorting into a hankie. That inspires me to do so too, out of sadness in large part, but also out of need, to expel the shock that seems to have clogged my throat and nasal orifices. Rome has fallen.

As if in prayer I say, "Lord, what am I to do with this?" It's hearsay, strictly speaking, inadmissible, but I am dizzy with the deeper implications. None of this was known in 1962. How differently I would have handled the case had this outrage come to light. The *naissains d'huîtres* are rebelling.

"There's more. There were consequences," April says. "Have some more tea. It's herbal, very soothing." A brutally suspenseful pause as she pours. "Mulligan impregnated Caroline Snow."

I nearly choke on the soothing herbal tea.

"I've written all this down, but let me summarize. Caroline didn't return to Pie Eleven after learning she was pregnant, and Ethel Brière did not hear from her for two and a half years. They

318

chanced on each other in Regina at the end of the war. Caroline Snow was then seventeen, working in the sex trade, supporting herself and her toddler. Sebastien. Sebastien Snow."

I lean back in my chair, feeling the colour drain from my face.

"And what ultimately became of Ms. Snow?"

"After Social Services took her son into care, she had a breakdown and had to be restrained from making noisy, unwelcome visits to the foster home. Ultimately she let her pimp take her to Vancouver, where she died in December 1957, at twenty-nine, of a heroin overdose. The band council located her death certificate. They are perusing Sebastien's foster care records. It appears that when he was fourteen he ran away, apparently intent on finding his mother. That would be not long before she died. No one back then seems to have bothered trying to trace him."

She touches my hand gently. "Are you okay?"

"I'll be fine." But I'm shaking.

"I'll have more in a few days. Apparently Sebastien has a police record. So, now tell me how I can help you with your prowling ex-wife."

I laugh hollowly. Numbly, as a distraction, I tell her the bare bones: Annabelle's return, my fear that she will make mischief, disrupt my life. "I'm looking for a safe house for a few days."

She suggests the Ritz, just a walk away, where Chinatown melds into skid road. I vaguely recall it as a Main Street dump with a pub, but April has heard it's been done over nicely into suites, the area gentrified.

~~~

Outside the Ritz, a skinny man with a sad, lined face extends a palm. "Can you help a friend out with some bus fare?" His breath sour with beer. In his sixties, about Sebastien Snow's age were he alive today. Indeed, there is a resemblance to Mulligan. Put horn-rims on, imagine him with more hair . . . I'm seeing phantoms again.

I give him a couple of loonies. "God bless," he says. "When my ship comes in, I'll pay you back."

The small lobby is clean, the clerk polite. As she checks me in, I put my glasses on to read a poster pinned to a notice board. "Have you seen this girl?" The missing fourteen-year-old, Kestrel Dubois: a new photo, taken only two days ago, in colour but not sharp. She wears a brown jacket and carries a small pack. Long hair, tied back. She is leaning over the railing of a B.C. ferry, contemplative. "Anyone seeing this person or who saw her aboard the *Queen of Coquitlam* on its Vancouver-to-Nanaimo run between ten a.m. and twelve-thirty p.m. on Tuesday, September 6th, please call 911 or contact GIS RCMP, Nanaimo."

The picture has also been in the newspapers, a blown-up cellphone image taken by someone unaware, until she showed it to friends, that a search was underway for this pretty girl. Kestrel disappeared from a Cree reserve at Lac La Ronge in Saskatchewan, and that has piqued my interest. It doesn't seem a typical case of flight from an unhappy home; her parents are obviously caring and quite distraught. A high school teacher and a nurse, they'd given Kestrel six hundred dollars for supplies and clothes for the coming school term and put her on a bus to Prince Albert for an overnight shopping trip. They haven't heard from her since.

My assigned room, though flashy – the style is bordello light, florid curtains, red sheets, pink pillows – will do for a short sojourn, a few days of boning up on the law with old Riley. But I haven't time to pop back to the office; I tarried too long with April Wu, reviewing her reports and interviews – an afternoon of sheer masochism, lashing myself as I recreated Mulligan in this new and awful light. *My white, polite, bourgeois brother, you worshipped him too . . .*

Had his rape of a child finally, after twenty years, devoured his will to live? Had he no longer been able to stomach his own perversity? Fondling the girl's undergarments . . . And now, of course, I go spiralling back to 1962, those pink panties tangled in tree roots on the banks of the Squamish. And I remember Gabriel's claim:

Whatever his atrocity, whatever his guilt, I can't believe I would not have forgiven him. But this was a sin beyond forgiveness. I can't believe Gabriel had knowledge of it.

Sebastien Snow, born March 1943, therefore sixty-eight now. Unless, like his mother, he met an early death on desolation row. Rendered to Saskatchewan Social Services as an infant, presumably put into foster care, so it's not likely he knew who his father was. Equally unlikely that Dermot Mulligan knew of his son's existence.

I must ponder how to relate this history in ways that will intrigue their lordships. If old Riley can find a way to wiggle around the rule against hearsay, and if the court buys it, then I can file Ethel Brière's affidavit and video. I must persuade them that Mulligan, ultimately overcome by guilt and self-hatred, took the easy way, the path darkly lit by Camus, Sophocles, Nietzsche, Shakespeare.

I check my cellphone messages. A lilting, husky voice too well remembered: "I just wanted to say hi, I'm here. No callbacks, please, darling, I know you're terribly busy. Ciao." A final punctuation mark: the soft pop of puckered lips.

All the old obsessive love and measureless pain come welling up. Why so much distress? I'm too old, too wise, too damaged to fall under her sway again. It's not as if she's some kind of omnipotent, spell-casting witch. She's more like a train wreck. How captivated I was – her masochistic prisoner, her slave. Hurt me, my love, punish me . . . Ah, but there's nothing there any more, Annabelle. Believe me, whatever it was (mindless infatuation, compulsive bondage?), it died many years ago.

With that firm pronouncement I am able to do my business, and I wash up and return to my messages. Hubbell Meyerson, reminding me of the dinner date at Hy's this evening. I barely find the strength to text him that I am sick and must decline.

That cathouse in Grandview? You were making out with that tawny little knockout . . .

I remember.

FRIDAY, DECEMBER 28, 1956

W as Caroline her name? A tiny preserved nugget of
memory tells me it was that, or just Carol. In her late
twenties, I assumed, though maybe the makeup hid a
few years. The dark, haunted eyes hid everything else.

Law school was on break and it was my birthday, so my room-
mate, Hubbell, even then a prodigious partier, had insisted we
celebrate with a trip to Vancouver's seamy side. This was not his
first visit to the Grandview bootleg bar, but it was mine, and I was
partaking only of its watered-down drinks, unable to brave the
tantalizing terror of bought sex.

Hubbell had no such constraints. Promptly on entering, he
began engaging the sex workers, jibing with them, coming on to
them – as if he needed to. But the satyr liked to enact his fantasies
of male seduction.

We were the sole customers. A house madam ran the bar and
three young women were languidly arrayed on a sofa. A fourth –
I'll call her Carol – was across the room, sitting on the shag carpet,
hugging her knees. She looked frail, was wearing a long-sleeved
blouse, presumably to hide the needle marks.

"Don't know which one of you ladies I'm in love with the most.
What's your name again, honey? Charlene? Lovely name. And this
can't be . . . Grace Kelly herself! Hey, Arthur, offer some companionship to that little lost soul over there. Cheer her up."

We had bar-hopped our way there, so I was well oiled, sitting
unsteadily on a backless barstool. Fearing I might tip over, I ejected
from it and wobbled my way to a safe landing on the thick carpet
near Carol. She was making no overtures, so I didn't feel threatened. I thought to entertain her, so for the next twenty minutes
I recited to her the entirety of Fitzgerald's translation of the
Rubáiyát. Then I moved on to Keats, and Byron.

Hubbell emerged at some point from his private session and

stood about for a while, hinting we should take our leave, but I was only vaguely aware of him, mesmerized by Carol's rapt, delighted smile. I was in fine form. *Maid of Athens, ere we part, / Give, oh give me back my heart!*

Hubbell finally wandered off and I spent the night with her, reciting, talking, never touching. At dawn I rose from my prostrate position at her feet and paid her everything I had in my wallet – fifty dollars – for the pleasure of her audience.

I hadn't asked her a single question. She had ventured few words, though she seemed often on the verge of tears. I learned nothing about her but was somehow persuaded she was one of the nymphs beholden to the goddess Diana. I never saw her again.

All of this may be irrelevant to my narrative. In truth, I haven't the faintest idea if my rapt listener was Caroline Snow. I want it to be her, crying to listen to the words of dead poets, and maybe remembering my kindness as she took that last, mortal hit into her arm. I want to believe I gave her one night of happiness.

I awake from a hideous dream into a strange place – a tarty bedroom, pink and frilly. Cognition comes slowly . . . I am in my room at the Ritz, my third morning here. The dream began in the Grandview cathouse but morphed into a vast library, an A-frame, Annabelle seductively undressing and offering herself to Dermot Mulligan, he in bra and panties. Irene drifted past us, ghost-like, and disappeared into a looking glass, and I fled for the Squamish River. My dreams are growing more freakish as the appeal date approaches.

I hope to get my work done today and make the last ferry back home, so I energetically complete my bathroom rounds, dress, pack up, and arrange for a late checkout. I am still flabbergasted over the bombshell from April Wu, and have instructed her to remain in steadfast pursuit of Sebastien Snow. Putting it in her cautious way, she has found "some further interesting details." She is to come by my office this morning.

Outside I try to detour around the skinny man who falsely conjured up the ghost of Dermot Mulligan. I know his name by now – Conway – as each of the last three days he has approached me for bus fare, having decided I am a mark. I unfailingly succumb.

He senses me behind him and turns. "Any chance you could help a friend out one more time?"

"Bus fare, Conway?"

"If it's not too much."

"Where do you go on this bus?"

"To visit my old probation officer. He ain't got no other friends."

This sounds so unlikely as to be true. I fish out a toonie. "God bless," he says, reaffirming his pledge to pay me back when his luck changes.

No longer sore-footed, I have been walking to Tragger, Inglis, and might have done so on this sunny morning, but I want my loaner handy for a fast getaway to the island. It's in a parkade, and my route there takes me past a pitiable skid road landmark, the streetfront where, as resident alcoholic, I defended down-and-outers for a few years, an interregnum from Tragger, Inglis memorialized in a few of *A Thirst*'s more depressing chapters.

My former building is boarded up, ready for demolition. A sign advises that something called the Downtown Eastside Recovery Centre will be built here. Gone will be a slice of my past. Annabelle supported me in my mission to serve the poor, I have to give her that. She must have had a social conscience at one time.

Neat car, says an anonymous note on the windshield of the Mustang. Each time it powers into life seems a miracle, probably because Stoney has burned me so often. Maybe the rapscallion has turned over a new leaf. Probably not.

~~~

Gertrude lays Annabelle's copy of *A Thirst* on my desk, open to the title page. I fiddle with a pen. *Fondest regards.* Too strong. *Welcome back to Vancouver.* Too sterile. I settle on something complimentary but distant: *You come off admirably in these pages.* As indeed she does. A sexy, passionate, scandalous social butterfly in contrast to the dull moth flapping around the lampshade.

"Any word from her?"

"Arthur, I'm sure she has lots of other people to catch up with. I imagine that's why she hasn't called. You may not be the centre of her life."

I'm not surprised Gertrude is siding with her; they always got along. "My sole concern is not to be caught up in one of her outrageous scandals." I feel bad, though. Perhaps I should not be so pitiless to a woman newly divorced.

"To business. Please fetch me a clean copy of Dr. Mulligan's memoir." I intend to spend some time reviewing it, seeking clues to the other Mulligan: the stranger, the violator of innocence. I wonder if there were others.

She produces a ring-bound copy, dusts it off. "Old Riley is waiting."

I turn to an early chapter, relating the trauma caused by his sister's youthful death. *There followed a wretched time – years, it seemed – when I ached for the smiles and hugs and words of comfort that Genevieve had unsparingly bestowed on me.* One would need a sage analyst, a Freud, to link Dermot's intense attachment to Genevieve with his ravishing of a child of similar age. A mad misplaced impulse to recapture that love?

~~~

I settle down with Riley, who has just filed an amended factum based on the second-hand account of Ethel Brière, produced sixty-nine years after the fact. He has been beavering away, seeking a loophole that will make the retelling of Caroline's story of defilement admissible. The rule against hearsay is ancient, and subject to few exceptions. In stripped-down form: a witness may not testify to matters told by another.

"You might argue the doctrine of recent complaint." Whereby a timely cry of rape – or even a frightened whisper – escapes the rule against hearsay. The rule was abrogated by Parliament two decades ago, but Riley will draft a Charter of Rights argument in support of its restoration.

"Just come up with whatever esoteric argument you can, something to confuse the court."

"There is also an issue of continuity. The circumstances aren't clear as to how the deceased's ruminations found their way into the National Archives."

After being alerted to its existence by the anonymous phoner, I instructed a lawyer from our Ottawa branch to get a certified copy. She also wangled a copy of a report from a questioned-documents examiner, who had no doubt the typing had been done on Mulligan's busy Remington on paper many decades old. The Attorney General has now conceded Dermot was the author, so I don't know why Riley is fussing over continuity.

"You might want to hire a student to comb through all his papers to see if anything else has been overlooked."

Sound advice. Who knows what other loosely bound revelations lurk in, say, the original copy of the truncated memoirs? But rather than hiring someone, I ought to go to Ottawa myself. I have recent, bitter memories of that town – a contempt citation, a botch-up that made me a laughingstock – but I might manage to stay out of trouble for a couple of nights.

The librarian calls me to the phone. I'm abstracted as I rise, wondering what Margaret's reaction might be to my descending on her. I don't want to stumble in on . . . what?

Gertrude is on the line, *sotto voce:* "She's here."

It takes me a moment to orient, to realize she's not referring to Margaret. I look wildly about for a hiding place, choose a narrow aisle of dusty old texts, grab one at random, bury my face in it, feeling pathetic because I know it won't take her long to ferret me out.

"Good morning."

I peek over the book. Annabelle is standing at the other end of the aisle, bag slung over her shoulder, hand cocked on hip, tall and stunning, a blonde now. Today's featured ghost: Annabelle thirty years ago, looking more like our daughter, Deborah, than herself.

As she approaches I find myself admiring the artistry of who-ever recomposed her face. "Annabelle, how delightful."

"Don't tell me I look decades younger," she says, still reading me easily after a dozen years apart. "I hate that even though it's true. You, however, are living proof that men age with more grace. You look fantastic."

"There's fresh coffee in the lounge. Can you stay a minute?" Delicately imposing a time limit, though I must admit to being flattered.

"I'm late for an appointment. I just wanted to thank you for signing the book." A continental kiss on both cheeks, the scent of something subtle and alluring. "Stop being so tense, darling. I'm not going to eat you." She pats me on the cheek.

"No, it's just . . . it's been a long time."

She pulls *A Thirst* from her bag, opens a bookmarked page: a photo from the seventies, the two of us arm in arm, she looking infinitely leggy in her mini. "Given my transgressions, I do come off rather entertainingly, don't I? The bad girl."

"More creatively portrayed than I, by a landslide."

"Not at all. I kept saying to myself, 'Yes, yes, this is the man I loved, this complex, insecure, beautiful being, who when he's not mesmerizing a jury can walk into the General Store with poop on his pants.'" She twists her head almost sideways to see the title of the book I'm holding. "*Eighteenth Century Origins of Modified Trusts.* How fascinating."

"Ah, yes . . . only makes sense when read upside down." With this feeble joke I return the book to the shelf right side up and usher her to the reading room, where she greets Riley, who rises and makes a pretence of bowing. The old fellow has been bent over tables for so long he can't stand straight anyway.

She protests but I insist on escorting her down to the parking levels. We are alone in the lift; I feel edgy, and in sensing her pull I am alarmed at its power. She is more assured and sexy than in her young womanhood, wiser, more confident.

She chatters on, confirming my reading of her postcard that hers was a divorce sans tears. "François was too immature, too romantically fascist, in love with Wagner." Her settlement? "He loved me too much to fight over the spoils. I have the Lucerne chalet and the condo in San Remo, and he the Bayreuth property and the ridiculous ranch – I can't imagine what he was thinking – in Brazil. I'm extremely well-off."

That sounds dangerously like an invitation to share. I take over with a sprightly updater about laid-back Garibaldi.

"And how is Margaret?"

"Constantly amazing."

"You must be so proud of her. Given your obsessive dislike of Ottawa, it was probably smart to return to your poky little island. Marriage survives best taken in short dollops. It's more like an affair that way."

"Deborah wrote that you and she shared some time in Sydney."

"Yes, she came to see *Lohengrin* at the Opera House. There was a sort of mending, but I doubt she'll ever forgive my treatment of you. I am sorry, Arthur. I was quite wicked, wasn't I?"

I suppress a polite impulse to disagree and say nothing. By now we have exited the elevator at parking level A, where Annabelle has appropriated for her late-model Jaguar one of the firm's reserved stalls. "Who's the office stud who drives the extreme machine?" She's looking at the Mustang.

"That would be me, Annabelle."

She tosses her hair, laughs at what she takes as an absurdity. "You're funny, Arthur. Look, they're throwing a do for me, a welcome-back party, next Friday evening. A lot of people you know will be there. Old friends, musicians, artists. They're all asking about you, of course."

"I'm afraid I shall be on Garibaldi. I'm returning tonight."

"If you find yourself wandering back, it's at the Orpheum, in the lounge. Saturday, seven to never. Ciao."

Another kiss, but on the lips, friendly, not over-familiar. And suddenly she is in her car and pulling away.

~~~

My childhood passion for the priesthood had little to do with God. In our family, in our parish, one accepted a supreme power without thought or hesitation. God was just there, plunked right in front of you, solid, like the kitchen range.

I have kicked my shoes off, am lying on my office couch with the memoir, reading with a newly jaundiced eye what I've read scores of times. A few pages ago Mulligan was mourning his sister, but this part is jaunty.

But, ah, the splendour, the glory of St. Joseph's Oratorio, of Notre Dame Cathedral. I was entranced by the grandness, the solemnity, the gaudiness, everything that young eyes see as awesome, and mature and wiser eyes see as pompous. And the costumery. Not for me the plebeian blackness of a priest's habit; give me scarlet! I would be an archbishop, maybe Pope Dermot the First.

But these dreams dissipated when I fell in love with teaching . . .

This style, this lightness of prose, seems forced. It's foreign to the professor's other writings and, as I recall, his lectures. He never joked, rarely smiled. Maybe he was trying to loosen up with this memoir, in contemplation of death and freedom from guilt.

Glancing up, I jump. April Wu is standing three feet away, smiling in her subtle, secret way.

"Come right in," I say.

"Forgive me, I'm neurotically snoopy." She bends her willowy form over the desk, recognizes what I'm reading. "I don't recall any thoughts of suicide in there."

"Let's assume he repressed them until he was no longer able to, and then the dam burst. How could he write about Pie Eleven without that memory flooding back? To escape the pain, he takes a great notion to jump in the river and drown."

"He who is drowned is not troubled by the rain." April perches, birdlike, on a chair and removes a file from her bag, two inches thick. "This is the life of Sebastian Snow."

"A busy one."

"A desperate one."

I leaf through her documents. The first several are copies of social welfare records from the 1950s, sections of which April has highlighted with a marking pen. They mention exchanges of correspondence between Caroline Snow and her son up to 1957. That year, after Sebastien turned fourteen, she sent him bus fare for a visit to Vancouver. He left Regina in August and after reuniting with her didn't return. It was assumed he remained with her until she took a hot shot of heroin in December.

"You won't see a mention anywhere of Sebastien's father." April can't sit still, goes to the window, admires the bold view of city and sea and mountains. "They use phrases like 'paternity unknown' or 'undetermined.' Nor is there any indication that Sebastien knew who his father was or that he was conceived from rape."

Sebastien must have lived on the street after Caroline died; there's no record of his doings until an arrest, at eighteen, for a break and enter in North Vancouver. There followed a series of convictions for theft, nuisance, assault, and narcotics, the usual pattern of those broken by the despairs of childhood trauma and poverty. Making the file weighty are the many reports from police, probation officers, and parole services.

"Let's find a typical pre-sentence report." Her smile is unaccountably impish. She gets behind me, leans close, locates a report from 1971. The offence: malicious damage. On the last page, the probation officer's summary is highlighted.

Mr. Snow presented himself politely throughout and seemed completely aware of his circumstances. Though over-cynical and clearly depressed, he is obviously intelligent, and his school grades confirm that. It's unfortunate therefore that his life has been so entirely unproductive.

His early difficulties in a strict foster home have been discussed above, as was the panic and the sense of hopelessness he suffered when his mother died suddenly. Despite the pity one might feel, given these antecedents, it cannot be denied that all previous rehabilitative efforts have failed, and at 28, Mr. Snow has an unenviable record of convictions. The crime is a senseless act, but I'm unable to advance any reasons why he should not be given the usual custodial sentence.

Senseless act . . . here it is: seven counts, a drunken windshield-smashing spree. I am suffering a kind of déjà vu, flickering old images. The closeness of the playful, feline detective, her hand on my shoulder as she flips a page, adds a further disorienting element.

I am staring at a brief transcript of the sentencing on the seven counts.

I am unswayed by your eloquence, Mr. Beauchamp. Nice try, but if this man is capable of reform, pigs can fly. Two years less a day.

There'd been so many legal aid cases, a dozen every week. I am again feeling my age. I'd hoped my body would go first, that I'd be allowed to keep my brain intact, but it seems this isn't being allowed.

A welcome reprieve from these thoughts comes with the aid of a mug shot, a memory of a skinny man in prison garb, handsome but scarred and aging fast. I'd interviewed him, read this probation report, but the prostitute mom, the tragedy of her death, was lost to me.

Suddenly I'm rewarded with a snatch of conversation. I had asked Sebastien why he'd done it. "It seemed to be the most sensible thing to do at the moment." A line I'd taken a fancy to, an odd, wry comment about a pointless act.

I repeat it to April and add, "Odd what one remembers. Odder what one forgets."

"A bird does not sing because it has an answer. It sings because it has a song."

I try to parse her aphorism, can't get a good grip on it.

She unhands me, gives me a sympathetic pat, glides away. "You may have swayed Sebastien, if not the judge. After he got paroled he turned things around for a while, dried out, went back to Cree territory for a new start."

So it appears that old bugger Scott did get it wrong. Pigs can fly.

April retrieves her bag. "I have to run off and follow someone. Skip to the last report, from Native Counselling Services."

In summary, Sebastien, a treaty Indian, was accepted into the Fox Lake Reserve in Manitoba, where he tried to live the traditional life, trapping and fishing, even marrying and raising a daughter. That lasted for nearly a decade, but the pattern of drink, drugs, and petty crime re-emerged. In 1985, after his wife died of complications from a miscarriage, he committed suicide in Stony Mountain Penitentiary.

When I look up from this tragic ending, April has vanished as silently as she came.

~~~

As I head off to the Ritz to get my bags and check out, my mind is whirling with lives destroyed, Caroline and Sebastien and a former man of faith who fell disastrously from grace. Whose sin was such an affront to Jesus's teachings that he abandoned Him, abandoned Rome. Mulligan could no longer believe, because that would mean believing in eternal hell. As a monstrous side effect to the suicide, Gabriel, whom he had loved, was jailed, brutally maimed, and after his escape banished from his homeland under threat of returning to serve his time.

On the surface Dermot seemed settled when I knew him in the 1950s, but he must have been suppressing a fierce trauma over the punishment he'd visited on Caroline Snow for speaking Cree. Somehow all the guilt he'd bottled up became uncapped. The signs had been there: his block, his inability to write about Pie Eleven, those two tortured pages of suicidal contemplation.

There was self-satire in the last sentence of his incomplete memoir, his greeting from "three hundred young voices in off-key choir, praising the coming of the Lord." Now I saw self-disgust too. Maybe it was that image – the innocent, trusting choir – that finally propelled him to the river's edge.

But why the semen stains on those frilly pink undies?

A bird does not sing because it has an answer. It sings because it has a song. Maybe that means it is futile to seek the truth. Only justice matters.

It has been a stressful week for this old farmer. He needs a dose of Blunder Bay, his own *angulus terrae. Happy is he who knows the rural gods,* sang Virgil.

I pull up in front of the Ritz's beer parlour – a loading zone, but I won't be long. Conway the panhandler appears out of thin air, and before I have unclasped the seatbelt he is at the driver's door, opening it for me.

I make him an offer. "If you guard my car while I bail out of here, I will drive you to see your lonely probation officer." He looks pained. "Alternatively, ten dollars."

He lightens. "God bless."

There is nothing much to steal in the open-top Mustang except a few garden tools: hedge clippers, a pruning saw, a trowel, a watering can to replace the one that our blind old horse, Barney, stepped on. Two sacks of fall rye seed in the trunk. I pocket the keys and leave Conway leaning possessively against the front fender.

It takes a few minutes to fetch my bags and a few more to raise the clerk. As she prints out my receipt I poke my head out the door. The Mustang is where it should be, outside the pub entrance, fifty feet away, but a bicycle cop has dismounted, a young woman, and she seems to be vigorously conferring with my security guard.

I am anxious to avoid a misunderstanding – might she suspect Conway is hovering about my car like a thief? – and equally anxious to avoid a ticket. So I grab my roller and suit bag and hurry down the street.

Conway parts from the officer and intercepts me, flustered. "I wouldn't of stole nothin' – I was only looking in the glove compartment, and she sneaked up behind me."

"Don't you go anywhere," she calls, leaning over the passenger door, poking around the front seats.

Conway hangs his head. "I hate to ask, but I think our arrangement was for ten dollars."

Despite my better judgment I pay off my fickle sentry; he was at least honest about his snooping. But this bicycle cop is just as bad. With majestic effrontery she is digging through the glove compartment. A raw recruit, with the dogged look of the overly resolute.

I stride up to her, demand to know what she thinks she is doing. She ignores that and pulls papers from a plastic envelope showing the car is registered to Loco Motion Luxury Rentals, proprietor Robert Stonewell.

"My own vehicle is in for repairs. This is a courtesy car." I lift my bags onto the back seat. "What is the problem, young lady?" An ill-thought-out form of address, but I am peeved.

She holds the envelope upside down and slaps it; two crumpled rolled cigarettes fall out. "The problem is I'm going to have your car seized so it can be gone over with a fine-tooth comb." She goes back into the glove compartment and retrieves from its litter a plastic pill bottle full of what I take to be cannabis seeds.

I watch, dismayed, as her hand sweeps under the dashboard, retrieving a small hash pipe held there by the masking tape. It has a carved miniature gargoyle head. Passersby are gathering, cars slowing. "Car's clean," Stoney had said. "I'll guarantee that with my dying breath." My confirmatory search was careless, slapdash.

While the concept of Arthur Beauchamp being busted for drugs is laughable, my main concern right now is avoiding the snarl of rush-hour traffic and making the evening ferry. "Miss, how long have you been on the police force?"

"Not Miss. Officer, Officer Wong. Do you have some identification, sir?"

I let go. "You, Officer Wong, are way out of line. You have no right to ask me for identification and no right to search this car in the absence of probable cause."

"I have very probable cause." She directs my attention to the rear end, the decals. *We stand on guard for weed. Bad cop – no doughnut.* "Now if you don't identify yourself, sir, I'm going to ask for a tow truck." Fingering the police radio at her belt.

By now a small, snickering mob has gathered. This fearless young constable is not going to back down in front of them, and I fear the impasse won't easily be resolved. There is no advantage to standing on principle, so I show my Law Society card. "Maybe it's best that you know with whom you're dealing. Arthur Beauchamp."

From her lack of expression it is obvious that Officer Wong has not read *A Thirst for Justice*. I look about, exasperated. People are gaping from shop doorways, from windows. Pictures are being snapped on cellphones.

I abase myself by importuning. "Miss – I mean, Officer Wong, I'd never set eyes on this vehicle until a few days ago. It's obviously had many users. Take the suspect goods with you; I have no interest in them. Now I beg you, I must be off to catch a ferry."

She holds the envelope to the light, looking for fingerprints, then slips it into a satchel. The container of seeds goes in there too, but not before she scrutinizes the newly bought gardening tools.

"What's in the trunk, sir?"

"Officer, this has gone too far." I'm embroiled in a ridiculous scene – street theatre, stores emptying, cars stopping, people speculating. *What did he do? It's Mr. Big.*

"What's in the trunk, sir?"

The curious horde presses closer, sharing her eagerness to see what's in that trunk. Grow lights, maybe, decisive proof Mr. Big runs a major op. Even what is in there – two thick sacks – will look suspicious.

In the face of my silence, Officer Wong announces she intends to read my rights.

"I know my rights." I get into the car and start it. She races to the front and puts her foot on the bumper. Several people cheer. "Officer 547 Wong," she says into her radio, "calling for backup. Officer being menaced."

I turn off the engine. I listen to the approaching sound of sirens.

FRIDAY, SEPTEMBER 9, 2011

I'm slow to get going because of a myriad of misunderstandings (though it isn't clear what they are), and once again I'm in a desperate race to make the seven-thirty ferry. But the going is sluggish. I can't get this old car up to speed, and it dies altogether when I'm halfway down the mile-long causeway to the terminal. I grab my bags and run and run, but the *Queen George* is sounding its departure horn.

I fall back on my pillow, exhausted from my imaginary run, and become aware of a light-hearted honking sound, then sunshine streaming through my open bedroom window. I pry my eyelids open and see nuthatches exploring the trunk of a fir, snorting their nasal calls. The dream stays with me, vivid, Chaplinesque. Wait . . . that was not a dream. It happened.

My memory cells finally yawn and stretch awake, and yesterday's *opéra bouffe* comes prancing back. The street scene with the mulish, thin-skinned cop. Groans from the crowd, but a few cheers too, when the bags in the trunk turned out to hold rye seed. The hours spent wrangling with senior officers, their call to Garibaldi, to Constable Pound, to check on the existence and integrity of Loco Motion Luxury Rentals and Robert Stonewell.

I finally managed to reach Deputy Chief Joe Collins, who couldn't stop laughing. By the time the Mustang was released to me, drug-free, I had a bare half-hour to get to my boat. That the tank would run dry on the ferry causeway was foretold. *The fuel gauge exaggerates, so tank up early and often.*

I spent the night in the terminal with my suit bag as a mattress, barely sleeping, surviving on Cheezies and corn chips from the vending machines. The abandoned Mustang remains in the custody of the ferry corporation, for I have declined to retrieve it or pay the tow and storage fee.

Reverend Al was disgustingly charitable when he met me at

Ferryboat Landing. "Show him compassion, old fellow," he said as he helped get my bags and tools into his car. I told him that, *au contraire*, I planned to strangle Stoney. After I showered and got some sleep.

It's already mid-afternoon as I pull on some country clothes. Framed in my window, Niko and Yoki seem like figures in a Constable landscape as they stroll from the orchard with baskets of plums. They spot me pulling up my suspenders and they wave. "Nice you sleep all day," says Niko. "We work."

There's no coffee and everything in the fridge is stale, or worse, so brunch consists of cornflakes eaten dry and an apple that I munch as I head off with my empty rucksack. On my way to the store I will pass by Stoney's. The Fargo had better be there, and ready.

Niko and Yoki are at our roadside stand, bagging up the plums for sale. "Bad night – no sleep, no car." Niko has summed it up admirably.

I ask if they've seen Stoney or my truck.

"Sorry," says Yoki, who is as thin and shy as Niko is plump and forward.

Tomorrow, Saturday, they will be off to Stan Caliginis's vineyard, his planting party. There's a ceremonial reward: planters earn a certificate entitling them, somewhere down the road, to a bottle of the fermented fruit of their labours.

"Free food," says Niko. "Whole island come."

"Whole island minus me."

"Sorry," says Yoki.

I take off. The sun is warm. When a warbler warbles, a bothersome aphorism returns: *A bird does not sing because it has an answer. It sings because it has a song.* Maybe the solution is to stop inquiring, stop complaining, enjoy that song.

~~~

I find myself out of breath early on Breadloaf Hill. Four days in the city and I'm out of shape – rich restaurant food and lack of exercise. It's too hot a day for September, my shirt sticking to my back. I pause, panting, on the Centre Road ridge, to take in the island's worst view: Stoney's scatter of rusting vehicles, engines, and transmissions and, next door, the Shewfelts, their roof already decorated for Thanksgiving, or perhaps Halloween, with a giant tethered blow-up pumpkin bouncing in the breeze. Gnomes and leprechauns cavort on the lawn.

They've built a ten-foot cedar fence to help shield them from what they term, in their plethora of bylaw complaints, "an unmitigated eyesore." The fence hides the metallic exoskeletons, but the Shewfelts can still see Stoney's shack on its knoll, and often Stoney himself, nakedly urinating from the deck.

He is not there this afternoon, however, nor is repair job one, the Fargo. I decide upon reflection that is good news; it means the Fargo is likely on the road. The bad news is Stoney has again, unfailingly, converted it to his own use, or, as he calls it, test-driving.

The way is mostly downhill now to Hopeless Bay, with fold-out views every fifty paces of little farms snuggled into the forest, then beaches, rocky inlets, and islets. These scenes remind me how much I don't miss Ottawa. I haven't let Margaret know I'm coming, and I must do so soon.

At the Mount Norbert turnoff, the general store and off-kilter saloon come into view. Ten vehicles down there, none of them the Fargo. I have a shopping list of toiletries and foodstuffs, but first I must attend at the mail counter.

I pause at the message board: a new Kestrel Dubois photo. In traditional costume this time, with a confident smile, she is accepting a certificate. Tall for her age, light-skinned, no bust to speak of. I heard her parents on the CBC, frightened for their daughter, stunned by her flight to the West Coast. It was inexplicable that she hadn't called home; I listened in pain to their pleas for her to do so.

I turn to see Makepeace holding an envelope to the light. On my approach he quickly tucks it under the elastic band of a packet of letters and clamps his hand on it.

"These here are for your wife, and if she signed a Form A-31, I ain't seen it."

"What nonsense are you talking?"

"She has to formally authorize you to accept her mail. I been lenient about this practice, but no more. The Postmaster General is tightening the rules because of national security concerns."

"Don't be ridiculous. Her mail can't be left gathering dust – she's a Member of Parliament." I bluster. "You could cause a constitutional crisis. She might have an invitation from the Queen."

"I can practically guarantee she don't." He hands me a Form A-31. "Her signature on a fax will suffice. Rule C-138."

After more squabbling and my written declaration that I am married to said recipient and not separated, Makepeace relents on a one-time-only basis. I slip out the envelope he'd been holding to the light. Handwritten. Underlined: _Personal_. From someone at Greenpeace, Ottawa – Les Falk.

"Given it's personal, I can't tell you what's in it." Makepeace pulls my own mail from the Blunder Bay box, mostly bills and magazines. The latest _Island Bleat_. "And one love letter for you too."

"What do you mean by that?"

Makepeace appears taken aback by the curt tone. "A joke. Bite my head off, why don't you."

The love letter, postmarked three days ago, turns out to be a formal invitation to Annabelle's welcome-back party next Friday. Penned on it: _In case you can't make it, write something terrible about me for the_ MC _to read out._

I stroll over to the bar, signal Emily for a tall-mug coffee, and take it out to the smoke-illegal patio. I wave off an invitation to join the beer-quaffing regulars at the next table and settle in with the latest _Bleat_. Forbish's lead article advertises Stan Caliginis and tomorrow's "ceremonial replanting of the grapes with a Wild West motive." I assume the editor means _motif_. The "respected millionaire" wants to "bring the community together to restore the historic old Bulbaconi Vineyard and Winery."

The latter is an imposing architectural disaster, castle-like, built of granite from the old quarry, and despite its sweeping views, proof that if you build it, no one will come. At least not many, Garibaldi being off the winery tour trail. A local dark theory has the vineyard under a curse.

"He ain't gonna suck me in." Ernie Priposki has seen me shaking my head over the article. "I'll go for the food and booze but I ain't lining up for no free labour."

"Well, I'm gonna show him what I can do," says Baldy. "He's hiring, and paying top dollar."

"You ain't held down a frigging job for fifteen years."

I interrupt this testy colloquy. "Any of you gentlemen seen my Fargo on the road recently?"

"You ain't heard, Arthur?" Cudworth Brown, bad poet and local literary lion. His face is strained. "Stoney didn't make the turnoff at Bald Rock. He rode that sucker two hundred metres down to the gully."

I jolt upright, coffee slopping from my mug.

"He's been coptered off the island, man. All we can do is pray." Cud wearily stubs out a cigarette.

Honk Gilmore sighs. "The Fargo didn't survive."

I have gone pale, speechless. I don't pick up that I'm being ribbed until Gomer Goulet snorts, unable to hold back laughter. The others join in: my history of victimization by Stoney, especially over the truck, has inspired much mean humour.

Seeking forgiveness, they send Honk to my table as an emissary; he's a mentor for the local growers. "Stoney's on the run, man. There was a scene here at lunch. Ernst Pound blew up at him over some beef involving that rent-a he loaned you. Stoney took off like a rabbit."

"In my truck?"

"In your truck."

"If you see him before I do, Honk, as I expect you will, tell him his car is in the B.C. Ferries pound. I want my truck back."

"Lights out," a sentry calls. A flurried butting of cigarettes and emptying of ashtrays. I tell Emily to set the boys up on my tab, and hurry down to intercept Constable Pound, who is just pulling in. He is clearly under worsening strain over his marriage breakdown, making wild tirades as he flails about trying to fulfil his arrest quota.

"What's going on?" I ask, climbing into his van.

"I know and you know that Stonewell is just a stoner with a scrubby little grow somewhere, but they want me to make a case and grab him. Someone at Integrated Drugs decided Loco Motion Luxury Rentals sounds like a trafficking operation."

I actually play with the thought of turning Stoney in. He proudly showed me his grow in June, in the broom patch behind the road maintenance depot. With some effort I retrieve my honour. "I want my Fargo, Ernst. I'm not going to get it if he's hiding from the law. Please put out word he's no longer on the wanted list."

I take Ernst's who-cares shrug as assent and return to the bar and my cold coffee.

Honk Gilmore shuffles back to my table with a hopeful smile. "You work something out for my man?"

"This is the deal: tell Stoney to return my truck or he'll never see his grow again."

~~~

I spend most of the evening, as usual, brooding – during dinner, and later over Darjeeling tea and the *Goldberg Variations* – fretting about the Swift appeal, my marriage, my truck, practically anything that comes to mind.

Maybe I'll find peace if I slay the dragon of Gabriel's guilty plea. It feels like the python of legend around my neck, the serpent the Romans believed was born from slime and stagnant waters. A plea bargain – such a bargain for Gabriel Swift, so eagerly snapped up by his raw young lawyer. If only I had known what I know today.

Before retiring I remember to set Margaret's mail on her desk, but I succumb to a temptation to examine that thin envelope from

Les Falk, Greenpeace, Ottawa. Dated two weeks ago – slow to get here. I hold it to the light, but I lack Makepeace's magic eyes. An environmental function they want her to attend. A speaking invitation. Could be anything.

Almost ten-thirty in Ottawa, so Margaret ought to be up, though there's no guarantee; politics has turned this rise-and-shine farm girl into a nighthawk. My hand shakes as I dial. I don't know why I'm so nervous about this proposed visit. Maybe out of concern that I'll be seen as intruding on her hectic schedule, an unwanted relative whose presence must be borne politely.

A clatter as she knocks the phone from its cradle. "Arthur?" A clearing of the airway. "Coffee, I smell coffee." Her maker has an automatic timer.

"I'm sorry, were you sleeping, darling?"

"Good God, ten-thirty! I have a meeting." I see her in pyjamas and slippers, padding off to the kitchenette of her paper-cluttered apartment. A thump of the fridge door. A sip of milk. A sigh. "Clean Oceans Conference; I was co-chair. The press conference ran late, reception ran later. Never mind, how are you faring? Is Blunder Bay still above the rising seas?"

I fill her in, rather too gaily, telling her of my preposterous misadventures with Stoney's rent-a.

She seems unsure whether to laugh or sympathize, and ends up gently chiding. "Oh, and he assured you the car was clean, did he? Poor Arthur, I imagine you were at your most bellicose with that young officer." Censorious, like Reverend Al. *I've been under great strain,* I want to say.

I bring her up to date on Blunder Bay, reassure her that the farm and I are mucking along just fine, mostly thanks to the enterprise and energy of Niko and Yoki, and that there's a bit of mail for her, nothing that looks important. Something from Greenpeace. Les Falk.

No response. She goes offline for a moment. "Sorry – call waiting. It's Pierette."

I hurry on. "I'll bring everything when I come to Ottawa this coming week. Along with the alarm clock you forgot."

She laughs, hesitantly. "Next week?"

I explain my plans to snoop through the Mulligan fonds at the National Archives. As I rattle on about the case I hear the shower start up, imagine her stripping, testing the water with her foot.

Finally she finds a chance to speak. "It'll be so wonderful to see you. I try not to miss you. Love you."

~~~

Buoyed by that sign-off, I am emboldened this morning to stall no longer and to grub out the chicken pen. So while the girls do the morning milk, I shovel manure into a wheelbarrow, and as I work up a good farmer's sweat I jettison my worries for the while. One gets gratification from honourable work.

With a barrow full of a sticky mat of straw and excreta, I exit the coop just as a monster pickup purrs down the driveway, pursued by Homer, and pulls up by the house. In the back are kegs of beer, cases of wine, coolers, several garden spades. I am not particularly surprised to see Stan Caliginis step out (I sense in him a propensity for stalking). Cowboy boots, white Stetson, ornate belt buckle. Presumably he's been in the city, laying in supplies for this afternoon's planting party, but why is he stopping here?

Homer, acting the butler, greets him with a sniff, then announces him, a barked message. *He means no harm, Arthur, though you ought not to be too effusive in your welcome.* I call out a greeting as I manoeuvre the wheelbarrow toward him.

Caliginis takes my hand in a hearty salesman's grip. "Phoned, no answer. Decided to come by. Heard you had no transpo." He pats the big truck's fender. "Just off the lot – 2011 Ford Super Duty, V-8 turbo diesel. Bought it for the farm. Have to spin back to the Big Smoke tomorrow. She's yours for the week."

"That's very neighbourly, Stan, but I've vowed to cut my carbon emissions."

Niko and Yoki have got all the goat milk refrigerated by now and have joined us to hustle a ride to the vineyard. "You like, we go early," Niko tells me.

"I like you go early. I not go."

Caliginis looks disappointed in me. I have spurned his generosity, failed in a duty of friendship that I can't recall undertaking. The woofers race off to their dwelling to change. I want to go in and change too, and shower, but am forced to be polite and stay put with my smelly pants and boots and wheelbarrow.

I can't imagine why the effluvium doesn't damage his refined olfactory senses, but he seems determined not to notice, even comes closer. "I have an apology. Didn't know you were AA until I got halfway through the book."

I ask him why that would be a problem. Because, he says, as a teetotaller I could hardly be expected to "enthuse" over his vineyard project. He doesn't want it to come between us. He is terribly sorry to have gone on the way he did about his favourite wines. (AAers often have to deal with this sort of thing. It's presumed that if we can't enjoy a drink we don't want anyone else to.)

"Fascinating woman," he says.

The quick change of subject startles. "Who?"

"Sorry, still caught up with *Thirst for Justice*. Annabelle. Your first wife. Gorgeous. Flamboyant. Reminds me a bit of my own first wife. Took me to the cleaners but I never got over her. Eudora. Remarried in haste, and that ended badly too."

I am dismayed to have become a repository of this personal oral history. I feel I'm being pressured to share.

Caliginis now retrieves a copy of *A Thirst* from the cab – shall I assume he carries it everywhere, or is it being used as a prop? He flips the pages, finds what he wants. "This photo from the early eighties, you and Annabelle in tux and gown . . . Owns that camera, doesn't she? Stunning."

"She looks exactly the same today."

Niko and Yoki are taking their time, so I see no recourse but to invite him to relax on the veranda while I wash up. In the course of changing into yesterday's fairly clean pants, I draw from a pocket the invitation from Annabelle. *In case you can't make it, write something terrible about me . . .*

Returning outside, I see the girls finally approaching, Yoki in a polka skirt and red bandana, and an old straw hat she must have found in the attic. Niko looks exotic in Daisy Mae cut-offs and a vest with a plastic sheriff's star. Caliginis insists on taking my picture with them.

I can offer no explanation why, as I see him to his truck, I present him with Annabelle's invitation. "Here's your chance to meet her."

An impetuous, mischievous act that haunts me the rest of the day. Was it motiveless or was I seeking to redirect Annabelle to him? Why wouldn't she thank me for hooking her up with a discerning tycoon with a nose for essence of hazelnuts and tropical fruit? *It was the least I could do, Annabelle – you reminded Stan of his only true love.*

I ought to have mentioned Annabelle to Margaret. I tell myself I'm protecting the leader of the *Parti vert* from distraction, but wonder if it's more complicated than that.

~~~

I have assumed Stoney will wait for the cover of darkness before returning my truck, but I don't expect him before midnight. So I am pleasantly surprised when, just at bedtime, sharp-eared Homer barks, *It's back! It's back!* I go out in time to catch the Fargo rolling down the driveway and stopping by the barn, engine off, lights off. Dog is standing in the back, riding shotgun with a pair of garden clippers.

Stoney swings down from the driver's seat in his slow, stoned way and waits for me to hustle over in my slippers. He's standing under the dim light of a hanging bulb, checking out the barn, seemingly enjoying its dense fecal odours. "Got a message you were concerned about me, sire."

My ruse seems to have worked, but I'm taking no chances, and I climb in the cab. The engine starts immediately, smoothly, its cough cured. Clutch, brakes, gearshift function; all the lights work except for the right bright, and there's even a quarter-tank of gas. I pocket the ignition key and climb out, holding my position between Stoney and the Fargo. I shall not fall for the predictable ruse: *We got no backup vehicle, man, so I'll return it in the morning.*

"Job one, as promised, eh, and it carries the usual warranty. As to the Mustang, I have arranged for a trusted emissary to retrieve it from the ferry monster. That will be Dog." He's still standing up there, his back to the rear window. "I have instructed him not to make inquiries about my cherished gargoyle pipe. Up until I heard about your altercation with the law, I was scratching my head over where I'd stuck it. I got too many things on the go – I get distracted, eh."

"Of course, Stoney."

He tamps out a cigarette. "So how's the, ah, heat situation, as far as I'm concerned?"

"Ernst will lay off you. You might want to thank him."

"I'll ask Filchuk if he minds letting Ernst have his grow. He's given up on it; it's all gone to seed."

Stoney blows a smoke ring that is whipped away by a gust, a wind change that sends the yard light swinging and causes the barn smell to be replaced by a sweet, pungent odour. I twist around, still protecting the driver's door, and peer at Dog, who in fact is not standing. He has actually been sitting, on a tarp, newly reaped marijuana plants piled beneath it.

"I figured you wouldn't mind," Stoney says. "They were a week away from prime, but I figured cut and run, man, just in case. Not that I mistrusted you to squeal, counsellor, heaven forbid. Anyway, me and Dog figured this old barn would be perfect for maybe an overnight or two. If that don't work out for you for some reason, we'll look for a different stash-hole and return the old girl in the morning."

"No, I will drive you and your cargo home."

Stoney is taken aback by that. "You okay with . . . like, driving a hundred K's of bud around this island?" Slow to recover, he picks up speed. "On a Saturday night, when both island cops are going to be out in force checking for drunks coming from that booze bash up at the vineyard? I believe you reported this here vehicle missing, so won't they be looking for it?" The disarming, apologetic smile says he thinks he has me.

And truthfully I am not at my sharpest, my mind clouded by Annabelle, still berating myself for pressing that invitation on Caliginis. But I am not going to stand here helplessly as Stoney disappears up the road in my 1969 vintage Fargo. "Haul those plants up to the loft behind the hay bales."

The Point Grey cliffs, Spanish Banks, English Bay, Lord Stanley's forest pass below, then the elegant arcs of Lion's Gate Bridge, then we glide into Coal Harbour. I am once again in the heart of über-livable Vancouver, delivered by a Syd-Air Beaver on its noon flight from the Gulf Islands.

I wasn't planning to be in Vancouver until tomorrow, and then only as a stopover to Ottawa. This sudden, unavoidable excursus also means I can't carry out my threat to burn Stoney's cannabis at sunset if it isn't hauled out of my barn by then. It was to have been gone three nights ago.

I have hastened here because Gertrude phoned just after breakfast, to tell me Jimmy "Fingers" O'Houlihan is dying to see me. Literally – he's in a hospice, on his deathbed. Soon as possible, he told her. His calendar was free for maybe the next few weeks. "He said it was about Dermot Mulligan; that's all I could get out of him."

I didn't keep up my relationship with O'Houlihan after 1962, other than bumping into him outside courtrooms as he waited to give proof of adulteries, and those were strained moments. Where he had been effusive, he became guarded. No mention of Mulligan and his affair with Rita Schumacher, no mention of the Swift case – it was as if he was embarrassed to be seen with me.

After Harvey Frinkell, his main revenue source, was disbarred, O'Houlihan closed up his detective agency and began flipping real estate in Florida. I heard he went bust in the Great Recession and returned to Canada to avoid fraud inquiries. He will be in his early eighties now. Liver cancer, Gertrude has learned. She will be meeting me, taking me to him.

Syd-Air has a berth at the Bayshore Inn, and that's where we four passengers alight. The hotel has had a few facelifts over time, a plush new tower, and though Trader Vic's is just a memory, I can never avoid hearkening back, when I am here, to National

Secretaries Day 1962, and the poor impression I made on nineteen-year-old Gertrude Isbister.

It's something she remembers quite well too. In the lobby, after we buss each other and she takes my arm, she recalls how I earnestly described over mai tais what goes into a Salish aphrodisiac. "I must say, Arthur, I tensed up."

She's joshing me. I don't remind her of her youthful feelings for me, embarrassingly revealed in my biography. *I don't know how many times I flashed him some leg.* That constant straightening of stockings.

Gertrude has brought a laptop and a video camera. I don't want to take a chance on O'Houlihan expiring before we record whatever relevant tidbits about Mulligan he withheld from me. The appeal is six days hence, and if Jimmy gives us value, we'll have to make immediate disclosure to court and Crown. Gertrude has assured me a DVD can be packaged and couriered in an hour.

Frinkell never did send me copies of the intimate photographs his private eye took from the balcony of the Schumachers' bedroom. With the case closed, I gave up pursuing the matter. But I retain vivid impressions: Dermot and Rita in rut, a dark exposure; Dermot putting on his horn-rims, his stumpy penis at rest; Dermot helping heavy-breasted Rita into her clothes.

I also remember an odd comment by Jimmy Fingers: *Missed out on a financial opportunity.* "How so?" I say aloud.

"Excuse me?"

"Sorry, Gertrude. I have been talking to myself incessantly, another side effect of age."

"Nonsense, you started doing that in your thirties. I do wish, Arthur, you'd stop making such a thing about your age. You really haven't changed at all, just found new things to worry about."

How true. A terrible scenario could develop if loose lips mention those hundred kilos of pot that Blunder Bay is harbouring. That has been bothering me all morning. How stupid of me, how unthinking – the repercussions for Margaret would be awful.

Gertrude turns north on Georgia, toward the park and Lion's Gate. The hospice is in the North Shore's hilly suburbs.

"I may have to delay tomorrow's flight to Ottawa."

She asks me why. I withhold details, explain it's about an unfinished matter on the island.

"Arthur, you're on WestJet out of YVR at ten. You will be just in time for dinner with Margaret at her favourite restaurant, La Bretonne. Afterwards she is taking you to the National Arts Centre. Carlos Prieto is performing Dvořák's cello concerto and they're doing Beethoven's Sixth, one of your favourites. It's all laid on. You will be on that plane."

~~~

The Loving Interlude Hospice is in Lynn Valley, down a wooded ravine – at a dead end, fittingly. A Cancer Society facility where patients end their days in as much comfort as their ravaged bodies will permit. Most of those in the sitting room are in wheelchairs, dolefully reading or playing cards. On a bulletin board, a tattered Kestrel Dubois flyer. There has been a tentative recent sighting of the young Cree, a dubious one, on the UBC campus. The story is slipping from the headlines.

A care worker takes Gertrude and me down a wing of suites, knocks on A-14, and pokes her head in. "Are we presentable?" Apparently, because she ushers us in. A small room with a balcony overlooking a mix of conifers. O'Houlihan is in his robe, sitting up in bed on a drip, bald, skeletal, but sharp of eye. He's been writing on a pad. Beside him, a few shelves with books, files, memorabilia.

"You have some guests."

"I will receive them."

"Is there anything we need?"

"We could use a hand job."

"You are being very bad. No more smoking. You've been warned."

"Hey, gorgeous, I ain't had a cigarette in forty years before I came here. It ain't going to kill me. Give a man his dying wish."

He blows her a kiss as she departs. "Bring a bottle, Artie?" Rattling laughter. "Forget it, morphine rocks. Anyway, I heard you sobered up, went AA. Tried it, couldn't stomach the rampant sincerity." To Gertrude: "He's my saviour – got me off a tough beef."

I ask, "Did you pay off that witness, Jimmy?"

"Sure did. That's a dying declaration." He cackles. Refusing help, he works his way off the bed and into his wheelchair. "Cirrhosis. I maybe got a month. But I ain't complaining. Never figured to make it to sixty, let alone eighty-one."

He picks up an inch-thick file folder and wheels past Gertrude as she sets up her computer and camcorder. "Can you help with the balcony door, love?" As she opens it, he switches on a desk fan, puts on a slouch hat, and pulls a pack of Rothmans from the pocket of his robe. "Trouble with morphine, it ain't addictive enough."

An eight-by-ten slides from the folder as he lights up, and he tucks it back. "Harvey and I figured to earn at least a champagne cruise off of this. He did the paperwork while I did the dirty. Phoned Mulligan, told him I wanted to avoid him some embarrassment. When he had the kindness to come to my office, I explained I was raising money for a highly recommended charity for the hungry." Another croaking laugh. "Frinkell set it up – all legit, even a bank account."

That speech was a physical effort, and he pauses awhile to wheeze out smoke, enjoying this, the story he'd kept cooped up.

"I suggested a substantial mortgage on his lovely house could help feed a lot of tummies. Mulligan looked them over, my photos, and went off to think about it." A theatrical sigh; he's playing to Gertrude's camera. "Our dreams of Caribbean cruises dissolved when he joined the choir eternal. Suicide, I figured, soon as I heard they found his clothes."

O'Houlihan flicks the remains of his cigarette over the balcony railing onto the grass, then navigates back to the bed, leaving the folder of photos with me. A dozen black-and-whites, all poorly lit because only a bed lamp had been left on. They disclose that Dermot did not go directly out the back way, as Rita had advised.

353

Instead he dallied, trying out her clothes. Stockings, panties, garter belt, a full-figure bra into which he stuffed socks. A girdle. A slip. A white blouse and dark pleated skirt. A splashy-looking party dress. Looking at himself in the mirror.

"These were real slow exposures. The perv was taking forever. My balls almost froze off. Last one's a beaut."

The last one, if I make it out correctly, has Mulligan wearing what look like stretch nylon panties and masturbating into them while standing before the mirror. I study it numbly, the literal climax to a sad little show.

Dermot finally got into his own clothes and made his exit, allowing Jimmy Fingers to come in from the cold. He retrieved the soiled panties from the laundry hamper, stuffed them in his camera bag. "Embroidered with little daisies, I remember. No idea what I did with them."

"Did you show these photos to Professor Schumacher?"

"Just the ones of them fucking. I still wanna laugh when I think of his expression."

"When did Mulligan come to your office?"

"Maybe four, five days before Easter, as I best recall."

"He came down from Squamish?"

"Yeah, that's where I phoned him. I was up there once, nosing around."

"Find anything?"

"Nope. Walked past his old lady but she had no clue who I was. Just a birdwatcher with his camera and field glasses." With that, he closes his eyes in sleep.

"A bird does not sing because it has an answer," I say, placing the photos in my briefcase. Gertrude gathers her equipment and follows me out, giving me a puzzled look.

"It sings because it has a song."

"Oh."

"Call Tim Dare at his unlisted number. Tell him I must see him today."

"Yes, I think it's about time you checked in with a psychiatrist."

From "Beauchamp Behind Bars," *A Thirst for Justice*,
© W. Chance

YOU WILL NOT HEAR BEAUCHAMP ADMIT IT, but his well-known antipathy to Ottawa stems mainly from a significant loss of face he suffered there. Until then he'd been rather a popular figure in the capital, beloved by the media, always ready with a quip, and he'd been garlanded for his international heroics in the Abzal Erzhan case.[*]

Beauchamp had been brought (*dragged* is how he put it) before the royal commission inquiring into the case and was accused of hiding vital information in an email from his deceased client. In declining to breach solicitor/client privilege, Beauchamp got into a spat with the chair and was ordered incarcerated until he purged his contempt of court.

No one expected that order to stand – expert consensus was that it would be quashed within the day. But unfortunately a supposedly respected counsel retained by Beauchamp turned out – and I choose my words carefully – to have a problem involving chemicals, and the motion to quash was fouled up. So poor Beauchamp spent three nights in a cell before matters were put right.

The whole episode has taken on the flavour of humorous folk tale told and retold where lawyers gather. All in all, a rather tragicomic note on which to end the legal career of Arthur Ramsgate Beauchamp, Q.C.[†]

---

[*] Detailed in Chapter 62. For a fuller history, see the appendix under *Snow Job*.

[†] For updates on his retirement years, see ThirstForJustice.ca/blog.

I am thirty-five thousand feet above the golden wheat fields of Saskatchewan. Far to the north is Torch River and the rubble of what was Pius XI Residential School, demolished two decades ago. Relics from the discipline room were retrieved for display in a Native museum.

April Wu has hit a roadblock in trying to track down a woman who may be the last remaining descendent of Dermot Mulligan. Marie Snow, born in Fox Lake, Manitoba, in 1978, daughter of Sebastien, who was born of rape. Marie lost both parents at seven – Sebastien to suicide, her mother after a miscarriage – and was adopted. The trail ends there, adoption records closed to public view.

Open in front of me is a learned article by Dr. Timothy Dare in which he calls for a firm diagnostic distinction between openly gay transvestism and the cross-dressing fetish of heterosexual men. I am finding it hard to concentrate, however; unable to suppress images of a tactical drug squad combing through my barn.

I tried to reach Stoney last night but he seemed to be out of range. I will keep after him, despairingly. I don't dare tell Margaret what I have allowed to happen. I already have a sense that over fine dining this evening she intends to explain why our marriage isn't working. She will tell me a little about Les, so daring and brave, yet tender, this Greenpeace activist. She hopes the Beethoven and Dvořák will soothe the pain. She hopes we'll still be friends.

No, that isn't Margaret Blake; she's more thoughtful than that. She will delay her announcement until the Swift appeal is done, knowing I am stressed enough. She has warned Les Falk not to contact her during the time I'm in Ottawa. Only two days. I have the stash-hole to worry about, and the appeal begins on Wednesday.

I return to Tim Dare's article. It is scathing about the DSM, the

Manual of Mental Disorders, for suggesting that a gay man who dresses as a woman might be suffering from a disorder. Tim has just published it, proudly, and was a little full of himself yesterday. But he gave me two hours. He is the coast's sharpest forensic psychiatrist, and a specialist in kink.

He was fascinated by my case, delighted by my ex-icon's history as the campus horndog, "getting nookie right and left," as that gossipy old bore Irvine Winkle put it. More fuel for Dare's thesis that most cross-dressers typically have strong masculine drives.

"We come out of the womb homo or hetero or something in between," he instructed. "Sexual orientation is something you come installed with. Paraphilias are learned. These are what we called perversions in more robust times – exhibitionism, fetishes." The latter involves sexual arousal spurred on by inanimate objects – in Mulligan's case, female clothing. Transvestic fetishism is the formal name for such cross-dressing. It likely finds its provenance in childhood, the result of a pattern or a trauma. An example of the former: a son getting the wrong signals from a mother who badly wanted a girl.

Tim offered a far more graphic and germane example of how a lengthy trauma could exert a similar influence: a boy in a deeply Catholic home (in Montreal, say) watches as his beloved older sister (let's call her Genevieve) wastes away from leukemia. *There followed a wretched time – years, it seemed – when I ached for the smiles and hugs and words of comfort . . .*

~~~

The Prius taking me from airport to city is Margaret's, and it's being driven by her elf of a parliamentary assistant, Pierette Litvak, whose youthful exuberance and optimism often leave me exhausted, even depressed that I no longer have that vigour. It's a crisp, clear evening in Ottawa, with a sharpness that warns of the brutal months ahead. The cruelty has already been felt, the outer branches of maples bleeding red.

"You're all set for tomorrow, Arthur. The archival officer who tends to the Dermot Mulligan collection is named Shaheed Khan, and he'll take you in hand. Expects you around ten."

I insist she's done far too much for me. She waves it off, takes a call through her headset. "Yeah, I got him." Pause as she glances at me. "No, not too bad. A little rumpled from the flight. Usual dour mood." Another pause. "I'll do that right now." Pierette passes along Margaret's air kiss. "Unless you feel a burning need to freshen up, we'll go straight to the Bretonne. I'll drop you off, then pick her up. She's running late."

"That's fine." Pause. "Running late doing what?"

"Ottawa Valley Environmental Coalition. The usual subversive elements. Heated debate about how to deal with threats to a fish stream. Some guys want an aggressive response – occupying a chemical plant."

"Ah. That would be coming from the Greenpeacers, I suppose." I take a breath. "They're there, I assume. Greenpeace."

"Of course."

I almost falter, but press on. "So I would imagine Les Falk is among the, uh, aggressive responders."

"Yeah. How do you know her?"

"Who?"

"Les. Leslie."

I'm hugely flustered. "I don't, really. Know her, I mean. As Leslie. I've brought a letter from her." Seeking an excuse to hide my flushed face, I swivel, fish around in my shoulder bag for Margaret's mail. "Yes, here. Les Falk, Greenpeace. Marked 'Personal.'"

Pierette glances at me oddly, as if suppressing an urge to call me a suspicious old goat. "It's a copy of the meeting notice. Les thinks slow mail is more secure. Maybe she's paranoid. Maybe she's right."

"She doesn't know our local postmaster." Suddenly I am looking forward to the evening with high anticipation. A terrific date, an excellent restaurant, a concert. Ottawa is a fine place to be right now.

~~~

La Bretonne is in a refurbished mansion, a genteel space with many dimly lit alcoves. It's too expensive for journalists, so cabinet ministers often come here with their mistresses or corporate sponsors. I have learned to identify the lobbyists: handsome, tanned men and charming, sexy women, skilled in the art of eye contact, casually bilingual, knowledgeable about food and wine, coolly indifferent to the cost of everything. The owner/chef is a secret Green, a contributor, and Margaret pays only for wine and cocktails. The one drawback to the place: a fellow at a baby grand playing routine so-called stylings.

I have Margaret's place of honour by a little bay window, and I am not here long before she hurries in. We embrace, and when she sits, still out of breath, she finds a glass of Merlot waiting for her. "You're a darling – I am in need of this." She looks a little overworked; there has been weight loss. What a tough life being leader of a small party, yet she's unflagging. Hearings, meetings, constant conflict, constant bullshit.

She sips. "Mmm, a majestic, fruity nose with subtle undertones of acorns roasting by the fire." More good news: she's no longer taking Caliginis seriously.

"And a gentle, teasing hint of pontifical grandiloquence." But I don't want to jest about the fellow; that could lead to a maze of complications. *What could possibly have been in your mind to give him Annabelle's invitation? And why haven't you mentioned her to me?* I can't imagine Stan has taken me seriously, that he will actually go.

I sort through my extensive repertoire of recent jokes upon myself and choose the contretemps with Officer Wong. I carry on at my self-deprecating best, and Margaret laughs merrily.

We have ordered by now and have our starters, her green salad, my onion soup. "Let me introduce you to the fascinating world of cross-dressing." Jimmy Fingers' tale of watching Dermot Mulligan trying on dresses and climaxing into a pair of panties gets us well into my Arctic char and her *canard à maquereau*.

Margaret seems content to let me ramble on about paraphilias and fetishes and cross-dressing, and I sense her relaxing. Though overworked, she seems happier here, in Ottawa, than on Garibaldi. We get along better here. Maybe it's as Annabelle said: *marriage survives best taken in short dollops.*

"We're talking about a male-only fetish, by the way. Ladies tend not to masturbate with men's jockey shorts."

I have said this too loudly – blame it on a pause between piano stylings – and am heard by a couple being led to their alcoved table, a portly older man and a pretty Asian woman some years younger. Both flick looks our way.

Margaret waits until they're gone, then leans forward. "Supplies minister on a clandestine date. He's pretending we didn't see each other." Darkly: "She reports to Beijing." She is on her third glass of wine and feeling quite gay. "I'm so relieved to hear women don't do it in men's jockey shorts. More evidence as to which is the more sensible sex."

The wine and a sobering coffee impel her to the washroom, giving me a window in which to pull out my cell.

This time Stoney answers. "Hey, man, am I glad to hear from you. They want two hundred bucks for towing and stowing my Mustang. I'm gonna have to call on your good offices –"

"Listen to me. Have you done the chore?"

"What chore?"

"I think you know what I'm talking about." Through my teeth: "Did you take out the hay?"

"Oh, that chore. Problem is I'm fresh out of wheels. My flatbed's out on loan, I can't access the Fargo, and they want an arm and a leg for the muscler. You caught me in a situation here, boss – I got customers. I'll call when I free up, that's a promise."

Before I can utter an oath or a threat, he has clicked off.

~~~

Margaret demands I give up my phone while we're still in the foyer of the concert hall. "I just don't trust you any more, Arthur. Disaster seems to stalk you." She ensures that both our phones are off and sticks them in her bag. I don't expect Stoney to call back anyway.

The playbill has the Pastoral Symphony on first. Next, after intermission, will be the premiere of an orchestral suite, "Loons Calling on Lake Nippissing," after which Prieto will straddle his cello.

I expected we might be hauling ourselves up to one of the lofty balconies of this vast gilded hall, but Margaret has many friends in the arts, and that has likely earned us these middle seats in the orchestra. My view is slightly impaired by the tall, bald gentleman in front of me; for some reason I'm distracted by the tufts of black hair bestriding his ears.

Though the Pastoral is lilting and lovely, perhaps I know it too well. I let it caress me, but by the second movement my mind has swung back twenty-four hours, to that illuminating session with Timothy Dare. Triggered somehow, I fear, by the unruly black tufts in front of me.

I must have expressed too keen an interest in fetishes, because Tim picked up something in my tone and body language. I asked, "What if it's not an inanimate object?"

"Like what?"

"Oh, like a foot. Body parts. Hair."

"Hair?"

That seemed to pique too much interest, and I tried to recover with a stale joke. "In my heyday I was known to be quite a breast man."

"Regrettably, that only makes you normal, Arthur, though possibly poorly nurtured. The disability is called partialism. You're obsessively preoccupied with part of a woman's body."

I squirmed under his gaze. I toyed with confessing, telling him about the au pair from Provence. But I held back.

Now the strings are joined in dance by woodwinds and horns. And I am overcome by a memory of Josette, her pillowy breasts, the wet-smelling hairy darknesses to either side of them. She shared our house for five years, until I turned twelve. She let me touch her breasts, even kiss them. And she would raise her skirt and give me a teasing glimpse of the lush junction of her legs – her garden, she called it. But I could not come into that garden, only her *petits jardins,* those thick, bushy pits into which she drew my guileless, palpitating young prick. Into which she took the sticky produce of my first ejaculation. One day, with no advance notice, my parents sent her away, and she was never spoken of again.

The stormy allegro awakens me, and I finally lose myself in the music.

Later, in the foyer, I follow Margaret about like a puppy as she performs the duties demanded by celebrity.

"Now we have to listen to some token Canadian content," I grumble as we take our seats. *Loons Calling on Lake Nipissing. Composed by J. Walter Prothero.* "Sometimes it's embarrassing to be a Canadian." Loud enough to get glances and a sympathetic snicker. Margaret shushes me.

The piece isn't as bad as I anticipated; in fact the call of the common loon is skilfully woven through the suite, even hauntingly. And when, during applause, Pinchas Zukerman calls for J. Walter Prothero to stand, I applaud vigorously, then freeze as the tuft-eared man in front of me rises. A spotlight finds him and I sink low in my seat, suffering the pain of Margaret's pinch.

~~~

My partner's small flat is more a workspace than a living space. Everywhere are clippings files, magazines, photos, maps, statistical charts – a politician's clutter. There is not much in the fridge. Alarmingly, I find evidence she has capitulated to the microwave oven, a device once reviled.

We have walked here from the concert hall, a quick, crisp stroll across the University of Ottawa campus to her low-rise, and are quickly into bed. Our after-dinner espressos are still working, and so is Margaret: marking up briefing notes for some hearing or other, giggling occasionally. I am rereading Dermot Mulligan's *After Constantinople: The Totalitarianism of Western Religion.*

Another snigger. "Can't take you anywhere."

Composer J. Walter Prothero never once turned to look at his maligner. That he chose not to embarrass us showed immense grace under pressure, a kindness that mollified her anger and my anguish, which evolved into merriment. It has been a splendid evening otherwise.

I pause at page 318 to study a quote from Camus about suicide being humankind's sole serious philosophical problem. It's the same quote that began Mulligan's undated, unsigned, uncompleted reflections on suicide. Earlier I found his Nietzsche reference as well, in a footnote of his *Clearing Judas's Name and Other Essays*. Absent from Dermot's musings was that philosopher's better-known quotation *The thought of suicide is a great consolation: by means of it one gets successfully through many a bad night.* The suicide note, if that's what it is, lacks the originality for which Dermot was so well-known, in his lectures as well as his writings.

Finally I turn off my light and Margaret follows suit. I am still wakeful, though, eyes open, my mind busy, words seeking egress. Margaret shuffles close, an arm around me, and I am emboldened. Maybe she will still love me.

"Darling, did I mention? Annabelle has suddenly returned to Vancouver. Seems her marriage went kaput."

"How sad."

"Popped by to have me sign the book. Asked about you. I told her you were amazing, of course."

"Ahmm." The sound made by a yawn. "Tell me all about it tomorrow."

This seems to be going okay. I try extending my luck. "Here's an oddity for you. I just learned I suffer from a disorder called partialism. It involves women's armpits."

Hearing only silence, I press on: Josette, my tainted youth, my paraphilia, Tim Dare's subtle diagnosis. I finally peter out, and there is more silence.

Finally, wearily: "Do you really want me to take this seriously?"

"I thought you might."

"Darling, the world is undergoing catastrophic climate change. Our seas and oceans are becoming cesspools. Countless millions are homeless and starving. Wars and terrorism never cease. You don't have the right to fuss over such a piddly thing."

She rolls away from me and is soon asleep.

A s was arranged, an obliging young archivist named Shaheed Khan takes me in tow at ten a.m. when I sign in at the National Archives building. He asks me to render up my pens and pencils but assures me copies can be made of anything I wish. I am led to a long table piled with boxes upon boxes of bundled manuscripts, letters, books, photos, and notes.

What is the task I've set myself here? Comb through all his papers, said old Riley, to see if anything else has been overlooked. But going through all this stuff – that will take days of bleary effort. I haven't put my mind properly to this. And I'm tired after a night of mentally kicking myself for coming across to Margaret as a self-absorbed weirdo. As to Annabelle's return, all she said this morning was, "She's your problem, not mine." A little touchy, I thought, but I was happy to let the subject drop.

"What's the history of this collection, Shaheed? How long have these papers been here?"

"They were bought from Irene Mulligan in late 1962. For fifty thousand dollars."

A fortune back then, but she'd earned it with her research, her hours at his old Remington. I am staring at thousands upon thousands of pages. No wonder a couple of them were overlooked by the experts evaluating this mountain of paper.

"How often is this collection visited by researchers?"

"On average, I would say fifteen times a year."

"For learned articles, theses, that sort of thing?" Out of habit, I am cross-examining.

"I believe another book is being written about him."

"Who's the author?" I ought to advise him to hold the presses.

"I'm sorry, Mr. Beauchamp, we don't release that information."

"Last March a significant two-page document came to light that was not listed in your fonds. Your office copied it for us and provided proof of authenticity. Have you learned who alerted you to it?"

"Your reopening of the case has caused a flurry of interest in these papers. I daresay it was someone who didn't want to be tangled up in the matter."

"What book was it in?"

Shaheed brings from a box a thick volume of Shakespeare's tragedies, published a century ago – an edition of value, enhanced by Mulligan's many pencilled marginalia, mostly references to literary or scholarly works. I look for act three, scene one, of *Hamlet*, the 'to be or not' soliloquy. *Take arms, Mulligan, take arms.*

Shaheed finally loses his aplomb and seems a little confused. "My goodness, that's the very page. That's where it was found."

"Indeed?" One of the cornerstones of my appeal has firmed up; here is the continuity that Riley said was missing. I find myself emoting, as if on stage: "*To sleep, perchance to dream: ay, there's the rub.* I will need to take your affidavit, my good man. Who was the last person to look through this material before you were alerted to these hidden pages?"

"I am really not allowed to say. Forgive me, Mr. Beauchamp, it's policy."

A subpoena will cut through the bureaucratic guff. But young Mr. Khan has been polite and helpful, so I will not threaten him. Lawyers from Tragger, Inglis's Ottawa branch will do that.

Shaheed says he'll be available should I need him, and goes off to report this conversation to his superiors. I call our Ottawa branch and put the head of litigation in the picture. He will send someone down here to help draft an affidavit. Before settling in with Mulligan's papers, I find a plug to power up my phone; I don't want to miss out if Stoney finds the decency and courage to make his promised call.

I merely riffle through Mulligan's personal letters – I've read them, in a UBC Press hardcover. He made several references to Gabriel, all complimentary: a "flower in the bleak wilderness of the Squamish Valley"; a reference to an IQ test in 1961 – "my acolyte ringing up a monster 165." Mulligan doesn't appear to have written to anyone after April 13, 1962, the date Harvey Frinkell sent out his demand letter. Which was compounded by Jimmy Fingers' shake-down. Suicide, milords.

I poke idly through other boxes, pull out manuscript drafts, shake them; nothing falls out but a few bookmarks. Nor does a similar effort produce anything from the three dozen books retained for their marginal comments. The vast bulk of Mulligan's library remains in the old A-frame by the river, now a literary shrine for grant-aided short-term-residence writers. I even delve into his McGill memorabilia, his yearbooks, where I find him portrayed performing in HMS *Pinafore:* a skinny young man in a sailor suit, belting out a song.

Presently a pair of young lawyers from our Ottawa bureau come by. Smart, eager young women, one with a copy of *A Thirst* to be signed, the other excited about doing "something cool" for a change. They have been on the phone with Justice Department lawyers, who will cooperate in shaping Shaheed's affidavit disclosing the finding of Mulligan's note but are balking at disclosing the names of those who accessed his papers. I tell the women what I want in the affidavit, and they fly off.

I spend the next few hours flipping through Mulligan's notes and papers, aimlessly and without reward. At mid-afternoon – noon on Garibaldi – I take a deep breath and call Stoney, who is usually up by then. All I get are a series of rings and this: "Loco Motion Luxury Rentals and Chauffeur Service, at your service twenty-four/seven. Please leave a message."

I disguise my voice. "Hello, sir, I represent a firm of venture capitalists planning a retreat on your lovely island –"

"I'm on it," Stoney says breathlessly. "Sorry we didn't pick up right away; my staff is on lunch break. This is Stonewell himself."

"Has the hay been hauled away?"

"The hay?"

"The crop."

It takes a moment to click in. "Nice try, counsellor, but I wasn't fooled for a second. I been meaning to call. Things piled up –"

"Is it gone?"

"Affirmative."

"Thank God for that."

"Well, I ain't sure if God had much to do with it. I'm gonna be up front with you here. We been robbed."

A joke. He's getting back at me. Nice try, Stoney.

"What happened was, when me and Dog went to pick it up last evening, the crop, it wasn't in the loft or anywhere. Just some broken stems and leaves."

"I see. Just disappeared, did it?"

"Yeah, and we went over to see Noki and Yoyo to ask if they seen anything suspicious, any cars, noises in the night. They didn't, like, know what I was talking about, eh. I got the impression they didn't know nothing."

I'm no longer sure this is a gag and am growing alarmed.

"I don't think it's the cops, and if it is, they're probably tapping the line, so we're goners anyway. My theory, it's more likely some common thief. That weed was gonna tide me through the winter, man."

He rambles on about the rampant dishonesty on Garibaldi until I cut him off. Do nothing, say nothing, I advise. I will see him tomorrow. Then I call our travel agent to book the next available flight to the West Coast.

~~~

"Windmills? How very Middle Ages, Lewison. Makes one think of Don Quixote."

"Jump in, my boy. Huge earnings potential in clean energy. Got to be savvy, though."

"Talk to me about it again when the oil sands run out – in about a thousand years from now."

It is eight o'clock and I am in Vancouver, finishing dinner at my club, eavesdropping on the filthy rich and suffering the kind of edgy feeling I long ago learned to associate with an urge to knock back a double martini. This, the Confederation Club, saw many of my extravaganzas after I'd had a few of those.

But I am sticking to tea. I am here only because I have become habituated to the jacket-and-tie atmosphere. However traditional – women have only recently breached its walls – the club gives impeccable service, and they usually have a bed for a charter member who is stopping over.

My plane got me to Vancouver shortly after seven, too late for flight or ferry to my island, but an early-bird Syd-Air charter will whisk me to Bungle Bay, where I will stage a last-ditch effort to save the reputations of a reckless old barrister and his celebrated life partner. Ex-partner, if I get busted for a hundred kilos of dope. *I'm sorry, Arthur, it was just not meant to be.*

"A sudden development after a successful day at the Archives," I told her in a hurried call. "Anyway, I'd be boring company on the weekend. Appeal begins in five days, and it's totally occupying my mind."

She took it in stride. Typical of the unpredictable fusspot.

On another front there is good news, though a little baffling. According to the radio, Kestrel Dubois has made phone contact with her parents. A collect call from a pay phone in Squamish – of all places – to allay their worries. She expressed her love and said she was healthy and safe and would call again in a week; she had "things to do" that she couldn't explain. Police and media have converged on Squamish but the fourteen-year-old has not been seen, has left no trail.

It is hard not to tease myself with the thought that Kestrel's journey parallels mine in some mystical way. I'm playing with asking April Wu to interview her parents, Samson and Marie Dubois, and ask if their daughter's mission might involve, in any remote way, *Gabriel Swift versus the Queen*. A lovely name, Kestrel, and so very appropriate – the fierce and determined little falcon they call the sparrow hawk.

"You actually think some of this global warming propaganda is true, Lewison?"

"Not our problem, is it? Leave it up to the next generation, old boy."

It is getting on toward nine o'clock, and a rigorous walk is in order before bed: a stroll down Granville to the so-called pedestrian mall, the theatre district. I head off, determined to take my mind off the crisis at home, to take in the glass and chrome and glaring lights, the lineups, the beggars and buskers, the wail of car alarms and sirens. To rediscover what I'm missing on Garibaldi Island.

The world's most liveable city lacks a vibrant centre, and I have fooled myself in expecting much to be happening on a Friday night. Not many louts around – maybe there's a football game at the stadium. Coming up is Granville and Smithe, and across the street, Vancouver's fine concert hall, the Orpheum . . . and I stagger to a halt.

There is a party of smokers outside the Orpheum. Quite a crowd, a dozen. At the centre of their attention is Annabelle Beauchamp.

I duck into a recessed doorway. No one seems to have noticed me. But there's too much light out here; I have to make a run for it. There's Hubbell Meyerson by a streetlamp, puffing on a cigar as he shields his eyes, trying to make me out. I swivel, turn up my coat collar, and sneak off the way I came, trying to still my panic. I can't understand how I could have forgotten this is the night of her party.

Now an added complication: a couple approaching at a fast clip, late for the event. I know them, gay, married, Fred and George, sets and costumes. I pretend not to see them but pause on hearing, "Arthur, I do believe you're going the wrong way."

"Just slipping off, Fred. Early flight to catch. Carry on, enjoy the party. Lovely night."

I meld into the crowd issuing from a movie house, then twist about to glimpse Fred and George conferring with Hubbell, confirming his sighting. By some means or other word will get back to Margaret that I was spotted decamping from Annabelle's soiree.

That word will be magnified, distorted. She will conclude that my real plan in quitting Ottawa early ("I'd only be boring company, my dear") was to hook up with Annabelle.

I berate myself all the way back to the Confederation Club. What is happening to my mind? I see phantoms, I do bizarre things, become irrationally jealous, get into pickles of my own making. I suffer breathtaking lapses of memory – *Friday, September 16* was in bold letters on the invitation. The one I gave to Stan Caliginis, another imbecilic act. I'm sure I saw him out there, hovering around, star-struck, lighting Annabelle's cigarette.

Maybe I purposefully forgot tonight was the night, some form of subconscious subterfuge at work. Maybe I have been denying a need to be here, to celebrate Annabelle's return. Maybe I seek something from her. Answers. Closure.

Maybe I should have a drink to settle me. A short one, for my nerves.

And then turn up in Appeal Court, if I turn up at all, piss drunk. My final dishonour to my client. It will not happen, my brother.

I crawl into bed. To sleep. Perchance to dream . . .

This was the dream, as I reconstruct it in a taxi to the float-plane dock: Wentworth rises from behind Mulligan's typewriter and demands to know if I'm ready to bear the whips and scorns. I am naked, ashamed, afraid. Annabelle, in a nun's habit, flicks her whip, and I find the pain thrilling. I sense that millions are watching on YouTube.

I am still parsing the dream as Syd's Beaver grunts off the inlet on this sunny weekend morning. The thrill of pain has to do with Annabelle's return, of course, with my former role as her pet masochist. Pain excites, a therapist told me; it arouses just as sex does – a turn-on, an aphrodisiac. It releases endorphins in the brain that are as addictive as opiates. I was hooked on pain. And some addictions, I was instructed, remain with us unto death.

What most gnaws at me from this dream is the vision of Wentworth Chance at Dermot's old Remington, challenging me to bear the whips and scorns. There is allegory here. Wentworth is chiding me for having failed Gabriel Swift, for having failed to right the oppressor's wrong, the law's delay.

We have conquered the Salish Sea and the islands are below us, farms and rocky bluffs and high, thick forest descending to looping straits and inlets. Here approaches Blunder Point; our forty acres come into view, our commodious house, the WOOFER house, the fearsome barn with its vanished cargo of cannabis. With relief I spot no official vehicles in the driveway, no SWAT team ready to pounce.

Syd manages to miss my crab trap by a foot, cuts power, and drifts his craft to my rickety dock. Seventeen minutes after leaving downtown Vancouver, I am home, disoriented by the sudden shift. I feel hopeless, incapable. Disaster looms and I have arrived without a plan.

Homer is quick to greet me, circling me, barking, *Problems here.*

Problems here. I leave my bags in his care, check to see that my Fargo is still safely chained by its undercarriage to the B.C. Hydro pole, then detour past the barn up to the goat-milking shed, where Niko and Yoki are at work.

Old Mathilda, who has become so cranky at milking time, is unusually serene under Yoki's gentle pulling. The other nannies are engaged in some playful bunting while awaiting their turns.

"Goats very happy," Niko says. "Geeses happy too, also cow and horse. Happy farm, no problem. Maybe you buy more extra-special good alfalfa. All gone."

PART FOUR

————

THE APPEAL

The Appeal Court Registry has let me know that *Gabriel Swift v. the Queen* will be called at eleven a.m. It is now nine, and I am staring out my office window at foaming seas and swollen clouds being bullied landward by Poseidon. *He spake,* sang Homer, *and round about him called the clouds and roused the ocean.* And did bathe Vancouver in such wet discharge that even gulls and geese were hiding. Below my forty-third-floor eyrie, street lights are still on. Cars scamper to underground garages for cover, umbrellas bloom at the exit doors of subway and buses.

I will not allow the weather to depress me. I will be the sunshine today. I will be bright before the court, carefree, confident. I will not lower myself to seek sympathy, to play the hoary old dotard embarking on his final, fumbling comeback.

Roy Bullingham has just walked in, affording me a chance to test that cheery formula. "Cleansing, isn't it, Bully – the rain. Causes this lovely city to sparkle when the sun finally comes out."

"It had damn well better clear up before the weekend." He is turning ninety-three then. There will be a large celebration, a garden party at a client's estate. Bullingham has two decades on me and he's lost nothing mentally, or physically – a little more gaunt, more loose skin, but he scrambles about with agility. Maybe there's hope yet for A.R. Beauchamp.

He joins me at the window. "Good luck on this one, Arthur, though I suspect you'll need not luck but divine intervention." He pats my shoulder. "Here we are, forty-nine years and five months after that foul-mouthed fool Pappas persuaded me to assign you this case. I ought to have resisted letting you handle it. You were too raw."

"I was about to quit the firm that day, Bully."

"I saw your determined look, thought you were about to ask for a raise. A chilling concept." A sly grin. "Your quitting, I mean."

"And you dangled the gift of a murder trial."

"Turned your life around, according to that fellow Chance. You'd have had a second-rate career had you not been scarred early. Fear of failure, Beauchamp – that's what makes for greatness." Another follower of the wisdom of Wentworth Chance, who cynically implies I practised on Gabriel and learned from my rookie mistakes.

I remain at the window after Bully leaves, watching clouds gather doomfully, working through that brief exchange, remembering my pencil-chewing anxiety when defending Gabriel, the drinking, the sweats, the gallows nightmares, trusting him, doubting him. Admiring him, fearing him. Discovering the brother I'd yearned for, as he must have too, another only child. Yes, Bully, I was too raw. And cowardly, and too in awe of Smythe-Baldwin.

The phone bleats. I've asked Gertrude not to put through anyone lesser than president, prime minister, or pope, but I'm almost thankful to be snapped out of this dreary reverie.

"What kind of court have you got, Arthur?"

"How lovely to hear from you, Ophelia. I was just about to jump in the river and drown."

"Yeah, I hear it's pissing there. I'm ever so happy here in the Okanagan drylands. Did you draw Webb?"

"Yes, thank God." Bill Webb, a charter member of AA's trial lawyers chapter and a liberal.

"That gives you a little leg up. I suppose the Chief Justice appointed herself to the coram?"

"To be sure." Martha Schupp, politically connected, more a formalist than a feminist. Catholic, anti-abortion. Stickler for rules, prickly, prideful.

"Martha loves her big media dramas. She never got ink when she was in practice. I don't know how you'll get around her. Your famous sex appeal ain't going to work. She has several cats – maybe there's something kinky about that you could play with."

"I'll add that crucial information to my arsenal. The third justice is Ram Singh. I recall he was a bit of a class clown when he was counsel. You served with him in the trial court."

"Wine, women, and song. All of which ingredients were in play during his affair with a lounge singer. Like most Tory appointees, he's without morals. He's probably known some racial intolerance, so that might help him relate to Gabriel. Careful how you use the word *Indian*. He's your wild card."

We chatted a little about personal things. She is alone, widowed five years, doing some writing, a memoir. "Won't be as scandalous as Wentworth's," she says with her throaty chuckle. Then, softer: "I'm so sorry I got on your case back then, Arthur. We were both too fond of Gabriel, but it's been harder on you. I called to wish you well today."

"It will be a test for the eroding brain cells."

"I'm not buying that. You're far fucking sharper than you were at twenty-five, and infinitely fucking wiser."

"You still believe I should have referred this to another counsel?" A concern she expressed a few months ago. It's too personal, the appeal needs someone with balance, with a perspective unclouded by feelings.

"No, I've changed my mind. Or maybe Wentworth changed my mind. Now he has an excuse to rewrite his final lousy chapter. For you it's an act of redemption. So mount your white charger – avenge injustice. Save your soul."

~~~

I have already made grumbling noises about the glass-roofed arboretum that is 800 Smithe Street, Vancouver's modernist courthouse. It's set within what planners call an urban park: an artificial hill, reflecting pool, waterfalls, manicured shrubbery. Within, a lattice of trusses supports an acre of sloping skylight that suffuses the Grand Hall and seven ascending galleries with a false greenish light.

The courtrooms of appeal are, befittingly, at the highest levels. Barristers may take a furtive back elevator from the ground-floor robing room or return to the Great Hall and ascend by a wide carpeted stairway. That is the way I choose, demonstrating to the throngs below that the old boy is still peppy and spry. Outside room sixty I pause to catch my breath – it wouldn't do for their lordships to see me panting – then smilingly enter, with the confident swagger patented by Cyrus Smythe-Baldwin. The heads that turn include those of several aboriginal leaders, including Chief Gibby Jacobs of the Squamish Nation, and a score or more of young faces – law students conscripted to attend. Only half a dozen reporters, but appeals aren't as sexy as trials; fireworks are rare.

There is a case ahead of mine, an appeal against a multi-year sentence for some thuggery or other. The judicial troika of Schupp, Webb, and Singh are chewing alive an inexperienced lawyer, who expends most of his efforts quailing and apologizing. They use rhetoric like, "Do you mean to stand there and say . . ." and "Are you seriously suggesting . . ." and "If I comprehend your drift – and I'm not sure I do . . ." These efforts are led by Martha Schupp, C.J., the meanest of our appellate justices. A pinched face, the expression of one with a permanent case of acid indigestion.

The Crown Attorney is Hollis Wotherspoon, Q.C., a lazy old boy from a proper Upper Canada family. He doesn't know much law but manages to blunder through. Right now he is relaxing, knowing he won't be called upon, and he swivels about to give me a wink as I settle on the counsel bench. He has checked and tested my new proofs from the National Archives, from Jim Borachuk, the DNA analysis of the foot, even the videotapes of O'Houlihan's deathbed repentance and his naughty photos, and has generously consented to their admissibility as fresh evidence. He has balked, however, over admitting the videotaped statement of Ethel Brière. The confidences of Caroline Snow about her defilement were "ancient, second-hand hearsay."

The young fellow ahead of me is reciting some rudimentary rule of sentencing. "We are well aware of that principle, counsel," Chief Justice Schupp tells the supplicating wretch. "We're not complete idiots, you know."

"I'm sorry, your Lordship, I didn't realize that." Not intended as a wisecrack, more of a verbal knee-jerk reaction.

Schupp ignores, or pretends to ignore, the poorly smothered laughter in the gallery. "We do not need to hear from Mr. Wotherspoon. Appeal dismissed."

The loser flees with his files. Wotherspoon is fighting for a straight face as he announces our case.

I take my place at counsel table and Ram Singh says, "I don't know if we're ready for you, Mr. Beauchamp, but I assume you're ready for us."

"Ready to try our fortunes, milord."

Singh smiles under his lavish moustache. He's a thickset man but athletic, a squash player. He is the one I will have to sway. I will not win over Schupp (unless I dazzle her with my love of cats) but I ought to be able to count on Bill Webb, a former corporate counsel who surprised everyone by being the court's sternest upholder of the Charter of Rights. His preferred manner is collegial, his look avuncular: bald but with a bushy outcropping on cheeks and chin. He's the justice who granted me leave to appeal.

All give me uninterrupted attention as I trace the history of why we are in this courtroom. They are not slow or lazy, like some of their lower-court brethren; they've read the appeal books and factums and know the issues.

I sense that Schupp is smarting from the wayward shot she took from the frightened rookie; with her look of pain, she seems determined to inflict some on me. When I finish my recitation of facts, she jumps in. "Can we agree, for the record, that your client has not given us the courtesy of being present in this courtroom?"

I was expecting this. "Let us say he is at liberty."

"It's a notorious fact, is it not, that he has fled the country? And that he faces a charge of escaping lawful imprisonment? I need not tell you there is ample precedent in such cases to order a stay of the appeal."

"Milady, the blunt truth is I have advised him not to appear, because of the risk, however slight, that I may not persuade this court to free an innocent man. Dr. Swift would then spend his remaining life in prison. As we speak he is in Bolivia, somewhere in the Cordillera Oriental in the province of Cochabamba, record-ing voices of aged speakers of a vanishing tongue. He is leading an initiative to preserve and revive Native dialects, a program that has the sanction of the United Nations, and from which he cannot break free. In the meantime, the Canadian government has made no recent moves to return him to this country."

"Is that right, Mr. Wotherspoon?"

Lost in other worlds, Wotherspoon seems puzzled for a moment, as if not quite recognizing his name, but finally stands. "May it please the court, the Canadian government has little recourse, be-cause Bolivia has granted him refugee status."

I add, "Ottawa has shown far less interest in his return than cer-tain of our high-ranking universities, which have honorary doc-torates waiting for him."

Webb and Singh have said nothing through this. They seem em-barrassed for the Chief, who has lost this one, particularly in the eyes of the press. "Proceed with the appeal," she says.

I hardly get going before she again pounces like a hunting cat, when I admit to taking on the additional burden that my client pled guilty.

"Surely that's an overwhelming obstacle, Mr. Beauchamp. Appealing a conviction based on a guilty plea is exceedingly rare. My sense is it ought not to be countenanced except in the most special and unusual circumstances."

Singh chimes in, grinning. "Especially when that guilty plea was advised by a counsel well-known for his mental acuteness."

"Milord, at that point in my career I was about as green as the young gentleman who preceded me today, and far less keen-witted."

Webb plays along. "You give yourself too much credit, Mr. Beauchamp."

My hope is that when these justices look at some of the pathetic boners pulled by the young Arthur, they will let him off lightly. But the Chief Justice, with her penchant for rigid rules, must be confronted about the guilty plea. "If special circumstances be the test, milady, this case is replete with them. You have an affidavit from a retired RCMP inspector that the two chief investigators lied under oath. There's evidence from a washed-up foot that, if I may be so crude, stank. Compelling fresh evidence is on offer that supports suicide. What circumstances could be more special and rare than those?"

"None of this proves your client's innocence, however." Singh, flipping through my books of cases. "That's your burden, isn't it?"

Have I already lost this lover of wine and women songstresses? I let him know I'm affronted. "I have never understood our laws as requiring any person to prove his innocence."

Schupp seeks to modify Singh's distressingly hardcore position. "I think what my brother Singh is saying is that your appeal can't succeed unless there is no reasonable chance the appellant was guilty."

"I submit, with respect, that the appeal ought to succeed on the traditional basis, that there is reasonable doubt – an excess of it. No jury properly charged would find it safe to convict."

Webb offers a helping hand. "I take it you're saying, Mr. Beauchamp, that the same rights and rules of appeal apply whether the appellant has been found guilty or has pled guilty."

"Especially when the plea was practically forced upon the defence to forestall the risk of a death sentence. The guilty plea was based on matters as they stood in August 1962. Recent developments have caused so much structural damage to the Crown's case as to give reasonable apprehension of an intolerable miscarriage of justice. Our courts are not in the business of sanctioning such miscarriages."

I get up quite a head of steam, leaning heavily on that grand phrase *miscarriage of justice*, associating it, for the benefit of her Ladyship, with abortion, though in the sense of a fiasco. And so it carries on through the entire morning, heavy wading but I'm up for it, no excuses needed, no pretence about the slowing mind. I am in a courtroom, therefore at home, in the comfort of debate, as others might be around their fireplace or television set.

When we break for lunch, I am too keyed up to deal with food. I head out through the West End, a peninsula of towers now, with few survivors of the sixties, those grand old houses. My old home on Haro has been spared, though. A stroll down the lane reveals a backyard swing set and a trampoline – evidence of normalcy, of happiness, the memory of Crazy Craznik erased.

Life was simpler then. I wasn't burdened by eminence; there were no high expectations. But now I sense those every time I walk into a courtroom. From the visitors' gallery, from the press table, from court staff and counsel. But I doubt that Dr. Swift shares those expectations. I have received no communication from him other than that crisp, chilly email authorizing the appeal.

I'm glad he expects so little of me. I don't care if I disappoint the *mobile vulgus,* though I fear I will. Nor have I impressed Schupp, who keeps buzzing around me like a mosquito, alighting for the occasional stab. But I wrote her off before we began. My main worry has to do with Ram Singh, the supposed wild card. A lot of light-hearted interjections from him but little substance. He's treating the appeal as a merry *divertissement* among more vital matters such as contested estates and corporate takeovers. His family has major timber holdings, so he's not likely to share the worldview of an anti-capitalist rebel. My best chance will be to appeal to his sense of self-importance.

I reach the rim of Stanley Park, the tennis courts, and watch a vigorous doubles match between skilled couples. But now I must head back to those other courts, to my own strenuous game.

~~~

Resuming the bench, Martha Schupp looks refreshed, ready to play another few sets. "Before you continue, Mr. Beauchamp, my brothers and I were having a little colloquy about the options we're looking at. What exactly are you seeking here?"

"I'm asking that the conviction be quashed and an acquittal entered."

"But alternatively you are asking for a new trial. And if there's any merit in the fresh evidence you are urging on us, that may be all you'd be entitled to."

Ram Singh: "I see that as a real problem. How does the Crown resurrect its case? There can't be many witnesses still alive. Exhibits have disappeared. According to the material filed by Mr. Wotherspoon, the key witness, Corporal Lorenzo, was murdered nearly two decades ago in a mysterious drive-by shooting."

That is what is bugging Singh – the 1983 slaying of Walt Lorenzo, an act few dared call random. The undercover specialist had built up a backlog of embittered enemies – corporate crooks, mobsters, drug cartel bosses – but none more prominent than Gabriel Swift. So it was widely speculated, though without an iota of proof, that Gabriel acted through agents, soldiers, for instance, of the American Indian Movement.

"It's troubling, isn't it?" says Schupp, appropriating the issue. "An unsolved murder. A brave and dedicated officer."

"Brave, no doubt," I say, "and dedicated to his job maybe. But not necessarily to the truth, as I will argue."

"You may argue that," says Singh. "But he faces insuperable difficulty in arguing back. Which returns me to my point. How can this court realistically order a new trial?"

"Milord, if Dr. Swift is to be denied a right to a new trial, there can be no alternative but simply to enter an acquittal."

Schupp, sharply: "Well, I'm far from persuaded he has a right to a new trial."

Bill Webb again tries to ride to my rescue. "Mr. Beauchamp, what I hear you saying is that if we find there's been a miscarriage of justice, our only reasonable and proper alternative will be to order him acquitted."

"Exactly."

By late afternoon hunger is punishing me for having skipped lunch. My complacent adversary, Hollis Wotherspoon, watches with pretend agony as I take my shots, occasionally exchanging knowing nods with the press. I continue trying slices, lobs, and drop shots against the aggressive doubles team of Schupp and Singh. They consider the fingerprints on the wallet to be telling, absent any testimony explaining them. They're unwilling to challenge Lorenzo's credibility. (Singh: "Even if, as Inspector Borachuk avers, two officers lied under oath, it doesn't prove Lorenzo also lied, does it, Mr. Beauchamp?") They are not swayed by his closeness to Knepp – the Reno and Disneyland trips, the cookouts.

They express themselves deeply troubled by the startling recollections of Ethel Brière about her teenaged tête-à-tête with Caroline Snow in 1942, but appear inclined to hold them inadmissible. Old Riley's brainstorm about evoking the doctrine of recent complaint finds no buyers – even Webb is against me. Maybe they're fearful of utterly trashing Mulligan's already tarnished name.

Nor do I get traction with the misidentified foot. Their attitude is *So what?* Singh, predictably, makes jokes: "Counsel seems not able to get his foot in the door." And (a loud titter runs through the courtroom), "This ground of appeal has one foot in the grave."

It is half past four, quitting time, and we are all getting a little silly with fatigue. I exit with a line about my getting off on the wrong foot and being ground underfoot by their lordships, then neatly segue into a mention of my adorable cats, Underfoot and Shiftless. Instead of warming to me, Martha Schupp wrinkles her nose as she recesses for the day. She probably names her cats properly, like Fluffy or Precious.

Wotherspoon, who'll be called upon tomorrow to answer me, commiserates as I pack my book bag: "Never say die." But I am desolate. All the thought and work and passion that I expended on this case may be for naught. A further appeal to Ottawa's ever-more-authoritarian Supreme Court seems futile.

As I turn to leave, I espy, rising from the back row and pocketing a notepad, a tall, wiry, bespectacled wonk in Lycra cycling shorts, clutching a bike helmet: Wentworth Chance. A strained smile says he's apprehensive about our imminent coming together.

~~~

A casual exchange of greetings, constrained on my part though not icy, wasn't enough for Wentworth, and he has tagged along from the courthouse to Robson Square and points north, walking his bicycle. I'd bumped into him only a couple of times since *A Thirst* came out, always in company, so there was no opportunity to have (in diplomatic language) a frank exchange of views.

And though there's opportunity now, I hold back. There's something about Wentworth that stops me – an inner frailty, a softness, a sense that a single sharp word from the icon will cause total disintegration. He is content to maintain this unspoken entente, not once mentioning the book. Or repeating any of the views expressed therein, such as that I'd choked during my first murder case and sold out Gabriel Swift.

But he does talk about the appeal, insisting I fill him in on the issues debated before he arrived, soliciting my views of the court's inclinations, sharing his, bringing me down further with his unalloyed pessimism. His tone is urgent, proprietary: "We've got to come up with something." What I'm hearing, though he doesn't say it, is: *You can't do this to me; it wasn't supposed to end this way.* I am to blame for the likely demise of this appeal. I've failed Gabriel again, and Wentworth too, a final betrayal not only of them but of my alleged prowess as a barrister.

He is a thief, Wentworth Chance, stealing from me my sorrow at this turn of events, my right to grieve. He stays with me up Howe Street, the financial district, confiding in a filial, self-absorbed way about his career as a lawyer. "I'll never get the great cases. Max and Brovak covet anything that makes headlines. I do the office scraps – the cranks and crackheads and loonies. By my age you'd already done d'Anglio and Smutts; you were already the heir presumptive to Smythe-Baldwin. I'm third rank; maybe I'll make it to second, maybe not. Maybe I'll just get out of it. Write books."

I can't think of anything to say that will not encourage him to carry on in this vein, but finally I find myself telling him, idiotically, to follow his heart. Rather than showing insult at this high-school nostrum, he becomes more ardent. Yes, that's just what he wanted to hear. There is something more satisfying than a big win (a fleeting event, after all); a book is permanent, its production has its own thrills. "Creation – using the right side of the brain, seeing it all in print, between covers – you can't beat that."

I'm tempted to remind him of Lord Byron's famous words: *'Tis pleasant, sure, to see one's name in print; A book's a book, although there's nothing in't.* But we don't talk about the book the right side of his brain produced. He fills all available audible time until we reach the Confederation Club building, jabbering at an accelerating pace, as if on drugs, maybe speed. But I assume he's simply nervous, in fear of what I might say about *A Thirst* if allowed a moment of silence.

"As you probably guessed, I am working on another writing project. I'm taking a leave from the firm for this one, so I'll have to earn my daily bread some other way. Teaching. I'll be doing some People's Law School stuff, how to get by in Small Claims Court, and, ah, doing some readings around the country – you can sell lots of books at those things. I got one coming up in the Squamish Library, as a matter of fact . . . And, ah . . . well, this is kind of ironical – I've applied and got a writer-in-residence gig at Mulligan House. Comes with a subsistence grant, so that'll get me through the winter. Dermot Mulligan's old house, where the Squamish River flows. Weird, eh?"

Weird.

The Confederation Club does not accept guests in spandex, so we must part. I worry about Wentworth as I sign in; the kid seems in trouble. Staying in Mulligan's shrine as writer-in-residence – that suggests he may be as obsessed with this case as I, though in a way less healthy.

~~~

I hoped for privacy in the dining room, a time to mourn the day and recharge for tomorrow, but the haunting continues. This time it's Hubbell Meyerson, who must have been lying in wait for me;

he rarely drops by the club. He signals me to his table, where he's working on a tall vodka tonic and a bowl of nuts.

I expect subtle accusations of spurning his oldest, dearest friend. But over our dinners – I could eat half a steer but settle for a share of its loin – he is convivial, supportive, encouraging me to fight on. He is more interested in my personal dramas, though, than the stale and dusty epic that engrosses me. Rather than chiding me for my cowardly flight from Annabelle's party, he sees it as a great joke.

"Ah, yes, we saw you spying outside the Orpheum, Annabelle and I. Having a little laugh at her expense, were you? Setting her up with that pompous, posturing fool Stan Caliginis, with his non-stop winey soundtrack."

This scenario – having a little laugh – I can live with, the sin of cruelty being preferred to cowardice. I have escaped major damage from the incident. I expected far worse than I got from Margaret when I phoned to tell her about my near incursion into Annabelle's welcoming party and to confess I'd hooked her up with Stan Caliginis. "How oddly you're behaving" was all she said.

Hubbell is still going on about Caliginis. "Big-time hustler in marginal stocks, junks, derivatives. I had him checked out, just to make sure he doesn't try to sell Annabelle a gilt-edged lead brick."

"Stan read *A Thirst* and was staggered by Annabelle's adventurous spirit and earthiness. She is steely, crisp, and juicy and has a very good length."

"I suspect he has a very good length himself, because the next day she asked me to pass on to you her most ardent thanks."

"She slept with him?"

"One assumes. He's also a major mover and shaker in the Liberal Party, so he'll be coming to Bullingham's ninety-third on Saturday. Annabelle has been invited, of course. Bully has always found her fascinating."

As does Hubbell, I suspect. He confessed a couple of times, years ago, while drunk, that he'd had fantasies involving Annabelle.

I am distracted by the entrance into the dining room of Justice Bill Webb and his wife and another couple. There is an awkward moment as they pass by, Bill pretending not to notice the fellow AAer he spent all day in court with. That he doesn't find the courage to meet my eye tells me I may not be able to count on him.

There is a presence behind me. I can feel it, something ugly from the past. I lay out my books, papers, and writing tools, and finally turn to look for whatever apparition I have divined in this courtroom. My eyes settle on a face near the back – aged, leathery, dark with an Arizona tan, an artificial, ill-meant smile – intended for me, the lawyer who dared impugn the honesty of the upholders of the law in the Squamish Valley. Roscoe Knepp, long retired in Tucson, could not resist returning to the scene of his crime, the Vancouver courts.

It's as if he's been summoned from the netherworld of my nightmares. Maybe the one that awoke me this morning, though I can't picture him among the dripping revenants crawling up the banks of the Squamish River, approaching me with their petitions. The lead haunter, as usual, was Dermot Mulligan, a horrifying sight with his horn-rims and stout penis, made up as a woman. Now that I think about it, this was a family scene, with Irene – oddly dressed too, as a man – and Mulligan's son, Sebastien Snow, in prison greens, and Sebastien's mother, Caroline. I can't remember any of their words but hers. *You could have saved me.*

I keep staring at Knepp as that dream spools through my mind. His cocky smile dissolves and he can't hold my gaze, checks his watch, frowning, as if he has a list of many things to do today.

As our case is called and Hollis Wotherspoon takes the floor, I stay trapped in that dream, wondering at Caroline Snow's challenge, hurting as I remember that frail young addict whom I wooed with Keats and Byron and deserted in the morning. Remembering her son, whom I defended for random acts of windshield-smashing anger. *It seemed to be the most sensible thing to do at the moment.* Sebastien Snow, who begat Marie Snow in 1978, who has disappeared into the closed systems of Manitoba's Adoptions Act.

She would be thirty-three now. She would have no idea who her grandfather was.

Wotherspoon's manner of litigating is old-school casual: unassertive, friendly, slightly underprepared, the occasional self-effacing joke, some stumbling about to reassure the judges he's not as bright as they. He is only vaguely adversarial and likes to preface remarks with phrases like, "If I may be of assistance to the court . . ."

Martha Schupp tells him she's "troubled" over the so-called suicide note, Exhibit One. Not troubled enough to leap to the obvious conclusion Mulligan was going to kill himself. Troubled by the note's provenance and how it came to have been overlooked in the Archives. "There is affidavit material affirming it was done on the deceased's typewriter and that the two six-by-eight sheets appear to be old, maybe by several decades. Are you happy with that?"

"If not happy, content. It may assist your Ladyship to know the document examiners were recruited from RCMP crime laboratories. Highly qualified; top people."

"This exhibit could be many, many years old, I suppose."

"Quite so, milady."

"Might have been created a decade or more prior to 1962, who knows?"

I stubbornly refrain from rising; I will not be the one to embarrass her. Bill Webb, on her right, takes on that task, leaning toward her ear, suggesting she might look more closely at Exhibit One, at the first line: *Albert Camus, who was unhappily taken from the world two years ago, wrote "there is but one truly serious philosophical problem and that is suicide."* Webb's advice that Camus died in 1960 causes Schupp to turn pink.

Loyally, Ram Singh tries to salvage her dignity by coming up with a light-hearted aside. "This reminds me of that case back in – when was it? – the fellow who allegedly hurled his accountant from his penthouse balcony. Does anyone remember the case? Something about a tainted suicide note and a massive bank deposit . . ."

I don't bother to rise. "I remember it well, milord."

"Oh, of course, you were defence counsel. What happened to your fellow?"

"He walked. All the way to the bank, I believe."

A rumble of face-saving laughter from the bench, Schupp looking more at ease, maybe even grateful I haven't rubbed salt in her wound.

As the morning winds down, she and her confreres take a few light shots at Wotherspoon, challenging him about O'Houlihan's recent admissions he'd tried to blackmail Mulligan. "Why do you say he ought not to be believed?" Schupp asks.

"I suppose because he's a generally untrustworthy character."

"He hasn't long to go, though, according to your own brief of evidence. Deathbed repentance – isn't that what we saw on those videotapes?"

Singh has a different take. "I thought he spoke more with pride than repentance."

"Maybe so, milord," says Wotherspoon, happy to concede anything to get through the day.

Singh expresses interest in the semen-stained panties and the missing socks, but Wotherspoon is unable this time to be of assistance. It's good that they're testing him, though likely only out of courtesy to the old trouper opposing him. They will reserve, of course, for the same reason, perhaps for a few weeks, long enough for Schupp and Singh to bend Webb to their wills. That may not be difficult; his body language, his apologetic glances inform me there will be no dissenting judgment.

Schupp notes the time and asks either counsel if they have anything to add.

"If I may summarize in a nutshell," says my learned colleague, "there's an excess of evidence to support a conviction, whether by guilty plea or not."

"Mr. Beauchamp?"

"It is obvious to the entire world that Gabriel Swift was the victim of a vicious conspiracy fuelled by revenge and racism. I trust it is as obvious to this honourable court."

That's for the press and, through them, the public – not even our highest courts are immune to the *vox populi* – but also, mainly, for Roscoe Knepp. The Chief gives me a stern look but suppresses the temptation to lay into me. "We will reserve."

As the gallery empties, Knepp, who is bent over and using a cane, turns to me and mouths, *You prick.* Age has not mellowed this fellow – he is not the glib, ingratiating staff sergeant we once knew.

The Southlands is a Vancouver enclave of the very rich, the horsy set: estates with paddocks and pools and high hedges to keep the gawkers away. It is on the rolling, manicured lawns of one such estate that the birthday of Roy Bullingham is being celebrated this afternoon. At least a few hundred people here. Tents for shade. Canapés on trays. The finest wines, some of which are being blind-tested in one of the parlours of the host's manse. A party game: guests are asked to guess the variety of grape, country, region, and price.

Martha Schupp is present, as are many others of the judiciary. A glass of champagne has transformed this cheerless auditor of regs and rules into a charm machine promenading about in her sun hat. "Splendid day, Arthur," she sings out as she passes by.

"How lovely to see you, Martha, in such a lovely setting." She is not fooled by my sunny response; she knows that I know I've lost.

Annabelle too is here, a woman comfortable with power and the powerful. Teasing, sexy, the old tycoons falling for her. Her escort is Stan Caliginis, who seems wowed by her, astonished by his good luck at being consort to a woman so vibrant, so attractively repackaged in her new skin. Annabelle has him where she likes them – at her feet.

I proceed into the house with Hubbell Meyerson. Gifts are piled by a table (mine is an eighteenth-century edition of Coke's *Commentary on the Laws of England*). The guest book must be signed, the array of old photos admired. Here is Bullingham in 1960, with the partners he outlived: absent-minded Geoffrey Tragger and Tom Inglis, unlovingly known as the Fat Man. They were oblivious to me until my glad-handing by Dief the Chief in 1962 – the year when my career began to soar, yet a terrible, terrible year, a year of shame and remorse.

We slip into the grand salon, where the Emerson Quartet is playing Beethoven's opus 131 for a small, rapt audience. But I am still in 1962, remembering the frightening thrill of taking on my first murder, remembering my early optimism, my earnest naïveté, my travels in the Squamish Valley, where I was ill-used by a rainstorm and the local RCMP. I've never returned to the upper Valley and probably never will, not even to pay homage at Mulligan's bookish shrine.

I remember the spirited debates with Gabriel, our growing shared respect – dare I say fraternal feelings, dare I say love. I remember my obsessive fear of losing him to the hangman. When the appeal court judgment comes down, I will have to be a man and deliver the news face to face. *It wasn't meant to be,* I'll say. *I gave it my all. Please stop hating me.*

I remember – too well – how during the trial I prospered one day and got trounced the next, how I caved in after Irene claimed to have recognized the size-eight foot. How odd that this foot had a similar vestigial toenail, though I've learned they're not so rare (nor, it turns out, are unidentified washed-up feet). I think now that Irene simply wanted it to be Dermot's, out of a need for closure. Yet I'm troubled by her signing of that affidavit so quickly and incautiously.

Hubbell shakes me out of this bleak cud-chewing, leads me off to the blind wine-tasting contest: a dozen brown-bagged bottles on the table, glasses to swirl and sip from. A pearl-bedecked matron is studying her score card. "Gracious, a two-hundred-dollar vintage. I was way, way low." The master sommelier running this show comforts her by saying she did well to identify it as a California Chardonnay; he gives her, generously, seventy per cent.

None of the twenty or so guests here comes forward when the sommelier asks for another volunteer, but then Hubbell cries out, gesturing at the doorway. "Here's our man!"

Stan Caliginis has just entered, Annabelle on his arm. Hubbell promotes him hard: "A famous connoisseur of the grape, a vintner himself, keeper of a cellar the envy of the Western world."

Caliginis is known by most here, and they applaud vigorously as Hubbell urges him forward. He wants to resist – I can see it in his frightened eyes – but Annabelle practically strong-arms him to the table.

"Ha, ha, wasn't expecting this. Not quite in shape for it, I think. Bit of a throat." The excuses tumble out in his staccato way of speaking. Annabelle gets laughs with her simulated rubdown, as for a prizefighter about to enter the ring. Caliginis sniffs, swirls, sips, then mouths a series of adjectives he's comfortable with: *flinty, steely, unoaked, apple-like acidity.* "A superior French Chablis, Burgundy region, of course, and I would put it about eight years old and priced at . . . oh, in the low hundreds."

The sommelier turns pink, as if flustered or embarrassed. "A joke," he says finally. "You had me there."

Caliginis goes "ha, ha" again. "Sorry, I just felt like having a little fun." He's fooling no one. He whispers something to Annabelle that seems to annoy her, then says something louder about expecting a call and heads off quickly with his phone.

"A rather uninteresting screw-cap wine, actually," says the sommelier, grimacing. "A Chilean Sauvignon Blanc, retailing for eight dollars at your local beer and wine store."

Annabelle sends me a weary look and takes Hubbell's arm. They walk out through the sun porch to poolside.

It is at this oddly gratifying moment that April Wu calls on my cell. "I am not a very good detective. I assumed you were home."

"I intend to be this evening. Where are you?"

"In your living room. I thought we would be able to avoid the media here. Marie is sitting beside me."

Momentary confusion. Marie . . . Mulligan's granddaughter. "Amazing! How . . . where did you find her?"

"In La Ronge, Saskatchewan. Marie Dubois."

I'm not as shocked as I ought to be; in fact, I have a sense of a fulfilled premonition. Marie, mother of Kestrel, who went missing three weeks ago on a quest for the same long-buried answers that have eluded me. For surely that's what she's doing in Squamish.

~~~

I pace the upper deck of the *Queen of Prince George*. I return inside to the little carrel where my bags and briefcase sit, dig some papers out, looking for something, though I'm not sure what. I wander off again, to the gift shop, to the forward lounge, then outside, where I pace again, fretfully.

With no flights available, I've had to resign myself to the mercies of a ferry busy with weekend cottagers and other undesirables. These include, below me on the car deck, Stan Caliginis, sulking in his monster pickup, and Stoney and Dog, quaffing beer in the bumper-stickered Mustang, which somehow they have rescued or stolen from the B.C. Ferries compound. Both give me headaches; I will try to negotiate a ride home with someone else.

I'm not ready yet to re-immerse myself in the picaresque pleasures of Garibaldi society. I am stressed because of the lateness of her cross-dressing highness the *Queen George*. We'll not be pulling in until well past ten-thirty, and I have guests – important guests.

I dig out my cellphone and ring April – for the third time – to confirm that the boat hasn't sunk and I'm still on my way. Everything is fine, she says. Niko and Yoki have come by to help them settle in and have stayed for tea. A bed has been prepared for Marie, who is exhausted from travelling and worrying.

Marie and her husband, Samson, spent several days on the coast hoping to regain contact with their fourteen-year-old, but Kestrel hasn't phoned since she called them from Squamish. They returned home a few days ago to their jobs, needing to be occupied. Now Marie has made a second journey, with April, who told me Marie is eager to speak to the lawyer she's read and heard about, the lawyer trying to solve the puzzle of her grandfather's death.

I was surprised to learn that Marie, though adopted at seven, knows about her antecedents. "How can that be?" I demanded of April.

"Patience," said April, "is the companion of wisdom."

"Lao-tzu?"

"Saint Augustine."

I'm back at my carrel, perusing the old RCMP exhibit list: items seized from Mulligan's desk, the outstanding one being Frinkell's letter, its accusation of adultery, its claim for damages. Casually tossed into his in-basket, unconcealed from his full-time attendant/researcher/secretary. Irene must have used that desk regularly for typing his manuscripts, handling his correspondence. Yet she claimed not to have known about it. There was no other working area she could have used, as I recall from my long-ago visit to the hobby farm. While Thelma McLean fixed us coffee, I'd snooped, found two decks of playing cards in a drawer of that desk, bridge decks in a clear plastic box. Irene's game, not Dermot's.

It is already ten p.m. as the *Queen George* putts into the Ponsonby Island dock, the last stop before Garibaldi. I pack up and descend to the car deck. The several island residents I encounter either have full vehicles or live far away from Potters Road, so I must choose between Caliginis and Stoney. A ride from the latter promises danger, but the grape connoisseur might prove even more distracted, now that his affair with Mrs. Beauchamp has imploded. I do not want to be driven off Breadloaf Bluff and land among the elves on the Shewfelts' lawn.

~~~

"Dog and me, we're sort of going that way anyway, so keep your wallet in your pocket. The mere pleasure of your company, sire, is reward enough, plus maybe out of the generosity of your heart a little pro bono advice." As we drive off the ramp, the top still down, Stoney pulls a massive joint from behind the visor and lights up in full view of everyone at the ferry landing. He passes it behind him to Dog, who exchanges a fresh can of Lucky for it.

Though I have insisted on sitting in the front, where there is a working seatbelt, I don't feel in any extreme peril. To give Stoney credit, he knows Garibaldi's roads so well that his responses to the dips, curves, and potholes are almost instinctive, automated, even as he smokes, drinks, and incessantly talks.

"This here's the situation. I had to pay off the ferry corp the flagrant amount of $357 and change for towing and storage. This was done according to my standard corporate practice, with a cheque on my business account."

"And how much is in that account?"

"Four dollars."

I earn my fare by telling him that a bounced cheque rarely gives rise to criminal proceedings.

"There ain't currently no law on this here island anyway, right, Dog?"

A grunt of assent. I ask, "What happened to the law on this here . . . on Garibaldi?" The second-hand smoke is getting to me.

"From various accounts we have pieced together, Ernst Pound got his ass suspended for punching the lights out of that pole-climber who's been poking his old lady. Zoller got the boot for standing by useless while this was going on outside the bar, and we ain't got no replacements."

Talking incessantly, he bemoans the loss of his cash crop – I dare not tell him the livestock ate it – but accepts the blame. "My problem is, though I ain't totally always aware of it, sometimes I rap too much when I do reefer, so some wrong ears musta overheard me mentioning in passing where I stashed my stash. No matter, I got friends with surplus, and anyway it's party hardy time on copless Garibaldi. The bar's gonna be rockin' wild all night, man. Metal Zombie is playing – they just got kicked out of Seattle for getting naked with some groupies on stage, right, Dog?"

"It was on TV." A rare entire sentence. Dog passes the joint back. Stoney fills his lungs, breathes out like a dragon, and orders Dog, through song, to "Roll another one, just like the other one."

Homer bounds up the driveway, announcing, *He's back!* April's car is outside my farmhouse, a nondescript Honda Civic suitable to the tasks of a discreet PI. She is out here too, but not quite so inconspicuous: she has found a pool of light, is leaning languorously against a veranda post, her jacket slung over her shoulder. One wonders if she once aspired to be a photographer's model.

"Man, who's the dream machine?"

"A friend." Stoney's on a need-to-know basis.

He grins. "I gotcha. Guess you ain't coming down to hear Metal Zombie."

I can already hear them, faintly, beyond the more salubrious music of tree frogs. I wish Stoney and Dog a happy time and remember to grab my bags and briefcase before they race away in a swirl of dust and smoke. I check to see that my Fargo is still moored to the utility pole.

"We'll let Marie sleep," April says, startling me by approaching suddenly and bussing me lightly, sweetly, before helping me with my bags to the veranda. "She has the room downstairs. I've made up the cot in your upstairs study. You don't mind?"

"Absolutely . . . I mean, of course not, my dear." I'm definitely feeling a bit high.

She takes my hand. "It's a magic night. Let's sit out here and count the stars." She leads me to a rise above the pebble beach, and we settle on my wonky handmade wooden bench. "Remember," she says, "no matter where you go, there you are."

I ask Ms. Enigmatic what that Confucianism means. She just smiles. I tell her I have given up parsing the one about why a bird sings. She shrugs, as if to say that explaining just takes the fun out of it.

The windless sea is like wobbling glass. Lethargic waves lick the shoreline with a gentle swish, the only other sounds distant wails and bass thumps, like heartbeats. An all-nighter – Abraham Makepeace is probably taking advantage of this lawless time to get out from under his punitive mortgage.

I have many questions to ask but must abide by April's fancy for dramatic waits. Finally: "Marie was adopted into a respected family at the Lac La Ronge Reserve – employees of the provincial park service – and she lived there until going to Saskatoon for a nursing degree. She returned to La Ronge to practise. At twenty-three, in 1996, she married Samson Dubois – I met him: quite shy, quite handsome. They have one child. Kestrel was born in 1997.

I gather she was a handful. They stopped there – they had careers." She shrugs. "I stopped before I started."

A wistful pause. I want to hug her but worry that the desire is cannabis-induced, and that she will read it as going beyond avuncular. On the other hand, she hasn't let go of my hand. I have never known quite what to make of this woman. I am well over twice her age, so she can't possibly have romantic feelings.

"Let's go back to when Marie was seven. That's when Sebastien Snow arranged for her adoption, after his wife died and while he was in prison. With all his troubles, he was a caring man. Marie says he met with her adopting parents several times, wanting to make sure they were right for his daughter. He told them his history as his mother had told him: that he was Dermot Mulligan's son, by rape – statutory rape, they called it."

And that was to have remained a secret, but like most great family secrets it wasn't kept. When Marie attained maturity, she was told about the famous professor whose genes were transferred unwillingly to Caroline Snow, then Sebastien, then Marie. Thence to Kestrel.

In her turn, Marie also swore never to tell her daughter. But that became too challenging a task in this era of Native truth-telling and redemption. Kestrel, who had been brought up to be independent, tough, and loving, and to respect her heritage, demanded the truth.

"Marie has a cellphone. Kestrel promised to call her this weekend. Is that enough for now? I'm almost too tired to sleep. Are you tired, Arthur? Do you want to go to bed?"

I feel incapable of answering any of these questions. They're either banally straightforward or too complex and cryptic.

She puts an arm around me as we meander back to the house. I cannot fathom her apparent feelings for me – they seem beyond teasing – and am made nervous by them, but also thrilled. I try to suppress silly imaginings prompted by her choice of my studio to bunk in, just off my bedroom. Ridiculous imaginings. April knows Margaret, and that I'm devoted to her.

In the kitchen we dally over tea, and talk turns to the personal. She asks if my ex-wife is still pursuing me. I'm not sure, I say, but I may have been given a breather. More awkwardly than delicately, I remind her I'm concerned about keeping my current marriage on solid ground, and recall her favourite aphorism: "If you don't want anyone to know, don't do it."

She looks at me oddly, as if missing my allusion. I'm embarrassed now with the turn our conversation has taken, and prompt her to talk about herself. She tells of her upbringing in mainland China, then Hong Kong, where she lived with her beloved grandmother, her inspiration, a student of Eastern philosophies.

I dare ask why she hasn't mentioned her parents. She says, "Tiananmen Square, 1989. I was nine when they were taken away. They died in jail." A long, melancholy pause. "My father was a great man, an intellectual, like you. I am in such pain when I remember him." Tears fill her eyes.

I hug her then, unutterably sheepish about the ludicrous thoughts I'd harboured.

I wake in the early hours from a dream I can't recall well. Just a snippet of speech: "He's here, darling," as flashbulbs pop outside and I scurry for my clothes but find only frilly underthings. I stare outside at the starlight for a long while, listening to the annoying *thump-thump* coming three miles from the bar at Hopeless Bay, wondering if that bit of dream is asking me to look once more at the photos by Jimmy Fingers.

Metal Zombie is still distantly pulsing at four a.m., a tribute to the staying power of the musicians, their fans, and their drugs. Also conspiring to keep me from sleep are Caroline and Sebastien and Marie and Kestrel. How does their familial history connect with the puzzle that has haunted me for almost fifty years? Is there salvation to be found for Gabriel Swift in this journey of generations? Yet another presence, quite near by, keeps me from subsiding back into the arms of Morpheus: April Wu on the cot next door, parentless April, veiling long-held sadness behind her saucy, cryptic persona.

When I awake a second time, the sun is streaming in, advertising another balmy day. The Zombies still haven't pooped out, but I can hear only a sole guitar. The more comforting sounds are of honking geese and prowling chickadees, and several women's voices downstairs. I recognize Yoki's and Niko's, their laughter.

I sense a presence in my doorway and blink away the sleep fog. April, with a portable phone and a mug of coffee, which she places at my bedside. "Good morning. Margaret called. She said not to wake you." She whisks off before I find my voice.

Margaret answers immediately, in a chirpy mood. "How enterprising of you to surround yourself with a harem of young women while I'm away."

April has filled her in as much as she can, and I embellish: a synopsis of my two tough days in court, which produces sympathy, and a rendering of Bully's party and the stripping away of Caliginis's sham show of expertise that produces delight.

"That did it for his prospects with Annabelle, I'm afraid. She walked off with Hubbell. Who knows what to expect from that?"

"Hmm," she says, communicating absolutely nothing. She changes the subject to Ottawa. She and her friend Leslie Falk took two days off to holiday in the Gatineau Hills. Parliament is in the helpless grip of ennui. Rumours abound that the prime minister's wife is having an affair with a policewoman.

"Also," she says, "I love you. I felt I needed to tell you that."

I don't ask why but suspect Margaret feels anxiety over Annabelle. An awareness she ought not to take good old Arthur for granted. Nobly, I will forgive this overburdened eco-warrior for her recent standoffish manner. Meanly, I thank Annabelle.

I sign off with Ms. Browning's famous avowal: "I love thee to the depth and breadth and height my soul can reach, when feeling out of sight."

~~~

Feeling like an outsider in a world of women, but showered, shaved, and combed, as ready as I can be, I descend to find them making pancakes with Saskatoon berry jam, a gift from Marie Dubois. She looks younger than in her TV interviews, and slighter, probably from weight-reducing worry. She greets me with a smile that isn't forced, one that must often comfort her patients.

Over the pancakes – ambrosial, I declare, a life-altering experience – I entertain with tales of yesterday's preposterously overdone birthday party. A tune interrupts this: the opening bars of "You'd Be So Nice to Come Home To," and I realize that Marie, poignantly, has set that as her ringtone. It's her husband, Samson, from La Ronge; she finds a quiet corner to talk to him.

Afterwards, when the woofers go out to woof, I invite Marie into the parlour and offer some consoling thoughts about her missing daughter, followed by a dose of hearty optimism. "I can hardly wait to meet this amazing, strong-willed young lady. And so bright. Top of her class, I hear."

"I'm sure she will call today," Marie says. April stands apart in the room's shadows, a listening ghost.

Gently I pull from Marie her perspective on Kestrel's quest. She begins by regretting she'd divulged her grim family secret to her daughter. "I didn't want her to know she was descended from him . . . from an act of criminal intercourse; it was long over, decades ago. She knew I was adopted and that my people came from the Fox Lake Reserve, nothing more. But all that truth-talking got to me – the truth and reconciliation stuff – and she was into it."

Kestrel researched the residential schools as a class project, read oral histories prepared for the Truth and Reconciliation Commission – maybe Ethel Brière's, but Marie isn't sure. "She pestered me, and I felt she had a right to know, so I sat down with her. And we had a fight. She was angry because I'd kept such a secret. I was part of the problem, I'd blinded myself to the past, a victim of white racism – that's what she said." She brushes away a tear, and April is suddenly there with a tissue. Marie thanks her and continues.

"She wanted to know more and more about her great-grandfather, even read some of his works. It was if she was after something, looking for clues about him, about why he did such a horrible thing. There's a book about Dr. Mulligan she read. And hordes of stuff about Gabriel Swift. Even a book written about you, Mr. Beauchamp. She was obsessed by it . . . her heritage, her dark heritage."

Yes, Arthur Ramsgate Beauchamp turns out to be a player in this teenage Homeric odyssey – Achilles storming the gates of Troy in pursuit of justice. My reopening of the case set Kestrel on the hunt a month ago, backpacking to British Columbia with two sets of clothes and six hundred dollars.

Marie believes Kestrel's resolute investigation explains her visit to Squamish and gives credence to reports of her daughter's sighting on the UBC campus. Clearly Kestrel was checking out Mulligan's former stamping grounds, probably surveyed his former house in

Point Grey. We speculate about whether she tried to track down Irene – still alive, though a century in age. I remember reading somewhere, in a "Where Are They Now?" article, that she's being cared for by a full-time nurse in a cottage in a seaside village on Vancouver Island: Fanny Bay, up the coast from Nanaimo. That might account for Kestrel's having been seen on a ferry.

But what does she expect to obtain from all this? What answers, to what questions? It seems more than a means of satisfying curiosity. Revenge? Making a claim to her birthright? Marie admits to being stumped, and I am too.

She is startled when I tell her I represented her birth father, Sebastien, and eager to hear more. Then she is saddened by the circumstances I relate, the purposeless shattering of car windows. Yet she smiles when I repeat his dry comment: *It seemed to be the most sensible thing to do at the moment.*

"Do you have any idea if Sebastien ever contacted Dr. Mulligan?"

"No. I was told some of his history. I know he was with his mom when she died. I know he tried to pick up the pieces; he gave it his best shot, and didn't make it. Didn't want to live."

More tears. Some are mine.

~~~

To allay the tension of waiting for Kestrel's call, I lose myself in the myriad tasks of the field for an hour or so while April and Marie, her cellphone at the ready, explore the shoreline and the gentle bluffs above it. Then, equipped with rucksack, I tramp off to the Hopeless Bay store and bar – a health walk, to be followed by some light engagement with the locals to let them know the old gunfighter isn't quite done yet.

I have no sooner got to Centre Road than I have to step off it to make way for a speeding, swerving minibus with a crudely painted logo: Metal Zombie. I assume its freaky-looking occupants are late for the eleven-thirty ferry. Their catch of the day is with them, waving from the windows, bleary and besotted: an omnium-gatherum of Nine Easy Pieces. In hot pursuit, a pickup with, I assume, a few irate boyfriends.

A sorry sight greets me as I begin the descent from Breadloaf Hill. Stoney has missed his driveway, driven his topless muscle car onto the Shewfelts' lawn, and dug himself in while trying to back out. He is passed out on the front seat. Dog is hard to pick out among the leprechauns, among whom he's found a grassy bed. On returning home from church, the Shewfelts, observant Pentecostals, may suffer an incalculable loss of faith: God is not always good.

Farther along, Cud Brown's beater sits in a ditch. Closer to the bar, Ernie Priposki on foot, wandering, lost. Baldy Johansson is literally being pulled by the ear by his spouse, down the steps from the bar to their car. To Baldy goes the award for last man standing – the bar is empty but for some fellow under a table and the girls from Mop'n'Chop cleaning up. The damage includes a shattered guitar and drum set. The cash register is open, empty. I am put in mind of the lawless West of the movies, after an outlaw has shot the sheriff. What they say is true: you never miss the police until you need them.

The bar's cash tray has not been rifled, as I suspected. It's on the store's checkout counter, where barkeeper Emily LeMay, bedraggled and exhausted, is counting out the take for Abraham Makepeace, who has just shown up, his normally solemn face gleefully lit by prospects of profit.

"Gets the mortgage out of arrears," he says. "Downside is we ran out of supplies. Have to wait for the beer truck tomorrow."

He catches me looking longingly at Blunder Bay's well-stuffed mail slot. "Not a snowflake's chance. This here's the Lord's Day."

"And the Lord bade us be charitable. I've been away all week."

"Rules ain't made to be bent, or you got anarchy."

"I see a special delivery there."

"That'll be the packet of Danish pipe tobacco you ordered. Available Monday. The rest is mostly bills and periodicals. *Canadian Goat* magazine. Postcard from Costa Rica – Brian Pomeroy, your former legal associate. Kind of a mental case, as I recall."

"And how is he?"

"Looks like he got into some jam down there. I ain't quoting him exactly, but he wonders if maybe you'd like to come down for a holiday and consult. And what else . . . oh, yeah, another card, from Wentworth Chance. He's teaching a biography-writing seminar. Mulligan House. Thought you might be interested."

"He deludes himself."

"I guess you're busy with other things." That sounds like a dig, but I don't get it.

Emily gives me a pat on the bottom as she edges past me. "You old dog."

Now I get it – their allusions are to the dream machine Stoney didn't get introduced to. Secrets distort quickly into base rumour on this island of genial busybodies. *Fere libenter homines id quod volunt credunt,* wrote Caesar. People readily believe what they want to believe.

The only customers in the store are the tank-topped organic growers we call Wellness and Wholeness, with their uncompromisingly furry armpits. I find myself unmoved by the sight – my paraphilia, so recently unloaded on Margaret, may be in robust remission.

~~~

By later afternoon I am back in my parlour, the Swift file out again. Still bugged by that dream – "He's here, darling," the flashbulbs going off – I am studying one of Jimmy Fingers' photos with a magnifying glass: Mulligan standing barefoot on the bedroom rug. Though the picture is dark and grainy, I'm persuaded I see a toenail on his small toe, where there should be only a hard little bud.

I'd focused so hard on the likelihood of suicide that I'd neglected the possibility he'd died at the hands of another, that in fact he may have been done in by his wife. Yet it seems incomprehensible she would be capable of such a deed, this reclusive, mousy collector of international bridge points. But have I been blindly resisting the possibility? Ignoring a glaring motive? His affairs, his trysts with Rita Schumacher . . .

I've always prided myself on recognizing guilt and evil when I look them hard in the face, but truly I didn't know Irene well – just those few conversations over the years. I don't know what darkness may have resided in her soul, what hidden anger, what simmering fires. But I ought not to be thinking of her in the past tense; she lives on, comfortably, on his insurance, pensions, royalties, the invested sales of home and hobby farm.

So there's motive and also opportunity. Irene usually took a late afternoon walk down Squamish Valley Road if it wasn't raining. She took such a walk on Saturday, April 21, 1962, at around four o'clock. A walk that could have taken her on a detour to the fishing hole whose location she disclaimed knowledge of. And what might have happened there between introverted Irene and her vigorous, outdoors-loving husband? The heap of clothes, the spermy panties . . . My mind can't come to grips with that; it defies credence.

All these thoughts I confide to April Wu when she joins me after her hike with Marie to Gwendolyn Park. I show her the photo of Mulligan's foot and she peers at it, magnified, a long time. "Really hard to say. Could be an imperfection."

April is my Ophelia now, someone with whom to play whodunit. She also plays Ophelia's role as devil's advocate. "Irene accepted his philandering, didn't she? Isn't that the sense you got from his friend, that history prof?"

Irvine Winkle. Irene let him have his affairs, he said, that was their deal. "But inwardly she must have smarted. Worse than that, maybe – revulsion at her role, a sense of outrage that finally erupted."

"Then what an awesome actor she must have been. Her tears. Her performance on the witness stand. And you, Arthur Beauchamp, such a wily observer, could you have been taken in so easily?"

"Wily is not how I would describe myself back then."

"But thinking back?"

What did I see then, in my interviews and watching her on the stand? Was there deception in that painted face, those damp, lowered eyes, her soft, hesitant voice? I'm not sure now; maybe I just wasn't looking for dissimulation. But I must concede April's point. "No, I didn't see a woman capable of murder."

"And if she was, why would she have been so supportive of Gabriel? I mean, he was her out. Why wouldn't she be bloody pleased to see him take the rap? Instead, she defended him totally."

"Maybe to put everyone off the scent. Me included." *He didn't do it, Arthur.* Her soft, trembling voice. Her seemingly dogged faith in Gabriel's innocence scuttled any suspicions I might have felt.

I didn't see her as a convincing actor, but maybe she picked up some tricks from her partner, with his flair for roles in college musicals. *I was fairly talented, I am not ashamed to admit, cutting quite a figure in my sailor suits.*

Goodnight, Irene; Irene, goodnight. There is more mystery to her than I thought.

Another odd bit comes back. She "wasn't real countrified," said Thelma McLean. Didn't like the horses, the whole rural scene – yet she held a master's degree in farm history. I remind April of that. She wanders over to my computer and clicks on to the Internet.

~~~

That evening after dinner, April returns to her computer tasks while Niko and Yoki demonstrate to Marie the art of goat milking. "First make Miss Goat happy, warm hands. Use hands this way, like loving." Yoki's English is steadily improving. "You try, yes? First message udder, like so."

Massage, but Marie understands, and does well with her gentle nursing touch.

This is part of our effort to keep her from constantly fussing with her cellphone, checking to see if it's on, if the battery holds power. None of us want to admit that Kestrel's promised weekend call may never come. There've been several – from Marie's husband, from her parents, other friends – but all understood their conversations had to be brief.

The tension has got to April, whom we find helping herself to the ten-year-old Laphroaig I keep for Reverend Al. Properly, she's taking it neat "Sorry, I can't resist superior malt."

I want desperately to join her.

Then I hear again the tinkling refrain "You'd Be So Nice to Come Home To." Marie starts, and her fingers, so sure with the nanny goat, fumble for the answer button. Then her eyes widen. "Oh, God, Kestrel, my darling, I've been so . . . never mind. Where are you, honey?"

For us, a wide smile. "My heart is racing."

Back to Kestrel, listening. Then: "Yes, of course we'll meet you there." A pause. "No, I'm not alone. Mr. Beauchamp, and a lovely woman helping him . . . Yes, Arthur Beauchamp . . . Well, that's good, because he wants to meet you too."

I n the morning, after April completes her research by computer and long-distance phone, we take off in her Civic, cross to the big island, over the high, steep-sided Malahat, and carry on to the hamlet of Buckley Bay, where the ferry will arrive from our northern sister island of Denman. That is where Kestrel has been shacking up – as Marie puts it disapprovingly – with a covey of young hippies. We are to meet her just before four o'clock and will make it with minutes to spare – the single-deck shuttle is just coming across a narrow sound.

April, Marie, and I hurry from the parking lot to the ferry slip and strive to make out Kestrel on the deck. But there's a dense group of walk-ons, some with bicycles, most with packs. Marie is having trouble spotting her daughter even as the boat nudges into the dock, even as it disgorges its cluster of travellers. She is clearly disappointed, but then her eyes suddenly light up.

A slender youth separates from the group: dark glasses, hair clipped short under a ball cap, running shoes, an over-large man's shirt, the below-the-knee shorts that are the apparel of the times for teen boys. The floppy shirt hides budding breasts, so the only feature to reveal she's a girl is the pretty face that emerges when she tucks her glasses away. Marie is aghast. "What have you done to your hair?"

But they are quickly in each other's arms. April and I return to the car, giving them their space and their time. We chatter with relief, admiring Kestrel's cleverness, her satiric cross-dressing disguise. She could pass for seventeen, is tall enough.

Marie is on her phone, likely with Samson, who is flying tonight to the coast to meet us. Eventually she and her daughter arrive at the car. On being introduced, Kestrel studies me intently, with an impish smile. She knows all about me, my achievements and my follies, my frailties and addictions – she's read Wentworth's exposé.

She and Marie climb into the back seat and April drives off, finding a winding uphill byway, seeking a secluded spot to confer and share the drinks and submarines we bought along the way. I pretend I'm not trying to hear the backseat talk, but I catch phrases:

"It was cool, Mom, they were friends I met . . ."

"But were you . . . I mean . . ."

"Oh, God, no! No one ever got that close . . ."

Something about the dangers of hitchhiking. "This isn't a war zone, Mom, it's *Canada*." I pick up that she was sheltered in Vancouver from time to time by a volunteer group called Cool-Aid.

April chooses a lay-by off a meadow with a view east to the mainland peaks above the Salish Sea. Below are Denman and Hornby Islands and little Fanny Bay strung along the shore, several dozen houses of the waterfront's well-to-do. In one of them, Irene Mulligan lives with her caregiver.

Kestrel is ravenous, and we adults haven't fed well today either. There is a time of quiet enterprise as we set to. Kestrel finally straws up the bottom bubbles of her Fanta, then leans forward to my ear.

"When can I meet Dr. Swift?"

I turn to her. "Why?"

"It's a big deal for me. I guess I've earned the right."

I'm not surprised. A hero to Canada's ever-more-politicized aboriginal peoples. Admired as Guevara was by rebels of a previous generation.

"I shall do my earnest best to make that happen, Kestrel."

"Is he still mad at you?"

"Kestrel, it is a very sad thing that happened between us. I carry the blame. I didn't have the courage or the strength of will to fight for his freedom, so I bartered for his life instead. But if I had lost him to the executioner, it would have been the world's loss too. And your dream of meeting him would have to wait for heaven."

"I'm not willing to wait for any heaven." The determined, spunky sparrow hawk. "Okay, I guess, yeah, it must've been tough. But is he still mad at you?"

"I'd say cool."

"He's cool?"

I laugh. "He's cool."

"He didn't do it, Mr. Beauchamp." To her continuing credit, it's *Beech'm.*

"You're sure?"

"No way. Not a damn chance in hell." She pulls her cellphone from her pack. "I'll show you."

~~~

"That's her house," April says, checking the number against her note-pad. A gabled cottage that a realtor might designate as a "charmer": two storeys, trimmed lawn, flowerbeds, picket fence with gate ajar, stone steps leading through forest to a rocky tidal shelf.

"Which is the main bedroom?" April asks.

"Facing the front, those tall windows," Kestrel says. "I knocked first. I saw someone moving inside and the lights were all on, but nobody answered. So I waited around awhile, then I decided to climb up onto that little balcony. Just like that dirty old dick who caught them screwing –"

"Kestrel, please!"

"Well, he *was* a dick, Mom. A private dick." O'Houlihan's video-taped testimony had been on the front pages; Kestrel must have read them avidly.

The sun is touching the hills behind us. We are parked several houses down, in the shadows of a tall fir. We can see no one outside but some roof repairers at a house across the way. Noise comes from the back of Irene's house – one of those ubiquitous, annoying leaf blowers.

Marie and Kestrel find a path through the trees to the beach while April and I stroll with feigned nonchalance toward the cottage. We pause as we glimpse in the backyard a long-haired, large-breasted Amazon working the blower.

"That has to be her nurse-attendant," April says. "Morg, she's known as. That's all I could find out, except she's probably a tough cookie – if she is a she; the neighbours I talked to weren't sure. Dotes on Irene. They've been together many years."

We swing the gate open and advance up the stone pathway to the front door. *Carpe diem.* Suddenly an alarm goes *wheep, wheep, wheep;* April points to the motion detector above the door. The leaf blower goes silent. I am already knocking.

Morg races to the front and stops short on seeing us. Fiftyish, the physique of a basketballer, big hands, good for grabbing the throat. But she doesn't resume her advance. There is recognition in her eyes, so I assume she watches the evening news. "You can't come here. She doesn't want to see you." Stammering. "It's her nap time; I tucked her in. Goodness, please, don't do this to us."

The alarm subsides and the door creaks open. "It's all right, Morgana. There's no point any more. They can come in." I am looking at a wizened face flanked by flowing grey hair, an incongruous stubble of beard. Eyes enlarged by thick rimless glasses, not the horn-rims I remember. A little paunch. A sweater and skirt, open-toed slippers. Normal toenails.

"I wish I could say it's a pleasure, Arthur." He is not too bent by age and, at ninety-nine, walks unaided with barely a wobble as he closes the door behind Morg and leads us into his living room. Bookshelves floor to ceiling, enough to stock a small public library. There, on a table, as if for show, is *A Thirst for Justice.*

"I take it you were expecting us, Dermot."

"Indeed. I gather that is the young lady who took my picture the other night."

"No, that was your great-granddaughter."

Dermot expresses no surprise, just a sigh of resignation. Kestrel told me, out of her mother's hearing, "I caught him with his cock and balls hanging out." That was two evenings ago. She snapped him with her flash, then ran off to join her waiting hippie friends, and they sped back to the Denman ferry. I spent a couple of stunned minutes staring at her cellphone screen. His thick, stubby penis, not much altered by the years.

He puts his desktop computer to sleep. "Online bridge. Quite a bit better than nothing."

I introduce April as my private investigator. He bows.

"I still keep some port about. Would you like a small glass to celebrate? No, that's not for you, is it, Arthur? I never quite saw you as an aspiring drunk. I suppose your biographer was right; it was the trial. I was about to make some tea, if you'd both care to join me."

"Very kind of you," I say.

"Please be comfortable." He leaves for the kitchen.

We lower our bottoms onto a sofa, stare dumbly at each other. April had found some records – Irene Mulligan's driver's licence, a marriage certificate from 1958 with the name Irene Middleton – items easy to come by in the fifties, before social insurance numbers, when governments were looser with paperwork. It had to be around then that Dermot developed the fiction of Irene. There was no Irene Middleton among the graduating classes of the Minnesota agricultural college.

Cross-dressers tend to grow into their fetish, Dr. Dare told me. I remember how flustered Mulligan was in the guise of Irene, when as a student I visited their home on the wrong day. Emboldened, he later made up scenarios, testing me, testing others, getting thrills from the game. That powerful performance when I interviewed his alter ego, who expressed such shock at seeing Frinkell's letter.

So many clues went over my head. The cloistered, boring life they ostensibly shared, never seen out for dinner or at entertainments. Gabriel didn't mention ever seeing them together; in fact he didn't see much of her at all during her brief times in the Squamish Valley. She never answered when Thelma McLean came calling. No photographs of them together.

Other clues: his talent for the stage, delighting audiences with his high tenor. In the lecture theatre: an uncanny ability to change pitch. In court: his clumsiness in high heels, overdressed, overpowdered. In the A-frame: no sofa where a couple might sit.

The modus operandi seems almost self-evident now. At the fishing hole he unpacked the women's clothes he'd brought, all but socks, and began taking on the guise of Irene. The excitement of the moment, the thrilling plan to disappear, and the erotic stimulus of the nylon tricot panties gave rise to an act of masturbation. An erring toss or an errant wind sent them flapping onto the tree root. He put his undershorts back on, finished dressing, fastened his wig in place, then made for Squamish Valley Road, becoming Irene taking her daily walk.

Heedful of Dermot's age, April rises when a kettle whistles, leaves for the kitchen to help. Wentworth's book is beside me. I ruefully flip through its pages and find a passage highlighted with two pencilled exclamation marks: *He was torn in another, deeply personal way over defending the suspected killer of a man who'd been his professor and mentor. He wondered if he'd be able to give it his all.*

Dermot's voice: "Thank you, young lady, you're very gracious indeed." I close the book quickly as they return. April sets the tea tray down but Dermot insists on pouring.

"New meaning is given to the plucky expression 'Never say die,'" he says. "A murder trial *sans mort*. No murder, no murderer. Novel, I suppose, even in the wide experience of so celebrated a counsel as you, Arthur. Wisely, you scorned my advice to become a classicist. The sheer, beautiful irony of it is not lost on us, is it?"

I am unimpressed by his sang-froid. Does he imagine he can seduce me with courtliness? "I hardly scorned your advice. You were no less a hero to me than you were to Gabriel." A gentle poke; too gentle. I'm fighting my emotions.

"I was appalled when he was arrested. I'd never thought such an eventuality might occur. You surely must have realized that I left that legal letter to be found by the police – a considerable motive for suicide. In the end I was left praying you would prove me wrong, would brilliantly demonstrate that your choice of the law was the right one." A poke back at me that I feel in the gut. "At all events, he's a folk hero now, either despite or because of my vast disservice to him. I, however, am now lost to history, a squalid figure of fun."

"The self-pity leaves me dry-eyed, Dermot." My idol. The great guru of moral values. What a repulsive person.

"So, Rome has indeed fallen. What was the precipitating factor, Arthur?" He is seated now, in a recliner, his feet up. "My supposed reflections parroting Camus and Nietzsche and Sophocles? Quotes cribbed from my works. I give the forger, whoever he or she may be, a failing grade."

"You may be relieved to know, Dermot, that the Appeal Court found it equally unpersuasive."

"Or were your endeavours inspired by that pair of repellent slime moulds Frinkell and O'Houlihan?"

"In today's tolerant society, your legacy might have outlasted the vulgar headlines prompted by a few titillating photos. But it would never have outlived the rape of a young teenager under your charge." An icy silence descends. "Sebastien visited you, didn't he?"

Dermot studies April, who has stayed out of this, though is alert, absorbed. "You must be very clever at what you do, " he says.

"It's your great-granddaughter you should thank, Dr. Mulligan. She's fourteen."

As Dermot reflects on the significance of that – Caroline's age when raped – the teacup shakes in his hand; he's struggling to maintain his self-assured manner. "Poor Sebastien. What was one to do? He was . . . what, nineteen? Drunk, when he appeared on my doorstep. Threatening at one moment, sobbing the next. A litany of injustices. A few thousand to tide him over – until his next fix, I suppose. I could have paid him, but what follows that? Can money ever cure such problems?"

My thoughts spin back to that windshield-smashing spree and Sebastien's wry reflection on his crushing sense of futility: "It seemed to be the most sensible thing to do at the moment." Anger has been welling up in me, the cumulative anger of weeks, months, decades, and I can no longer master it.

"Sebastien was your son! You denied him his birthright! As callously as you ravished his mother, an adolescent, your student! You condemned her to a life of prostitution and addiction! And by God, you were no less pitiless during the trial. Brilliantly playing the tearful widow over an unclaimed human foot, knowing it would further sabotage the defence of a young man who admired you unstintingly. Whom you contrived to sacrifice to the hangman at what you dare call a murder trial *sans mort*. Were you so desperate to retain your legacy that you'd have sent him to his death? I believe so! I believe you have the heart of a murderer. Damn you!"

This is not me. I never let go like this, I am a great masker of anger, but now I'm fighting tears of wrath and revulsion, and I look away, look out his open windows, where a wren is sweetly carolling. I murmur. "A bird does not sing because it has an answer. It sings because it has a song."

"One of the great sage's loveliest aphorisms. How apt."

I want him to decrypt and solve this riddle. I can't help myself; I'm his student again, impatient for his knowledge.

He takes a mere second. "Don't look for obscure motives." He puts his cup down, yawns. "Well, I wish I could offer more hospitality, but it is getting on. These old bones demand some respite." Unruffled, calm in the storm.

We rise with him. We have no right or power to do anything more. The rest is up to the authorities.

"Oh, let me not forget. Would you do me the honour, Arthur, of signing this lip-smacking inverse *argumentum ad hominem*? In the jargon of the pop critics, unputdownable."

I open *A Thirst* to the title page and inscribe: ὁ δὲ ἀνεξέταστος βίος οὐ βιωτὸς ἀνθρώπῳ.

Dermot's face crinkles into a wry smile. The words are Greek to April, and he interprets for her: "Plato. The unexamined life is not worth living."

He holds the door for us. April has the last words, and speaks them first in Cantonese, which she must translate in turn. A Confucianism: "Do good, reap good; do evil, reap evil. Thank you for the tea."

"You are most welcome. Adieu." There is desolation finally in his aged, weakened eyes as he closes the door.

As we walk by, Morg barely looks up from her task, raking the leaves that escaped the blower. We carry on toward the beach, through the woods, and find Marie and Kestrel perched on a shoreline rock, close and confiding in the dying sunlight. We let them be, and my passion cools in the crisp evening air.

I play with my cellphone awhile. I'm at a loss as to whom to call. I have Hollis Wotherspoon's home number, and it would be pleasant to ask the senior prosecutor how soon our appeal court panel could be called into emergency session. I look forward to seeing Martha Schupp, C.J., fall all over herself, to watching Ram Singh struggle to find something funny about this outcome.

There will be reparations for Gabriel, of course. Many millions – the state must pay for what it stole. I ought to call my travel agent. I hope Kestrel and her mother have passports. But maybe Gabriel can be persuaded to meet us here, in the country of his former persecution.

Marie cries out, "Look!"

April and I turn. She starts running along the grassy verge above the high-tide line, but I can't see why. Twilight has set in. I search the dimness, the rocky beach where Marie and Kestrel are pointing.

A skinny naked figure is wading into the ocean. Dermot Mulligan. His clothing is sitting in a clump on a barnacle-encrusted rock. He is up to his thighs, his hips. April is clambering across the rock-strewn shoreline. Now I am running too, all of us are, including Morg, who is thundering toward the water.

But Dermot will have his suicide after all. The wind has risen and the tide is up, a big tide, and a wave quickly catches him. He may have been caught in a swift current, because he is swept off, disappearing, a sandaled foot rising from the chop, vanishing.

April is hesitating at the water's edge, contemplating a treacherous rescue. "Don't even think of it!" I shout.

Even Morg has stalled, up to her knees. She slips and makes a great splash, flounders a while, then crawls back to shore, wailing. Neighbours are out by now, and two young men rush a skiff into the water, clamber in, lowering its thirty-horse engine. But darkness is enshrouding the strait as they take off, and the only living creature bobbing in the water is a curious seal.

April has just finished calling 911 when I catch up to her.

"Goodnight, Irene," I say softly, staring at the voracious sea.

"I wish I could join you in court," Margaret says. "Sorry to miss your big day."

"You didn't. My big day was November 18, 1994."

"I only married you then because you're such a great bullshit artist."

We came off the *Queen George* a short while ago and are heading to the airport by taxi. She has already extended her Thanksgiving weekend and can't afford to miss her spot in question period tomorrow.

I will continue on to Vancouver but return forthwith, after my duties in court. I left my Fargo in the lot at the Garibaldi ferry, not chained to anything, a ripe target for the trucknapper whose Mustang has been impounded for bad brakes and bald tires by a newly installed constable, determined to restore law and order on the island.

I'm feeling rather pillowy after the long weekend – meals with the Nogginses, the Sproules, and an event at the community hall. I had a dream last night about being pursued by turkeys, and I woke Margaret up by going, she claims, *gobble, gobble.*

"Let me try this on you." Margaret has her Blackberry out and is thumbing words onto the screen. "Question for the Honourable Minister of Energy. How much longer does he plan to be giving blow jobs to the oil bosses?"

"Too subtle."

We're nearing domestic departures, and she tucks the device into her bag. "Try to come to Ottawa before Christmas. Not for a few weeks, though; I'll be pretty cramped." Her friend Les Falk has split up with her boyfriend, will be batching awhile with her. "You should really treat yourself to a holiday."

"I have an invitation for Costa Rica."

"Brian Pomeroy? Oh, I don't know, he'll just get you in trouble . . . What the hell, do it."

A kiss, a hug, another kiss, declarations of love, and I proceed away, wondering what's going on with her and Les Falk. I laugh at myself for falling prey to suspicion. Ridiculous. Utterly ridiculous...

~~~

I have plenty of time to stop at the office and pick up my court gear. Gertrude isn't here; she's off to Hawaii with her daughter and grandkids (and why shouldn't I go to some similar tropical clime?). Bully is here, though, who denounces holidays as wasteful exercises in indolence. As he escorts me out I make my standard declamation of final retirement.

He scoffs and offers to bet a hundred thousand dollars, then laughs when I fail to take him up on it. "Junkie," he calls after me.

I fear there's something to that. I still get an irrepressible thrill on entering a courtroom with all my senses on alert. I am indeed a junkie – for the theatre, the clash of minds, the play of language, the exquisite intricacy of ancient rules and routines. Even the foolishness and the flaws, the false assumptions of unfailing justice.

There's a crowd outside the Law Courts' main entrance: a mix of media, lawyers, academics, local politicians, prominent aboriginals. A dozen members of the Squamish Nation, in traditional blankets, have formed a ceremonial circle. An elder is speaking solemnly, as if reciting a prayer or, more likely, giving thanks. Several drummers, in a smaller circle, await their turn.

They are here, of course, to honour Gabriel Swift, who by now must be en route from the airport, escorted by yet another welcoming group. The appeal is set to resume at eleven – time enough for him to arrive, to play his central role in this act of redemption.

He was to have been here yesterday, but there was a snafu at the stopover in Los Angeles – the immigration authorities of Fortress America sought to detain him as an undesirable. After high-level intervention he was sped on his way to Seattle but missed his connector to Vancouver.

424

He will have met Kestrel Dubois and her parents by now, torch-bearers for the airport greeters. Gabriel and the Dubois are sharing a ride to the courthouse, so Kestrel will have her chance to commune with her hero. He will be staying in Green College at UBC, where tomorrow he is to give a lecture hurriedly organized by the Vancouver Institute.

As I enter the courthouse, my gown bag over my shoulder, the circle opens and the drumming begins; voices are raised in enthusiastic, chant-like song. I am slowed by tributes as I head to the robing room, my self-effacing responses spurned. A small media scrum descends, which I smilingly, silently skirt.

In the changing room I am required to pose for a photo – a pair of young barristers I've never met, with their arms about me. I am distressed at being treated as such a hero, given my unworthy role forty-nine years ago. I'm reluctant to harbour any illusions that Gabriel will show similar warmth when we meet.

I escape to the bank of Tragger, Inglis lockers, remove my suit, and change into pinstriped pants, waistcoat and wing collar, then draw my robe from its bag. Not my black silk one, but the fur-trimmed nobility robe I've kept since its purchase from Celia Swift, well maintained and mothballed. I settle it over my shoulders, proudly and shamelessly, as if I've earned the right.

I am stared at, of course, as I stride off to the Great Hall; I don't care if onlookers suppress giggles. But most of them are focused on the assembly outside the wide glass doors. The chief of the Squamish Nation is making what seems a vigorous speech, which he concludes as a sedan pulls up. The ceremonial circle quickly closes. A roar goes up as Dr. Gabriel Swift alights from the back seat.

He is seventy, bronzed and lined, has kept his hair, and is scarred in a way that adds to his handsomeness. He is casually dressed: slacks and a handcrafted Bolivian sweater. Turning, he extends a hand to Kestrel, who emerges from the car in the dress of her people, the Cree of Lac La Ronge. Samson and Marie get out too, and all engage in a flurry of greetings. More drumming, but it's silenced as Gabriel speaks – words of appreciation obviously, during which he looks about as if seeking someone. I have a feeling that someone is me, but I stay rooted at the top of the stairs. The sheriffs are out there now, urging everyone inside. It's eleven o'clock.

Entering, Gabriel hesitates upon seeing me, adjusts his glasses, then carries on up. And we are face to face. His intense dark eyes betray little weariness. I am probably looking as numbed as I feel.

"It's been a long journey," he says.

"You look well, nonetheless."

"I meant our journey, Arthur." He adjusts my robe. "Wear it with pride."

~~~

I recall from the 1962 trial the clerk looking aghast at Ophelia in her pants, but his present-day counterpart just smiles at me in my nobility robe. Hollis Wotherspoon demands to be informed about its provenance. "*Comme il faut* in the court of the Salish chiefs of yore," I explain, then usher my client to a seat at counsel table.

"Order in court!"

Entering, Martha Schupp widens her eyes on observing my unorthodox dress, then redirects her look – as if she's noticed nothing amiss – to the overflow gallery. It includes, standing at the back, Wentworth Chance, who came panting up the stairs late and must have cajoled or bribed the sheriffs to be allowed in. Near the front, with the chiefs, is the Dubois family. Mulligan didn't prepare a will, I'm told, so what he left goes to them, his nearest kin.

Dermot's body wasn't found until the morning, washed up just outside the town. There will be a funeral, of course, more solemn and better attended than that of the foot. On a bizarre note, the Vancouver Transvestite Association is planning a tribute, presumably farcical in intent.

Bill Webb smiles at me, happy at my success, doubtless relieved that he won't have to grapple with denying my appeal. Ram Singh looks too hungover to care much about what is going on.

"We have read the material newly submitted," Schupp says. She still won't look at me. "The appeal is allowed and the verdict set aside on the ground that it is unreasonable, pursuant to Section 686(1)(a)(i) of the Criminal Code." Then she finally abandons her ritualistic façade. "Dr. Swift, I can only hope that you will find forgiveness in your heart for the grievous wrongs you have been subjected to. You are free. Is there anything you wish to say?"

Gabriel stands and speaks a few phrases in the Squamish tongue, then translates: "Madam Chief Justice, I have always been free, in my mind and my heart, and I can only pray that those of your tribe will one day find the compassion, strength, and humility to share that freedom."

The Chief Justice is flustered. "Yes, well, thank you. We will adjourn."

~~~

Outside the Law Courts the media demand audience with Gabriel. They obviously want him to hunger for vengeance, but he's calm and reflective. "I'm merely one of the lesser, luckier victims of the grand experiment to crush, like a defeated enemy, our aboriginal societies. Fortunately, history has a bias for truth and rebels against the received wisdom of the times, the lies told, the crippling intolerance. That I'm here today, free, is merely incidental proof of that, but proof hard won." He goes on to laud Kestrel and her parents, who stand by beaming, and even mentions his "accomplished and dedicated counsel," without whom he would still be a homeless wanderer. "But I have come home."

Gabriel spends some time with his supporters, who reluctantly disperse upon being advised that he and I have lunch plans. Wentworth is harder to escape from, making his move as we head to the taxi rank. "I am dying to meet him, Arthur."

"Not literally, I hope." I make the obligatory introductions. "Wentworth is my biographer. Be careful he doesn't ask to do one of you." I signal a waiting cab.

"Maybe you've heard, Dr. Swift, I'll be at Mulligan House this November, writer-in-res. It's been pretty well restored to the way it was in sixty-two, in case you want to see it one last time. I can't imagine it will survive all this – I'll probably be the last funded writer." He rambles on, blocking our entrance to the taxi, and we're not allowed to make our getaway until I promise Wentworth I will meet with him at length. Gabriel wisely makes no such promise, though he accepts Wentworth's card.

In the car we exchange brief remembrances of Jim and Grace Brady. They faced hard times after Mine, Mill got taken apart, and couldn't afford a trip overseas to visit him. They died within a year of each other, after the Wall came down and the system they believed in failed. I let Gabriel know I attended their funerals, that I was one among a thousand others who mourned. "I heard you were there," he says, "and that you honoured them with some thoughtful words. I'm grateful."

He volunteers that he broke down and read *A Thirst* last month – several friends had mailed him copies. "It caused a rethinking of events that I'd tried, often successfully, to forget."

I don't press him on that. He muses, "I've had several approaches for the rights to my life; I've toyed with the idea of doing my own. Then I remembered the impulsive, arrogant young refusenik who acted without a lawyer on his sentence appeal."

~~~

It wouldn't be fair to frighten members of the Confederation Club by taking Gabriel there, and it has been years since he's had sockeye salmon, so we have chosen a little seafood place near Fishermen's Wharf. He tells me he'll stay in Vancouver a few days, long enough to visit his parents' graves and those of Jim and Grace, and then will return after he finishes his work in Bolivia.

He has already had approaches from academic headhunters in Canada, and hopes to take one up. "Politically I want to be a part of what I've missed. There is movement here – not fervent, a little too cautious for my taste – but movement nonetheless. A healthy abundance of land claims. A push for self-government. I want to push it harder." Smiling. "I'm not too old to be a troublemaker."

I admit to envy, recall how he made me feel, so many years ago, as a man of settled convictions – tame, orthodox.

"And, if your biographer is right, a man of too much rectitude. He has persuaded me that the lawyer I foolishly fired embodies the four great virtues: justice, prudence, fortitude, and – though I gather it was some time coming – temperance."

The cardinal virtues of ancient Greece, which Gabriel mocked in our youthful jailhouse debates as flabby philosophizing. He has me smiling. I realize I have never before seen him relaxed.

He adds, "And a man of enough compassion, I hope, to forgive my unrelenting impoliteness over the years."

It is I who must confess, and I do, to my lack of confidence as his counsel, to my lack of ancient Greek fortitude. Everything Ophelia Moore said was true. *Old Smitty reeled him in like a fish.* A quote that prompts just a shrug from Gabriel. It's the past.

After exchanging more *mea culpas* and forgivenesses, we jointly pledge there'll be no more apologies. I am relaxing too, finally, feeling relief and a threatening wetness of eye. I find a diversion: tales of Garibaldi, the supposedly bucolic island where I am in supposedly relaxed retirement.

Gabriel commends me for my good sense in finding such a partner as Margaret Blake, and expresses the hope she has knocked some of the conservative stuffing out of me. He broadly supports her agenda. Like most thinking members of this besieged planet, he is of a view it ought to be preserved. *Progress* is a word he abhors; it's synonymous with destruction, not only of the environment but of the earth's fragile cultures.

He no longer sees a panacea in old-style communism. "My Rome was too despotic, too top-heavy not to fall like Humpty Dumpty. Gods have failed, though ideals survive. What I was, I no longer entirely am. But that is the way of growth. Maturity comes slowly, arrives too late. And then we are old, my brother."

"Si jeunesse savait, si vieillesse pouvait."

He laughs. And we carry on about this and that and everything, close and lively – comrades finally, the brothers we were
meant to be.

Stoney tuned up the Fargo last week (he was under my watch throughout) and did a competent job of it. Like a housebound dog finding freedom, she is enjoying a long gallop up the Sea-to-Sky Highway. The Stawamus Chief looms forbiddingly through the mist; the Howe Sound fjords are grey and gloomy. I drive past the Squamish Nation's Totem Hall, a proud, imposing structure, and ease off on the gas as I enter the town. Its economy is now based as much on tourism as resources, a way station for hikers and skiers. A modern police station, modern provincial court, malls, and microbrewery.

It is Remembrance Day weekend, all too appropriate for my return to the Squamish Valley after these many years. I've been to the town proper for the odd preliminary hearing, but until now have never ventured north of it – my camping days are long over. A sense of guilt brings me here, after a month of dithering, to honour my pledge to Wentworth Chance to record sound bites for his revised *Thirst*, soon to be available in quality paperback.

Leaving town, I head up the narrow asphalt road that leads into the Cheakamus Reserve, Gabriel's childhood home, and along the east bank of the Squamish River. Where the reserve ends, the wealthy have taken root: large landholdings by the river with rambling showpiece homes. I stop at the driveway that once led to the hardscrabble farm of Buck and Thelma McLean, since pulled down, and now pastureland for several grazing horses. The driveway to Mulligan House has been paved. The little barn is still there, with a fresh coat of paint, and the A-frame and its once modern protrusion seem untouched by time. The river is timeless, though, and rolls past with a weary majesty.

On seeing me pull up, Wentworth races from the front door like a man chased by bees, pumps my hand and won't let go, towing me inside, chattering like a kingfisher. "Thank heavens, because I'm on deadline. Got it down pretty well, but it needs an insider feel. Bulletin: the Holy Roman Church has finally confessed that some long-dead prelates were covering up for Mulligan, knew about his rape; they suppressed reports from a Pie Eleven teaching nun. The chickens will now be flocking home to roost."

He pulls me through the ill-lit A-frame, its giant library still intact, into the study, which is not much altered either: the old turntable, the record collection, but now with baseboard heating replacing the airtight stove and indigenous art on walls and table-tops. A large rectangular shadow on the wall where Mulligan's portrait may once have hung. The same massive desk, even Mulligan's old Remington, but it's been shoved aside for a computer monitor and a printer. A great clutter of paperwork, reference works open, piles of transcripts.

"I published too early – the book desperately needed a completion. Not some boring retirement on a funky island but a hero's return, redemption. I'm calling the new final chapter 'Never Say Die.'" He fiddles with his computer, jumpy as an addict on speed. "My biography seminar was a bit of a bust – only one showed up. On the bright side, I'm shortlisted for the Drainie-Taylor Biography Prize; I guess you heard that. I'll set this up in a jiff, voice-to-computer. Darn, I'm a lousy host. There's coffee or . . . it's tea in the afternoon, isn't it? God, if anyone should know, it's me. Orange pekoe, of course, milk, no sugar, right? Give me a sec, I'll brew some up."

"Hold. Stay." I am behind the desk now, tapping on the keys of the Remington. They all seem to work. "What exactly did you think you were doing, Wentworth?" It isn't panic I see, but something close. "You were doing some research here earlier this year . . . sometime in March, wasn't it?"

"I, uh, yeah. Spent a couple of days. They opened it for me. Checking out the scene in person – that's the key to solid research, right?"

"The problem I have with that is your manuscript was already at the printers." I pull a volume from the shelf – Bertrand Russell, a 1950s first edition. "Not much of a task to scissor out a couple of blank end pages from a book like this. A lot more work excerpting appropriate quotes from Mulligan's texts. Sophocles, Camus."

Wentworth sags. "Didn't pull any wool over your eyes, did I?" A laugh so tight it squeaks, then silence. Then, softly: "Arthur, you needed a push. I was forcing you to be a hero. Erasing the blot on your career." His voice rising. "Damn it, your biography was incomplete. Your life was incomplete, your one great challenge un-resolved. I had to goad you back to court." He starts to weep. "You were a god to me."

"Make us some tea, Wentworth, and let's get going."

AUTHOR'S NOTE

I was received warmly into Squamish by its historical society, whose president, Bianca Peters, helped bring me into contact with several knowledgeable locals, including Helmut Manzl, Lesley Keith, Susan Steen, Trevor Mills, and Paul Lalli. Chief Gibby Jacobs of the Squamish Nation had some words of wisdom for me, and Squamish pioneers Corinne Lonsdale and Spen Hinde generously offered aid.

Eric Andersen, an energetic Squamish historian, supplied a plethora of pertinent historic documents and photographs and led me to the sites of the old police station, prison, and courtroom, and finally to the Squamish Library, with its excellent archival collection, which includes a powerful recorded interview with Squamish elder Shirley Toman, movingly describing her years in a residential school.

Debbie Millward, chief librarian for the *Vancouver Sun* and *Province* newspapers, kindly set me up with a microfiche viewer. I spent several days at it, refreshing my memory of Vancouver in 1962 (a year during which, coincidentally, I was a *Sun* reporter, working my way through law school). George Bowering, Canada's first poet laureate and an old Vancouver hand, helped me tweak some of the Vancouver scenes from that year.

Long-time friend Louise Mandell, Q.C., one of Canada's leading Native rights lawyers, reviewed my next-to-final draft, and the novel has benefited from her wise counsel in important ways.